PAINTED DOLL

The Only In Tokyo Mysteries

NIGHTSHADE

FALLEN ANGEL

IDOLMAKER

PAINTED DOLL

Jonelle Patrick

PAINTED DOLL

An Only In Tokyo Mystery

BANCROFT & GREENE, PUBLISHERS LLC Published by Bancroft & Greene, Publishers LLC, 80 Santa Paula Avenue, San Francisco, CA 94127 USA

This is a work of fiction. Names, characters, places, and incidents either are the product of the author's imagination or are used fictitiously, and any resemblance to actual persons, living or dead, business establishments, events, or locales is entirely coincidental. The publisher does not have control over and does not have any responsibility for author or third-party websites or their content.

PAINTED DOLL

A Bancroft & Greene book / published by arrangement with the author

PUBLISHING HISTORY   Bancroft & Greene print edition / December 2016; Bancroft & Greene ebook edition / December 2016

Library of Congress Control Number: 2016942230

ISBN-10: 0-9975709-3-8
ISBN-13: 978-0-9975709-3-9

PAINTED DOLL

THURSDAY, DECEMBER 4

•

A pillow of white capped her gravestone, the first snow of winter.

He frowned at the dead flowers. Brown heads forever bowed, the dried chrysanthemum stalks shivered in the wind. Didn't her family care enough to keep them fresh? He lifted the withered stems from their stone vases and set them aside, then drew a stick of incense from his pocket. His hands were cold. It took him two tries with the lighter before a thread of smoke curled toward the leaden sky. He poked it through the icy crust on the altar.

Uncapping the bottle of water he'd bought at the vending machine down the street, he emptied it over her gravestone. The snow dissolved, leaving the pale granite beneath bare and gleaming. Setting the empty bottle carefully on the ground, he drew a pack of cigarettes from his pocket and stripped off the wrapper. Placing one between his lips, he held the flame to the tip, closed his eyes, and tasted the harsh tobacco that reminded him of that day. Taking it from his mouth, he laid it next to the smoldering incense, watching as the twin streams of smoke mingled and twisted toward heaven.

Sinking to his knees, he folded his hands, wincing at the twinge that was new since the last time he'd knelt on this patch of cold ground.

Nine years, he thought. Nine death anniversaries. Tomorrow would be the tenth. He always came early, so he wouldn't cross paths with the remnants of her family. He always came on the day he'd actually killed her.

WEDNESDAY, JANUARY 1

•

Kenji Nakamura stepped off the train onto the Tabata Station platform and felt an icy finger of winter slip through a gap in his hastily wound muffler. The platform at this stop was deserted, even though it was New Year's Eve. Actually, he corrected himself, New Year's Day. Midnight was long gone.

Beyond the sheltering roof, snow now plummeted down in earnest. He stopped to unwind the old gray scarf that had been his mother's last gift before she died. Gritting his teeth against the chill, he shook it out and put it on more carefully, stuffing the ends inside his coat and buttoning it up a notch. The button came off in his hand. He frowned, dropping it into his pocket. He needed a new winter coat, but shopping was such a chore—the largest size of the Japanese brands was too short for him, the foreign styles cut too wide.

The platform's warning bell rang and the train pulled away, riffling Kenji's hair and leaving a maelstrom of snowflakes spinning crazily in its wake. He shoved his hands into his pockets and began trudging toward the exit at the end of the long platform. How could it turn so cold, so fast? Six hours ago, he and Yumi had shared an umbrella, not letting a little rain dampen their giddiness that she was free at last. Her engagement to the man she'd met through an arranged marriage *o-miai* had officially ended yesterday.

Now they could be together, the way he'd dreamed of since the day his third grade teacher stood her up in front of the class and introduced the new girl from America. He should be with her right now. He should never have returned that missed call.

Just his luck, this was the one time a year that trains ran all night. If there had been no easy way to get to his father before morning, he would still be snug in his warm futon, with Yumi by his side, maybe even finishing what they'd . . . . Well, after last night, he was sure there would be other nights. They didn't have to rush things. He smiled, remembering how she had tucked herself in even closer to him after she fell asleep.

Stepping onto the escalator, he let it bear him up toward the south exit, then beeped his way through the turnstile without slowing. Feathery patches of snow began to spot his coat as soon as he left the protection of the overhang. Angling himself against the wind, he set out for the police box manned by his father on this loneliest of nights.

Even the most far-flung families reunited for the holidays, but ever since Kenji's mother had died ten years ago, his father had volunteered for duty every New Year's Eve, on the one night a year that nobody wanted to be at work.

It wasn't an accident.

That's what his father had said on the phone tonight. How could he suddenly know—after all these years, in the middle of the night—that Kenji's mother's death hadn't been an accident?

If it wasn't an accident, what was it? It hadn't been suicide. The investigation had ruled that out. And it couldn't have been a crime. Kenji knew about crime. As a police detective, crime was his business. But crimes were something that happened to other people, people who put themselves in harm's way, people who invited bad luck upon themselves. Crimes didn't happen to policemen's wives. Crimes didn't happen to policemen's *mothers.*

Crossing the street by the *pachinko* parlor, head down, clumps of falling snow pelted his face and melted as soon as they hit. An icy trickle ran through his hair and down his neck.

He should have grabbed his dad's old felt hat before he left. He trudged up the hill, squinting into the wind. Two more blocks.

Why had his dad dropped this on him *now*? His mother had died ten years ago. In a train accident. *A not-accident.*

Sergeant Nakamura had been working the graveyard shift that night, too. He'd come home the next morning to find his wife's slippers lined up neatly at the edge of the *tatami* and an empty space in the shoe cupboard where her winter boots usually sat. There was no note, so he hadn't worried. No note meant she'd be back soon, that she'd gone out to do something that wasn't worth an explanation. That she'd be back before the family woke up and realized she was gone.

Kenji's father had gone to bed thinking nothing was amiss, but when he awoke in the early afternoon, he'd found both sons sitting in the kitchen, strangely silent and more than a little hungry. Two half-finished bowls of rice sat on the table, every grain still rock-hard in the center. Even though Kenji and his older brother were in high school, they still hadn't known how much water to put in the rice cooker. The refrigerator was filled to bursting, but they hadn't dared touch the plastic-wrapped trays that their mother had made for her upcoming high school reunion, the ones papered in sticky notes scribbled with "DO NOT EAT!"

Sergeant Nakamura had phoned his sister first. His wife had gone out early, he said, but wasn't back yet. Had Sachiko stopped by to see Ayako and her family, by any chance? No, sorry, they hadn't seen her, but tell her thanks for recommending the new acupuncturist. Uncle's headaches were much better.

Next, his dad began calling the rest of the relatives, then friends, then everyone he could think of. By the time he slowly hung up the phone for the last time, worry had replaced the irritation that she hadn't returned in time to make breakfast for the boys.

Then Kenji remembered the note that had been stuck to the dinner plate his mother had left on the table for him last night. He dug through the trash to retrieve it. *Sorry, had to run out for a bit and take something to one of my high school friends.* They all looked at each other. Who *were* her friends? None of them had ever stopped to wonder how Sachiko Nakamura occupied herself, in between the cooking and cleaning and washing that kept their lives running smoothly.

Her friends' numbers would be on her phone, wouldn't they? Kenji asked. They searched for it, but it was gone, along with her purse.

They didn't know what to do next. None of them could remember her saying anything about helping a neighbor or getting in line early for a sale. Of course, that didn't really mean anything—every day she told them plenty of things that went in one ear and out the other.

I'm running out to the store to buy some fish for dinner.

I think I'll get you some new socks on the shopping street. They're having a sale.

I'll be a little late, because I'm picking up Mrs. Kimura's prescription for her.

And then the phone rang. A female accident victim had been found near the tracks of the Toyoko Line. Kenji's father went to the hospital alone, to identify the body that had been spotted by a hungover high school student on his way to weekend basketball practice. The local police were conducting an investigation. Two days later, they'd pronounced it an accident.

It wasn't an accident.

Kenji turned the corner at the top of the hill and saw the police box ahead, its wide front window glowing like a beacon for lost children and victims of minor crimes. Every neighborhood had a *koban* like this, manned by officers who knew everyone on their patch by name, thanks to the visits they made twice a year to update the particulars of each household.

The police box officers were as much a part of everyday life as the mailman, consulted not only if you wanted to report a crime, but also if you needed directions to the new café, had lost your cat, or found a dropped glove on the street.

As a boy, Kenji had always stopped to look at the wanted posters on the bulletin board outside, wondering what bungles had caused a fugitive to be missing joints on both pinky fingers, or why a suspected murderer had only three remaining teeth. But tonight he didn't even glance at the sketches as he strode past, slowing only as he approached the door of the narrow stucco-clad building with the Tokyo Metropolitan Police's bronze star over the door. Through the window, he could see his father seated behind a wide metal desk, official notices tacked to the wall beside him. A well-thumbed book of local maps sat neatly squared on the corner of the desk. The gold buttons on his uniform gleamed, and his hat was firmly settled on his graying brush-cut hair.

But tonight Sergeant Nakamura wasn't sitting ramrod straight, he was hunched over a red clay teacup, staring into its depths. It was one of the pair he and his wife had bought on their honeymoon.

He looked up as Kenji pushed through the door. He wasn't alone.

"Happy New Year, Ken-*kun*." A man with sad eyes bowed from the doorway to the back room.

Kenji returned the bow, recognizing his father's longtime poker crony, who had just retired in November.

"Happy New Year to you, too, Officer Toyama."

It was the first time Kenji had seen the ex-policeman out of uniform. In his plaid flannel shirt and fleece sweatpants, he looked . . . smaller. Had Toyama-*san shrunk*? Kenji remembered him from boyhood, an imposing figure who always had a riddle for the boss's son and would fish a piece of candy from his pocket if Kenji guessed right.

"What are you doing here in the middle of the night, Toyama-*san*?" Kenji asked, pulling the door shut behind him.

"He came with me," said a voice Kenji hadn't heard since high school. A younger version of Officer Toyama appeared behind his father.

"Sho-*sempai*! Happy New Year."

Mr. Toyama's son returned the greeting with the same lopsided grin he'd worn when their high school baseball team won the division championship. Sho had been Kenji's mentor, his *sempai*—a senior pitcher when Kenji was a first-year rookie. Sho was shorter, but made up for it by being built like a brick wall. As expected, Toyama Junior had followed in his father's footsteps and gone straight to the police academy after graduation.

"You still working out of Saitama Station?" Kenji asked.

"No, they transferred me to Shinjuku two months ago." He grimaced. "Just in time for the quake."

Ten days ago, a 7.9 temblor had given Tokyo a severe shaking. Every division was still working around the clock to deal with the criminals who had been caught with their pants down in the chaos that followed.

"And actually, that's why I'm here," Sho explained. "I was one of the locals assigned to help bag and tag a scene for the First Investigative Division after a warehouse in East Shinjuku collapsed."

"Why were the big boys involved in an earthquake accident?" Kenji asked. The First Investigative Division was only called in to take over when an incident turned into a major crime: extortion, robbery, rape, murder.

Sho snorted. "It turned out that the janitorial service headquartered in the building was storing more than mops and wax there. A bunch of illegal Chinese girls were locked in a back room, and one was in the wrong place at the wrong time when a stack of crates fell. The scumbags moved her body outside, trying to make it look like an accident, and a patrol officer caught them dumping her purse and passport into a storm drain. When we searched what was left of the building, we discovered the traffickers had stripped the girls of everything they owned, and locked their stuff in a storeroom marked 'Toxic, Keep Out,' along with a couple of crates of Chinese handguns. At the very back, we found . . . *that*."

He nodded toward a small suitcase sitting beside the front door. Cobwebby and coated with dust, it had once been dark blue. "Inspector Mori got pretty excited when he opened it up. He made me take it to the crime lab right away. Said it was tied to a case he'd worked on ten years ago."

Ten years ago.

"What kind of case?" Kenji asked, suddenly uneasy.

"Don't know, except that it's an unsolved."

So it couldn't be his mother's death. That had been ruled an accident. *It wasn't an accident.*

Kenji turned to his dad. "But what does this suitcase have to do with Mom?"

His father's frown grew deeper.

Sho answered for him. "Inspector Mori wasn't actually interested in the bag—it was the passport and stuff packed inside he wanted. But they found a receipt for three bus tour tickets in one of the side pockets, along with a luggage tag that had your mom's name on it. He figured the bag belonged to her, asked me to return it when the lab boys were done with it."

Kenji raised an eyebrow at his father.

"It's hers," Sergeant Nakamura admitted. "She bought it right before she went on that damn trip to the Ise Shrine with her old high school friends."

"And . . . ?"

His dad scowled. "Mori wants me to come in, ask me a bunch of questions that I won't know the answers to. He's going to try to make this into something it's not."

"Hey, now," Mr. Toyama chided. "Just because Mori-*san* wants you to come in and talk to him about that suitcase doesn't mean Sachiko's death was anything but an accident. Sho said it was only the stuff inside he was interested in. Who knows how some illegal Chinese girl ended up with that bag? Maybe your sister gave it away after the funeral, and didn't realize there was anything still in it that belonged to your wife."

Sergeant Nakamura shook his head, unconvinced.

Kenji crossed the small room to stand before his dad's desk. "There's only one way to find out," he said. "When you go see Inspector Mori, I'm going with you."

•

Kenji's father shot to his feet, scooping up his empty cup, said something about getting more tea. But when he got to the back room, he dropped his cup on the counter by the hot water pot and detoured to the toilet instead, pulling the door shut with a bang. Flipping the lock, he spun around and braced himself on the sink, hung his head, breathing hard.

Get a grip, Nakamura. Breathe. Breathe. In, *two, three, four,* hold it, *two, three, four,* out, *two, three, four.* Again. Again. Slower. Again. He straightened and raised his chin, draining the tears back inside. Manly sniff. Clear. Swallow. Good. He frowned into the mirror, grateful to the *sensei* who had taught him how to control his weaknesses. He'd hated the old bastard for how he'd done it, but he'd never have become the man he was without that unforgiving taskmaster. Certainly never would have made it through the police academy. And if he'd never made it through the Academy, he never would have married Sachiko.

That first day at the *koban*—filling out her missing bicycle report as slowly as possible, giving himself time to think of a way to see her again—she'd told him her father had been a sergeant at the police box on the other side of the train station. That her uncle was a beat cop in Chiba.

For a long time, he'd figured that was why a tall, sparkly girl like Sachiko had chosen a quiet, solid guy like him—she came from a family of cops. It wasn't until they were arguing over how to handle the bullying that Kenji's brother Takeo started getting in first grade, that he realized how determined Sachi was to raise a family that was nothing like the one she grew up in. She'd agreed to let him find Takeo a judo teacher, and he'd agreed to let her have a quiet word with the bullies' moms and find someone to help Takeo with his stutter. Something had worked, because both the bullying and the stuttering had stopped, and they still got New Years postcards from the bullies' families.

Twisting the cold water faucet, he splashed water on his face, rubbing it dry with the towel he'd brought from home, freshly laundered for the new year. Sachi had always insisted they start the year right: house clean, debts paid, apologies made. She'd always tried to do the right thing. And so had he. Until the day she died, he'd tried his damndest to be everything she wanted him to be.

Fear clamped his chest again. Sho told him that Mori had found clothes, makeup and a metallic blue Nikon CoolPix camera inside that suitcase. They didn't know that was the same kind of camera Sachi had owned, the one that had never reappeared after her death.

Breathe, dammit, breathe. He slumped over the sink. Fucking Mori. He had to stop Kenji from coming to that meeting. Couldn't let his son hear the questions the Inspector would ask, the same questions he'd been asked ten years ago. The questions he'd pretended he didn't know the answers to.

•

Boom. Boom. Boom. Boom.

Yumi drifted up from sleep. Pulled the pillow over her head. Who was beating a drum at this hour of the. . . ? Oh. This wasn't her room. Kenji's house was a lot closer to the Komagome Shrine than hers. *Kenji.* She turned to peek at the face she'd never seen defenseless in sleep before, but her happiness evaporated when she saw his side of the futon was empty. Where was he? Did he get up early to see the First Sunrise of the New Year? Without her?

She listened. The house was quiet. Feeling around for her phone, she clicked it on. 5:54.

Maybe he'd gotten up to make tea. First Tea of the New Year. First tea *together*. She climbed to her feet, wrapping the comforter around her shoulders like a royal robe. Switching on the light, she looked around for her slippers, found them. Smiled. They didn't match: last night he'd given her one blue plaid, one brown. The First Mismatched Slippers of the New Year.

Scuffing them on, she reached for the doorknob, then hesitated. Had her mascara run while she was sleeping? Yumi swiped beneath each eye with a finger, just in case. She didn't usually wear makeup to bed, but last night after washing her face, she'd put a little back on.

Then she realized what time it was. 5:54. Didn't Kenji's father get off work at six? How long did it take to get to Komagome from Tabata? What if he came through the front door and caught her barefoot, wrapped in Kenji's bedclothes, wearing only her underwear and his son's old baseball jersey?

She looked at the unappealing pile of cold clothes she'd abandoned on the *tatami* last night. Taking a deep breath, she dropped the comforter and scrambled for her tights and skirt. Goosebumps prickled against the chilly t-shirt as she pulled it over her head. Poking her arms into her hoodie, she zipped it up, stuck her hands in the pockets and jumped up and down a few times. Even her bedroom at home was warmer than *this*.

Slipping into the hall, she spied the door to the bathroom standing open and ducked inside. Peering into the mirror over the chipped enamel sink, she experienced the First Regret of the New Year. She never should have cut her hair. Tugging at the short ends near her face, she sighed. It would grow. Eventually.

Leaning in, she examined the mascara that had survived the night and decided it would do.

Hustling down the dark hall toward the kitchen, flipping on lights as she went, she hugged herself, hoping Kenji had turned on the old kerosene heater and started tea brewing. But as she rounded the corner, her steps slowed. The kitchen was dark. No heater, no tea, no Kenji. She stopped, confused. Had he gone out? Had he left her here *alone*?

She found the light switch and flicked it on, illuminating the old-fashioned green linoleum floor, the scarred countertops, the blackened gas burner sitting on the counter. Crossing to the low table surrounded by faded floor cushions, she looked for a note. Nothing but a police exam cram guide, splayed face down where Kenji had left off studying.

Last night, he'd told her about the test that would catapult him into an assistant inspector's uniform in the First Investigative Division if he passed it next May. A promotion to the elite murder squad would mean he'd be set for life. Once he'd stepped onto the career escalator that would steadily raise him into the lofty heights of police administration, he'd be able to afford a car, a house, a family. *A wife.* They'd avoided the word "marriage" because this thing between them was still too new. But she knew how Kenji felt about her. And she no longer had to hide how she felt about him.

At the moment, though, she wasn't feeling so great about his choice of career. Had he been called out on a case? In the middle of the night? On New Year's Eve? Why couldn't criminals take a day off, like everyone else?

Picking up the study guide, she thumbed through it. *Proper search procedure. Hostage situations. Guidelines for use of deadly force.* She quickly set it back on the table, not wanting to be reminded that knowing how to shoot meant that others could be shooting back, and someday he might go to work and never come home.

Turning off the lights, she retraced her steps. Stood in the entry, unsure what to do, but not wanting Kenji's father to come through the front door and find her there alone. That would be . . . awkward. Then she remembered there had been unread messages on her phone when she checked the time. She went to fetch it from Kenji's room.

Sure enough, the one sent at 2:41 a.m. was from him: *got a call, will try to get back before you wake up*

Well, he hadn't.

5:17 a.m., Kenji again: *sorry, still tied up here, not sure when I'll be back. call you later?*

Disappointment closed her throat, as the day that had stretched ahead with such promise shriveled and died. Instead of wandering hand-in-hand among the festival booths at the Komagome Shrine, laughing as they tried to scoop up goldfish with paper nets, sharing sticks of grilled squid and *yakitori* chicken, she'd be stuck with her parents in their drafty old house, eating cold New Year's food, and being dragged along to exchange dutiful New Year's greetings with her father's university colleagues. If Kenji had been assigned to investigate something serious, he'd be on duty until further notice.

Yumi glumly unhooked her coat from the rack. Shrugging into it and winding her muffler around her neck twice, she pulled on one glove, then stopped to see who the other text was from.

12:37 a.m. Her mother. *Where are you? Come home immediately. We have some things to discuss.*

Ugh. It looked like she was about to have the First Fight of the New Year.

Hoping Kenji wouldn't mind if she borrowed one of the umbrellas propped by his front door, she slipped out, angling it against the storm. It was still dark. She trudged through the familiar streets, silent except for muffled crunches as her boots poked holes in the fresh snow. She fumbled a tissue from her pocket and wiped a drip from the end of her nose, skirting a jumble of bikes pushed over by the wind. Her footsteps slowed as she turned the corner toward home.

Snowflakes swarmed down like insects through the cone of light cast by the streetlamp in front of the Hata family's house, settling in the rickety planter beside the front door. The chrysanthemums her mother had been so proud of in November had withered in the sudden cold snap, the stalks now bent under heavy caps of white.

The Hatas' old wooden house huddled between two modest apartment buildings, one clad in grimy stucco, the other in beige tile. The neighborhood had survived the World War II firebombing, but not the temptation to modernize afterwards. Those who could afford it tore down the drafty old wood-and-paper structures their families had lived in for generations and put up multi-story boxes with aluminum windows and a separate floor for the in-laws. But Yumi's grandparents hadn't been among them. The Hata family home was still made of unpainted cedar, stained so dark by years of weather that the wood grain was barely visible anymore. The roof was tiled in dark gray, each crack and dip now outlined in white. Her grandparents had replaced the paper in their *shōji* screen windows with pebbled glass, and stapled thick electrical cords ending in a single boxy outlet to the baseboards of every room, but nothing short of tearing the place down and rebuilding would keep the old house warm in winter and cool in summer.

When Yumi and her parents had moved back from America so her father could take a lecturer's position at Toda University, they'd planned to renovate. But as her dad was passed over time and again for promotion, the plans to tear down the old place and rebuild a home that Yumi's mother could be proud of slowly curled up and died. Over the years, they'd replaced the two burners sitting on the kitchen counter with a real stove and traded the weathered front door for one made of stamped metal and frosted glass. Her mother considered it an improvement, but Yumi secretly thought it looked like lipstick on a washerwoman.

She paused outside, dreading hearing what things her mother thought they needed to *discuss*. Then she realized the windows were still dark. Maybe she'd be able to sneak into her room, shut the door, and sleep past the time her parents left to make the obligatory New Year's visits.

Pulling off one glove with her teeth, she pawed through her purse in search of her key and stepped up to fit it into the lock. *Thwap.* She winced at the sound, slid the door open just wide enough to slip inside, listened. Silence. Easing the door shut behind her, she stood for a moment to let her eyes adjust to the dark, then unwound her muffler, plucked off her hat, and hung her coat by the door.

All she had to do now was get past the squeaky patch in the hall, avoid tripping over the recycling bag in the kitchen, and remember to lift the door to her bedroom as she slid it open, so it wouldn't catch. Slipping out of her boots, she crept down the hall, located the recycling with a cautious toe, then aimed at the door on the far side that led to her bedroom.

"It's about time."

Yumi groaned. Her mother. Sitting at the kitchen table. In the dark.

Mrs. Hata climbed stiffly to her feet and flipped on the lights, wincing at the sudden brightness. A cup of cold tea and a half-finished Sudoku puzzle sat on the table. Hair lopsided from dozing during her vigil, Yumi's mother squinted at her watch, then glared at her daughter.

"Sorry," Yumi muttered.

"What do you mean, 'Sorry'? Why didn't you answer my calls?"

"I'm twenty-six years old," Yumi reminded her.

"And you're unmarried and you live at home, which means you at least owe us the courtesy of letting us know where you are."

"Sorry," Yumi repeated, feeling even less sorry than before.

Silence.

"I didn't want to wake you up, coming in at two in the morning after we visited the shrines, so I crashed at . . . a friend's house."

"I certainly hope that 'friend' wasn't Kenji Nakamura."

Holy crap! How did she know?

"I ran into Haruko Matsumoto on the way home last night," said Mrs. Hata. "She mentioned she'd seen the two of you at the Komagome Shrine, around midnight. What in heaven's name do you think you were you doing? You're supposed to be engaged to Ichiro Mitsuyama!"

"But I'm not!"

"As of yesterday. Which nobody knows. Yet."

Yumi felt a twinge of shame. She hadn't thought about how being seen with Kenji would look to everyone who didn't know the wedding was off. The news had yet to be broadcast on the neighborhood grapevine. Tokyo might be the most populous city in the world, but living in Komagome was like living in a small town. Most of the businesses on the shopping street had been handed down for generations, and most of the residents had grown up together. And their parents had grown up together. And their *grandparents* had grown up together. Gossip from fifty years ago was still repeated as if it had happened yesterday.

"Sorry," Yumi muttered again.

"If you had an ounce of common sense," her mother scolded, "you'd realize that people would jump to the wrong conclusion if they saw you in line at the shrine on New Year's Eve with someone who's not your fiancé." Her eyes narrowed. "Or was it the right conclusion? What's going on, Yumi? Were you carrying on with that Nakamura boy while you were engaged to Ichiro?"

"No!"

But Yumi's face burned. She'd never technically cheated on the man she'd been cornered into marrying after his family arranged for her father to become a tenured professor at Toda University, but she hadn't been able to entirely resist the attraction that had blazed up six months ago when she and Kenji had crossed paths again for the first time since high school.

"I don't think you realize how important it is to let people know about this business in the right way." Mrs. Hata's aggrieved tone told Yumi she had yet to forgive her daughter for turning her back on the match of the century. "If people hear you were already out with someone new on the very same day your engagement was broken, they'll assume you were the one who deserved to be dumped."

•

The sun poked a tentative beam through the trees surrounding the Komagome Shrine, and Kenji breathed a sigh of relief, watching his father laugh for the first time since the blue suitcase had reentered their lives. Toyama Senior had talked them into cutting through the shrine grounds on their way home, where they ran into another poker buddy, busy setting up the grilled squid stand he manned every New Year's Day. Two hours later, the tide in a party-size bottle of saké had been lowered, and they were still there, wearing dark blue festival coats and reddened holiday faces.

Behind them, the shrine's red and gold eaves spread like benevolent wings, soaring over the parishioners as they stamped their feet in the snow, waiting to toss their coins into the slatted wooden offering box. Bright banners snapped in the breeze all around, touting everything from fried octopus balls to roasted sweet potatoes. Fragrant smoke filled the air as the first chicken, squid and skewered sweetfish began to sizzle over charcoal fires. The squid stand enjoyed a choice spot among the vendors lining the main path to the shrine, and a long line of locals arriving to make the new year's first offering had been tempted into detouring for a tasty skewer as they waited to climb the steps to the offering box.

But Kenji and Sho had made their First Shrine Visit the night before, so instead of waiting in line, they were listening to Mr. Toyama reminisce about epic poker games past.

"There you are!" Mrs. Toyama arrived at the stand, towed by a foxy-looking shiba dog. She fixed a baleful eye on her husband and son. "How long does it take to deliver a suitcase, anyway?"

Toyama winced. "Sorry. We got to talking and—"

"—and then Ken-*kun* came, so we had to catch up—" Sho added.

"—and then they stopped by to give me a hand," supplied their squid-grilling friend, beaming with holiday cheer.

"Looks like they've been giving you a hand with that bottle of *dai-ginjo* too," Mrs. Toyama observed dryly, spotting the half-empty saké bottle.

The dog whined and gave her a reproving look.

"I know, sweets," she said, slipping it a treat. Turning to Sho, she said, "Kaiju still has to leave his calling cards at his favorite bushes, but Haru-*chan* asked me to bring her a rice ball for breakfast. Are you going home soon? Could you stop by the Family Mart on your way back?"

"Sure." Sho heaved a party's-over sigh.

Kenji turned to him and said, "That reminds me: congratulations. I hear you're having a baby."

"Yeah, Haru's due any day now. What about you? You married yet?"

"Not yet, but . . . . " Kenji grinned. Yumi. Last night.

"Anyone I know?"

Kenji hesitated. It was still too early to tell anyone. But he smiled, remembering the way her hair fell over her cheek as she slept, how her . . . *oh shit*. What time was it? He checked. How could it already be 9:20? He'd meant to message her long before now. The suitcase had pushed everything else from his mind. He pulled out his phone. *good morning & happy new year! meet me at the shrine? i'm at the squid stand.* Send.

"Hey, by the way," Sho said, "did you hear about that girl you had such a crush on in high school? Yumi Hata? Haru told me she's engaged to some super rich guy, family owns the Mitsuyama department stores. Every girl in the neighborhood is wondering how she got so lucky. I mean, she wasn't even popular in high school." He laughed. "Except with you."

"Actually," Kenji said, a smile spreading across his face as he pocketed his phone, "I hear that wedding is off."

•

Yumi awoke with a start as the phone still clutched in her hand pinged. She must have dozed off after the First Fight.

Text from Kenji. Yes! The First Date of the New Year was back on. She squinted at the time. 9:21.

See you soon, she typed, then flung off the covers and made her way across the cramped room, scooping up last night's dirty clothes and dumping them in her laundry basket. Sliding open what used to be the futon closet, she shivered, rummaging for the pants that would go with her new . . . *kawhumph.* The clothes bar slipped from the wire loops that had been temporarily rigged fifteen years ago and every piece of clothing she owned collapsed in a heap on the floor.

Crap. Why did this always happen at the worst time? It would take half an hour to unhook all the hangers, stick the bar back where it belonged, and re-hang all her clothes. Forget it, she'd do it later. Pawing through the heap, she found the pants she wanted and pulled them from the tangle, then rescued a squashed shopping bag with the sweater she'd been saving for her date with Kenji.

Plucking fresh socks and underwear from her clean laundry basket, she ran to the bathroom for a quick wash.

Fifteen minutes later, she waited until she heard her father cross the kitchen floor, rinse his teacup and head back down the hall, then slung her bag onto her shoulder, and tiptoed to the front door. Pulling a slouchy knit hat down around her ears and grabbing her coat, she muttered a barely audible *"itte kimasu"* and was out before anyone had a chance to reply.

A biting wind was pushing the clouds around the sky and the temperature was dropping. Yumi squinted against the snowy glare, buttoning her coat and pulling on her gloves.

Everything from the corner vending machine to the stone bollards in front of the station had been capped with snow beanies. Yumi slowed to join the throng funneling through the shrine's pi-shaped *torii* gate.

She had already given the gods their due last night when she visited the shrine with Kenji, so she didn't stop to join the four-deep line of people waiting to make their First Offering. A shorter line stood before the jumbo bin that was built specially for New Year's trash, and she was sorry she'd forgotten to bring last year's good-health amulet to burn with the sacred garbage. A shiny laminated sign was tacked to the front of the bin, forbidding people to throw in stuffed animals, good luck Daruma figures and baby dolls. The priests were probably tired of being exposed to the toxic fumes that roiled up as plastic parts went up in smoke, but Yumi couldn't really blame people for wanting to honorably cremate childhood toys that had acquired a soul after years of being loved.

She detoured to the shrine store to buy a wooden prayer plaque screened with this year's zodiac animal. Taking her *ema* to the nearby counter, she flipped it over and penned a wish that she and Kenji would be happy together in the coming year. She took it to the rack already stacked ten deep with her neighbors' hopes and dreams, looking for a peg that wasn't quite full yet.

Making her way back through the crowd toward the food booths, she spotted Kenji behind the counter of the squid stand, smiling and handing two skewers to someone who looked vaguely familiar. Was that their middle school math teacher? Mr. Ito used to be young and crush-worthy! When had his hair turned *gray*?

Kenji looked up and saw her coming. He grinned and waved. Excusing himself, he whipped off his head cloth and shed his festival coat.

"Hey," he said, shouldering through the crowd and handing her one of the squid skewers he'd grabbed on his way out.

"Hey."

"I'm really sorry about last night," he began. "I mean, not all of last night." His face reddened. "Just the part where I left while you were still asleep. Were you still there when you got my messages?"

"No, I went home around six for a shower, some clean clothes and the First Lecture of the New Year."

"The what?"

"My mom heard we were together at the shrine last night, and now she's worried that everyone will think I'm a brazen hussy because they don't know the wedding is off."

Kenji groaned. "On no. I hadn't thought about that. I'm really sorry. I—"

"Don't be. It's stupid. I mean, what is this, the Edo era? Why should we care what people think?"

Kenji was silent. He looked away, suddenly uncomfortable.

"You do care," she said. Her heart sank.

"I'm sorry, Yu-*chan*. It's just . . . I don't just live here, I'm stationed here. It's not that I don't—" He looked around. "Look, can we talk about this somewhere that's not so crowded?"

She fell in behind him as they aimed for the shrine garden, threading their way through the scrum of festival goers. Arcs of split bamboo leapt in and out of the snow, fencing the stone path that led to the gate. It creaked as Kenji pushed it open.

While Kenji brushed the snow from a bench under the bare plum trees, Yumi looked around, thinking how different the familiar garden looked when it was blanketed in white. The moss and low bushes had become undulating hills, with sparkling crests and blue-shadowed hollows. Overhead, crisscrossing plum branches framed fast-moving clouds. In a few weeks, they'd be robed in frilly pink, but today the flower buds knobbing the twigs were still gray and hard as knots.

Kenji sat, pulling her down next to him. Keeping hold of her hands, he said, "Don't get the wrong idea. You know how I feel about you. How I've always felt about you. But . . . . "

"I understand," she said with a sigh. "It's Ichiro's family, isn't it?"

Her ex's father had friends in all the right places, and the ones in the loftier heights of the Police Administration had turned a blind eye last spring when Mitsuyama Senior had forbidden Yumi to testify in one of Kenji's cases. If any of them heard gossip that Kenji was responsible for breaking up the Mitsuyama heir's engagement, it wouldn't matter how mistaken they were, they still might block him from rising any further up the career escalator.

"Hey," she said, seeing his glum face. "Cheer up. I can't believe that the gossip mill in the Mitsuyamas' social circle is any less efficient than the one in Komagome. It shouldn't take long at all for 'Tokyo's most eligible bachelor Ichiro Mitsuyama is back on the market' to be Topic A at the City Club. And I'm sure my mother has already been moaning to her friends about the big fish that got away, so by the time Matsumoto's Coffee Shop opens tomorrow, it'll be on the menu there too." She squeezed his hand. "While we're waiting for word to get around, we can still see each other, can't we? We just have to meet in some part of town where the Great and Good fear to tread."

Kenji was looking a little more cheerful. "Like…?"

"I dunno, Sugamo? Takadanobaba?"

Kenji cracked a smile, recognizing the name of the area known for street markets that sold lucky red long johns to the over-sixty set, and the neighborhood that boasted the highest concentration of outlandish makeup and beauty schools in Tokyo.

"I'm sure there are plenty of places that the Mitsuyamas have yet to conquer," he said. Sobering, he added, "I'm really sorry it has to be like this, Yu-*chan*. I—"

"Shh!" she stopped him, laying a finger on his lips. "Save the apologies for something you *should* be sorry for. Like running out on me in the middle of the night, so I had to face the First Cold Tatami of the New Year alone." She withdrew her hands and tucked them into her jacket pockets. "What happened? Did you get called out on a case?"

"Yeah. Sort of." He fell silent.

"Ken-*kun* . . . ?"

"It was my dad. He called about my mom."

"Your mom?"

"Yeah. He thinks her accident . . . wasn't an accident."

"What?"

Kenji explained about the blue suitcase that had been found in the aftermath of the big quake, a suitcase that had belonged to his mother.

"How did your mom's luggage end up in a basement full of Chinese immigrants?" she asked.

"That's what I'd like to know. My father said she bought the bag for a bus tour to the Ise Shrine, but I'd never seen it before." He shook his head. "Something about this is really upsetting him. I'm going with him when he talks to Inspector Mori tomorrow, to find out what I can."

"But why did he tell you your mother's death wasn't an accident?"

"I don't know that either. I asked him, but he never really answered. The guy who found it told me that the stuff packed inside was tied to an unsolved case from ten years ago, but I don't know why my dad thinks it has anything to do with my mom. I mean, the bag was hers, but the things inside weren't. What's worrying me is that he said Inspector Mori was going to 'try and make this into something it's not.' Sounds like there's some history there, something he's not telling me. Which is why I want to go with him tomorrow and hear what Mori has to say."

Yumi nodded. She wanted to know more about what exactly had happened to his mother, but from the look on his face, now was not the time to ask. She shivered. Cold was seeping through her clothes. Her stomach growled.

She jumped up and put on a smile. "Want to get in line for the First Octopus Balls of the New Year, before the line gets too long?"

"Sure." Kenji climbed to his feet and held the gate for her as they waded into the crowd outside, which had swelled while they'd been talking. The shrine grounds were now a roiling river of merry locals. All round them, people were hailing neighbors they hadn't seen since at least yesterday, stopping to bow and exchange new year's greetings. But as Kenji steered them upstream toward the *takoyaki* stand, a different kind of cry rang out over the hubbub.

"Doctor! We need a doctor! Is anyone here a doctor?"

Heads turned toward a flurry of activity. It seemed to be centered at the squid stand. Kenji craned his neck, then abruptly changed course and began pushing his way through the crowd. Yumi followed as best she could in his wake.

"What's going on?" he called to Mr. Toyama, who was standing behind the grill, stabbing at the keypad of his phone.

"It's your dad! He just . . . collapsed!" Putting the phone to his ear, Toyama shouted, "Hello? *Moshi-moshi*? We need an ambulance! Right away!"

•

Kenji's father lay motionless on the ground, his face ashen. He twitched, opening his eyes. Disoriented, he tried to sit up, but Kenji knelt next to him. "Dad, don't."

The elder Nakamura lay back and looked at his son as if he didn't recognize him. "What? Where—?"

"Just lie still, Dad. The ambulance will be here in a minute."

A faint siren grew louder, then stopped nearby. The crowd parted to allow two white-coated medics to push a gurney through. In a moment they were behind the counter, one kneeling to flip open the latches on the mobile diagnostics case, one moving to Kenji's father's side to begin examining him.

"Stop! What are you doing?" Sergeant Nakamura raised himself on an elbow, trying to sit up. "Get away from me! I'm fine!"

Struggling to his feet, Kenji's father backed away, refusing to let the EMTs near him.

"Who called the white coats?" he protested, shakily brushing bits of dried leaves from his festival coat. "I don't need them!" He glared at the onlookers, who turned away, embarrassed they'd been caught staring.

Kenji stepped up and said, "Dad, just let them check your blood pressure and—"

"I'm fine!" he snapped.

But Mr. Toyama had fetched a chair and Sergeant Nakamura grudgingly allowed himself to be lowered into it as the emergency crew strapped on a blood pressure cuff.

"A man ought to be able to have a few cups of saké after pulling a night shift without calling in the cavalry," he grumbled.

Kenji tried to drape his own coat over his dad's festival jacket, but Sergeant Nakamura shook him off, protesting that he wasn't an old woman and didn't need to be treated like one.

But the paramedic's face was grim as he pulled Kenji aside, showing him the numbers he'd jotted in his work log.

"Dad," Kenji said, kneeling next to the chair. "Why don't you go with them to the hospital anyway, so they can give you a thorough check-up and make sure everything's okay. The paramedic says they want to give you some saline because your blood pressure is dangerously low, and your heart rate is—"

"Of course it is!" his father barked. "Yours would be too after—"

His gaze faltered and his face pinched into the grim mask Kenji hadn't seen since the terrible days after his mother died.

It wasn't an accident.

Kenji turned to the paramedics and thanked them, apologizing that they'd been called out for nothing. He promised them he'd get his dad home and make sure he took it easy the rest of the day. They left the elder Nakamura with stern instructions to rest, drink plenty of water, and avoid alcohol.

Kenji glanced toward Yumi, who was hovering on the other side of the counter, a worried look on her face. He ought to go over there, tell her what was happening, but there were too many people watching, including a couple of Traffic Division officers who'd like nothing better than some fresh gossip to chew over with their grilled squid.

He pulled out his phone and keyed in a message. *sorry, i have to take my dad home. can i call you later?*

A moment later, he saw her reach into her purse and bring out her phone, then type in a reply. *i understand. do you want me to come along? i could help.*

Kenji glanced at his dad. Sergeant Nakamura's gaze was turned inward, his mouth creased in a deep frown.

thanks, Kenji wrote. *but I think i'd better handle this myself. i'll call you later.*

He watched her read his response, saw the disappointment on her face. But all her reply said was, *sure. call me.*

•

The sun had arced across the sky and was on its way down again as Kenji turned his back to the eye-watering breeze that was blowing a glittering plume of snow from the eaves of Sanjo-in Temple. He hunched into his coat, wishing his father would hurry back from the hut where the grave-visiting supplies were kept. He balanced the two skinny bunches of cellophane-wrapped chrysanthemums on a corner of the cemetery's utility sink and shoved his gloved hands into his jacket pockets.

Sergeant Nakamura had gone straight to bed once they got home, ordering Kenji to wake him before 3:00 so they could go to the family New Year's gathering together. But Kenji wasn't convinced that the annual nephew wrestling and saké drinking was such a good idea, so he'd let 3:00 come and go. His father had been so irritated when he woke up at 3:30 that he'd charged around like a bull, angry that they were going to be late. Kenji hadn't dared suggest further changes to the day's plans, so here they were, making their usual visit to the family grave on the coldest New Year's Day he could remember.

His father returned with a wooden bucket and dipper. Kenji took the bucket emblazoned with the Nakamura family crest from him and filled it, as his father picked up the flowers and stalked off into the graveyard. Kenji followed him around the back of the main temple, slipping a little on the snow that was hardening to ice as shadows reclaimed the walkways.

The sun slanted low through the trees as they followed a wide avenue already trampled by dozens of feet since last night's storm. This was an ancient graveyard, in an old part of Tokyo, and only the newest plots had gravestones with spaces for individual names. Family names and crests were all that marked the final resting place of most of the souls spending eternity at Sanjo-in. Family plots lined the path like miniature skyscrapers. Some were topped by polished slabs of granite carved with the family name, others were marked by obelisks. Many had fresh flowers in the vases flanking the headstone, and fresh ashes in the carved stone incense altars that crouched below.

It was easy to tell which graves had been visited today—freshly washed, they were wet and bare, naked-looking next to monuments still cloaked in white. As they made their way to the Nakamura family plot, Kenji saw personalized offerings that told of a mother remembered, an uncle mourned. A favorite cup, filled with tea; a can of beer, to be enjoyed in the hangover-free afterlife; sometimes a pack of cigarettes with one left smoldering beside it.

Right again, then left, the scuffle of footprints narrowing to a path, then a single pair. Those stopped before a rough-hewn slab carved with the crossed-arrow Miura crest. A parting ray of sunlight glinted off a small bottle of saké, the cap cracked open. Whoever had visited the Miura family grave had bought flowers at the same shop as Kenji's father—Kenji recognized the lace-patterned cellophane and the chrysanthemum mix sold by the flower shop near the station.

His father's steps slowed as he approached the stone marked with the Nakamura plum blossom crest. A black cat crouching on the plinth tensed as they approached, then flowed off its perch, pausing to give them a final yellow-eyed stare before disappearing into the bushes.

The tall lotus-topped slab that rose behind the incense altar sported a white cap, and little commas of snow had blown into the deeply carved characters that read "Nakamura." Made of pale granite, the marker had been smoothed by a century of wind and rain. It was scrubbed clean every August before the holiday when spirits returned to visit, but patches of pale gray and black lichen had begun to spot the base again, and were creeping up to claim the incense altar.

Kenji pulled a small trash bag from his pocket, then noticed that someone had already removed the dried chrysanthemum stalks he'd expected to find in the flower holders. Who had visited his mother's grave since they were last here? Had Takeo been here, and not told them?

Kenji's older brother didn't come often, and never at New Year's. He was technically no longer a Nakamura. After high school, he'd landed a job at a venerable sushi restaurant out in Jiyugaoka, and married the owner's daughter. His wife's family had no sons, so the Watanabes had formally adopted him. As Takeo Watanabe, he would someday inherit the restaurant that had been in the family for seven generations. His first duty as eldest son was now to his new family, not the one that had been broken wide open when his mother died.

Kenji's father stripped the cellophane from the flowers and settled them into the holders, while Kenji dipped water from the bucket and ladled it over the stone. When the entire monument was wet and gleaming, his father filled the teacup on the altar from the thermos he'd brought, then fumbled in his pocket for the bundle of incense. Kenji held a lighter to the end until it glowed. His father laid it atop the pile of last visit's ashes, and a coil of smoke began its climb toward heaven. As the wind shook the stiff chrysanthemums in their vases, father and son knelt to pay their respects. Kenji squeezed his eyes shut and folded his hands.

He didn't feel his mother's presence here. He never had. He hated to think of her trapped in the cold, dark vault beneath the plum blossom crest, with only the ashes of long-forgotten Nakamuras for company. A minute ticked by. Two. His knees hurt, but he didn't want to stand up too soon and reveal just how empty these visits were for him.

The breeze changed and the sweet melancholy of incense filled his nose. He opened his eyes a slit and watched the bright orange ends begin to curl. The wind was eroding the pile of ash around it, revealing something small and white.

Was that a cigarette butt? Kenji felt a stab of irritation. This wasn't the first time he'd found one here. He ought to speak to the priests, tell them that kids were using the place as an ashtray. Or it could be vagrants. One year, he'd found a can of cheap beer sitting on the stone too. He stole a glance at his father, his silver head bowed, face hidden. What was he thinking? Was he praying?

The one thing Kenji knew he wasn't doing was crying. Sergeant Nakamura never cried. Not at the funeral. Not at the cremation. Not when they stood around her ashes, picking up the bleached coral shards of her bones with chopsticks and depositing them in the urn.

When they got home, his father had set the white brocade box containing all that was left of Sachiko Nakamura on the family altar, then sat silently before it the rest of the day. And the next, and the next.

Kenji's Aunt Ayako had come to feed the boys and keep the household running, but her brother had made no effort to emerge from his shell-shocked half-life. The family decided it would be best to send Kenji and Takeo to their uncle's family in Osaka until the forty-nine day memorial service. When the boys returned, the white brocade box was gone, and their father was functioning again. A little shaky, but functioning. And Aunt Ayako began coming every day to teach them how to cook and clean and do all the household chores they'd never really thought about before. The one thing she couldn't teach them was how to stay together after the heart of their family was gone.

•

Umph. It was harder to kneel in front of Sachi's grave than the last time he'd been here. Well, it was cold out, wasn't it? Anyone's knees would get stiff, kneeling in a graveyard when it was below freezing. Nothing to fret about—he was still as strong as any of those young bucks he commanded at the police box. He'd have to hide it from Kenji, though—the last thing he wanted was to have to ask for help when it was time to climb to his feet again.

Hiroshi Nakamura stole a glance at his son, then cautiously took a deep breath through his nose. Slowly . . . carefully . . . . Hold it. Let it out. Good. No tightness. No pain. All he'd needed was a few hours' sleep.

The only thing that was wrong with him was that damn suitcase. It had still been waiting there in the entry when he woke up. Reminding him that he'd have to face Inspector Mori again. When the call came, he'd have to go. Didn't have a choice.

But his *sensei* had taught him how to deal with the likes of Mori: *Wait for the right moment, then use your opponent's strength against him.* He'd show up, find out what Mori knew, and not give him a damn thing. *Be like water.* In a contest between a rock and a stream, the stream always won.

Water. Why was his mouth so dry? He could use a cup of water. Or tea. Which reminded him, he had to remember to bring glue with him next time. When he'd filled Sachi's teacup today, he'd noticed it was leaking, and he didn't want Kenji to know he'd accidentally dropped it last year. He'd have replaced it with an identical one if that were possible, but this was the other half of the set they'd picked out on Sado Island. Their first purchase as Mr. and Mrs.

The artist had explained how the cups would become shiny and smooth with years of use—just like a married couple, he'd said with a smile—somehow guessing they were on their wedding trip. They'd debated longer than necessary about which design they liked best, even though neither of them really cared. They'd been painfully self-conscious, needed something to focus on besides the fact that the night before, they'd slept together for the first time.

He still remembered how exhausted he'd been. He'd lain awake beside her most of the night, fretting over whether she knew it had been his first time too.

Did you guess, Sachi? If you did, you never told me.

He'd pretended to be asleep, of course, when she slipped out of the room sometime around 3:00 to use the toilet down the hall. Neither of them had used the private one attached to their room that weekend; they were both too afraid of making embarrassing noises or—even worse—leaving a smell.

Fortunately, things got easier. Sachi was the one who had finally let loose a little burp after drinking half a glass of beer at dinner a few weeks later, her cheeks glowing pink, covering her mouth as she laughed a little, making it okay to be human.

You were so good at that, Sachi. Making things okay. Being human.

She was the one who mended the broken toys, tended the broken hearts, knit their family together again after angry words. His throat closed and he squeezed his eyes tighter. None of them had noticed how good she was at it until after she was gone, when nothing was okay ever again.

Especially Takeo. The son who was so much like him, in so many painful ways. He'd tried to be a good father, tried to keep him from making mistakes he'd later regret. But after Sachi died. . . .

He'd seen Takeo here, in the cemetery. Last year, on Sachi's birthday. Watched his son disappear through the back entrance. Takeo must be doing well—his coat looked new, the flowers he'd left weren't cheap. Was he happy with his new life, his new family? The restaurant had a good reputation. They were famous for the chef's seasonal specialties, so when people asked, that's what he told them. He never admitted he hadn't tried them himself, that he'd never set foot in Takeo's restaurant. Not because he didn't want to, but because he'd never been invited.

A cold breeze flung a sprinkling of ashes onto his coat as a pair of crows rose, squabbling, from a nearby tree. He raised his head. Bracing himself, he slowly climbed to his feet and straightened his jacket, muttering about the cold.

•

Kenji plucked the cigarette butt from the ashes and dropped it into the trash bag, then knotted it and pushed it into his pocket.

The shadows had lengthened in the time they'd been there. He returned the bucket and dipper, then rejoined his father to walk toward Ayako's. He wondered what Yumi was doing right now.

"When we get to your aunt's house," his father said, interrupting his thoughts, "I don't see any reason we need to mention what happened this morning at the shrine."

"What?" Kenji cried. "Why not? Are you afraid she'll make you go to the doctor?"

"She'll certainly try," his father said, his face grim.

"But what about the suitcase? Don't you think we should ask her if—"

A ringtone sounded from his dad's pocket. Sergeant Nakamura fished out his phone and frowned at the unknown number. Held it to his ear.

"This is Nakamura."

He stopped in his tracks, then bowed to the unseen person at the other end of the line. "Ah. Inspector Mori, happy New Year to you too, sir." He listened. "Yes, he did. Yes, it belonged to my wife." Listened. "Tomorrow? Yes, sir, tomorrow would be fine."

Kenji waved his hands to get his father's attention and mouthed the words, "Nine o'clock. Ask if we can meet at nine."

His father turned away. "Yes, eleven would be fine, sir."

"Not eleven, nine!" Kenji yelped. "I have to work! Ask him—"

"Thank you, sir. I'll remember. Fifth floor, Chiyoda Ward headquarters, eleven o'clock. See you tomorrow, sir." He ended the call.

"Why didn't you tell him I'm coming too?"

"Because you're not."

"Why not?"

"You have to work."

"I'll talk to Section Chief Tanaka."

"No."

"Last night you didn't object to me coming along."

"I changed my mind. Inspector Mori wants to talk to me, not you. You don't know anything that will help him."

"And you do?" Kenji challenged. "Anyway, it's not about helping Inspector Mori. It's about finding out why he thinks mom's suitcase is connected to his old unsolved."

"There's no connection."

"Then why did her bag end up in a Shinjuku warehouse full of Chinese illegals?"

"I don't know. And that's what I'll tell him. End of story."

"You said mom took that bag on her trip to the Ise Shrine, but did she bring it home with her? She'd have told you if she'd lost it, right?" Kenji pressed. "Or did Aunt Ayako give it away, like Toyama-*san* suggested last night?"

"It doesn't matter," his father said, face tight. "She's gone, and that suitcase doesn't have anything to do with anything. I don't want you in Inspector Mori's office, hurting your chances of getting into the First Investigative Division next May."

Ah. So that was it.

"Look," Kenji said, his voice softening. "I promise I won't say anything to annoy him. I know I'm not his favorite underling."

"You wouldn't be mine either if you'd made me look like an ass in front of my men. Even if you were right."

A few months ago, Kenji had been working on a case that was taken over by Inspector Mori's elite murder squad. Even though he'd been assigned the lowly task of being the Inspector's driver, Kenji had discovered something that forced Mori to abandon the suspect he had in custody and reconsider his star witness.

Kenji's father shook his head. "I'm doing this for your own good. Butting in on this interview could hurt your career, and it won't be good for your mother's memory if you ask a lot of questions and make him think this connection is something it's not."

"Mori's too good a detective for that," Kenji said. "I don't like the guy, but he's not stupid."

"Don't be so sure. You know how policemen are about the ones that got away."

•

"Aunt Ayako?" Kenji called, appearing in the kitchen doorway with a ravaged food tray that needed refilling.

If his mother had still been alive, their kitchen might have looked like this one—the ancient oil-spotted burner replaced with a shiny stovetop, the creamy walls and cupboards repainted more recently than twenty years ago. Aunt Ayako's refrigerator didn't hum quite so loudly, and the cloth covering the much-scrubbed kitchen table wasn't mottled with faded stains. Only the linoleum on the floor was the same, it's once-shiny surface dimmed by countless moppings. His aunt crouched in the middle of it, tugging at the lid of an old-fashioned storage well in the floor.

She looked up and stood, wiping her hands on her apron.

"Ken-*kun*!" She smiled, her eyes crinkling behind the cat's-eye glasses she'd worn forever, regardless of fashion. "I was wondering when we'd have a chance to talk. I never get to see you, even though you're working right here in the neighborhood."

"Well, that's your fault," he replied. "You haven't been committing enough crimes." He nodded toward the under-floor storage. "Can I help you with that?"

"I only go into it on New Year's," she explained as Kenji took her place. "And the cover sticks worse every year."

He poked his finger through the pull ring that usually sat flush with the floor. At first it didn't budge, but just as his finger was starting to hurt, it popped open. He lifted the square of linoleum-topped wood and set it aside. "What do you want from here?"

"Those trays on top," she said. "Thank you. You can put them over there."

Kenji set them next to the sink, as his aunt began to fill the teapot.

"Join me for a cup?" she asked.

"I'm sure nobody will starve if I don't bring back the snacks right away," he replied, fitting the cover back onto the floor well.

He plucked two cups from the drying rack as his aunt cleared a space on the low table, setting out the teapot and two red lacquer saucers. Crossing to the refrigerator, she returned with a plate of homemade *o-hagi*.

"I've been saving these for you," she said, peeling off the plastic wrap.

Kenji grinned. Sticky balls of sweet rice covered with red bean paste had been his favorite since childhood. The plate barely made it to the table before he grabbed one, blessed it with a quick "*Itadakimasu*" and bit it in half.

"No one even comes close to your *o-hagi*," he moaned around a mouthful of starchy sweetness.

She gave him a catlike smile. "I can't wait to tell that to Etsy Matsumoto."

"No, don't do that!" he yelped. The *o-hagi* from Matsumoto's Coffee Shop were his second favorite.

"I might consider keeping my mouth shut," Ayako said, pouring the tea, "if you tell me what's wrong with your father. Instead of helping the uncles finish their bottle of saké, he's been playing cards with Chiho's youngest boy all afternoon, drinking tea. When I asked him what was the matter, he told me he was getting over a 'bug.'"

"A 'bug'?" Kenji sputtered. "He called something that knocked him out cold in the middle of the squid stand this morning a *bug*?"

By the time he finished telling his aunt about her brother's scare, Ayako's brow was furrowed with disapproval.

"He's such an idiot when it comes to taking care of himself," she fumed. "If you don't make him go straight to the hospital tomorrow, I will. In fact," she rose and began to pull off her apron, "I'm going out there right now to—"

"Wait." Kenji stopped her. "Let him be. He's really got his back up about this, and he's not in the mood to listen to either of us right now. Besides . . . . " He hesitated. "It might just be shock. Last night, Toyama-*san* showed up at the police box with my mother's old suitcase."

Ayako sank back onto her cushion. "What suitcase?"

"A small, dark blue one. Apparently, she bought it for a trip to the Ise Shrine, right before her accident. The police found it two weeks ago, in a storage room, at the back of a Shinjuku warehouse full of illegal Chinese women."

Ayako lowered her voice. "How did your mother's suitcase end up in Shinjuku?"

"That's what I'd like to know. Do you remember seeing it when you went through her things?"

His aunt reflected for a moment. "I don't remember any bags that were small and dark blue."

"You're sure you didn't give it away when you got rid of her clothes?"

Ayako shook her head. "There was a beat-up red suitcase I used to pack up her shoes, but nothing small."

"Then don't worry about it," Kenji said, helping himself to more tea and topping up his aunt's cup. "It'll probably turn out to be nothing. Tomorrow my dad is meeting with the Inspector who discovered it and I'll find out what there is to know."

•

Yumi picked up the last blouse from her closet floor and straightened it on the hanger, making space for it next to the dress she'd reluctantly worn to wish her father's colleagues a happy New Year. Her mother's brittle mood had continued throughout the day, fueled by a new resentment that they ought to be receiving the obligatory visits instead of making them. Although her husband now held a full professorship at a prestigious university—thanks to Yumi's ex-fiancé's father hastily elevating his status before the engagement was announced—their house was far too small and dingy to display to colleagues.

Yumi had escaped to her room as soon as they got home. Flopping onto her futon, she tried calling her best friend again. It rang once. Twice. Why wasn't Coco—

"*Moshi-moshi.*"

Yumi could barely hear her. "Hey, happy New Year!"

Silence. Then a small voice replied, "Happy New Year to you too. I guess."

Uh oh.

"Did you just wake up?" Yumi probed. "How was last night?"

Silence.

"Coco?"

Sniff.

"Hey, what happened?"

Sniff.

What could possibly have gone wrong while her best friend was visiting shrines with the girls she moonlighted with at the Queen of Hearts hostess bar?

"Coco," Yumi said firmly. "You. Me. Coffee. Now."

"Okay." Sniff. "Where?"

Good question. The Tea Four Two and Matsumoto's Coffee Shop would both be closed for New Year's.

"The McDonald's by the station?" Yumi suggested.

"Okay." Pause. "Let me . . . let me just fix my mascara first. See you in, I dunno . . . ten?"

Yumi smiled, ending the call. Whatever was causing Coco's First Tears of the New Year couldn't be too awful if she was planning to fix her makeup before venturing out. She wouldn't, of course, be dolling herself up to Queen of Hearts standards, but even meeting a girlfriend at the local fast food shop would require curling the hair she faithfully bleached to the color of milk tea, applying eyelid glue to achieve the wide-eyed innocent look favored by Princess Gals, and putting on her fake lashes. Yumi doubted her friend would be going full Princess—winter was challenging for fashion cultists whose wardrobe consisted mostly of short, frilly, babydoll dresses—but even in mufti, Coco wouldn't be there in less than thirty.

But Yumi was itching to get out of the house, so she peeked into the kitchen, found it blessedly deserted, then scurried to the entryway. Grabbing her coat and hat, she eased the front door closed behind her with a muttered "*itte kimasu,*" and headed toward the station.

Once outside and free of the old house's gloom, she felt better. Maybe after she dispensed the necessary amount of sympathy for whatever had ruined Coco's New Year's celebration, she could drop a few hints about what was happening with Kenji and do her part to start the neighborhood grapevine humming. She'd have to be careful, though—Coco had cast her as some kind of modern Cinderella when her engagement to the son of the Mitsuyama Department Store chairman was announced, and when things hadn't worked out, Yumi had been surprised to discover that her friend was more than a little disappointed. Even a little . . . disapproving.

Stamping the snow off her boots, Yumi pushed through the heavy glass door into the McDonald's. It was deserted, except for a young couple ordering coffee to go. The guy behind the register must have been pressed into service after barely completing his training, because he was painfully slow, nervously checking a cheat sheet beneath the counter at every step. Yumi hoped whoever was manning the coffee machine knew what they were doing—anyone with a shred of seniority would naturally avoid working on New Year's Day.

"Medium coffee, for here," she said, stepping up to the counter.

As she dug through her purse for change, a voice behind her said, "Make that two."

Coco reached past her and slipped a five-thousand-yen note onto the pay tray.

Yumi turned, surprised. She offered the coins, but Coco waved her off with a half-hearted smile and a "Happy New Year."

"Thanks." Yumi picked up their drinks as the clerk counted out the change with painful deliberation. "How did you get ready so fast?"

Coco pointed a bejeweled nail at the curls cascading from under her fur-trimmed deerstalker and said, "Wig."

"That's a wig? Really? It looks like your real hair. Where did you get it?"

"This girl I work with at the Queen of Hearts told me about a shop in Kabuki-chō, where you can get any kind of wig for cheap. That's how she changes her hair color so often without turning it to straw."

They stopped to raid the cream and sugar stand, then Coco led the way upstairs to a table by the window, in the smoking section. After they shed their coats and doctored their coffee, Coco pulled over an ashtray and lit up.

"Okay, spill," Yumi commanded. "What happened? You went shrine hopping with the girls from the Queen of Hearts, and . . . ?"

Coco tipped her head back and blew smoke at the ceiling. Sighing, she admitted, "I wasn't with them the whole night."

Ah. Should have known. *A man.*

"Was it that customer you told me about?" Yumi guessed. "The one who was begging you to go to that really expensive restaurant at Skytree with him?"

"Yeah." Coco gazed out the window. "It was so clear that night, you could see the lights all the way to Saitama."

"Wait . . . you went? And you didn't tell me?"

"I couldn't." Coco busied herself tapping her ash. Then she glanced at Yumi and admitted, "I didn't want to tell you, because you were in the middle of breaking up with Ichiro and—" She hung her head. "He's married."

"Coco!"

"I know. I know it was stupid. But he was so sweet, and he swore he'd never been in love before—not like this—then he gave me a little diamond necklace and said he was planning to leave his wife, but he couldn't do it until after he got his year-end bonus, and—"

Coco fell silent.

"And . . . ?" Yumi prompted.

"Well, I had this idea. I bought us these really cute matching keychains and thought I'd surprise him at his local shrine at midnight on New Year's. You know, after he got his bonus and told his wife and all."

"Oh, no." Yumi groaned. "Let me guess. He showed up with her."

Coco didn't say anything.

"And I bet it didn't look like she was getting the boot anytime soon."

"Or ever." Coco stubbed out her cigarette. "She was eight months pregnant."

Yumi's mouth dropped open.

"Don't say it," Coco warned. "Just don't—"

"I have to. What an asshole!" Yumi shook her head. "The thing I don't understand is why you'd even consider settling for someone like that. I mean, you've had guys chasing you since you were thirteen."

"Yeah." Coco sighed. "Chasing. Not asking me to marry them." She frowned. "You don't understand, because it was so easy for you. You got engaged to the first guy you met."

"Yeah, but that didn't work out so great, did it?"

Coco's face softened. "Yesterday was the day, wasn't it? Did you really break things off with Ichiro?"

"And his family." Yumi grimaced. The undoing of the arranged marriage had required a carefully scripted sit-down, at which both sets of parents stiffly exchanged formal apologies and agreed to reparations.

"Was it awful?"

"Yeah. Pretty awful."

"Well, at least it's over. Now you can get on with your life." Coco sat up and tried to smile. "Good timing, too. We can be single again together!"

No they couldn't. Yumi opened her mouth to tell Coco about Kenji, then clamped it shut again. How could she drop the news that she already had another boyfriend, when her best friend had just been dumped? Fortunately, Coco was rummaging in her purse and didn't notice her sudden discomfort.

"You know," Coco said, pulling a slightly crumpled flyer from her bag. "We'll both feel a lot better if we get out and swing the bat again right away. I was saving this to give to you, but now we can do it together."

She handed the glossy leaflet to Yumi.

MEET HIGHLY PAID PROFESSIONALS
SEEKING WEDDED BLISS.

Yumi frowned and opened it. Flowery lettering, a soft-focus shot of a bride and groom, handsome men and women walking hand in hand under blooming cherry trees. Free consultation, it said. Which undoubtedly meant their other services weren't.

"Paid introductions?" Yumi flipped it over, looking for a fee schedule. LuvLuv Match had left that part out. She'd heard that matchmakers charged for every step on the road to matrimony, and love didn't come cheap.

She handed the brochure back. "No can do. A successful hostess like you can probably afford it, but not a lowly part-time translator like me."

"Actually," Coco said, leaning across the table. "I can get us a deal. I know one of the owners. I called him this morning."

"What?"

"He says that he can offer us a deal, and assured me the men who've signed up so far are all on the up and up. He checked them out thoroughly."

Checked out their wallets, more likely, Yumi thought. "No thanks. What kind of L-O-S-E-R is so desperate he needs to pay someone to find him a girlfriend? You'd have better luck asking Auntie Ayako to fix you up."

Coco made a face. "And end up with someone we've known since kindergarten? Or, more likely, their *uncle*? I mean, Auntie Ayako must be older than my mother." Coco dropped the flyer back in her purse. "Unless . . ." She cocked an eyebrow at Yumi. "You think she'd set me up with her nephew?"

"Nephew?" Yumi sat up in alarm. Komagome's unofficial matchmaker had been Ayako Nakamura before she married. "You mean Kenji?"

"Yeah. Ever since he got that mole fixed . . . . "

The Mole. Even Yumi had failed to consider Kenji Nakamura as boyfriend material when they were in high school, because of the big black carbuncle that used to sit right next to his nose.

". . . I mean, who would have guessed that frog would turn into a prince?"

Oh no, was Coco interested in—?

"Ha, what's with the face?" Coco laughed. "I'm joking, duh. Mr. Police Detective isn't my type." She fixed Yumi with a stern glare. "And he's not yours either, missy. Now that you're single again, let me remind you of the first rule of happily-ever-after: never fall for a guy who loves his job more than he loves you."

"Come on, Coco, he's not really like that. You just happened to—"

Her friend stopped her by holding up a well-manicured hand. "Hey, all I know is that when I asked him to go with me to that kimono event at your ex's store last fall, the only women he was interested in talking to all night were witnesses. I know you two are buddies, but honestly, don't let him rope you into helping him catch bad guys for a while. It might take more time than you think to replace Ichiro."

"Coco, honestly," Yumi objected, "I'm not really in that much of a hurry to—"

The first few bars of "Don't Need You" blared from the jewel-encrusted phone on the table. Coco picked it up, scanned the message.

"Who's it from?" Yumi asked.

Coco smiled. "Hoshi."

"I thought you were over him," Yumi said. With his bleached rock star hair and flashy suits, Club Nova's number one hostboy looked like the kind of prince every Princess Gal dreamed of, but his attentions came at a price. His specialty was making every woman who sat at his table believe they were first in line to be his girlfriend. He poured them drinks, whispered sweet nothings into their ears, and charged them handsomely for the privilege.

"What does he want now?"

"To do me a fa-a-vor," Coco said with an arch smile. She keyed in a reply, then turned to Yumi. "And you'd better be free Friday night, Miss Newly-Singlepants, because we've got plans."

•

The sushi knife stalled on the sharpening block as Takeo's thoughts were hijacked again by the phone call from Kenji.

It had been a long time since he'd examined his feelings about his father. Like a ticking clock he couldn't quite bring himself to throw away, he had buried that relationship as far away as possible from his everyday life, hoping that the batteries would run down. That someday, being reminded of his dad would no longer infuriate him.

This morning he'd been surprised to discover it had worked—when his brother had called to tell him their dad had collapsed at the shrine's squid stand, Takeo had felt a stab of loss, fearing the old man was dead. Not so long ago, he would have been relieved to hear that he never had to see his father again, that he'd never again be reminded that he hadn't measured up. He wondered if it was becoming a Watanabe or just the passing of time that had defused his anger . . . .

"Takeo, have you finished with the knives yet?" His father-in-law appeared with a tray of fish. "It's almost opening time."

"Sorry. Almost done."

He resumed sharpening, using the familiar repetitive motion to distract himself from the other thing that had been needling him since his brother's call. He badly wanted a cigarette. But that craving hadn't been brought on by the news about his dad—it was because of the other questions Kenji had asked. Questions about a suitcase. Takeo hadn't known anything about it, and had said so. But his younger brother was a detective now, and poking into things is what detectives did. It sounded like he was going to try and find out what had happened the day their mother died. Dig everything up. Dig *everything* up.

Sharpen, sharpen, sharpen. Takeo wanted that cigarette. Wanted it more than he'd ever wanted one since the day he quit. Since the day his mother died.

•

Kenji locked the front door of their house as his father excused himself to get ready for bed. The sound of running water came from the bathroom as Kenji swept the entry and made himself a cup of tea. He settled himself at the kitchen table to do some test prep and tried to concentrate on interview protocol, but his thoughts kept straying to the dusty blue suitcase sitting near the door. His dad had wedged it into a space next to the shoe cupboard, as if not letting it past the entry would keep the uncomfortable questions it raised from intruding any further into their lives.

As soon as snores began to rattle the door of his dad's room, Kenji closed his study guide and made his way down the hall to fetch the bag. Laying it on the kitchen table, he noticed that the dust wasn't all from the warehouse—some was fingerprint powder. Had the crime lab found anything? Kenji made a note, so his father could ask Inspector Mori tomorrow.

He stared at the suitcase, wondering if it was as empty as it felt. Taking a deep breath, he unzipped it. Lifted the lid. Disappointment and relief. The contents Sho had mentioned were gone. Nevertheless, Kenji ran his hand inside all the compartments. Not even a safety pin. Zipped it back up. He checked the outside pocket. A luggage tag. With a pang, he recognized his mother's neat handwriting. Her name, their address. He set it aside and reached into the pocket again, drawing out a white business-size envelope with a folded sheet of paper inside. The receipt Sho had mentioned.

Happy Holiday Bus Tours, Ise Shrine, 11/27–11/28. Three round trip tickets, sold to Sachiko Nakamura, paid for by JCB credit card, Total: ¥78,900.

He skimmed the tour description. In addition to the Ise Shrine, they had stopped at Toba ("Pearl Growing Capital Of Japan"), spent the night at a traditional inn, and stopped to view the autumn leaves at Korankei on the way back.

The 27th—what day of the week had that been? He looked it up. A Saturday. His mother and her middle-aged friends had probably been the youngest tourists on the bus. The only reason anyone under thirty would go see autumn leaves on a weekend was to give them an excuse to hold hands with their main squeeze, and you didn't need to go all the way to Korankei for that.

He checked the bottom line again. Three tickets. Credit card. His mother must have made the arrangements, then her friends had paid her back. In cash? Sure enough, there was a crease in the envelope, right where it would be if had been folded around a stack of yen notes.

What had happened to the ¥52,600 her friends had given her for the other two tickets?

THURSDAY, JANUARY 2

•

Another rainy day. Kenji didn't have to check his watch to know that if the squad room was emptying, it must be noon. By 12:05 he was alone, sitting at his desk, slurping up the last of his instant ramen from its Styrofoam cup.

Unlike his neighbor, Detective Oki, who worked amid an ever-growing collection of framed snapshots of his students receiving their judo black belts, Kenji's desk was almost bare. In-box, laptop, pencil cup, phone.

He drained the rest of the ramen broth. As lunches went, it was bottom of the barrel, but at least it was fast. He wiped off his personal chopsticks and stowed them in his desk drawer, then walked his trash over to the recycling bin. Checked the time. Surely his dad's interview with Inspector Mori would be over by now. He returned to his desk and called.

"This is Nakamura."

"Hey Dad, it's me. How did your meeting with Inspector Mori go?"

"Fine."

Kenji waited for more. It didn't come. Why was trying to get information from his father harder than prying a confession from a criminal?

"What did he ask you?" Kenji persisted. "Why does he think Mom's suitcase is tied to his unsolved?"

"He's grasping at straws."

"What kind of straws?"

"The kind you can't build a case from. You know how some guys let the ones that got away eat at them? Well, Mori's one of those. Just because they found her bag in a warehouse with illegal aliens, he thinks it's tied to some case he worked when he first got kicked upstairs."

"But—"

"But nothing. There's no connection, and I told him so. I'm glad you called, though, because I wanted to remind you I'll be out tonight, so you're on your own for dinner."

"Where are you going?"

"The Komagome Volunteer Firemen's Association New Year's Party."

A drink-a-thon if there ever was one. *Rest, drink lots of water, avoid alcohol.*

"Dad, are you sure you should go? Maybe it would be better if you took it a little easy, after—"

"I'll be back late. Don't wait up." Click.

Kenji scowled at his phone, then tossed it on top of his in-box. Flopping back in his chair, he gave an exasperated sigh.

"Already giving up on catching our underwear thief?"

Detective Oki dropped a bottle of hot tea and two packets of fried pork sandwiches on the desk next door, and eased his bulk into his own chair. At the staff meeting yesterday, the pursuit of a man who'd been stealing women's panties from clotheslines had been reassigned to Kenji, so Oki could concentrate on a string of store burglaries.

"Nah," Kenji replied. "I figure it's only a matter of time before you break down and confess."

Oki gave a snort of laughter. Suspects often saw only his good-natured face and burly build and were fooled into thinking they could outsmart him, right up to the moment he tricked them into confessing. He had ten years more experience than Kenji, and although he wasn't on the elite career track, he'd nearly had a psychology degree in hand when he transferred to the police academy.

"So, why the big sigh?" the detective asked.

Kenji told him about the suitcase and the frustrating conversation with his dad.

"Why don't you call Mori yourself?" Oki suggested, unwrapping a sandwich.

"You think he'd take the call? He doesn't like me much."

"And neither would I, if I were an inspector in the First Investigative Division and I had to share the glory for my biggest solve of the year with a lowly Komagome Station detective." Oki took a bite. "But I'll give him one thing—he likes to close his cases. If you really want to get his attention, maybe you should offer him the help he didn't get from your dad."

Kenji hadn't thought of that.

"It's worth a shot, anyway," the big detective said.

Kenji picked up his phone. Inspector Mori's number was still in his Contacts, from the case they'd worked together last year. He dialed. Left a voicemail.

"Mori-*san*, this is Kenji Nakamura from Komagome Station. My father came in this morning to talk to you about a suitcase you found in Shinjuku after the earthquake, and I suspect he didn't give you what you needed." He hesitated. "But I've been thinking—maybe there's some way I could be of assistance. Please let me know if there's anything I can do to help."

Ending the call, he began reviewing Oki's notes on the panty thief. Nine local women had complained of missing underwear since early November. The thief had only taken sexy garments, but not all the victims were the kind of women one expected to own sexy underwear. In fact, a few of them—

Kenji's phone rang.

"Nakamura."

"This is Mori." They exchanged New Year's greetings out of politeness, then Mori got straight to the point. "Are you actually volunteering to take a crack at the Sergeant Nakamura who failed so spectacularly to help me this morning?"

"I apologize for any inconvenience he may have caused you, sir," Kenji said. "He had a health scare yesterday, and he's not himself."

"Really? Because he seemed *exactly* like the same stubborn man I called in ten years ago when we were investigating a murder in Shimbashi. The same stubborn man who asked his detective buddy at Shinjuku Station to run a search on the license plate of a brown van belonging to our main suspect in the Painted Doll murder."

"What? Sir?"

"It was the first case I worked as an Assistant Inspector— the death of an illegal, a Chinese prostitute. She was dumped in the gutters of Shimbashi. We only had one witness, a vagrant, dossing in a doorway. Under hypnosis, he remembered a partial license plate on a brown van he saw speeding away from the scene. That was our only lead, so when I got a call that someone had run a check on a plate that matched what the witness had given us, I called your father down to headquarters."

"Why was he running the plate?"

"Because your mother came back from some trip to the Ise Shrine and said she saw a man shoving a woman into that very same van, against her will."

"My *mother*? My mother was a witness to an abduction? And she didn't go to the police?"

"She did go to the police. She just went to the *wrong* police. I called her in, but your father had made her promise not to talk to us. She wouldn't tell us anything, just sat across from me with her hands in her lap, saying, 'I don't remember, I don't remember.' And because she refused to help us," his voice took on a bitter edge, "we never caught the killer. Which means he's still out there, eating ramen, drinking beer and getting laid, while the girl he killed went home in a box."

Kenji was stunned. Why had his father forbidden his mother to talk to the police? He couldn't really blame Mori for not wanting to let that one go.

"I'm sorry my dad didn't help you," Kenji said. "But maybe I can. What was it you wanted from him?"

"I want to know how your mother knew the victim."

"I'll try to find out for you, sir. Anything else?"

"I want the picture."

"What picture?"

"The picture of that brown van. Your father claimed there wasn't one, but I'm sure you know how unreliable eyewitnesses can be. When suddenly faced with a women being shoved into a van against her will, I doubt even a policeman's wife would have the presence of mind to memorize all ten characters and numbers on a license plate. There has to be a photo. I want it."

"I'll do my best to find it for you, sir."

•

"Could you please excuse me for a moment?" Yumi bowed to the head of the Toda University history department over the lunch table. "I'm afraid I need to find the . . . . " She let her eyebrows communicate the indelicate word "restroom."

Then she excused herself in English, bowing to the American scholar who was being interviewed for a fellowship.

Trying not to feel the foreigner's eyes roaming all over her legs and *oshiri* as she retreated, she wished that the orange and brown uniform of the International Interpreting Company was even uglier than it already was. The American professor's wedding ring had disappeared sometime between his interview at the chairman's office and sitting down at the restaurant. For the past forty minutes, he'd been making a critical career error, relentlessly chatting up his interpreter instead of giving the history chair a chance to hold forth on his favorite subject, Elizabethan barge traffic.

Yumi was counting the minutes until she could be rid of them both, silently thanking Kenji for returning her call. Locking herself in a stall, she called him back.

"Nakamura here."

"It's me," Yumi said.

"Hi, me." He paused. "Uh, I'm really sorry I forgot to call you back yesterday—"

"That's okay. I understand. How's your dad?"

"Fine. Sort of. He's refusing to admit anything's wrong." Kenji sighed. "He made me take him to my aunt's for the family New Year's party yesterday, even though I didn't think it was a good idea. And he went to see Inspector Mori this morning. Alone."

"Why didn't you go with him?"

"He refused to let me come. But I called Mori, and he believes my mother's bag is linked to a case they called the Painted Doll murder."

"A murder?"

Yeah. An unsolved murder. Mori thinks—" Kenji covered the mouthpiece and said something she couldn't hear, then returned to say, "Sorry, Yu-*chan*, I'll have to tell you later. Gotta run."

"Wait!" Yumi cried. "How about dinner tonight?"

"Sure. But where? You know we should be careful about—
"

"I'll find somewhere good in an obscure neighborhood and let you know."

She returned to the table just as the department chair was paying the check and the fellowship candidate was refusing a tea refill. Apparently, five minutes in each other's company without being able to communicate about their pet subjects had convinced them both it was time to leave.

Outside on the sidewalk, she bowed to the chairman, thanking him for lunch and accepting his thanks for interpreting. Then she thwarted the American's attempt to plant a kiss on her cheek by thrusting out her hand and giving him a quick, businesslike shake, pretending she was out of business cards so he wouldn't be able to contact her.

In her haste to get away, she charged off in the opposite direction from the station. Crap. Well, she didn't want to wind up on the same train as Mr. Unwelcome Advances, PhD, anyway. It wouldn't hurt to kill a few minutes drinking a cup of coffee somewhere and checking her messages.

Yumi chose an inviting café by the bridge and climbed the stairs to the second floor, settling into an empty seat next to the window. The view wasn't much—a coffee shop, a *yakitori* restaurant, a canal with steep cement sides that plunged down to a trickle of water that was all that remained of what had once been a river. A lone cherry tree arched over its banks, branches bare and shivering.

But inside the Ten Degrees Cafe, conversations hummed companionably around her, as young men in suits did business over their cappuccinos, friends met for a quick gossip, and students hunched over their keyboards, brows furrowed, fingers fluttering.

While she waited for her coffee, Yumi noticed a little sign that explained why the place was so busy: Free wifi. Pulling her laptop from its sleeve, she typed in the access code, checked her messages, then opened a window and sat for a moment, trying to recall the name of the case Kenji had mentioned. Something-doll. Baby Doll? Rag Doll? No, Painted Doll.

Scrolling through the first four pages of search results—how could there be so many fetish hobbyists in Tokyo? —she found what she was looking for.

The top article was headlined "Painted Doll Killer Claims Second Victim." A foreign illegal had been found dumped in a gutter in the middle of the night, but she hadn't been the first. Yumi skimmed the piece, noting the name of the first victim, and did another search.

Her coffee arrived, and she settled in to read. Victim number one had been a 28-year-old Chinese woman, who had recently quit her job as a sex worker in the Kabuki-chō red light district. Dumped on the side of the road in Ueno, sometime after two in the morning, she'd been found dressed in a flight attendant's uniform that was considerably shorter than regulation. Her makeup was flawless, her hair professionally styled. A vagrant interviewed by the reporter said he thought she was drunk, that he'd tried to wake her up. She looked like a doll, he said, a doll that had been tossed into the gutter when her owner tired of her.

Six weeks later, when another foreign woman was dumped in Shimbashi, the reporter resurrected that quote and suggested a connection between the cases, dubbing them the Painted Doll killings. Police denied the link, pointing out that although both women worked in adult entertainment and had been found wearing what looked like professionally-applied make-up, the second victim had been left by the side of the road in a completely different neighborhood, and was dressed as a nurse, not a flight attendant. Plus, they'd died in different ways—the first victim had been strangled, the second, stabbed.

Yumi examined the artist sketches that went with the articles. Both victims were young, Asian and beautiful. How had girls like that ended up dead in a gutter, so far from home? And why had there been no follow-up articles?

She scrolled back to the top and found the byline. Jack Goldman. A foreigner who wrote for a Japanese newspaper? Why did his name sound familiar?

Then she remembered scanning the upcoming work roster on the office website this morning. The International Translating Company had just posted a request for two Japanese-to-English translators and three Japanese-to-Chinese translators for professors attending next week's Symposium on Organized Crime in the Asia-Pacific Region. "Renowned reporter Jack Goldman" was one of the keynote speakers.

Yumi composed an email to her supervisor, asking if the Japanese-to-English translator slots had been filled yet.

•

Kenji stepped into the warm restaurant Yumi had chosen, grateful to be out of the snow that had started up again as he walked from Takadanobaba Station.

Pulling off his gloves as the door slid closed behind him, he nodded to the server who greeted him with an "*Irasshaimase!*" as he brushed past to deliver a fragrant order of grilled mushrooms.

Seats lined a polished wooden counter surrounding an open kitchen, where whole chickens and salt-crusted fish roasted over a crackling fire. Spotlights washed the rough plaster walls and touched the faces of the diners with a warm glow as they sat at the counter and joked companionably with the chefs.

Kenji scanned the room. There she was, seated at the end of the counter, next to the wall, her head bent over the menu. A wave of nostalgia swamped him. From this angle, she still looked exactly like the schoolgirl he used to steal glances at over the tops of his books while she was studying in the school library. The way she twirled a stray lock of hair while concentrating, the slight frown as she puzzled over *kanji* characters— Suddenly, all he wanted to do was leap across the restaurant, pull her to her feet and say "Forget dinner." He'd tell her his father was drinking with the Volunteer Firemen tonight, and—

Yumi looked up and saw him. She smiled, waved. He took a deep breath and shook off the crazy. What was he thinking? Later would be soon enough. His dad wouldn't be home until past midnight.

Making his way across the room, he accepted a hot hand towel from the server and ordered a beer as he slid into the seat next to her.

"So, will there be a quiz?" He laughed. "When I saw you across the room just now, I remembered how I used to watch you studying in the library. Not that you'd have noticed, even if I weren't hiding behind my book. I don't think you'd have looked up, even if an earthquake had flattened the building around you."

"That's because it took me forever to get through my homework." She grimaced. "I could barely read Japanese when I got here."

"Yeah, but you sure could speak. Remember the look on what's-her-name's face? You fooled us all at first, because you didn't say anything but 'yes' or 'no' when the teacher stood you up in front of the class."

"You wouldn't have answered either," she retorted, "if the questions were as stupid as 'Did you ever see anyone get shot?' and 'Do you know Bart Simpson?'"

Now he was sorry he'd mentioned it—clearly she wasn't as fond of that memory as he was. It had taken their classmates nearly a week to discover that even though the new girl couldn't read or write *kanji* characters, that didn't mean she was stupid. A few days later, Yumi had overheard a pair of girls talking about her at lunch, and she had marched over to set them straight, teaching them some new words in the process. The astonished queen bee had run to the teacher, and Yumi had been scolded for using language that was more appropriate coming from a movie gangster than a third-grader. After that, though, word got around that she spoke Japanese as well as they did. Better, if you counted the *yakuza* swear words.

"I still sometimes have trouble with the characters for weird ingredients," Yumi admitted, scooting closer. "Do you know what this one is?" She shared the menu, pointing to a description of the seasonal green beans called *soramame*.

A few minutes later, food on the way, he sat back in his chair and smiled. "The food here looks good. How did you find this place?"

"I asked the server at the café I was at this afternoon. It's right down the street." She took a sip of her wine, then said, "They had free wifi, so I looked up that case you mentioned. The Painted Doll murders. Why does Inspector Mori think your mom's suitcase is connected?"

Kenji sighed. He wished he knew. He'd spent every spare minute that afternoon searching for information, but he'd ended up with more questions than answers.

"Ten years ago, my mother apparently saw a man shoving a woman into a van that had the same license plate as the one seen speeding away from the murder scene," he explained.

"Your mom saw the Painted Doll killer's van? Where?"

"I don't know. It was while she was on that bus trip to the Ise Shrine, but I don't know where she saw it. And neither does Mori. My mom told my dad, but he refused to let her say anything to the police."

"What? Why?"

"I don't know. He shuts me down every time I ask about it, and when I searched police records, I discovered that the whole Painted Doll investigation has been sealed off behind a password-protected firewall. All I know is what Mori told me and what little was reported in the press."

They were interrupted by the arrival of their wood-roasted chicken with fresh wasabi salsa, along with two prawn croquettes. A salad sprinkled with tiny dried fish, and a dish of grilled *soramame* followed close behind.

The talk turned to Coco's New Year's debacle and Sho Toyama's baby. A stack of empty plates, two bowls of rice and another beer later, Kenji called for the check. Yumi returned from the ladies' room, pulling on her woolly gloves.

They stepped outside and stopped, transfixed. While they'd been eating, the world had changed. Giant snowflakes floated down through the glow of the red lantern across the street, deepening the white cloak that had been draped over the footprints and ruts in the alley outside. Now that the students who usually thronged Takadanobaba's streets had gone home, it felt like they had the city to themselves.

"Want to take the long way back to the station?" Yumi suggested.

"The long way?"

"We could walk along the canal. Nobody we know would see us together."

She was looking up at him expectantly, eyes shining, snowflakes turning to jewels on her eyelashes. His heart skipped a beat.

"I have a better idea," he said. Popping open his umbrella, he grabbed her by the hand and pulled her along the street toward the station.

His father wouldn't be home for hours.

•

Stifling their laughter so they wouldn't attract the attention of the neighbors, they stamped their feet on the back step of Kenji's house to get the snow off before he unlocked the door. They'd avoided holding hands as soon as they neared Komagome, and taken back alleys from the station, but the moment they stepped into the kitchen, Kenji didn't even flick on the light before Yumi was in his arms. The fresh scent of winter filled his head as his lips met hers. He crushed her against him, letting go briefly to fumble with her coat buttons, unwinding her—

A loud snort came from down the hall. They jumped. It turned into a snore. They looked at each other in dismay.

How could his father already be home? He never left the Volunteer Firemen's parties before the last saké bottle was empty. Worried now, Kenji put a finger to his lips, slipped off his shoes, and crept down the hall to check. Sure enough, his dad was already in bed. The elder Nakamura muttered something in his sleep and turned over.

Kenji eased the door shut and returned to Yumi, but disappointment had thrown the switch on the electricity that had been sparking between them, and she was already buttoning her coat. He bent to put his shoes back on, so he could walk her home, but she stopped him.

"It's only a few blocks," she whispered. "I should probably go by myself, in case my mom's still up."

Kenji couldn't disagree. "Tomorrow?" he suggested. "It's Friday, so maybe we could catch a movie or something?"

She grimaced. "Sorry, I can't. I promised Coco I'd go somewhere with her." Seeing Kenji's raised eyebrow, she added, "Don't ask, because I don't know. I'd have said no if she hadn't just been dumped by a guy she was seeing, but I think I ought keep an eye on her so she doesn't fall into Hoshi's clutches again."

"What about Saturday?"

"Yes." She stretched up for a final kiss, then he helped her tuck in the end of her muffler. They held each other for a long moment, then she pulled away and cold air took her place as she slipped out the door.

Kenji locked it behind her, then took his coat to its peg in the entryway, frowning as the snoring coming from his father's room reminded him that all was not well.

Returning to the kitchen, he scooped up the teapot from the drying rack and dropped in a spoonful of leaves. Tipping it to fit under the hot water pot's spigot, he began to fill it, but the water gurgled to a stop before the teapot was even half full. Kenji's worry deepened. His father had never forgotten to refill it before he went to bed before. Something *was* wrong. Tomorrow he'd have to insist they go to the doctor, whether his dad wanted to or not.

He filled the hot water pot from the tap and plugged it in. The old clock above the table read 10:15. Too early to go to bed. Would it be safe to look for his mother's camera, try to find that photo Inspector Mori wanted so badly?

The room where his father slept was off-limits, but he could search the rest of the house. It wouldn't take long, because the camera obviously hadn't been stored in the bathroom, and he knew his own bedroom cupboard was filled with baseball trophies, old comic books, and the futon his brother hadn't used since he became the official eldest son of the Watanabe family.

That left the kitchen.

The Ready light flicked on atop the hot water pot, and Kenji finished making tea. He took a sip from the stained mug that had somehow become his over the years, then turned slowly, surveying the room where he and his father ate nearly every meal together.

The cupboard above the counter was stacked full of the dishes they used every day; he knew it wasn't in there. But what about the cardboard box sitting atop the refrigerator? He lifted it down and set it on the floor, brushing off the dust and prying open the flaps. Inside were the vases his mother had used to display cherry and plum branches, and a set of red lacquer bowls painted with golden pine needles. She had unwrapped those only at New Year's, and for a moment he could almost smell her *ozōni*, the fragrant holiday soup filled with baby vegetables and melting rice cakes. Pushing away the sorrow that he'd never taste it again, he closed the flaps and shoved the box back in its place.

The taped-up carton on the pantry floor proved to be full of spices gone gray with age, and the box squatting at the back of the cabinet under the sink held only lacquer polish, a *tatami* brush and other seldom-used cleaning supplies.

Kenji stood and stretched the kink from his back. Frowning, he surveyed the kitchen. There was nowhere else to look, unless— Was there a storage space beneath the linoleum, like at Aunt Ayako's? He set down his teacup and walked the floor, looking for a pull-ring. He pushed the table aside and rolled up the area rug. Nothing but a spider, scurrying to safety.

He looked around, saw the door to the pantry standing open. Crossing the floor, he moved the box of old spices, shifted half a dozen unopened bottles of beer, and dragged out a 20-pound bag of rice.

Yes! No wonder he'd never known it was there. Kneeling, he poked a finger through the ring and tugged until the square cover reluctantly gave way, with a sticky sound. Beneath was a well, exactly like at Aunt Ayako's.

The first thing he saw was a squashed paper shopping bag, a pale green tag dangling from one of its handles by a loop of frayed elastic. He flipped the tag over. It was printed with the characters for Toritsu-daigaku Hospital, a case number written on it with a thick black marker. A sick feeling bloomed in the pit of his stomach. He'd never been to Toritsu-daigaku Hospital, but he'd seen bags like this before. Bags from the morgue.

Ten years ago, someone in blue scrubs had stood outside the viewing room, bowed apologetically to his father, and handed him this bag. Everything his mother had with her when she died would be in it, except for the things that were . . . unsalvageable.

But why was it still stapled shut? Had no one looked inside since she died? And how had it ended up pushed into the storage space under the pantry floor?

It couldn't have been his dad who put it there, Kenji decided. His father wouldn't have been able to sit at the kitchen table all these years—reading his newspaper, sipping his beer—if he'd known this was right beneath the floor. It must have been Aunt Ayako. Kenji imagined her finding it after the funeral, looking around for somewhere to stash it out of sight, somewhere his father wouldn't chance upon it and be reminded of things that would send him spiraling back down into the darkness.

Kenji pulled the staples apart and looked inside.

A purse. The one they'd looked for ten years ago, before they'd gotten the worst phone call of their lives. The purse his mother had been carrying when she died.

Kenji lifted out the brown leather bag and set it on the kitchen table. There was more. He drew out an inventory sheet from the hospital, the signature seal stamped at the bottom too smeared to read. Setting it aside, he pulled out a pair of knit gloves, the ones his mother had bought at his brother's school fair when he was in fifth grade. Then Kenji saw what was beneath them, and his vision blurred. Slowly, he lifted out his mother's winter hat.

The month before she died, he'd been out one night with his baseball teammates. They'd stuffed themselves at a restaurant that had an all-you-can-eat-in-ninety-minutes special, and a touchscreen button they'd solemnly pushed, swearing that none of them were underage. The beer they'd drunk was fueling their laughter as they meandered back down the street toward the station. They'd passed a lone shop that was still open, knitted hats laid out on a small table outside the door. Kenji's teammates made a lark of trying on every one, before chasing each other back to the station. But Kenji felt sorry for the grandmotherly woman who'd come out to see if they needed help, apologized for his teammates, and bought one. A red one. He'd given it to his mother for her birthday.

He held it to his face. The vanilla scent of her shampoo filled his head. The bottle had always been kept in the hall cabinet, outside the bathroom, so the boys wouldn't—

His eyes brimmed and then there was no stopping the tears as he pressed the hat to his face and let out a muffled sob. Silently, he cried, swallowing the sound the way he'd taught himself, so no one would guess he wasn't strong enough to keep the grief inside.

Kenji's brother hadn't held it in. He'd cried. Even though he was older, Takeo had cried when his father came home with the news. He'd cried at the funeral. He'd cried until his father had yelled at him to stop. Kenji had saved his tears for his pillow at night, afraid that if he cried too, what remained of his broken family would splinter into a thousand pieces.

But even though he'd tried to hold it together, his family had still cracked apart. His brother had given up his spot at the police academy, and as soon as he graduated the following spring, he'd moved away, and never come back.

Kenji's tears finally slowed, then stopped. He took a shaky breath and wiped his face on his shirttail. Folding the hat, he settled it back in the bag with the gloves. He sat for a long moment with the purse in his hands, then unzipped it. Item by item, he emptied it. Wallet. House keys. Reading glasses. Mobile phone.

He stopped and turned over the silvery-blue case. It looked so outdated. Ten years was like a hundred in phone-years. Kenji flipped it open. The screen was absurdly small, with a keypad to match. How could this old thing ever have looked state of the art? He shook his head, remembering when all 48 phonetic characters had to be typed with ten buttons and two thumbs. He turned it over. There was a tiny lens set in the back, and he recalled the day his mother got it. This was the first phone she had owned that had a camera, and she'd chased him all over the house, begging him to show her how to use it, asking to take his picture.

She had eventually figured it out, no thanks to him. He remembered waiting impatiently while she aimed it at autumn leaves on the way to dinner, remembered feeling his smile go stale as she fumbled with the settings after one of his baseball games. She hadn't used her phone for taking pictures very often—only when she was caught unprepared, when she wasn't carrying her real camera.

Like, for instance, when she unexpectedly saw a woman being forced into a van against her will? Kenji stared at the phone in his hand. Had she used it to take the photo Inspector Mori was looking for?

Kenji pressed the On button. Nothing. Well, what did he expect, after ten years? Crossing to the junk drawer, he pawed through the jumble of orphaned items; outdated stamps, dull scissors, cords for long-dead appliances. No phone chargers. Where could he get one for something this old? Did the phone company still sell them?

He slipped the phone into his pocket to deal with tomorrow. Returned to the purse. Lipstick. Nail file. Grocery list. Two yellow slips of paper, stapled together. The top one was a receipt, apparently for camera repair. Across the top in 1950s-style brushed characters was printed, *Komagome Camera—Prints • Sales • Service*. It was date-stamped December 4th, but jotted in red pen next to the description in the Repairs Needed box were the words "Factory service recommended, picked up 12/4." Did that mean his mother had taken her camera in for repair, gotten the news that it couldn't be done at the shop, and picked it up the same day? Or that it had been picked up on the 4th for shipment back to the factory? He made a note to find out.

He flipped to the second slip. It was for a set of prints, the snapshots promised for the following day. His heart sank. The 5th was the day they woke up to find her gone. No one had gone anywhere that day, except to the morgue. And the claim check was still in her purse, which meant nobody had used it to pick up the photos later, either. If the van photo had been among them, it was long gone.

He'd visit the shop anyway—if it was still in business—but he knew the chances they'd kept an unclaimed order for ten years were slim to none.

He sighed and unzipped the last pocket. There was something inside. He pulled out a thick envelope, with the familiar Mitsubishi Bank logo printed in the upper corner. Lifting the flap, he peered inside. A stack of crisp ¥10,000 notes. He frowned. How much did his mother usually carry with her for the household shopping?

Then he remembered the missing money for her friends' bus tour tickets. He began to count it, but before he was halfway through, he slowed, stopped. It was way too much.

He finished counting and sat back in his chair, stunned. Why had his mother been carrying ¥300,000 in cash on the night she died?

FRIDAY, JANUARY 2

·

"And was anything else missing?" Kenji asked the indignant twenty-something woman who sat opposite him in her tiny box of an apartment. She had called Komagome Police Station that morning to report another underwear theft.

Her scowl looked out of place on her doll-like face; her fake eyelashes and sparkly pink lip gloss seemed more suited to flirting than outrage.

"Isn't a pair of lace panties and my favorite Rilakkuma thong enough?" she retorted. "Or do you only arrest thieves who make off with the matching bras too?"

Assistant Detective Suzuki's face went red all the way to the edge of his shorter-than-regulation haircut as he perched next to Kenji on the edge of the victim's sofa, taking down the particulars.

"Have any of your neighbors experienced similar thefts?" Kenji asked.

"Not likely," she answered with a snort. Rising, she crossed the room to the only window and threw open the curtains.

Kenji joined her and gazed at the laundry that was drying outside other apartments in the complex. Underwear was pinned to nearly all of the square racks that hung outside each door, and Kenji spotted several pairs of long johns, a number of generously cut grannypants, and more than one pair of the lucky red underwear given half-jokingly as sixtieth birthday gifts.

"I see. It looks like quite a few of your neighbors are retired. Are they home during the day? Do you know if anyone saw or heard anything?"

"You can ask," she said. "But please don't tell them it was my stuff that was stolen." She made a face.

"I understand."

Kenji nodded at Suzuki and the assistant detective stood, stowing his pen and notepad with obvious relief.

"You'll let me know when you catch this guy, won't you?" The young woman followed them to the door. "Because I want my stuff back. Underwear is expensive, you know."

"We'll keep you informed," Kenji promised. They bowed their goodbyes.

Half an hour of door knocking later, they'd added nothing to what they already knew. None of the neighbors had seen or heard anything out of the ordinary.

"What now, sir?" Suzuki asked, closing his notebook.

"Well, at least we know it's the same guy," Kenji said. "And we discovered that he likes cute bears as much as he likes lace."

Suzuki colored again. His stomach rumbled.

"Time for lunch?"

"Not yet, sir," Suzuki replied, dutifully checking the time. "It's only 11:53."

"I won't tell if you won't. I have to run to the crime lab over lunch, so why don't you get something to eat and I'll meet you at one to regroup?"

"Would you like me to bring you some *soba*, sir? I could stop at Ikeda's."

Being a *sempai* did have its advantages. A bowl of homemade buckwheat noodles would be a huge step up from the instant ramen Kenji had been planning to wolf down at his desk when he got back.

"Thanks. That would be great. Get me whatever the special is today." He dug in his pocket and produced a thousand-yen note.

"Yes, sir. I'll bring you the change." Suzuki bowed instead of snapping off a salute—a big improvement over their first weeks as partners—and disappeared up the street toward the noodle shop. Kenji turned to make his way to the train station.

His mother's cellphone weighed heavily in his pocket. Crime Tech Tommy Loud had suggested looking for a charger in the crime lab department he called "The Graveyard."

As Kenji beeped through the turnstile and boarded the train, he rubbed the smooth blue phone case like a talisman. There was a good chance every photo his mother had ever taken was still on it—he doubted she knew how to erase them—but he also knew that early cellphone cameras were designed to take tiny snaps that could be shared in text messages, not pasted in albums. If she'd used it to take a picture of the Painted Doll killer's van, would the resolution be good enough to tell them anything they didn't already know?

Kenji walked the short distance from the station to the building that housed the forensics lab. He submitted his name at the front desk, and a few minutes later, a ginger-haired Australian strode from the elevator. Tommy Loud bowed and greeted him in perfect honorific Japanese, tossing him a visitor's badge.

The two officers signing the book at the reception desk turned to stare, but Kenji was no longer surprised to hear the gangly foreigner use Japanese like a native. He could speak so well he'd swept the Superintendent General's daughter off her feet over passionate coffeehouse discussions on the novels of Yasunari Kawabata. Now they were married, with a baby.

"Long time no see, Rowdy-*san*," Kenji said, pronouncing Loud's name as closely as he could in Japanese. He winced at the sight of the tech's face, which today flamed redder than his hair. "Ouch. That sunburn looks like it hurts. Okinawa for the holidays?"

"Nah, took the wife and kid to Sydney over New Year's to see my folks, and I didn't buy sunscreen quite fast enough after we got off the plane."

Loud pointed him back toward the elevator and punched B2, complaining about his wife's penchant for Louis Vuitton leather goods. Apparently, the stuff was nearly as expensive in Australia as in Tokyo. The elevator descended, then opened onto a long concrete hallway. Their footsteps echoed as they made their way to a door stenciled "Technology Archive."

Loud opened it. "After you."

The officer manning the desk looked up from his computer screen. His face broke out in a smile when he saw Tommy, and he pulled off his reading glasses. "Rowdy-*san*! To what do we owe the pleasure?"

"Sorry to interrupt, Doc, but Detective Nakamura needs a favor that's right up your alley." He turned to Kenji. "Hashimoto-*san* is our resident expert on all things obsolete. And," he added, "he really is a doctor."

"Wrote my dissertation on 'Obsolescence in Electronic Devices as a Function of Sociological and Technological Pressures,'" Doc explained. "In other words—" He gestured at the shelves of outdated equipment arranged in the room behind him. "—how this all became junk."

"A noble calling," Kenji acknowledged.

"But I sense you're not here today to discuss Moore's Law. How can I help you?"

"Detective Nakamura has an old phone he needs to find a charger for. Think you might have something like that lying around?"

"You bet. What model?"

"It's ten years old," Kenji said, handing his mother's phone across the counter. "I know it's a long shot, but . . . . "

"Ha, you call this old?" Doc grinned. "Come on back."

He lifted a hinged section of the counter so they could pass through to the inner sanctum. Kenji and Loud followed him past rows of metal shelves lined with everything from electric toothbrushes to electric screwdrivers, most still in their original packaging.

"Police departments from all over Japan send us stuff for analysis," he told them as they passed an aisle anchored by the brick of a "mobile phone" that now inspired gales of laughter when it appeared in movies from the 1980s. He added proudly, "Most of them are in perfect working order, too."

He stopped to pull a large box from a shelf near where the aisle opened up into a workshop. Dropping the carton on a workbench lined with electrical outlets, he pried open the top flaps and upended it. Dozens of tagged cords and docks spilled onto the scarred wood.

He flipped open Kenji's mother's phone, checked the model number, and began pawing through the mountain of chargers, tightly wrapped in their cords.

"Aha!" He triumphantly held up a small bundle, unwound the cord and clicked the blue phone into the cradle, plugging the charger into the wall.

"Is it working?" Kenji asked.

Doc pointed to a glowing LED.

"How long before I can check the photos on it?"

"Five minutes, if you don't need to look at them long."

While they waited, he took Kenji on a tour of the racks, and they hooted at the size of the first home video camera. Kenji spotted a twin of the videotape player his brother had worn out as a child, watching the anime classic *My Neighbor Totoro* over and over.

They returned to the workbench. Doc detached the blue phone and pressed the power button. The keypad glowed to life.

Kenji navigated to his mom's photos. His own scowling 16-year-old face filled the tiny screen, half obscured by the hand he'd held up to keep his mother from taking his picture.

Kenji felt a pang of regret. If he'd known that his mother had less than a year left to live, he'd have been nicer.

He quickly paged through her other early experiments, knowing the charge wouldn't last long, skipping through dozens of shots of himself, far away on the Koshikawa High School pitcher's mound.

Restaurant food, more baseball, a flower arrangement, then two smiling middle-aged women standing in front of a bright green tour bus, making peace signs like schoolgirls. Kenji stopped to examine the photo. He didn't recognize either of them. But the next photo was of the same women, same bus, plus his mother. She was wearing the red hat he'd bought for her birthday, so the picture must have been taken right before she died. On the Ise Shrine trip? Sure enough, the next one showed her two friends sitting in their bus seat, grinning and brandishing bottles of hot tea in their mittened hands.

But that was the last photo. No brown van.

Disappointment burned, as he realized how much he'd been counting on coming up with the evidence he'd promised Mori. Now his only hope was that the Komagome camera store never threw anything away.

•

Where was Coco? Yumi stopped at the top of the wide stone steps leading out of Shinjuku Station, breathing hard. She'd forgotten to set an alarm to remind her when it was time to stop studying the jargon she'd need to interpret next week's "Symposium on Asia-Pacific Trans-Border Crime," and she'd barely had time to change clothes before running to catch the train.

"Couldn't you find anything cuter to wear than *that*?"

Yumi turned, to find her friend standing behind her, eyeing her outfit critically. Coco was in full manhunting attire: dangerously high pink heels, an orange and pink chiffon dress that barely fluttered past the hem of her short leopard-print jacket, and a pink rabbit fur muff.

"Do I *need* something nicer than this?" Yumi asked warily. "You didn't tell me where we were going."

"That's because it's a surprise." Coco sniffed. "To cheer you up after your big breakup. Come on."

She linked her arm through Yumi's and towed her toward the melee of pleasure-seekers heading for the red light district, one eye on her phone map. Neon signs and flashing lights vied for their attention, as barkers accosted passersby, trying to hustle likely customers into the restaurants and clubs. They passed the Arabian Rock, the Pasela Resort, the Cupid Club.

Yumi stopped in her tracks, suddenly suspicious. "We're not going to a host club, are we? Because you know I have zero interest in guys who get paid to pretend I'm the best thing since instant ramen."

"I know." Coco rolled her eyes and pushed her along the sidewalk. "That's not what we're doing tonight."

But Yumi's misgivings multiplied with every step. Club Top Dandy. Hotel Afrodite. Love Bar. They were deep into Kabuki-chō and heading deeper.

Coco stopped, checked her phone, then backtracked a few steps to a building lit up like the palace of Versailles, with a red-carpeted staircase spiraling up to a pair of golden doors.

"This is it."

The far-too-dandyish doorman bowed them over the threshold, and Yumi reluctantly followed Coco into a dark corridor lined with spotlit decanters of expensive liquor. A parade of crystal chandeliers overhead threw rainbow sparks onto the walls, as each step took them closer to the glittering script on the wall ahead that read "Club Dymond."

"I thought you said we weren't going to a host club," Yumi grumbled.

"We're not. I mean, this is a host club, but that's not why we're here."

What could they possibly do at a host club that didn't involve drinking—and paying—far more than she felt good about? Unfortunately, it was too late now, because Coco was already shrugging out of her coat and handing it to the smiling young man who had materialized to usher them in.

The moment they stepped through the padded leather door into the dark room beyond, they were hit with strobing laser lights and a deafening throb of J-pop.

Coco leaned close to the young man's ear, raising her voice to be heard over the din. "We have an appointment with Hoshi. Please tell him Coco and Yumi are here."

The greeter held out his hand for Yumi's jacket, then went in search of his boss. While they waited, handsome hosts wearing shiny suits and silver jewelry hustled past with buckets of ice and bottles of Dom Perignon. The music shifted to a song Yumi recognized, but couldn't quite—

"Coco-*chan*! You look stunning, as always!"

A striking man stopped in front of them, then leaned in to kiss Coco's cheek.

Yumi squinted at him. Was that . . . Hoshi? Where was the platinum-haired, rock star look-alike she remembered? This Hoshi had black hair, cut fashionably short on the sides, long on top. Dressed in a dark suit, white shirt, and Hermes tie, he was still unnervingly handsome, but looked nothing like the professional gigolo Coco had been head over heels for a few months ago.

"Yumi-*san*! Long time no see!" he beamed, turning to take her hands. "I was so happy when Coco-*chan* told me you were coming." He stood back, admiring her from head to toe. "You're perfect!"

Perfect? For what?

"Come this way, ladies—let's go to the VIP room, where it's a little quieter."

He ushered them through the main club to a back room filled with private leather booths. Sinuous jazz replaced the club beat. He bowed, parting a shimmering curtain of crystals surrounding a table in the corner. They slid in.

Hoshi seated himself in the booth across from them and wrapped a white linen napkin around the bottle of pink bubbly that was already chilling in a champagne bucket. Pulling it from the ice with a flourish, he popped the cork, filled three flutes, then handed them each a glass.

"*Kampai*!" He touched his glass lightly to each of theirs.

They sipped.

"Hosh', could you explain to Yumi about your new company?" Coco said. "I wanted it to be a surprise, so I didn't tell her anything."

He smiled at Yumi. "Of course." Pulling a brochure from his jacket pocket, he handed it across the table, offering it with both hands, like a precious gift. "It's called LuvLuv Match."

"So this is *your* company," Yumi said, as the penny dropped. *I can get you a deal. I know one of the owners.* "Coco showed me this the other day. It's a matchmaking service, right?"

"Yes. But what's special about LuvLuv Match is that we do coaching too."

"Coaching?" She regarded the pamphlet dubiously. Hoshi had never struck her as the sporty type.

"Relationship coaching," he explained. "For men."

"What?"

"Let me explain." Coco said quickly, before Yumi's disbelief could turn into dismissal. "You know how host clubs are packed every night with women who just want to be treated nicely? Flirted with a little? Listened to, for a change? Well, most Japanese men aren't very good at that, so Hoshi's starting a service that teaches them how to treat us the way we deserve."

"By teaching them to be like . . . hosts?"

"No. To be considerate. To think about what women want, not just what they want."

"And then we find them the perfect match," Hoshi said smoothly, leaning in to top up their glasses. "Which is why I invited you here tonight."

Yumi tried not to groan. Did Coco really think her so-called breakup blues would be cured by going on a date with some guy who let a host do his matchmaking for him?

She turned to her friend, but Coco saw the look on her face and said, "Stop. I know what you're thinking, but the guys Hoshi has already signed up aren't hosts. They're totally your type. They all work for big companies, or for the government. Show her, Hosh'."

He passed his phone across the table. Yumi scrolled through studio shots of nine men. Okay, she had to admit that, much to her surprise, none of them were hideous—one was actually quite handsome—and although they all had the kind of haircut that screamed Salaryman in a Big Boring Company, they'd been posed casually, in suits and ties that were subtly more fashionable than the ones they probably wore to work. And—if Hoshi hadn't already taught them to lie like hosts—the places they worked were more than merely respectable: Mizuho Bank. Daiwa Securities. Ministry of the Environment.

Which, of course, made them even bigger losers. With resumes like that, these men ought to have women lined up around the block. There must be something seriously wrong with them if they needed a guy like Hoshi to help them find wives.

"It'll cost a hundred thousand yen to be a LuvLuv member when we're up and running," Hoshi explained. "But as a special introductory offer, we'd like to offer a few lucky ladies the chance to join for free." He smiled. "And I'd like you to be the first. What do you say?"

Coco sat up and clapped her hands. "Oh, Hoshi, that's so sweet of you! Sign me up!"

Hoshi picked up his glass and clinked it with hers, then turned to Yumi. "And what about you, Yumi-*san*?"

Not in a million, trillion years. "I, uh . . . . "

"I heard about your broken engagement," Hoshi said quickly. "I'm so sorry. It must have been hard."

"Yes, well—"

"But what better way to get over your heartbreak than to meet someone new?"

She already had someone new. "I don't know. I just don't think I'm ready to—"

"Come on, Yu-*chan*," Coco said. "You have to put Ichiro behind you. I know you got lucky once, but the truth is, it's harder to meet decent men than you think."

"I'm sure you're right, but—"

"You're not thinking of saying no, are you?" Coco gave her a wounded look. "I mean, I called Hoshi specially and begged him to help you get over Ichiro, and then he offered to give us a special break on the price, and—"

Then Yumi understood. Coco had convinced herself she was doing Yumi a favor, but the truth was, she was the one who wanted to sign up for LuvLuv Match, and she didn't want to do it alone. One look at Coco's hurt face, and Yumi knew she couldn't say no, especially since telling her friend the real reason she was dragging her feet would make her feel even worse. Once Coco found the love of her life—or at least had someone in her sights—it would be easier to tell her about Kenji.

Yumi turned to Hoshi. "Do I have to go out with anyone I don't want to?"

"Of course not." Hoshi smiled. "But I'll do my best to tempt you."

Good. She would sign up and just say no to any dates until Coco was safely set up with someone promising, then back out gracefully.

"Well, I guess—"

"Yay!" Coco's face lit up as she clapped her hands. She turned to Hoshi. "When do we get started?"

Hoshi checked his calendar.

"How about tomorrow morning for your first consultation? Say, ten o'clock?"

Tomorrow morning? Way too soon. Yumi pulled out her phone, hoping she had a conflict. Damn.

"Come to this address, fifth floor," Hoshi instructed, handing each of them a business card. His name was printed over the title President. "You'll need to bring a couple of different outfits for your photo session. Give me your contact info, and I'll send you the guidelines. I'll attach the membership agreement too, so you can look it over. Copies will be ready for you to sign tomorrow morning."

He poured out the rest of the champagne, raised his glass and smiled. "To love, success and happiness, ladies!"

Not necessarily in that order, Yumi thought, watching Coco drain her glass.

SATURDAY, JANUARY 3

•

Kenji set his cup of green tea on his desk and hung his jacket on the back of his chair. It was Saturday morning, and still early enough that the squad room was quiet. Only the officers on rotation had to come in on the weekend, and today Kenji wasn't one of them. But he hadn't owned a personal computer since he was a student, so he needed his police-issue laptop to take a closer look at the pictures he'd found on his mother's phone.

He took a sip of tea, then opened his email. Yesterday, Doc had helped him send the snapshots on his mother's old phone to Kenji's personal account. If he could locate one or both of her friends, he could ask what they knew about the woman being forced into the van. Maybe they'd even been there when it happened. Finding a new witness would be even better than finding a photo of the van, which was looking less and less likely.

Last night, on his way home, Kenji had detoured to the address on the photo order slip, only to discover that not only had he arrived twenty minutes past closing time, Komagome Camera had become an "imaging" shop. There were still photo-related displays in the front window, but the change of ownership made it even less likely that a set of unclaimed vacation photos had survived for ten years. He'd try again today, before he met Yumi at the movie theater, but meanwhile he'd work on what might turn out to be a more promising line of investigation.

Kenji didn't like to admit it, but his father was right—he needed to climb out of the hole he was in with Inspector Mori and impress him with what a good team player he could be. Mori had good reason not to like him, and the Inspector really could hurt his chances of joining the First Investigative Division next spring, after he passed the assistant inspector's exam. *If* he passed the exam. Between his recent caseload and spending time with Yumi, his test prep had suffered. He vowed to burrow into his study guide the moment he got home this afternoon.

But now it was time to get to work. He zoomed in on the faces of his mother's friends. Neither of them looked familiar, but if they were close enough friends to be road trip companions, their numbers ought to be among the ones stored on his mother's old phone.

He picked it up and switched it on. A trip to the Ise Shrine would have required planning. He checked her email folders, but they were empty. That seemed odd until he remembered that few women in his mother's generation had learned to thumb type, and most of them saw no reason to send a message when they could speed dial. His mom had probably called her friends to discuss the details. He navigated to her call records to see whom she'd talked to in the weeks before her death.

Eleven matched names in her Contacts file. He copied their names and numbers into his notebook to save the old phone's battery, skipping Ueda and Akiyama, because he suspected that people listed by last name were local shopkeepers or distant acquaintances, not friends.

The remaining nine numbers were attached to first names. Women's first names. There were two Yokos—YokoK and YokoS—as well as two Keikos, a Momoko, a Michiko, a Satsue, a Haruna, and a Yuri.

He clicked back to her Contacts and added all the women who were identified by first name to his list. He'd start with the ones she'd talked to right before she died, then call the rest.

Taking out his own phone, he keyed in the first number on his list.

•

Name. Birthdate. Height. Weight. Blood type. Education. Hobbies. Yumi frowned. Hobbies. That one always stopped her. Clipboard propped on one knee, she sat on a folding chair filling out the LuvLuv Match questionnaire in the corridor outside the professional hair and makeup studio where Hoshi's stylist was readying Coco for her profile portraits.

Earlier that morning, Hoshi had met them in his tiny office two floors above. Yumi suspected it had been decorated with cast-off fixtures from the host club he now managed, because the crystal-draped light fixture and white leather furniture all looked a bit too large and nightclubby for the cramped waiting room.

After presenting them with contracts to sign, he'd explained how the photos they would take that morning would tell their "stories" to prospective matches. The guidelines he'd sent suggested they bring along "business wear," "day off" casuals, a glamorous "date" outfit, and something they might wear while enjoying their favorite sport or hobby.

Yumi looked up from her perch as two young women made their way down the hall, chattering in a language she didn't understand. The taller one was glancing from a business card to the names on the doors. They stopped before one near the end, knocked, and were admitted.

Yumi returned her attention to the questionnaire. She didn't really have any hobbies. Since she'd reconnected with Kenji last year, she'd spent nearly all her free time helping him catch criminals. Somehow, that didn't seem like the sort of thing Hoshi's wife-hunting clients would want to hear.

Should she make something up? After all, she had no intention of going out with any of these guys—what did it matter? She was just tagging along to keep Coco company until she found the right time to drop the news about Kenji.

What about "foreign travel"? That sounded legit. And it was something she'd actually done, if not exactly for pleasure. She double-checked her electronic dictionary for the proper characters before writing them on the form.

"Yu-*chan*?"

Coco's head poked out the door. Yumi stared. This was probably the first time Hoshi's stylist had spent more time taking off someone's makeup than putting it on. Coco hadn't gone out in public with eyes that were their natural tilted almond shape since she started gluing her eyelids in middle school. What's more, they had changed color since this morning, from turquoise to brown. And Yumi hadn't seen her friend with black hair since elementary school. It had to be a wig.

"Can I, um, borrow some of your clothes?" Coco asked. She lowered her voice. "The stylist thought the dress I brought for 'business attire' was for the 'glam date night' shot."

Yumi smiled and passed her the garment bag. "Help yourself."

"Thanks. I owe you one."

Coco and clothes bag whisked back inside.

"Excuse me."

Yumi looked up to find a girl with golden skin and long-lashed narrow eyes standing before her. She thrust a pink-and-white business card at Yumi.

"Please, where is . . . ?"

Yumi peered at the card. It was from an outfit calling itself "Perfect Love International," but she couldn't read the squiggly foreign characters beneath. The girl saw her mistake and flipped it over. The back was in Japanese, the street address the same as LuvLuv Match.

"Oh," Yumi said. "You're on the wrong floor. You have to go up two more. 'Perfect Love International' is on five."

The girl regarded her blankly.

Yumi handed the card back, pointing at the suite number in the address. Then she showed five fingers and said "five." She pointed at the ceiling. "Up."

"Oh!" The girl broke into a smile. Folding her hands together and bowing quickly, she said something Yumi understood to be a "thank you" and scurried back toward the elevator.

What kind of writing was that? The girl looked like she could be Vietnamese, but Vietnamese was written in English characters fancied up with pronunciation marks. Maybe Thai? Yeah, probably Thai. Yumi got up to stretch her legs and meander over to the directory next to the elevator, curious about why this building attracted so many foreign visitors.

There were quite a number of businesses on each floor—none of them could be much bigger than Hoshi's. She looked at the names. Lovely Face. Glamatic Studios. Wedding Bell Introductions. It looked like the second and third floors were filled with hair and makeup studios, eyelash extension salons and nail artists. The fourth was mostly photo studios, and the fifth was wall-to-wall matchmaking companies like Hoshi's.

The stylist's door opened.

"Your turn." The strange new Coco looked down at her outfit, suddenly nervous. "This feels so weird. I haven't worn a skirt this long since middle school. Do you really think . . . ?"

"You look great," Yumi assured her, then picked up her clipboard and slung her purse onto her shoulder. "Like every future CEO's dream date."

She opened the door, wondering if she'd emerge looking as unlike herself as Coco did.

•

"Okay, I think we've got what we need."

The photographer beckoned Yumi off the white seamless backdrop, where she'd been shot from all angles, pretending to read an English guide to the wonders of Hawaii.

She moved over next to him, and watched him cycle through the shots on the back of his digital camera. Ten shots of her sitting at a computer in her navy blue suit, pretending to make changes to the presentation on the screen. Six shots smiling down at a realistic-looking stuffed poodle on a leash, wearing a short skirt and her red Mary Janes. Eight takes gazing over the rim of a champagne glass in a cocktail dress. Finally, ten shots with the Hawaii guide book.

Yumi breezily okayed the photos, randomly picking one of each to send to Hoshi. She didn't really care if they were the most flattering. In fact, as the elevator took her back to the fifth floor, she was sorry she hadn't taken time to choose the ugliest, so she wouldn't have to deal with any real interest from inexplicably unpopular salarymen.

As she made her way down the hall to rejoin Coco and Hoshi, she glanced at the names on the doors to see if she'd been right about the fifth floor tenants.

Princess Match. Elite Meet. Picture Bride.

Picture Bride? What a terrible name for a matchmaking service. Who would sign up for that? "Picture bride" was what they'd called the unfortunate women who had been shipped over to marry Japanese laborers in the Hawaiian cane fields, sight unseen. She shook her head. The owner probably thought it meant "pretty as a picture."

She breezed through Hoshi's waiting room and knocked on the conference room door. Hoshi and Coco looked up from his laptop screen as she entered.

"So, how does this work?" Yumi asked, skirting the table to study Coco's new profile page over Hoshi's shoulder. "Do the guys just look through the profiles and send messages to the women they like?"

"Oh, no," Hoshi said. "We carefully pair people according to their interests, so nobody wastes time dating someone who's not a good fit."

In other words, Yumi thought, whoever was paying the most got the cutest girls.

"And then they contact us?" Coco asked.

"I will contact you," Hoshi said, "with the member's profile and some suggestions for a perfect first date."

Yumi had noticed that as soon as they'd signed the agreements, the grand "we" that suggested a consortium of powerful backers had quickly dwindled to a more honest "I." Hoshi had admitted that he was the "active" partner and that the start-up had been funded by the owner of the host club he managed.

"But I can still say 'no' if I don't like the guy, right?" Yumi asked.

"Of course. But if you recall, in the contract you signed this morning, you agreed to go on three dates in the next six months, so—"

Oh crap. She ought to have read the damn thing first. How was she going to explain this to Kenji?

Her dismay must have shown on her face, because Coco said, "Yumi, I know it's hard, but you've got to face it—Ichiro is history, and résumé-wise, nobody's going to top him. You've got to face reality, though, and I don't think you should be so quick to turn up your nose."

"Sorry. You're right. Being single again is just all . . . so new."

Coco turned to Hoshi. "So, how soon do you think . . . ?"

"If you could keep next weekend free, ladies, I'm sure I'll have something for both of you by then."

Next weekend? No! "Um, I don't think I—"

Coco and Hoshi turned.

"I mean, I think I'm busy."

"Doing what?" Coco demanded.

But Hoshi raised a conciliatory hand. "No hurry. I was only thinking that you might be eager to move on with your life. But don't wait too long to say yes—I have an excellent candidate in mind for you, but I'll match him with someone else if you're not ready. Why don't I send you his profile, and you can decide how 'busy' you are?"

"Well, okay. Sure."

They stood, and bowed their goodbyes. As Hoshi ushered them toward the door, Yumi asked, "Are all the offices on this floor matchmakers?"

"Most of them, I think. Why?"

"Do some of them cater to foreigners?"

"I wouldn't know," he said, suddenly uncomfortable.

"The reason I'm wondering is that I ran into a woman while I was waiting for the stylist, and she asked me for directions. She was pretty and spoke a little Japanese, but it didn't seem like she knew enough to go out on a date with someone, if you know what I mean."

Hoshi murmured that he didn't know much about his neighbors, and bowed them into the elevator.

"She might have been a hostess," Coco suggested, as the doors closed. She pressed the button for the ground floor. "A few clubs in Kabuki-chō specialize in foreigners. This building is famous for inexpensive hair-make and photo studios, and a lot of hostesses come here to get their pictures taken for their staff pages."

"But if that girl was a hostess looking for photos, why was she headed to the fifth floor?"

"Well . . . . " Coco paused, choosing her words. "Not all the women who work as hostesses are like me, part-timing a couple of nights a week for spending money. Some of them work six days a week and moonlight at another club on the seventh. The Japanese girls who do that are usually in deep with a loan shark and trying to work off their debt, but the foreign hostesses work like crazy to send money back home to their families."

"What does that have to do with matchmaking companies?"

"Well, you need at least a one-year visa to get a work permit, but a lot of the clubs that hire foreigners don't bother with that. They sign up women who come in on 90-day tourist visas, no questions asked. The girls start making more money than they ever dreamed of, so they stay on past the limit and work until they get caught and deported. Or," she said, "they get married to a Japanese man."

"For a visa?"

"Yeah."

Yumi thought about that for a moment. "Okay, I can see why women like that might use a matchmaking service. And I'm sure there are men who want to marry a beautiful woman, even if she's not Japanese. But what Japanese man would let his wife keep working as a hostess after they get married?"

"Some don't," Coco admitted. "But in that case, the poor dope will probably wake up someday and discover both his wife and his savings are history."

•

Kenji stood outside what used to be the camera store and studied the "Open" sign propped in the window. It read,

Northwest Tokyo Digital Print Specialists
Everything for your imaging needs

A bell jangled as he pushed through the glass door into a cramped shop with a glass-topped counter at one end. The walls displayed examples of the digital miracles on offer, everything from photo retouching services to advertising banners. A young man with bleached hair and black-rimmed glasses looked up from the workbench behind the counter. An array of precision screwdrivers and clamps hung on the wall beside him, but the tool in his hand was a drawing tablet attached to a computer with a professional-sized display.

"*Irasshaimase,*" he said with a smile, standing and taking his place behind the glass counter. The name "Takuya" was embroidered over the breast pocket of his uniform shirt. "How may I help you?"

"I was actually looking for Komagome Camera—I think it used to be at this address . . . ?"

"It still is. This was my grandfather's shop. I took over from him three years ago."

"Do people still bring in film to get prints?"

"They do. A handful of my grandfather's old customers haven't quite made it to the digital age." Takuya's mouth quirked in a smile. "But you don't look old enough to be one of those."

"Actually, my mother was. I'm kind of embarrassed to ask, but a long time ago she came in to get prints made, after a trip to the Ise Shrine. I was wondering if, by any chance, you still have them." Kenji produced the yellow claim slip.

The young man's eyebrows shot up when he saw the date, and he shook his head slowly. "I hate to say it, but I'm pretty sure we don't. We don't usually keep stuff for more than three years past the pick-up date, but let me take a look in the back anyway."

Yellow paper in hand, he disappeared into the storage room behind the counter. Kenji heard him rummaging around. Cabinet doors opened and closed. A heavy box scooted along the floor.

Then Kenji heard him mutter, "Ah. There you are."

The imaging specialist returned, carrying a shoebox. Kenji's hopes dwindled further. It wasn't nearly big enough to hold ten years' worth of abandoned vacation photos.

"When I took over, we cleaned out the storeroom," Takuya explained. "But there was some stuff my grandfather wouldn't let me get rid of."

He placed the box on the counter, lifted the lid and set it aside. Pulling out a bulging envelope, he snapped off the rubber band that was holding the flap shut. An assortment of digital camera cards spilled onto the counter, and he began pawing through them, checking the tags for a match with Kenji's claim slip.

"Found it!" He held up a large, flat square. "I'm sorry to say we didn't keep the prints, but the photos your mother took should still be on this card." He handed it to Kenji.

Kenji stared at the windfall in his palm. "I can't believe you still have this," he marveled, shaking his head.

The card was nearly the size of a saltine cracker, the words 16MB emblazoned on the label. Camera cards now had hundreds of times the memory and were a quarter the size. Which might be a problem, he realized—it was much too big to fit in his computer's card reader.

"How can I look at the pictures on this?" he asked.

"Well, your best bet is to try to find a retro card reader that'll import them to your photo app. Or I could put them on a portable drive for you."

"How long would that take?"

"If you've got five minutes, I can do it right now."

•

"Sorry I'm late," Kenji said, coming to a halt next to the table Yumi had staked out in the café upstairs from the Sunshine City cinema in Ikebukuro. He held up the small device he'd brought from the camera store, unable to contain his excitement. "Look! Here are the photos I told you about."

She smiled and opened the laptop sitting before her, as he scooted his chair around to her side of the table so they could both see the screen.

When he had called to ask if they could go to a later movie because he needed to use his work computer to look at pictures from his mother's camera, Yumi had rescued their date by offering to bring along her interpreting company laptop. They had nearly an hour before it would be time to claim their reserved seats in the theater downstairs.

Images jumped onto the screen. Water. Leaves. Sunset. Lobster. People. *Torii* gate. Faces. Food. Leaves. Leaves. Leaves. Face.

"Wait, who's that?" Kenji cried, as the thumbnails arrayed themselves. "May I?"

Yumi angled the laptop toward him, and he clicked on the last shot, a close-up of a man's angry face, three red scratches raking across his cheek.

Kenji didn't recognize him. He paged to the previous shot. Blurry autumn leaves dominated the upper left corner, but in the background, a woman was running straight toward the camera, pursued by a man in a black knit cap. The man was pitching forward as his foot caught on a pink duffel bag.

Mori was right. His mother hadn't merely witnessed that abduction, she had the photos to prove it.

Excitement mounting, Kenji clicked to the previous shot. The same red maple leaves filled the corner, but this time they were sharp. Out of focus in the background, a man wearing a black knit cap was helping—or pushing?—someone into the back seat of a brown van. A woman stood nearby, a pink duffel bag over her shoulder.

Brown van. From the side, though. No view of the license plate. Heart pounding, Kenji clicked back one more. The leaves in the corner were blurry, because the camera had focused on something beyond. Two women were walking away from a bright green tour bus, one towing a small, dark suitcase, the other with a pink duffel bag slung over her shoulder. Beyond them, a brown van approached.

"Yes!" Kenji exclaimed, pointing to the license plate on the front of the van. "Can we zoom in on this?"

The number emerged. 新宿 07 ま 44-09.

Kenji gave a yelp of triumph and pulled out his pen and notebook.

Yumi asked. "Is this the van that was used in the Painted Doll murders?"

"It matches the description," Kenji said. He had the photo Mori wanted!

He paged back one more, but it was of a brilliant red maple towering over a small wooden building. No more abduction photos.

"Is the man in the last picture the Painted Doll killer?" Yumi asked.

Kenji looked up. "He could be."

He returned to the shot of the man, whose blurred hand was reaching toward the camera and partially obscuring his angry face. The man's lips were curled in a snarl and three scratches raked across his cheek, with tiny beads of blood beginning to ooze along their length.

"Where do you think he got the scratches?" Yumi said.

"They look fresh. Maybe the woman he's chasing gave them to him." He scrutinized the man's face, then paged back to the photo of the woman being "helped" into the van. Zoomed in. Studied it.

"There had to have been more than one," he said.

"One what?"

"Man. In the van. One to drive, and one to grab the women." Kenji frowned, thinking. "The thing is, two men and a van suggests an organization. Inspector Mori thinks he's looking for a lone killer."

"He could still be right," Yumi countered. "It was the van that was seen at the crime scene, not the man. Just because the killer had access to the van doesn't mean he had anything to do with this abduction."

"But the killer and the abductors are both connected to whoever owns it." Kenji flopped back in his chair, frustrated. "I've got to get access to that Painted Doll file so I can get the names on Inspector Mori's suspect list. He came up empty handed, but he didn't know who he was looking for. He probably talked to this guy and let him go."

He leaned in again and clicked back to the man's face.

"You know," Kenji said, studying it, "he's close enough that he couldn't miss the fact that my mother was taking pictures. And see how blurry his hand is? Do you think he was trying to grab her camera?" He looked at Yumi. "You know, I found a camera repair slip stapled to the claim check for the prints. Maybe this is how it got broken."

"You think Mr. Cheek Scratches knocked it out of her hand?" Yumi pulled the laptop closer. "But why would he stop chasing the woman to do that?"

"Good point. And why didn't he pick it up and take it with him?" He paused, thinking. "Let's go back to the first shot and walk through it, see if we can reconstruct what happened." He clicked back to the first abduction shot. "Okay, here they are, walking away from the bus with their luggage. The van is coming toward them. It stops. Then," he clicked to the next photo, "one of them is getting into the van."

"Or being pushed," Yumi said.

"Or being pushed," Kenji agreed. "The woman with the pink duffel bag gets spooked for some reason . . . " He paged to the next photo. ". . . so she drops her bag and runs. But where did she go after that picture was taken? Where is she while her abductor is trying to grab my mom's camera?"

"Maybe he caught her, put her in the van, then came back to deal with your mom."

"Is there an electronic timestamp on the shot?"

Yumi clicked on the photo app's info feature. "Yes, there is, but no, the shot of his face was taken just six seconds after the one of him tripping over the duffel bag."

"Okay, let's think of this another way. She was running straight toward my mom in the third photo. Why?" Kenji considered the possibilities. "Was she hoping my mother would help her? Or was she aiming for somewhere else?" Kenji clicked back to the photo taken right before the abduction shots. When he enlarged it, he could see the icons for "Men" and "Women" hanging outside the doors of the building under the red-leafed maple.

Yumi asked, "Why did she take a picture of a bathroom?"

"I think she was taking a picture of the leaves," said Kenji. "She was a fiend for autumn leaves." He compared it to the previous shots, then said, "How much do you want to bet that the leaves on that tree are the same ones that are in the corner of the next pictures? See how that branch hangs down in front of the ladies' room door? I bet my mother took the next photos standing with her back to the bathroom. I don't think that woman was running toward my mom—I think she was trying to escape by running into the ladies' room."

Yumi nodded. "It's not a bad idea. Most men would hesitate to follow her in there."

"I'm not sure that guy is one of them, though," Kenji said, shaking his head. "And I'm sure my mother would have tried to stop him, but she wouldn't have slowed him down for long."

"So what happened?" Yumi mused. "Do you really think the guy broke her camera, then charged into the ladies' room, grabbed the foreign girl, and hauled her off, right in front of your mom?"

Kenji frowned. Even the stupidest criminal wouldn't continue committing crime after crime in front of a witness.

"Maybe someone else intervened," he said, thinking aloud. "What if someone else was in the parking lot, and stepped in to help? Maybe the guy suddenly found himself outnumbered, and had to get out of there before he got caught." His eyes widened as possibilities suggested themselves. "Which would mean there was another witness."

"But who would be hanging around the parking lot while everyone else went to look at autumn leaves?" asked Yumi.

They pondered that for a moment, then their eyes met, and they both said, "The bus driver."

Yumi leaned in and clicked back through the photos. "There. On the left side, in front of the green bus." She pointed to something blue at the edge of the frame. "What's that?"

"Looks like an arm." Kenji zoomed in further, but the image became too pixelated to make out any detail.

Yumi said, "Okay, let's say the bus driver gave those women their bags, then took a few minutes closing up the luggage compartment. He sees a man get out of the van and begin to chase one of the women. He'd run over to help, wouldn't he?"

"Let's find out," Kenji said. "I bet the tour company still has a record of who was driving that day."

Yumi's phone alarm chimed, reminding them that the movie would start in ten minutes. While she ran to the ladies' room, Kenji zoomed in on the brown van's license plate.

新宿 07 ま 44-09.

The first two characters told him it been registered in Tokyo, Shinjuku ward, but that's all the information he could get without running the plate. Unfortunately, he didn't know anybody in Motor Vehicle Registration who would help him. Detectives in TV dramas were always "calling in a favor" to get someone to trace license plates for them off the record, but the truth was, the people at Vehicle Registration got really annoyed if you asked them to do work they couldn't charge to an active case number. Not only would they refuse, the next time you had a legitimate request, you might find yourself waiting an extra week for results.

But there were other ways to get the information. Both Inspector Mori and his father had tracked that plate down ten years ago. Kenji didn't want to tell his dad he was looking into his mother's death until he discovered something worth risking the trauma it might cause, but maybe he could get the information from Mori. Normally, an inspector on the elite murder squad wouldn't even consider sharing information like that with a lowly local detective—especially one he already had reason to dislike—but would Mori show him the Painted Doll file in exchange for the photo of the brown van that he wanted so badly?

Maybe. He'd be more likely to grant access if Kenji could tell him something he didn't already know. Like, where the photo been taken. He blew it up so it filled the screen. A row of old-fashioned shops lined the end of the parking lot, but their signs were too blurry to read. Beyond them rose a mountainside covered with trees blazing red and yellow in autumnal glory. It had to be one of the stops on the shrine tour, but which one? He pulled out his phone and located the snapshot he'd taken of the ticket receipt from his mother's suitcase and skimmed the tour description. Toba. Tojishima fishing village. The Ise Shrine. Korankei. It had to be one of those, or one of the highway rest stop complexes that offered bathroom and tea breaks on the long stretches between.

Yumi returned, but as they walked out the door, his phone rang. Unknown number. Maybe one of his mother's contacts, calling him back?

"Go on in," he said to Yumi, handing her one of the tickets. "I have to take this, but I'll be there in a minute."

He answered the call. "*Moshi-moshi*? This is Kenji Nakamura."

"Oh, I'm so glad I caught you!" A woman's voice. "Is this Sa-*chan*'s son? The younger one, right? The baseball player? This is Momoko Fujimoto. You called me this afternoon?"

"Yes," Kenji said, pulling his notebook from his pocket. He found "MomoF" on his mother's contact list and scribbled "Fujimoto" next to it. "The reason I called was that I wondered if you were one of the friends my mother traveled to the Ise Shrine with ten years ago, right before she passed away."

"Why . . . yes. Yes, I was."

Kenji's pulse quickened. "I hope you can help me, then. I just found her pictures from that trip, but there were some I couldn't explain. One was of a brown van, taken in a bus parking lot. I know it was shot somewhere on your trip, but I have no idea where she might have taken it, or why."

"A van in a parking lot? That's a strange one. She took pictures of everything from the Grand Shrine to the lobsters we had for dinner, but I don't remember her taking any pictures of vans."

Damn, Momoko hadn't witnessed the abduction.

"What else was in the picture?" she asked. "Maybe I can help you figure out where it was taken."

He described the parking lot, the old-fashioned shops, the mountain covered with red and yellow trees in the background.

"Korankei," she said.

"How can you be so sure?"

"The autumn leaves were late that year, and Korankei was the only place where they'd really changed color."

"And you didn't notice my mom taking a picture in the parking lot?"

"No." She paused to reflect. "But she might have taken it when she went back to go to the bathroom. After we took the group photo, your mom told us she was sorry she hadn't stopped at the ladies' room before we left the bus lot. She said she'd run back, then meet us."

"And did she?"

"No. By the time she caught up with us, we were halfway back to the bus. I remember, because it was such a shame— she'd really been looking forward to taking pictures of the autumn leaves, but I ended up having to send her copies of mine. I told her she had time to run and take a shot of the maples hanging over the famous bridge, but she said she couldn't, because her camera was broken."

"Broken? What happened?"

"I don't know. I just assumed she dropped it."

So his mother hadn't told her friends what had happened in the parking lot. Why not?

"Wasn't there another friend who went with you on that trip?"

"Yes, Keiko."

"Keiko . . . ?"

"Sato."

He found "Keiko S" on his list and wrote "Sato" next to her name. It belonged to one of the disconnected numbers. He'd left messages or talked to someone at all the numbers from his mother's phone except four, because those were no longer in service. The 03 prefixes told him they'd been old-fashioned landlines, the kind that used to serve a whole family. They'd probably been replaced by cellphones in the years since his mother died.

"You don't happen to know how I can contact her, do you?" he asked. "The phone number from ten years ago has been disconnected."

"Just a second." Momoko paused to look it up, then rattled off a 080-prefix mobile number.

"Thanks. That helps a lot."

"Anything else?"

"Just one more thing—do you remember the suitcase my mother took on that trip? It was small. Dark blue."

"You mean the one that was stolen?"

"Stolen?"

"Well, that's what Keiko and I thought. When we got back to Shinjuku Station and the driver unloaded the luggage, it was missing. After all the bags had been claimed, your mother's was gone. There was one left over that sort of looked like your mom's, but it wasn't. Turned out, it belonged to one of the foreign girls."

"What foreign girls?"

"The two who were on our trip. The ones who didn't get back on the bus when we stopped at Korankei."

The women who'd been abducted were foreigners, and neither had made it back to the bus? Had both of them ended up in the brown van?

"Why didn't they get back on the bus?" he asked.

"The driver told us they'd decided not to return to Tokyo that day."

But that wasn't true—they'd been abducted against their will. The driver was lying. But why? Was he involved? More importantly, why had his mother let him get away with it? Why didn't she speak up?

"Isn't that kind of strange?" he asked Momoko. "Leaving a tour in the middle of the trip? How did they plan to get home?"

"I don't know. But they certainly had enough money to go anywhere they liked, after they stole your mother's bag."

"What do you mean?"

"Your mother charged all our tickets on her credit card, then Keiko and I repaid her in cash. Over fifty thousand yen. I remembered those girls standing near us in the waiting room at the bus terminal before we left. They saw us hand over the money and watched your mom unzip her bag to put it inside. We all noticed them, because they were so much younger than everyone else, and they were dressed so . . . inappropriately."

"What do you mean?"

"Well, let's just say that if I had a daughter, I wouldn't let her leave the house looking like that."

"You said they were foreigners—do you have any idea where they were from?"

"No. But they were sitting right ahead of us on the bus, and I don't think they were speaking Filipino or Korean. Keiko thought they might be speaking some kind of Chinese."

"So they got off at Korankei and didn't get back on."

"That's right," Momoko said. "We never saw them again."

If they'd been abducted by the man in the Painted Doll killer's van, maybe nobody had.

Kenji thanked Momoko and ended the call.

His mom had witnessed a crime, and there were pictures to prove it. Why hadn't his father allowed her to give Mori the evidence he needed to arrest the men who had done it?

He switched his phone to vibrate as he made his way down the corridor to join Yumi. He was going to have a hard time concentrating on the movie.

•

"So, what did you think?" Yumi took a sip of her white wine. After the movie, they had decided to grab a bite to eat at a restaurant near the train station.

"Uh, I thought it was pretty good," Kenji said. "What did you think?"

"Well, I pretty much agreed with the reviews," she admitted. "The action scenes were well done. And the special effects were excellent." The film had been far from her first choice, but it was the only one they'd both been able to muster a little enthusiasm for. She added, "I thought the final chase scene could have been about ten minutes shorter, though."

"Yeah." Kenji nodded, taking a sip of his beer. "I agree."

Yumi stared at him. He was *agreeing* with her? The guy who'd told her his favorite guilty pleasure was re-watching "The Bourne Identity"? Yumi's irritation grew, her suspicions confirmed. Kenji hadn't been watching the movie at all! He'd apologetically slid into his seat half an hour late—plenty of time for her to become hyper-aware that she was surrounded by happy couples, and imagine how they were pitying the lone woman with an empty reserved seat next to her—and then he hadn't even paid attention once he was there. He'd absentmindedly taken a handful of popcorn from their shared bag occasionally, but she'd gradually become aware that he wasn't laughing at the funny parts, nor sitting on the edge of his seat when the hero was in danger of being thrown out of a plane/crushed by falling debris/set upon by ridiculously well-armed bad guys.

"Were you even watching?" she snapped.

"I, uh—" His guilty look supplied the answer. "I'm sorry, Yu-*chan*. It's just that the call I got right before the movie was from one of the women my mother went to the Ise Shrine with."

"Oh." Well, at least that explained it, although Yumi still wasn't quite willing to excuse it. "What did she say?"

Kenji explained that, after talking to Momoko, he was pretty sure that the women in his mother's photos were two young foreigners who had been on his mom's tour, and they didn't get back on the bus after it stopped at Korankei. That Momoko believed one of them had stolen his mother's bag.

"Is that why your dad said your mother's death wasn't an accident when the suitcase turned up again?"

"I don't know. All it really explains is how it disappeared. I still don't know why my dad claimed not to know what happened to it. Or why he refused to let my mother give Mori what he wanted."

"Do you think your mother told him that the suitcase had been stolen?"

"I can't believe she wouldn't. But in the past few days—" He fell silent, shook his head. "I'm beginning to think I didn't know my parents as well as I thought."

Yumi heard the sadness in his voice, saw it in his eyes. Her irritation about the movie suddenly felt petty. How could she resent that he wanted to know what had happened to his mother? She couldn't blame him for that, or for not wanting to quit until he found out.

She sighed. Whether she liked it or not, the only way for him to get past this was to find out the truth. And if she wanted that to happen sooner rather than later, she had to help him.

SUNDAY, JANUARY 4

•

Yumi hugged herself against the cold, stamping her feet—maybe a little too loudly—as she waited for the salaryman ahead of her in line at the shrine to finish his lengthy petitions.

Kenji had called to apologize, just as she was walking out the door. Instead of coming with her to hunt down the bus driver, he had to take his father to the hospital. His dad had been up all night, feeling sick and faint, and he was scared enough that he'd agreed to let Kenji take him to the emergency room.

Yumi had said she hoped it would turn out to be nothing serious, then stood teetering on the doorstep, trying to figure out what to do with the day that suddenly loomed empty before her. Then she'd pulled on her gloves. It didn't take two people to get a bus driver's name, did it?

As she neared the Happy Holiday Bus Company terminal, she'd spotted this shrine and figured it wouldn't hurt to enlist the gods' help in today's quest. Stepping up to toss her coin, bow, and tug on the bell rope, she asked the *kami-sama* to look favorably on her search. Belatedly—and somewhat guiltily—she added a prayer for Sergeant Nakamura's health, feeling ashamed of herself for being slightly irritated that he was sick right now, on top of everything else that was thwarting her relationship with Kenji. She bowed again and retraced her steps, crossing the street to the tall office building that housed the bus terminal.

Loosening her muffler as she blew through the automatic doors, she stopped and looked around the vast, granite-paved lobby. The Happy Holiday waiting room was on the far side, next to a Tully's coffee shop.

Tossing her empty tea bottle in the Family Mart's recycle bin as she passed, she approached the glass wall dividing the building lobby from the bus waiting room. Stepping up to the glass, she peered between a poster depicting Mt. Fuji frosted in white and one featuring an enormous Totoro snow sculpture grinning over Hokkaido's Winter Festival.

The departure lounge was filled with molded plastic seating, and a wide aisle ran down the center to the check-in desk. Twice a day it was probably packed—every morning, when the company loaded the buses that streamed out to all parts of Japan, and every evening, when they returned—but in between, the place was nearly deserted. A couple of pensioners dozed here and there, but they looked more like refugees from the winter weather than would-be tourists.

Two women in navy blue vests and white blouses manned the counter under an orange and yellow Happy Holiday logo. One riffled through a stack of flimsies with a managerial frown on her face. The older woman with the smile lines around her eyes looked more promising.

"May I help you?" she asked, as Yumi stepped up. Her nametag read "Takeda."

"I hope so," Yumi said.

"Would you like to book a tour?"

"Actually, I'm here because of my mother." Yumi launched into the story she'd come up with on the train. "She went on a Happy Holiday trip to the Ise Shrine ten years ago, and has never stopped talking about it. The bus driver was very kind to her—he rescued her from an unpleasant situation—and she says a prayer for him every New Years. Her sixtieth birthday is coming up, and I was hoping to surprise her by having him sign the memory book I'm making."

Mrs. Takeda beamed. "What a lovely idea."

"The problem is—" Yumi put on her most appealing smile. "—I don't know his name, and if I ask her, she'll want to know why. Does Happy Holiday keep records of who might have driven the bus on her trip? It was ten years ago. They left on November twenty-seventh and returned the next day. I know it's a long time, but is there any way you could find out his name and put me in touch with him?"

A crease appeared between Mrs. Takeda's brows. "I'd love to help you, but even if I had access to company records, I'm afraid I'm not allowed to give out that kind of information." She bowed apologetically. "I'm very sorry."

"Of course, of course," Yumi said, glancing at the manager, who was working within earshot. "I wouldn't want you to do anything that would get you in trouble. But if by any chance you discovered who he was, would you mind passing along my name and asking him to get in touch with me?" She offered one of her International Translating Company cards.

The woman shook her head, but accepted the card. "If I knew his name, that might be possible, but I'm afraid that records of past trips are stored at headquarters, and I'm not authorized to look at them. I'm really very sorry."

Yumi returned her bow and thanked her, disappointed. Well, it had been worth a try. Maybe Kenji would have better luck with his police ID.

Out in the lobby, she paused as a blast of cold air blew in through the automatic door, along with two men in overcoats with a dusting of snow on their shoulders. She decided the walk back to the station would definitely be improved by a bottle of hot tea. She wasn't thirsty, but it would make a good hand warmer. She detoured to the Family Mart by the entrance.

Standing in front of the hot drinks display, she heard someone call her name. She turned. It was Mrs. Takeda.

"Miss Hata? I'm sorry I was so unhelpful just now," the travel agent said. "I think it's a lovely idea that you want to surprise your mother on her sixtieth. I can't look up the name of the driver from your mother's tour, but I was thinking that if you had a picture, I might recognize his face. I've been with the company a long time, and I might know him."

Damn. All they had was a piece of his arm.

"I wish I did, but . . . . "

"What about the group photo?" Mrs. Takeda suggested. "Did your mother order a copy of the picture they always take near the end of the tour?"

The group shot. Of course. No tour experience would be complete without a photo, even if most of the people in it were strangers. Had Kenji's mother ordered a copy?

"That's a wonderful idea," Yumi said. "I'll look for it. If I find it, can I bring it here to show you?"

Mrs. Takeda handed her a slip of paper with her email address on it. "If you send me a message, I'll meet you on my tea break." Her face creased in a smile. "I'll be having my sixtieth birthday in April. I hope my own daughter is as thoughtful as you."

•

Kenji ended the call with Yumi, elated. As soon as she mentioned the tour group picture, he remembered the plastic sack full of mail he'd seen beneath the morgue bag when he'd lifted it out of the well in the pantry floor.

He started down the hall, then stopped. Should he risk his father appearing in the kitchen while he was digging around in his mom's old things? It wouldn't be good for him to sustain another shock, after what the doctor had said this morning.

The heart specialist had sent them home after giving his dad a thorough exam and a prescription for blood thinners, promising test results in a few days. But he'd taken Kenji aside and told him he suspected heart disease, with risk of stroke. He warned Kenji to keep an eye on his father until they knew for sure, and he could prescribe a course of treatment. Fortunately, it was his dad's day off, so Kenji didn't have to fight with him about whether slogging to the Tabata Police Box in the biting wind was the best idea.

The murmur of the TV came through the door of his dad's room. Kenji knocked, then peeked in. His father was reclining on his futon, watching . . . a cooking show? Ah. His eyelids were closed. The previous show's host must have discovered the best ramen in Akita Prefecture while Kenji was on the phone with Yumi.

Kenji eased the door shut and retreated to the kitchen. He opened the pantry door, moved aside the clutter, and pulled on the floor ring. Lifting out the bag with his mother's purse inside, he spotted the Tokyu Store bag he remembered, stuffed with envelopes addressed to his mother. He dumped it out on the floor.

The largest piece was from Korankei Memories, a thin, stiff, envelope that was just the right size to hold an eight-by-ten glossy. Setting it aside, Kenji bundled the rest of the mail back into the bag and stuffed everything back into the storage space.

Grabbing a worn paring knife, he took the discovery to his room and shut the door. After slitting open the envelope, he removed a photo of mostly elderly women standing on bleachers in front of a picturesque red lacquer bridge framed by red maple trees. He moved to the window and raised the blinds for better light.

There was his mother in the middle row, wearing her red knit hat. Her friends stood next to her. The bus driver was at the end of the back row, wearing a sky blue uniform jacket that matched the color of the sleeve in his mother's snapshot. He looked to be between forty and fifty, receding hair combed straight back from his forehead. He had a long face, jowls already beginning to sag.

Was he still working for the bus company? That would make him between fifty and sixty now, so it was possible.

Would the woman at the bus company recognize him? Kenji pulled out his phone to ask his aunt if she could come over and stay with his father for a few hours.

•

"Wait here," Yumi said to Kenji, stopping outside the Excelsior Café, three blocks from the Happy Holiday terminal. "I told Takeda-*san* that I needed the bus driver's name for my mother's memory book, and she'd think it strange if I show up with a policeman."

"Hey, it's not like I'm wearing my uniform. Can't I pretend to be your brother, or something?"

"No," Yumi said. "I know you too well—the minute she tells me anything, you'll go into interrogation mode. If there's something you want me to ask, tell me now."

The wind buffeted the café's awning and Kenji said, "Okay, but let's do it inside. It's too cold out here."

They stepped into the warmth of the café, and Kenji waited in line while Yumi hovered near the table of a businessman who was packing up his laptop.

When they were settled across from each other at the table with their hands wrapped around cups of hot tea, Kenji said, "Okay, first of all, if this woman recognizes the bus driver, ask her if he's still working for the company."

"And if he is?"

"Find out which routes he's on now. And when he's next scheduled to drive."

"Okay. And if he doesn't work there anymore?"

"See if she knows where he went. If not, find out if he retired or quit. If he quit, ask why. That might tell us if he's likely to be working at another tour company or not."

Yumi nodded, then checked her phone for the time. "I'd better go. Takeda-*san*'s tea break starts in ten minutes." She stood.

"Good luck."

Yumi put her gloves on and pushed back through the door. The cold hit her with an icy slap. She trotted to the Family Mart, head down against the wind.

•

Mrs. Takeda found her standing, pink-cheeked, in front of the hot tea shelves.

"Thank you so much for meeting me today," Yumi said, pulling the stiff manila envelope from her bag. "I can't begin to tell you how much I appreciate your help."

The travel agent slid out the picture, then reached into her purse for her reading glasses. She peered at the bus driver, and a smile of recognition creased her face.

"That's Kuma-*san*," she said. "His first name is Hideo, I think. I didn't recognize him at first—he looks different with all his hair. But—" She looked at Yumi apologetically. "I'm afraid he doesn't work for Happy Holiday anymore."

"How long ago did he quit?"

"He didn't quit, he retired. Last year. Happy Holiday is an old-fashioned company, and when you turn sixty, you get a sayonara party, a lifetime tour pass, and your walking papers." From the look on her face, Yumi guessed that Takeda-*san* wasn't looking forward to her own last day.

"Any idea where Kuma-*san* lives?" Yumi asked. "Or where I could find him?"

"You could ask his son."

"His son?"

"A van with 'Kuma Dry Cleaning' painted on the side used to wait for him at the curb after work. I assumed the young man driving it was family, because of the name."

Yumi made a note, then bowed deeply.

"Thank you so much for your help, Takeda-*san*. I really appreciate it." She extended the small shopping bag she'd brought. "Please accept this insignificant token of my thanks. My mother enjoys this kind of tea, and I hope you will too."

•

How long did it take to identify a face in a picture? Kenji checked the time. Twenty minutes had passed. He stared at the Excelsior Café's door, willing Yumi to walk through it. His phone began to vibrate. Unknown number. He scooped it up and headed for the door to take the call outside.

"*Moshi-moshi*?" he said, as the cold wind reminded him he shouldn't have left his muffler and gloves on the table.

"Is this . . . Sa-*chan*'s son?"

Sa-*chan*. A nickname used by childhood friends.

"Yes . . . ?"

"My name is Keiko Sato. Returning your call . . . ?"

Keiko Sato. Wasn't she the other friend who had been with his mother at the Ise Shrine?

"Thank you for calling me back," Kenji said. "I'm sorry for suddenly contacting you after all these years, but recently I discovered something that happened right before my mother passed away, and I was wondering if I could ask you a few questions."

"Of course. What about?"

Stepping around the corner, out of the wind, Kenji confirmed she was the third woman on the Ise Shrine trip, then described the series of pictures he'd found on his mother's camera chip.

"Oh my goodness!" Keiko said when he'd finished. "I had no idea. Did all that happen while Momo-*chan* and I were looking at the leaves? I did think it was strange those foreign girls decided not to get back on the bus, but I'm afraid you know more about it than I do."

"My mother didn't say anything to you about what happened? Even when it was time to leave and those two women were still missing?"

"No. It was Momo-*chan* who noticed they weren't on the bus, and told the driver not to go." Keiko paused, then asked,

"Did something happen to them? Is that what you're trying to find out?"

"Yes. But the photos my mother took don't show their faces very clearly. Can you tell me what they looked like?"

"Actually," Keiko said, "I might be able to do better than that. They didn't have cameras, so I offered to take their picture in front of the *torii* gate at the Grand Shrine and send it to them."

"Really?" She had a picture! "Do you have their address?"

"No, I'm sorry, I'm sure I didn't save it. But I might still have a copy of the picture. Would you like me to check?"

"If it's not too much trouble."

"I'll look for it, then call you back."

Kenji stood in the alley, stamping his feet. Should he wait here, or go back inside? He'd just decided to return to his tea before it got too cold, when his phone buzzed again.

"Sorry that took so long," said Keiko. "I had to dig it out of my closet. I didn't paste that picture into my photo album, but I found it in an envelope of outtakes in the back. Shall I drop it in the mail it to you?"

"Actually, would it be all right if I came to pick it up in person?"

She hesitated. "I have to meet a friend in half an hour. Are you anywhere near Toritsu-daigaku?"

Toritsu-daigaku. His heart began to pound. That was where his mother's body had been found. Was this the friend she'd been meeting on the night she died? If so, he had a lot more questions to ask her, but he didn't want to do it over the phone.

"I'm afraid I'm all the way across town in Shinjuku right now," he said. "But would it be all right if I came tomorrow? Around six, after I get off work?"

"Of course. I'd be happy to meet you at the station, but if you have time for a cup of tea, we could walk to my house from there."

"Thank you. I'd like that. I'll be there at six."

They said their goodbyes, and he let out a whoop of triumph.

"Looks like someone just got good news."

He spun around to find Yumi's pink-cheeked face smiling up at him.

"Who was that?" she asked.

"The other friend my mom went to the Ise Shrine with. She has a picture of the abductees."

"Really? Did she email it to you?"

"No. It's a print. I'm going out to Toritsu-daigaku tomorrow to pick it up. And," he added, "she might be the friend my mother was meeting the night of her accident."

"Really? Is that where it happened?"

"Yes."

"Kind of far from Komagome, isn't it?" Yumi commented, as Kenji held the door for her.

"Yeah. After my mother's forty-nine day memorial service, I asked my dad what she was doing so far from home that night, but all he told me was that she'd gone there to see some old high school friend. 'Cookie-*chan*', he called her. But there was no one by that name on my mother's Contacts list."

"'Cookie-*chan*'. Sounds like a nickname, doesn't it?"

"That what I thought too. But I have no way to figure out who it belonged to, and none of the other women I talked to live near Toritsu-daigaku."

They returned to their table, and Kenji waited for Yumi to get settled in her seat before leaning forward eagerly to ask, "Did you get the driver's name?"

"Even better." Yumi told him about Hideo Kuma being picked up after work by his son. "On the way back, I did a search on my phone, and there's only one shop in Tokyo called Kuma Dry Cleaning. They specialize in linens for big events."

"Are they open on Sundays?"

"I just sent them a message to find out."

Yumi's phone pinged.

"Yes," she said, skimming the reply. "They're open today until six. And Kuma Senior will be at the shop all afternoon. Fancy a trip to Ningyo-chō?"

"Let's go."

•

The sound of thunder greeted them as they climbed the final flight of steps from Ningyo-chō Station. Yumi checked the map while Kenji popped open his umbrella.

Rain was washing away the last pockets of dirty snow on the Ningyo-chō town clock as they passed. The nostalgic fragrance of roasting tea wafted from an open door and followed them down the street as they passed a seaweed seller, a pickle store, and a sweets maker whose plum blossom-shaped *okashi* looked too beautiful to eat.

Yumi checked the map again. Their destination should be ahead, on the next block. Yes, there it was. Rain was trickling down a sign propped open on the sidewalk that read, Kuma Dry Cleaning, Event Linens Our Specialty.

Yumi stopped to peer through the rain-streaked glass. Formica counter, cash register, wheeled metal racks beyond, stuffed with plastic-shrouded tablecloths on hangers.

An automatic chime rang as they stepped inside, followed by a recorded voice chirping, "*Irasshaimase!*" A woman wearing her hair in two stubby braids emerged from the back room, her hand resting on a stomach as big as a watermelon. Her baby must be due any day now.

She smiled. "How may I help you?"

"My name is Yumi Hata. I exchanged email with someone here earlier today . . . ?"

"Oh! Yes. You wanted to talk to my father-in-law, right? Just a minute, I'll get him."

While they waited, Yumi idly perused the business cards thumbtacked to a bulletin board next to the counter. Plumbing. Odd jobs. *Shamisen* lessons: classical and jazz. They were clustered around a yellowing newspaper clipping headlined, "Cultural Group Honors Local Man." In the accompanying photo, the bus driver from the Ise Shrine group photo was receiving some sort of framed certificate from an elderly man who was wearing what looked like an old-fashioned Japanese military uniform. Behind him, a banner emblazoned with the Rising Sun read *Great Japan Restoration Society*.

"Hello. You wanted to see me? I'm Hideo Kuma." The man who had emerged from the back room had lost more of his hair, and the creases framing his mouth had grown deeper since the picture was taken on that Ise Shrine trip.

Yumi stepped forward and bowed. "I'm Yumi Hata. This is my friend, Kenji Nakamura. You used to work for the Happy Holiday bus tour company, right?"

He nodded, puzzled.

"We were hoping you might remember something that happened on a tour you drove to the Ise Shrine. It was at the end of November, ten years ago."

"Ten years ago?" He shook his head. "I'm afraid—"

"It was a two-day tour," Yumi said. "When you stopped at Korankei to see the leaves, there was an incident."

"An incident?" His voice became wary.

"A man in a brown van chased one of the women on your tour into the bathroom by the parking lot, and I think you ran over to help. We think you saved the woman's life."

"What?" He bridled. "Why would I—"

"Dad? Is everything all right out here?"

A young man with the same long face as his father appeared in the doorway, a worried expression creasing his brow.

"I'm sorry," Yumi said. "We were just asking about a bus tour to the Ise Shrine, back in—"

"I need a smoke," Kuma said abruptly.

"Dad," the son objected. "You know the doctor said—"

The bus driver ignored him, grabbing an umbrella from behind the counter and pushing out through the front door. Yumi made an apologetic bow to the son and they hurried after him.

"Wait! Kuma-*san*!" Yumi called, as they dashed down the street. They caught up with him at the light.

He rounded on them, his face ugly. "You're one of them aren't you?"

"One of what?"

"A traffic watcher."

"What?"

"You should all be deported," he spat. "You and those dirty foreigners you like so much. There ought to be a law against them coming here, taking our jobs, preying on hardworking Japanese, raising the crime rate."

"Raising the crime rate? What are you talking about?"

Kuma poked a finger at her. "You know what I'm talking about. Good riddance to bad rubbish."

"Are you talking about what happened at Korankei? Those women were victims, not criminals!"

"Victims? They were here illegally—that makes them criminals." His eyes narrowed. "And more power to anyone who helped send them back where they came from."

"Is that why you didn't go to the police?" Kenji asked.

Kuma's jaw jutted. "The police are paid by Japanese taxpayers to protect Japanese citizens."

"They're also paid to investigate crimes," Kenji countered. "And you witnessed a crime."

"What crime?" The driver's face hardened. "I didn't see anything."

"You did," Yumi insisted. "You're in a photo that was taken while it was happening."

"A photo? What photo?"

"Do you remember a woman on your tour named Sachiko Nakamura? She was taking pictures of autumn leaves outside the bathroom, and you're in one of them. Along with two foreigners who look like they're being abducted by a man in a brown van."

"I don't know anything about it. Why are you asking me? If that Nakamura lady thought she saw a crime being committed, why aren't you asking her?"

"We can't," Kenji said. "She's dead."

Kuma's eyes widened. "Dead?"

"She died ten years ago. Right after that trip. It looked like an accident at the time, but two weeks ago, the Metropolitan Police's First Investigative Division uncovered some evidence that makes me think it wasn't." He pulled out his own badge.

The color drained from Kuma's face. He backed away. "I didn't see anything. I didn't tell anyone anything."

He spun around and ran back toward his shop.

Yumi and Kenji stood there, staring, then went after him. But by the time they reached Kuma Dry Cleaning, the door was already locked. Rain streaked the window as the bus driver flipped the Open sign to Closed.

MONDAY, JANUARY 5

•

Rain was still beating against the window behind the section chief's desk the next morning as Kenji stepped out of the elevator into a squad room filled with officers toting umbrellas and complaining about crowded trains and wet shoes. He made his way to his desk, still chewing over yesterday's encounter with the bus driver.

They'd been dead wrong about Kuma. He hadn't run to the aid of the foreign women—quite the opposite, in fact. But why did the bus driver think the women were being hunted down in order to be deported? The men in the van couldn't have been from the immigration service—illegal immigrants were chased with paper, not muscle. So who were the abductors? And what had spooked Kuma so badly that he'd run away when he heard Kenji's mom was dead?

I didn't see anything. I didn't tell anyone anything. What did he see, and who was he afraid of?

"Nakamura." Section Chief Tanaka appeared next to his desk. "What progress are you and Suzuki making with our underwear thief?"

Kenji grimaced, hooking his umbrella on the back of his chair and shedding his wet raincoat. "Not much, sir. Nobody saw anything. Nobody heard anything. Nobody is saying anything."

"You think they're scared of talking to the police?"

"No, I honestly think they don't know anything."

"Somebody must have seen something," Tanaka insisted, his frustration showing. "This guy has stolen underwear from ten women now. In broad daylight. He's making us look like idiots. Are you sure you talked to everyone who might have seen or heard anything? What about that map you made? Any patterns? What about the time of day? I want this thing solved. It hasn't made the papers yet, but if some joker gets a hold of this and writes about it on the Internet —"

Kenji groaned. He hadn't thought of that. An uncaught underwear thief was exactly the sort of story that could go viral, and the name Kenji Nakamura would be front and center as lead investigator.

"Suzuki and I will go out and re-canvass the neighborhood, sir."

"This time, get some results," Tanaka growled, stalking off.

"Easy for him to say," Kenji grumbled to Oki, who had arrived partway through the section chief's tirade. "I'm beginning to think this creep is a ghost."

"Or he's invisible."

"Same thing."

"Not necessarily." Oki perched on the edge of his desk. "What time does the mailman deliver your mail?"

"What? How should I know?" Kenji groaned. "Oh. That kind of invisible."

He swiveled toward his laptop, bringing up the map of Komagome that Assistant Detective Suzuki had made on Friday. Ten red dots marked the addresses where the thief had struck, all over the neighborhood.

"I don't see any pattern," he said, frustrated. "Do you?"

Suzuki arrived, looking uncharacteristically bedraggled, with a plastic Family Mart bag looped over his arm. Something inside was poking it into an odd, angular shape. He bowed and extended a slip of paper with both hands.

"I apologize for being late, sir."

Kenji examined the late train chit. The Chuo Line official had generously punched the hole that would have given the assistant detective an excuse to be up to two hours late, but Suzuki had still managed to arrive a mere eight minutes after starting time.

The assistant detective spied the map on Kenji's computer. "Did you figure out a pattern, sir?"

"No. And Tanaka-*san* is getting antsy about our lack of progress. It looks like we'll be out knocking on doors again, but first, he suggested we look at what time of day this guy did his dirty work. Could you take this map and code each incident with the time it happened? It probably won't help catch him, but it'll make the chief happy."

"Yes, sir. I'll get right on it, sir."

Suzuki picked up the bag containing his wounded umbrella and made his way back to his desk, leaving a trail of drips in his wake.

Ugh. As soon as he figured out a new way to ask the same old questions, he and Suzuki would be out pounding the pavement. In the rain. Or snow, if it got any colder. He wasn't looking forward to it, especially since his right sock was wet, a sure sign he had a hole in his shoe.

He pulled his computer toward him and powered it up. Before he got to work on the panty thief, he had an email to send.

To: mori@tmp.jp.gov
From: nakamura@tmp.jp.gov
Subject: Brown van photo

Mori-*san*,
I think I found the photo of the van you were looking for. But when I searched the Tokyo Metropolitan Police database to make sure the license plate matched the one associated with your Painted Doll case, I discovered the files

were password protected. In order not to waste
your time, if you can give me access, I'll check
before I send you the photo.

Nakamura, Kenji
Detective, Komagome Station

Send.

Mori would understand the unspoken tit-for-tat implied
by the offer to send a photo that he could easily have attached
to the email. He was sure the Inspector hadn't climbed into the
lofty heights of the First Investigative Division without learning
that if you wanted to make a withdrawal from the favor bank,
you had to make a deposit first.

Kenji took a notepad from his desk drawer, pondering
how to rephrase the panty thief questions. A message pinged.

To: nakamura@tmp.jp.gov
From: mori@tmp.jp.gov
Subject: Re: Brown van photo

Nakamura-*san*,
Thank you for your help. I would appreciate it
if you'd send me the photo you mentioned at
your earliest convenience.

Mori, Matsuo
Inspector
First Investigative Division

Fucking Mori. Now he had no choice but to send the
picture, and Mori wasn't going to give him a damn thing in
return. Kenji wrote a terse message and attached the file,
deciding he'd hand over the one with the van's license plate, but
he'd be damned if he gave Mori the rest. He pressed Send. The
Inspector must still be pissed about sharing the spotlight on
their previous case, and didn't want to take the chance he'd
have to do it again. *Asshole.*

Kenji's phone rang.

"*Moshi-moshi?*"

"Mori here. Thank you for sending that picture." He paused. "I wanted you to know, it wasn't me who denied you access to the Painted Doll files."

Right.

"Don't take it personally," Mori continued. "When I tried to check the license plate in your photo against the file, my own password didn't work." A note of frustration crept into his voice. "The case must have gotten attached to some other investigation that I don't have access to."

"Do you remember who the license plate traced back to?"

"Yeah. It wasn't a who—it was a corporation. And I'll tell you for free that it didn't go anywhere. We interviewed everyone who worked there. I was hoping the photo would give us something new to work with. Where did you get it?"

"I found the memory chip with my mother's pictures on it." He paused, then asked, "Did my father say anything to you about what happened to her camera when you talked to him?"

Mori snorted. "He didn't say *anything* when I talked to him. But funny you should mention the camera, because when I showed him the nice blue Nikon CoolPix we found in your mom's suitcase—along with a Chinese passport and all the worldly possessions of the second Painted Doll victim—he went white as a sheet. You want to ask him why? Maybe you'll have better luck than I did."

Kenji sat there, stunned. A camera exactly like the one his mother had owned had been found with the Painted Doll victim's clothing. And his father knew it.

"I will, sir," he promised.

"Was there anything else on that chip that might tell us what your mother witnessed that day?"

Kenji hesitated, then waffled. "I haven't had a chance to look at everything yet, sir,"

"If you find something more, let me know."

"Yes, sir."

"Appreciate it," Mori said. "I'll be in touch." Click.

Kenji lowered his phone. Why had his father lied? Why had he told Kenji that the suitcase didn't have anything to do with anything, when he knew from the start that Mori had found his mother's camera inside?

Kenji sat back in his chair. He needed to know more about the Painted Doll victim. He needed to see the old files. But Mori couldn't get into them either. If he sent the other pictures, would that be enough to get the Inspector access to the investigation that had swallowed the Painted Doll case? And if so, how appreciative would he be in return?

•

The stormy sky was darkening toward night by the time Kenji got on the train to Toritsu-daigaku. His luck was turning, but instead of the usual rush that accompanied a breakthrough in a case, all he felt was a sense of foreboding. In less than an hour, he'd have a photo of the two women who were abducted at Korankei, and he'd be that much closer to finding out how his mother and the Painted Doll were connected. But the more he found out, the closer he'd be to learning what his father was hiding, and he was beginning to fear that was something that wouldn't help him sleep at night.

As the train sped through the southern suburbs, Kenji watched skyscrapers give way to low-rise apartment buildings. The rain must have stopped earlier out here, judging by how many balconies were festooned with drying laundry.

The train slowed. Next stop, Toritsu-daigaku. It eased up to the platform and Kenji stepped out.

Déjà vu hit him hard.

He looked around, bewildered. Had he been here before? Wide platforms curved alongside the tracks under a peaked roof, ten subway cars long. Built from no-nonsense beige concrete blocks, billboard ads covered the walls between wired-glass windows that obviously hadn't been scoured by anything but the elements for a good long time. Open at both ends, the station offered protection from rain and snow, but not from the cold. Toritsu-daigaku was a minor station, a local stop on the Toyoko Line, and Kenji was sure he'd never—

Then he remembered. The day after his mother's funeral, Aunt Ayako had taken him and his brother to leave flowers and say a prayer for the safe passage of his mother's soul at the spot where she'd been found. This was the station where they'd gotten off.

Kenji hadn't made it to the site. He'd been overcome with nausea. He hadn't actually thrown up, but he'd spent a cold and miserable hour huddled on a bench, waiting for Aunt Ayako and Takeo to return.

He shook himself. Now was not the time to dredge all that up. He had a job to do, a photo to collect, a witness to interview. Trotting along the platform, he took the stairs two at a time.

Rounding the corner with a sense of relief—this part of the station was reassuringly unfamiliar—he slowed, scanning the faces of the people huddled into their winter coats outside the ticket gate. There she was, a middle-aged woman in a puffy knee-length coat, anxiously searching the arriving crowd. He recognized her pointy chin from his mother's photos, although she wore her hair shorter now, in a chin-length bob. Pushing through the turnstile, he stopped in front of her, bowed and introduced himself.

"You look just like your mother!" she exclaimed. Then, embarrassed to have said something so personal to someone she'd just met, she hastily bowed and added, "Won't you join me for a cup of tea? My house isn't far."

He fell in beside her as she turned onto the street bordering the station. They crossed under the tracks. Small houses lined the lane that ran alongside the Toyoko Line, but modest apartment buildings were beginning to crop up in between, as families rebuilt to add rental units that would help pay for the privilege of living a ten-minute ride from Shibuya.

A train roared by on its way toward Jiyugaoka, leaving the air shimmering in its wake. Ahead, the gates barring access to a foot crossing lifted, and a young mother began bumping her stroller across the tracks.

Keiko guided him around a corner into a narrow lane and stopped in front of a thatch-roofed gate, probably a relic of the old-fashioned house that had once stood there. All over Tokyo, sprawling one-story wooden structures with gracious gardens had been replaced by three-unit stucco buildings like this one, with an entrance on each floor, so three families could live where only one had been before. Keiko dug into her handbag and found her keys, then led him up to the middle flat.

"Excuse me for intruding." Kenji murmured the formal phrase his mother had drummed into him, as he stepped into the cramped entryway.

He waited while his mother's friend dug through the basket of slippers, searching for a pair that would fit him. She took his coat and hung it in the closet, then motioned for him to follow her into a small living room.

"Please have a seat," she said, gesturing to a chair that was a little too low for Kenji's long legs, but was obviously the "good" one reserved for guests. She excused herself to make tea.

The room was furnished in comfortable, if somewhat dated, Western style. The Satos' TV was big, but it hadn't been replaced since the time when big also meant half a meter thick. A compact computer desk sat next to it, home to a neat stack of bills and a bulky laptop that had been new several generations ago. A plate of wrapped Yoku Moku butter cookies and a bowl of rice crackers had already been set out on the coffee table, next to a photo album with a blue cloth cover and plastic-filmed pages. Kenji longed to snatch it up and flip to the back to search for the snapshot of the two foreigners, but it would be rude to do so before being invited.

On a shelf above the TV sat a clutter of framed snapshots. Kenji rose and crossed the room, wondering if there were any of Keiko and his mother together.

No, they all looked like family shots. A much younger Keiko in her red wedding kimono, white cranes winging across it toward eternal faithfulness. Keiko again, with a toddler—a son, apparently—in a sailor suit. An older Keiko and a tall man in a blue uniform, posed with a young man holding a diploma. Kenji picked that one up to study it more closely. She was married to a policeman?

Keiko reappeared, bearing a tray with a blue and white teapot, delicately painted with camellia blossoms. Kenji returned to his chair. She poured and handed him a cup, then poured one for herself.

"Please, help yourself," she said, pushing the cookies and rice crackers closer.

"Thank you for making the time to see me today," Kenji said after taking a polite bite of rice cracker. "So . . . you and my mother were old friends? From high school?"

"Yes. She was actually my older sister's friend, but we needed a vocalist for our band, so she introduced us."

"My mother was in a *band*?" He wasn't sure whether to be embarrassed or impressed.

"We weren't very good, but we had fun," Keiko said, her face softening. "We only did it for a few months, but after that, we were friends for life." She shook her head, sadly. "We had so much in common. She was more like my sister than my real sister. We talked about that a lot, over the years—how eerie it was that our lives had turned out so much alike."

"Because you both married policemen?" Kenji nodded toward the photos.

"Yes." She smiled. "But that wasn't coincidence—your mother introduced me to Shin. His father was your dad's judo *sensei*."

"And your husband works in Toritsu-daigaku now?"

"He did, when we first moved here. Now he commands a police box in Jiyugaoka, the next station over."

"And how old is your son?"

"A year younger than your brother. Satoshi is a profiler now," she added with pride.

"In Tokyo?" Kenji asked.

"No, Nagoya."

"Your husband must be proud."

"Actually," she said, "My husband tried to talk him out of going to the Academy. Said he should go to college and work with his brains, not his back. So they compromised—Satoshi went to college, then he applied to the Academy."

"I did the same," Kenji said. "Except my dad wanted me to go straight to the Academy, and I talked him into letting me go to college first. My brother was supposed to go, but—"

"I know. My husband helped him get a job at that restaurant."

So that's what happened. Kenji had always wondered how Takeo had ended up as a sushi chef in Jiyugaoka.

"He was kind of lost, after your mother passed away," Keiko said. "And your father—"

His father had been furious. The night Takeo broke the news that he'd gone to the police academy administration center and withdrawn his name from the next class of cadets, Kenji had barricaded himself in his room with his music turned up high, trying to drown out the angry words that were flying through the house like bullets. He hadn't ventured out again until he heard the front door slam behind his brother.

"But everything worked out for the best, didn't it?" Keiko said, attempting a smile. "I know your mother would have been happy that Takeo finally found his way, that he's happily married, with a good future. She was always worried he wasn't cut out for police work. We talked about it on that trip to the Ise Shrine, and I suggested she speak to Shin. I think that's what they were discussing on the night she—" Keiko fell silent.

"On the night she died? She was here? At your house? Are you 'Cookie-*chan*?'"

"Yes, that's what your mother used to call me." Keiko looked surprised. "How did you know? It was my high school nickname."

"After the funeral, when I'd recovered enough to wonder what exactly had happened to my mom, I asked my dad why she'd been in Toritsu-daigaku the night of her accident," Kenji explained. "He told me that she'd been visiting someone he called 'Cookie-*chan*', but until now, I didn't know who that was."

"I'm surprised he remembered." Keiko sighed. "While we were drinking tea after the funeral, I went to your dad to offer my condolences, and tell him how sorry I was that the accident had happened while she was visiting me. I thought he'd want to know more, but he didn't ask any questions at all, just said, 'Thank you for coming' as if he hadn't really heard me."

"I'm sorry he was so . . . unresponsive," Kenji said apologetically. "I think those are the only words I heard him say to anyone that day. He was in bad shape. We all were."

"I'm not surprised, and honestly, I didn't blame him a bit."

"What I've been wondering, though, is why she was here? All her note said was that she was taking something to a friend."

Keiko looked puzzled. "I don't recall her bringing anything with her that night, but it's possible that she did, and I just don't remember. I walked in the front door after spending the evening with my mother, and found your mom standing in the entry, talking to my husband. She said she'd just stopped by, hoping to see my pictures from the trip, so I made her take off her hat and coat and stay a while. Of course we got to talking, and by the time Shin came out to remind us what time it was, she had to run for the last train." Keiko shook her head. "The next morning, I heard the sirens, but I didn't realize— Shin came home from work that night and told me the sirens had been for her, that she'd been in an accident."

She glanced at his face, watched him blink back the tears that had welled up as she spoke.

"I'm so sorry," she said. "I didn't mean to rake this all up again. That's not what you came for, is it?" She pushed the photo album closer to him. "Please, go ahead and look for that picture you wanted. Excuse me for a moment."

She scooped up the empty teapot and disappeared, to give him some privacy.

Not now, he told himself, swallowing the lump in his throat. Not here. Get the photo, then get out. Opening the album and flipping quickly past the reminders of how much his mother had enjoyed life before it was cut short, he found the yellowing envelope of snapshots in the back.

Shuffling through them, he recognized the Ise Shrine, even though he'd never been there. He and Yumi had become friends when they'd been assigned to make a model of it together, in third grade. He flipped past shots of the bridge over the nearby river, and a stream of pilgrims flowing through an imposing peeled cedar *torii* gate toward the Grand Shrine. The next series was of a patient crowd inching its way up wide granite steps to the offering box, then finally, two young foreign women posing at the foot of another wooden *torii* gate, dark trees towering behind them.

He studied the picture. The young women were trying to make peace signs like Japanese schoolgirls, but getting it slightly wrong. One was giving the camera a saucy grin that revealed a little gap between her front teeth. The other's round face looked more foreign, her golden skin and delicate brows accentuated by straight, dark hair pulled into a ponytail. Her full lips curved in a shy smile.

Why did the saucy one look familiar? With a jolt, he remembered where he'd seen her face. He pulled out his phone and searched for the second Painted Doll article, scrolling to the artist's sketch. A beautiful young woman with a gap between her front teeth stared up from his screen.

She would never make peace signs the wrong way again.

Keiko returned with a fresh pot of tea. She poured.

"Can you tell me anything about these girls?" Kenji asked, dropping his phone in his pocket and handing her the snapshot. "Did you talk to them at all?"

"Just the sweet one, with the ponytail." Keiko pointed. "She thanked me and told me that she hoped my prayers were answered. The other one . . . . " she bit her lip. "At one of the rest stops, I saw her sneak a bar of chocolate into her pocket and walk out of the store without paying. At the end of the trip, when your mother's suitcase was missing, we thought she was probably the one who stole it."

"Do you remember her name?"

Keiko shook her head and handed the photo back. "Sorry, no. It was something foreign. Chinese, maybe."

"That's okay. Don't worry about it." He stood. "Thank you for making the time to see me. I really appreciate your help. I'll return the picture as soon as I scan it."

She smiled. "Keep it as long as you like."

•

Kenji turned to give Keiko a final bow from inside the ticket gate before starting up the stairs to the train platform. Tomorrow he'd scan the photo and send it to Mori, along with a link to the artist's sketch from the newspaper article. Surely that would convince the powers-that-be that at least one of them should be allowed access to the file.

He now had zero doubt that the camera found inside the suitcase belonged to his mother. Keiko had been asked to take the two victims' picture because they didn't have cameras of their own. Now he just had to figure out how that blue Nikon CoolPix had ended up in the stolen suitcase, while the memory chip that had been inside it was lying in the back room of the Komagome Camera shop.

And something else was puzzling him: Keiko's explanation of why his mother had been there that night. His mom never just "stopped by" to see her friends, not without calling first. She never would have gone all the way out to the southern suburbs of Tokyo without making sure Keiko was home and it was a convenient time to visit.

What was she really doing in Toritsu-daigaku that night? There must be another reason, one that might explain the ¥300,000 in her purse.

The money was bothering him more and more. If he'd found that much cash in an accident victim's bag, he'd be asking some uncomfortable questions. Who did it belong to? Was she paying someone, or had they paid her? And what for? Goods or information? Legal . . . or illegal?

Worrying about what his mother had gotten herself into, he stepped onto the Shibuya-bound platform and was hit again with that unwelcome jolt of familiarity. He stopped in his tracks, then made himself walk to the markings for car number four, the one that would stop closest to his transfer gate in Shibuya.

He gazed across at the outbound platform. Had his mother stood in this same spot that night? No, Aunt Ayako had taken his brother outside, somewhere beyond the station. From his perch on his bench, he'd spotted them walking along the road that bordered the tracks. His mother must have been standing farther down when it happened.

Across the tracks, a local rumbled in. Passengers poured out. The departure bell rang, the doors closed, and the train eased away, gathering speed as it headed toward Jiyugaoka. The crush of just-arrived passengers bottlenecked as they flowed down the stairs leading to the exit.

On this side of the tracks, people were steadily filtering onto the platform around him, lining up behind the marks that showed where the doors of the next train would open. The arrival sign began flashing a "Stand back, the next train does not stop" warning. A moment later, the ends of Kenji's muffler were thrown in his face as an express roared through.

He jumped back, staring after it. His mother had ended up in the path of *that*? The horror of it hit him full force, and he spun around, walked away from the tracks. He stood, head down, breathing hard.

It wasn't an accident.

Stop. Get ahold of yourself. He swayed, suddenly dizzy. Dropping to a crouch, he hung his head. *Breathe. Breathe.*

"Are you all right?"

Shined leather shoes, the hems of sharply creased blue pants. Kenji looked up to find a young station attendant in a peaked cap and wire rimmed glasses bending over him.

"Yeah, sorry," Kenji said. "I . . . I just felt a little dizzy there for a moment. Give me a minute. I'll be fine."

"Do you need help getting to the restroom?"

The attendant must think he was drunk.

"No, I'm fine," Kenji said, clambering to his feet to demonstrate that he wasn't about to throw up all over the shiny shoes.

"Are you sure? Would you like to lie down?"

"No. Thank you. I'm fine. But I appreciate your concern. Thank you," Kenji said, willing him to go away.

"Perhaps a cup of tea?" the attendant persisted.

Damn. Now the guy thought he was a jumper.

"Tea, yes, that would be great, but please don't trouble yourself. I'll get some at the vending machine over there." Kenji gestured down the platform. He dug some coins from his pocket and picked out the right ones, giving the attendant what he hoped was a reassuring smile. "I'm fine now. Really."

The young *eki-in* didn't look convinced. Instead of returning to his post, he watched Kenji move to the vending machine nearby and feed in the coins.

Thunk. Kenji scooped up his purchase, then moved further down the platform. Hands warmed by the hot bottle, he cracked the top and took a slug. Oddly enough, the familiar flavor did calm him a little.

A local train arrived, but he stepped back, finishing his tea, let it go without him.

Feeling better, he pushed his empty into the recycle bin, then turned to gaze at the far end of the platform. If he wanted to know what really happened the night his mother died, he needed to go down there. See for himself.

He started to walk. This far from the stairs, long after rush hour, nobody was waiting. Even at peak times, it would be less crowded at this end.

Another express train barreled through, windows blurring by like high-speed film, but this time he didn't flinch, he kept walking. In the wake of the train, silence.

At least it had been quick, he told himself. At least she didn't suffer. He stopped and looked around. A wall blocked the end of the platform and protective barriers lined the edge, but those were recent. Ten years ago, train stations didn't have anything that prevented people from falling into the path of an oncoming train.

Is that what had happened? He recoiled, as the implications horrified him. It had not been an open casket funeral. How had his father been able to—? *No. Don't think about that. Don't. Don't.* A green light flashed at him from between the tracks. He stared at it, letting it push the unwanted images from his mind. *Flash. Flash. Flash.*

Green lights were supposed to deter jumpers. The police had told his family that she hadn't committed suicide, but how did they know? There must be a report. Actually two reports— one from the police and one from the train company. He was pretty sure they would confirm what the family had been told, though—if the Toyoko Line investigators thought his mother had stepped off the platform on purpose, they'd have charged the Nakamura family for every minute the trains were stopped. That would have been a financial hardship nobody could hide.

But if she didn't jump, did she fall? Kenji thought about the crowds that surged onto the trains at rush hour, pictured the drunken commuters he'd seen, running hell-bent for the last train's closing doors, just before midnight. Did the investigators think she'd been jostled? Pushed?

"Excuse me, but I just wanted to make sure . . . . "

The station attendant again. Kenji realized that by standing at the end of the platform and staring at the suicide prevention light, he'd practically issued him a gilt-edged invitation.

"Thank you, but I'm feeling much better," Kenji assured him, as another local train pulled into the station. A clutch of teenagers toting electric guitars got off. "Excuse me, but this is my train."

Kenji boarded, feeling the eyes of the attendant follow him. As it pulled away, the young man began speaking into a walkie-talkie, brow furrowed. No doubt he was giving the stations between Toritsu-daigaku and Shibuya a heads-up that a tall potential suicide in a black coat and gray muffler was coming their way.

Kenji leaned against the end of the seats, by the door. The train wasn't crowded, but he preferred to stand; he thought better on his feet. Rain began to speckle the windows.

He needed to see the accident reports. Had his family been given copies? The investigating officer had probably asked his father to come in, so he could deliver the findings face-to-face. Kenji pictured his dad sitting ramrod-straight in an interview room, a cup of tea growing cold before him, not flinching as the words tore through him like shrapnel.

His father couldn't have done that alone. Ayako must have gone with him. She would have taken charge of the reports and tucked them out of sight. He pictured the kitchen floor storage well, but he was pretty sure there hadn't been any official-looking envelopes in it.

As soon as he got off the train, he'd call and ask where she put them.

•

A scrum of chattering schoolgirls coming through the ticket gate at Komagome Station passed Kenji, drowning out the voice on his phone. He covered his other ear, so he could hear his aunt.

"—seven-thirty! Now that he doesn't have to work late, your uncle informed me there's no reason we can't eat earlier. What's he talking about, *no reason*? He might be retired, but I'm not. How can he expect me to be home every day by six o'clock so I can have his dinner ready by seven-thirty?"

"If you'd rather I came by later—" Kenji offered.

"No, no, come now," Ayako said. "You can keep me company while I slave over a hot stove."

Ten minutes later, Kenji was sitting at his aunt's kitchen table, a cup of tea before him. The knife in her hand flashed as she slivered carrots for *kinpira*.

"So," she said, "What's the occasion?"

"I wanted to ask if you have copies of my mother's accident reports. There should be one from the police and one from the train company."

"Her accident reports?" She turned to face him. "Why do you want those? If you have questions, I'm sure I can answer them."

Kenji shook his head. "I'd rather see the reports for myself. I'd like to go over them, see if the investigators missed anything."

"Ken-*kun*, are you sure you want to dig this up again?"

"Auntie, I'm a police detective. It's what I do."

Ayako sighed. "There's a reason they don't let people investigate cases involving their own families, you know."

"I know," Kenji said. "But nobody else is going to do it."

Ayako turned off the stove and wiped her hands on her apron. "Okay. Let me go find them."

She left the room and came back a few minutes later, hugging two large envelopes to her chest, one white, one manila.

Kenji had seen envelopes like that before, filled with the dispassionate findings of investigators, medical examiners, crime techs. Suddenly he didn't feel so eager to know what was inside.

"Thank you," he said.

"Are you sure?"

He nodded.

"Promise me you won't let your father see these."

He promised. She handed them over.

"Is that all?" she asked, resuming her stirring.

"Actually . . . ." Kenji hesitated. "There is one more thing."

In most Japanese families, it was the wife's job to manage the household money and pay the bills. Because the lights had stayed on and hot water had continued to flow in the weeks after his mother's death, he suspected his aunt had helped his dad with that chore too. She might know if the ¥300,000 in his mother's purse had been withdrawn from the family account. She might even know why.

"After my mom passed away," he began, "did you help my dad with the finances?"

"Yes." Ayako picked up her knife and returned to the carrots. "Why?"

"When you looked at the bank statements, did you notice anything . . . unusual?"

She hesitated, then scraped the slivers into a bowl and picked up another carrot. "What do you mean 'unusual'?"

"I don't know, anything that didn't match the regular deposits or withdrawals."

She didn't answer, kept chopping.

"Auntie?"

Ayako's knife stilled.

"There was something, wasn't there?"

Somewhere outside, one schoolgirl called to another.

"Someone took five hundred thousand yen out of your parents' savings account on the day of your mother's accident," said Ayako.

¥500,000? But there had been only ¥300,000 in his mother's purse when they found her. What had happened to the missing ¥200,000?

"When I asked your father, he said he didn't know anything about it," Ayako continued, her face troubled. "I asked if your mother might have used it for something without telling him, and he got upset. He said no, she'd never do that. But—" Her gaze faltered. "I think he was lying."

"How do you know?"

"Because he told me not to worry about it. That it wasn't important." She shook her head. "Five hundred thousand yen is a lot of money. It was even more, ten years ago. It's not possible that my brother—the brother who worked nights at a convenience store to put himself through the police academy— didn't care what happened to that much money. I think he was shocked she'd made the withdrawal, but he didn't want me looking into it."

Kenji's worry deepened. The question was, had his *father* looked into it? Or did he already know why his wife had withdrawn that money from their savings? Whatever the reason, he obviously didn't want his sister to know. And that meant he probably wouldn't want his son to know either.

Of course, Kenji though grimly, that wasn't going to stop him.

TUESDAY, JANUARY 6

•

Kenji's first cup of tea was almost gone. He looked up at the window behind Section Chief Tanaka's desk, surprised to find the inky sky lightening to gray.

He'd intended to open the envelopes from Aunt Ayako last night, as soon as his father went to bed. But while washing the dinner dishes, he'd noticed that the outside of the pan they used for grilled eel had become blackened with burnt-on oil and needed a good scrubbing. Then he'd discovered a pickle juice spill in the fridge and ended up taking everything out to wash the shelves. By the time he finished ironing a few uniform shirts, it had been too late, so he'd put the envelopes in his briefcase, set his alarm, and come in to work while the streetlights were still on and the night shift officers were still manning their desks.

Half an hour later, his stapler freshly refilled, his computer screen cleaner than it had been in months, and the dried-out pens in his desk drawer moved to the trash, the reports still sat on his desk, unopened.

He started up his laptop in order to take notes, and saw the reminder to send Mori the photo he'd gotten from Keiko. Crossing the squad room, he scanned the picture of the two women who had been abducted at Korankei, then opened a new message and keyed in the Inspector's address. He composed an email to accompany the attached picture, including a link to the artist's sketch of the second Painted Doll victim that had accompanied Jack Goldman's article.

"Haven't seen one of those in a long time."

Detective Oki propped his umbrella against his desk and peeled off his waterproof jacket. "Must be eight or ten years since the Toyoko Line used that logo," he said, nodding at the envelopes on Kenji's desk. "What's a train company got to do with your underwear thief?"

"Nothing," Kenji said. "These are the reports from my mother's, uh, accident."

"Ah." Oki regarded him silently for a moment. "I see you haven't opened them yet. Would you like me to take a look first? Get a feel for what's in there?"

Kenji felt a great weight lift. "Yes. Yes, please." He handed the envelopes to the other detective.

"What exactly are you looking for?" Oki asked.

"I don't know. I guess I just want to know what happened. Why they thought it was an accident."

Kenji explained what he'd discovered about the suitcase since he'd mentioned it to Oki last week. He concluded by saying, "Everything I'm learning makes me think they were wrong to classify it as an accident."

Oki nodded. "So you want to know what happened. What evidence they had to support their verdict. And if there were witnesses."

"Yes." Kenji said. "All of the above."

"Okay." Oki flipped the latches on his briefcase and dropped the reports on top of his other paperwork. "I'll read them when I get a break, try to get back to you before the end of the day."

•

Yumi hoped she wasn't too late. Finally rid of the Australian criminology professor she'd been translating for at the symposium on organized crime, she pushed through the door to the main lecture room.

Relieved to see that audience members were still lining up on stage to introduce themselves to the keynote speaker, she hustled down the aisle to join the queue waiting to meet Jack Goldman. Last night, when Kenji had called to update her on what he'd discovered about his mother's connection to the Painted Doll case, she hadn't mentioned her plan. She wasn't sure she'd get a chance to speak with the journalist who had been responsible for naming it, and didn't want to get his hopes up. If she found out anything interesting today, she'd surprise him with the news.

Up close, she saw that the reporter was closer to fifty than forty—he'd looked younger from the 27th row. The first foreign writer hired by a big Japanese newspaper, he'd made his reputation by exposing the dirty doings of the *yakuza*. Twenty years later, he no longer worked at the paper, but continued to report on how gangsters took advantage of changing laws and a shrinking population. A head taller than the Japanese waiting to speak with him, he was heavier than in the photos taken around the time he'd written the Painted Doll stories, but he still looked fit. Gray peppered his no-nonsense buzz, and the shrewd eyes now fixed on the face of a professor who was asking him about a well-known underworld figure looked like they had seen it all, and then some.

When Yumi had signed up to work this conference, she'd intended to ask him about the Painted Doll killings because he was the writer whose byline was on the stories. But while she'd been interpreting one of this morning's other lectures, she'd realized he might be able to help her with more than that.

The earlier talk had been on smuggling and piracy, and as she hummed along translating Japanese into English, she'd been mildly interested to learn that digital content was more profitable to pirate than gold, and that human beings were the hottest commodity being smuggled today. The speaker had used the Japanese *yakuza* as an example, citing their exploitation of the foreign and domestic laborers they supplied to radioactive cleanup sites, and the women they enslaved to feed the voracious prostitution trade. Then she'd been brought up short by the name of an organization the speaker mentioned: Human Rights Traffic Watch.

Was that what the bus driver meant when he'd accused her and Kenji of being "traffic watchers"? Had the abducted foreign women been brought to Japan by the modern version of slavers? Had they escaped their captors, bought cheap bus tour tickets and run away?

Maybe one of the groups that monitored human trafficking had helped them. And if the second woman had managed to elude the man in the brown van, maybe that organization knew what had happened to her. If they could locate her, Kenji could ask her what really happened that day at Korankei.

All Yumi had to do was discover which outfit had helped the two women escape, and she thought there was a good chance Jack Goldman could help her. He'd been billed by the conference organizers as one of the country's foremost experts on human trafficking.

She stepped closer, as the line ahead of her dwindled to a single gray-haired man, who was in the midst of a flowery speech, laden with honorific Japanese. Goldman parried, exchanging escalating phrases of appreciation, then graciously allowed his adversary to utter the loftiest parting words. As the scholar strode away, the journalist straightened from his final bow. She caught a look of weariness on his face before he noticed her standing there and replaced it with a professional smile.

She held out her hand and said, in English, "I enjoyed your lecture very much, Mr. Goldman."

His smile became considerably more genuine as he shook her hand. "I'm glad there's one beautiful woman in Tokyo who's interested in organized crime."

"Actually," Yumi said, "today I was interpreting for a visiting professor, but I'm also trying to track down someone who I think was a victim of human trafficking. I was wondering if you could give me some contact names at the Japanese organizations that help foreigners."

"Glad to. You're an interpreter?" His eyes crinkled at the corners. "Do you have a card? I often find myself in need of interpreting services."

Right. She'd heard that line before. Jack Goldman spoke Japanese like a native and probably hadn't needed an interpreter for years, if ever. Nevertheless, she handed him a card.

He examined it. "Well, Miss Yumi Hata, Interpreter and Translation Specialist, how is it you come to be looking for this human trafficking victim?"

"Um, it's kind of a long story, and I'm sure you're busy. But if you could just—"

"Hang on a sec," he said, digging for his phone. "I have to meet my next appointment at four, in Ginza, at . . . " he pulled up an email, ". . . some coffee shop called Café Bechet. Do you know it?"

She shook her head.

"Let's grab a cab and let the driver find it for us. I'll buy you a coffee and help you however I can, until my guy shows up."

Ginza was in the opposite direction from Komagome, but how could she refuse?

"I'd be delighted, Mr. Goldman," she said, bowing.

"Call me Jack."

Yumi would have preferred to continue being Miss Hata, but she had no choice but to ask him to call her by her first name, answering questions about her American childhood as their taxi crawled through traffic, the windshield wipers squeaking back and forth.

The driver slowed as they approached Ginza Itchome Station, and pulled over to the curb in front of a narrow, seven-story building. A sign for Café Bechet hung outside, among the ones for dentists, day spas and other small businesses. They dashed across the sidewalk to the entrance, looking for a directory. No luck. They'd almost decided to climb the stairs, hoping the café wasn't on the seventh floor, when a man with a newspaper tucked under his arm emerged from a door in a shadowy alcove. The mingled aromas of coffee and cigarettes followed him out. Café Bechet looked so much like a bar, they'd walked right past it.

Jack caught the door before it closed. "After you."

Inside, they blinked, as their eyes adjusted to the gloom. Although it was only mid-afternoon, the café existed in a sort of twilight time slip, the dark wood furnishings dating from the days when men wore snap-brim hats, and newsreels flickered across movie screens. The music of a long-dead clarinetist surrounded them with pre-war jazz as they seated themselves at the long wooden bar. At the far end, four battered copper coffeepots with long spouts sat on burners ringed with blue flame. Jars of coffee beans were lined up on shelves behind, along with china cups and saucers displayed with regimental precision. An old-fashioned balancing scale and industrial-grade grinder gleamed from years of daily use.

A young woman handed them a menu, and they discovered why Jack's next appointment claimed this place brewed the best coffee in town: it was all they served. There were over twenty different varieties on the menu, roasted in small batches daily, weighed out bean by bean for each order, then ground and dripped by hand so slowly through a cloth filter that Jack had pried Yumi's entire life story from her by the time their cups were reverently placed on the saucers before them.

Jack breathed in the aroma, then took a sip. He smiled with satisfaction. "Now *that's* coffee."

Yumi tried hers and agreed. Japan might be a nation of tea drinkers, but this was by far the best coffee she'd ever tasted.

Jack set down his cup. "Now, what is it you wanted to know? You're looking for some human trafficking victims?"

"Yes. I was hoping you could give me a few contact names at organizations they might have been working with."

"Are they male or female?"

"Female."

"When did they disappear?"

"Ten years ago."

Jack's eyebrows shot up. "That's a long time. Can I ask why you're only starting to look for them now?"

"A friend just got some new information about the day they disappeared, and now we're worried that something bad happened to them."

The journalist pondered the possibilities for a moment, then said, "Ten years ago, most human trafficking victims in Japan were women brought in for the sex trade. Were the women you're looking for sex workers?"

"Maybe. They were young and beautiful, so it's possible."

"Where were they from?"

"I don't know."

"Asian?"

"Yes."

He put down his cup and drew a spiral notebook from his pocket, flipping to a fresh page. "Back then, the biggest organization operating in Japan was the Institute for Trafficked, Exploited and Missing Persons."

He pulled a pen from his breast pocket, wrote "ITEMP" and underlined it, then wrote out the name, in both English and Japanese. "They have branches all over Japan, in all the cities big enough to have red light districts. Call them and ask for

Shoko Kawasaki. Tell her I sent you." He jotted down Shoko's name, adding the proper *kanji*.

He thought for a moment. "You could also try WomanWatch. Natsumi Jones runs that one." He added her name to the list, his mouth twitching into a half-smile. "It's probably better if you don't mention my name when you talk to her."

He ripped the sheet from his notebook and handed it to Yumi. "Try Shoko first. She's been doing this for twenty years, and if ITEMP wasn't the outfit helping your victims, she can tell you which other groups were operating back then. It's a small world, and even if some of them have disappeared, she can probably tell you who was in charge and where they are now."

He picked up his coffee cup. "Where were your victims last seen?"

"Korankei. It's a famous leaf-viewing spot. Do you know it?"

"Near the Ise Shrine?"

"Yes."

"What were two sex workers doing in Korankei?"

"They were on a bus tour. They were abducted from the parking lot when the group stopped to see the leaves."

"How do you know?"

"I saw photos."

"Photos?" Jack raised an eyebrow. "And there's no police report? Are you sure the victims are still missing?"

"We're pretty sure at least one of them is. We think she became the Painted Doll killer's second victim."

Jack stared. "You're shitting me."

"I know you wrote the story," Yumi continued. "I saw your byline when I searched. You're the one who came up with the name 'Painted Doll,' right? You tried to convince the police that the guy hadn't stopped at one victim. Why didn't they believe you?"

"They did believe me," Jack shook his head, old frustration boiling to the surface. "But they didn't want anyone else to believe me."

He paused for a sip of coffee. "You have to understand—for years, I was the only foreigner working at a Japanese newspaper. They hired me because they figured the mob bosses would talk to me. Here in Japan, the police, the media and the gangs have worked out an elaborate system of mutual obligation, but I'm not Japanese, so I don't fit into the hierarchy. I don't have to play by the rules, and neither do they."

He set down his cup. "After I got my first death threat, I figured out the other reason they offered me the crime slot: no Japanese reporter wanted to investigate stuff that might get him—or his family—killed. I was young and crazy, so I figured what the hell?" He drank his coffee. "My beat wasn't exclusively organized crime, but any dumped body makes the cops think 'gangsters,' so I'm the one they called when that first girl was found in the gutter. I talked to the homeless guy who saw the van the killer used, and convinced the cops to try hypnosis. They got a partial plate out of him.

"Then, when the second girl was found, I was the first reporter on the scene. It was obvious the same guy killed her. I filed the story, but the day after it ran, the boss of the organized crime unit called me downtown to police headquarters. He said they were putting together a task force to catch the guy, but they didn't want anything published about the manhunt or the murders until it was over. They didn't want the good citizens of Tokyo panicking about a serial killer on the loose. Especially," Jack gave her a grim smile, "since it appeared that the only people in danger were foreigners.

"They promised I'd be the first to know when they had a suspect in custody, that they'd give me an exclusive in exchange for my silence. I could have refused, but by then I knew how things worked in Tokyo: If I didn't take the carrot, they'd use the stick. I'd never get another lead from the police again." He shook his head. "But I was there at both scenes. They had nothing. The only way they were going to catch the guy is if he kept killing."

"But he didn't."

"No, that's the problem. He did. I've got friends in morgues all over Tokyo, I've seen the reports. The task force swept the others under the rug, but there were at least three more—all foreign illegals, all young women, all dressed and styled and ready for their close-ups. And I couldn't publish a word of it."

Yumi's heart raced. Five women! Three plus the two they knew about. The Painted Doll killer had murdered five women, and nobody knew.

"Is it okay if I share this information with my friend who's investigating the abduction?" She added quickly, "He's a police detective."

"On the Organized Crime squad? What's his name? Maybe I know him."

"I doubt it. He's stationed in Komagome."

"Why is a Komagome local investigating the Painted Doll killer?"

"Because it was his mom who took the pictures of that abduction at Korankei, and she died right after she got back from that trip. In an accident, supposedly. But—"

"But what?" Jack's interest sharpened another notch. "Does your detective friend think whoever abducted that girl was involved? That he's connected to the Painted Doll killings?"

"We don't know. Yet."

Jack took out a pen and opened his notebook. "You mind if I take a few notes?"

"No, go ahead."

"Why does your friend think his mother might have died because of what she saw at Korankei?"

"A few weeks ago, the police found the suitcase she took on that trip, in a warehouse full of human trafficking victims.

Inside was stuff that belonged to the second victim. We found out the bag was stolen on that trip, probably by the second victim. We have a picture of her wheeling it away, and—"

"And?"

Yumi hesitated. "I think I should check with my friend before I tell you any more. I just realized he might not like it if he knew I was talking to, you know, a reporter."

Jack slapped down his pen.

"That's right," he said sarcastically. "Because we all know that reporters like nothing better than to ignore gag orders." He glared at her. "Can I remind you that this reporter has kept his goddamn mouth shut for ten fucking years—pardon my French—on a story that could have bought me the Japanese equivalent of a Pulitzer? I want to solve this one as much as the cops do, because I can't publish one word until some brassbutt a lot further up the food chain than your detective gives me the go-ahead. That gag order is ten years old, but I still have to honor it. Not least because some very senior heads will roll if word gets out that all the king's horses and all the king's men couldn't catch one creep who's been preying on women in this city for ten years, despite their best efforts." He leaned in, "Tell me what you know."

Yumi bit her lip. Would Kenji be mad if she told Jack that the Korankei van's license plate matched the one from the Painted Doll killer's van? Would it hurt his chances at being promoted to the First Investigative Division? *Car, house, family—*

"You'd be doing your friend a favor, you know," Jack persisted. "A local detective who hands the big boys the break they need to get this unsolved off the books will be papered with so many commendations, he won't be able to refuse a promotion. And," he added, "I can help you. I know people, on both sides of the law. I don't have to play by the same rules as the police."

He had a point. He was an expert on organized crime. He had information that Kenji didn't. And he wanted to find out what happened at Korankei as much as they did.

"Tell me," he urged again. "I can help. What's the connection?"

"Okay," she said. "It was the van. The license plate of the van that abducted the women at Korankei matches the one that dumped the first Painted Doll victim."

"And you have a photo to prove it?"

"Yes."

"Show me."

"I don't have it. My friend has the pictures."

"Pictures plural?"

"Yes."

"Can you describe them to me?"

"Well, there are four. In the first one, the two foreign women are walking away from the tour bus with their luggage. In the second, a guy is pushing one of the women into a van. In the third, he's chasing the second woman toward the camera and tripping over the duffel bag she dropped when she ran. The fourth one is a close-up of the guy's face."

Jack's pen stopped mid-scribble and his head snapped up. "You have the abductor's picture?"

"Yeah, but I don't think anyone would be able to identify him from it unless they already had a pretty good idea who he is. He's wearing a knit cap pulled down to his eyebrows, and his hand is covering half his face."

"I want to see it."

"I'm not sure my friend will share. I can ask him, but—"

"Then describe the guy. Maybe I'll recognize him. Was he tall? Short? Fat? Thin?"

Yumi reflected on the photo she'd seen. "Compared to the woman he was chasing, he was big," she said. "But that's about all I can tell you. At first he was too far away, then he was too close. The only thing I can really remember about his face were the three fresh scratches across his cheek."

"Serious enough to leave scars?"

"Couldn't tell."

Jack flipped back through his notes. "Okay, you said there were two women. What happened to the one who ran away?"

"We don't know. That's who we're looking for."

"And you think the one who was already in the van became the second Painted Doll victim?"

"Yes."

"What did the van look like?"

"It was brown."

"Any markings?"

"No. Plain brown. At least, what I could see of it. It was kind of far away."

"What about damage? Unusual fittings?"

Yumi cast her thoughts back. "It was hard to tell from the pictures, but now that you mention it, I think there were some sort of grills over the windows. Painted the same color as the van."

"Right wingers," Jack said, sitting back. "Could be right wingers. You know, those convoys that roll through the streets of Tokyo, blasting nationalist slogans and patriotic music?"

"Those guys? Ugh." Yumi made a face. She always covered her ears until they passed.

"You're not the only one who thinks they're dickheads," Jack said, smiling at her reaction. "They put those grills on the windows to protect themselves from rotten tomatoes and worse. How much do you know about them?"

"Not much," Yumi admitted. "Just that they're always blasting slogans about restoring the emperor to power and kicking out foreigners."

"Yes. But they differ about which foreigners they want to go to hell first. For example, the Great Japan Patriotic Party wants Japan to unite with South Korea and the United States against Russia and China, while the Patriotic Way group demands that all Koreans leave Japan. The Great Japan Restoration Society wants to deport anyone who's not a hundred percent Japanese, even if they have one Japanese parent. And a few of them—"

"Wait a sec," Yumi interrupted. *Great Japan Restoration Society.* Wasn't that the name on the banner hanging behind the bus driver in the newspaper clipping tacked to the dry cleaner's bulletin board? The bus driver had been getting an award. What had he done that pleased the Society so much? Had he helped them rid Japan of two foreigners? She wished she'd noticed the date on the clipping. Was he more than just a reluctant witness to the abduction at Korankei?

"The Great Japan Restoration Society," she said. "You say they want to deport everyone who's not Japanese. Are they all talk, or . . . ?"

"Do they act on their rhetoric?" He sipped his coffee. "Most of these groups confine their attacks to verbal ones and demonstrations in neighborhoods with big foreign populations. It's only the ones linked to *yakuza* outfits that occasionally cross the line."

"Is the Great Japan Restoration Society one of those?"

"Yes. Why are you asking?"

She explained about the bus driver.

"You think he could have been involved?"

"I don't know. He refused to tell us anything, and said he sympathized with anyone aiming to kick those two women out of the country. But he didn't really look like a gangster. I mean, he didn't have tattoos or anything. And his job was driving a tour bus, which doesn't seem too, you know, gangster-ish."

"True. But the low-level guys have to work day jobs, just like any other chump climbing the ladder. What about the man who was chasing the woman through the parking lot? Did he look like a gangster to you?"

She shook her head, doubtful. "I couldn't tell from the pictures."

Jack leaned toward her. "Talk your friend into sending me those photos. I know a lot of players in the *yakuza*. And I remember what they looked like ten years ago. If I recognize the guy, your detective can pass the info on to whoever will give him the biggest promotion."

The café brightened for a moment as the door opened and closed behind a grizzle-bearded man in a shapeless overcoat. Stuffing his wet cap into his pocket, he grinned at them as he crossed to the bar.

"Jack, you old dog," he said, his accent putting his origins far north of London. "What's this lovely young lady doing in a dark coffee bar with a guy like you?"

"Angus." Jack rose, and they clapped each other on the back. He introduced Yumi, then said, "We were just discussing our patriotic friends in the loudspeaker vans."

"You can have 'em. Not my beat, and glad of it."

"Angus is more of an anti-nuke guy," Jack explained.

"More of a let's-clean-up-this-bloody-mess-before-you-make-another-one guy," the other journalist corrected him. "Although today I think we're here to test how serious the government is about prosecuting people under their bloody secrecy laws."

Yumi smiled and pushed back her stool.

"I'll leave you to it, then," she said, gathering her things. She turned to Jack. "Thank you. For everything."

She dug in her purse for her wallet.

"No, no, put that away, this is on me," Jack said.

"No, I insist," Yumi said, finding the right coins and setting them on the counter next to his cup.

He picked up the money and grabbed her hand, folding the coins into it.

"Absolutely not." He smiled. "But I won't forget you owe me."

He produced a card and wrote a number on the back. "This is my personal mobile number. My email is on the other side. Send me those pictures." He handed it to her. "You won't be sorry. I promise."

"Watch out, young lady," the other reporter warned. "That's the card of the most notorious ladies' man in Tokyo."

"Wrong-o," Jack said. "That's the card of a reporter who knows a good story when he sees one."

•

Everyone in the squad room was beginning to tidy their papers and power down their laptops by the time Kenji ended his call and checked the last number off his list. Post office, messenger services, department stores, grocery shops.

Suzuki's new color-coded map had surprised everyone by handing them a breakthrough in the underwear case. Correlating the panty thief's crimes with the time of day they'd occurred had revealed that the crime scene dots traced a swirl of fire through Komagome: yellow for morning slowly changing to orange for afternoon, then into red for evening. Nothing before two in the afternoon, nothing after eight at night. The flame swooped from the neighborhood west of Rikugi-en garden to the streets east of Komagome Hospital, suggesting that whoever was stealing panties worked the same route on a regular basis. So instead of slogging around the neighborhood in the rain that afternoon, Kenji and Suzuki had spent the day on their phones, calling local businesses to gather names of deliverymen who worked the streets of the neighborhood.

How many potential panty thief suspects were on the list so far? Kenji counted. 106. Tomorrow he'd start running them through the police database, but now it was time to call it a day. He stood and stretched. Finally, it felt like they were making progress.

Kenji walked back to Suzuki's desk, where the assistant detective was just ending a call to a local noodle shop. The long list on his laptop screen told Kenji that they had tomorrow's work cut out for them.

"I found fifty-six local restaurants that deliver, sir," Suzuki said. "If nothing else, the next time it's raining, I'm going to let someone else get wet bringing our lunch." Suzuki glanced at the wall clock. "Do you want to go out and start interviewing people now?"

"No," Kenji said, noting that it was five minutes to five. "Let's get started first thing tomorrow morning, and hope the storm blows through by then." He dismissed Suzuki for the day with an "*O-tsukare-sama-deshita*," thanking him for becoming honorably tired while working hard for the good citizens of Tokyo.

Back at his desk, he checked his email and groaned when he spied the unsent message to Inspector Mori sitting in his Drafts folder. He'd forgotten to finish it over lunch. He reread the note, hesitated, then attached the additional shots from his mother's camera. Send.

The elevator doors opened, and a weary-looking Detective Oki emerged, followed by Assistant Detective Aya Kurosawa. Water from their umbrellas was pooling at the bottom of the flimsy plastic sleeves dispensed inside the front door, and Oki's brush-cut hair was standing up in wet spikes all over his head. Curly tendrils had escaped Aya's no-nonsense ponytail, making her look more girlish than usual.

Kenji refrained from mentioning how becoming that was, lest she treat him to the scowl she reserved for morons, but he thought it would be quite useful if it were raining the next time he needed her to watch his back. The bad guys would never guess a girl with a halo of curls and a sprinkling of freckles across her nose had a third degree black belt in judo. Assistant Detective Kurosawa was so small, she could be mistaken for a child from the back, which made it extra-humiliating to find yourself suddenly sailing through the air, smacked down hard before you knew what hit you.

"*O-tsukare-sama*," Kenji said.

Aya bowed in return. "And thank you for your hard work too. Sir."

She was getting better at remembering he deserved an honorific. Kenji and Oki were the only ones at Komagome Station who knew that Aya was one of *those* Kurosawas. That she'd grown up in Kabuki-chō where her father was king. Or rather, *oyabun*. The head of the Kurosawa-*gumi* crime family had disowned her the day she'd graduated from the police academy.

"I noticed you're not signed up for the throws clinic on Friday," she said.

Kenji groaned.

"You could use the practice, you know," she added. "Sir."

He'd been ignoring the sign-up sheet for the judo clinic at the Bunkyo Ward Sports Center, hoping some other engagement would crop up and give him an excuse not to go. Aya was one of the instructors, and inevitably she chose him as a demonstration victim. She threw her superiors to the mat as ruthlessly as she slammed the raw recruits, oblivious to how much that shocked everyone who hadn't grown up in her world, where rank was based solely on who you could beat, not how much gold braid was on your uniform.

"Um, it's at seven, isn't it?" Kenji stalled.

"Yeah. And if the weather report is more right than usual, I expect lots of guys who could really use the practice will skip out because they don't want to get their little tootsies wet." She grinned. "Which means the ones who come will get an extra-good workout."

Great. Not only would he get cold and wet walking over there, he'd be rewarded by extra smackdowns. But she was right; he did need the practice.

"I'll put my name on the list," he said.

She nodded and disappeared toward the ladies room.

"Well, that was a miserable way to waste a day," Oki groused, shedding his dripping rain poncho and hooking his umbrella on his desk.

"No luck?" Kenji asked.

The big detective shook his head. "You?"

"We made a little progress." Kenji woke up his computer so Oki could see the map. He explained Suzuki's color code.

"Lucky you," Oki said. "A thief who punches the clock. Wish our guy was that organized."

"If it's any consolation, tomorrow it'll be me and Suzuki pounding the pavement. He found fifty-six local restaurants that deliver, and I tracked down a hundred and six guys with regular routes through Komagome."

"Throw a coin to the shrine gods on your way home," Oki advised. "Maybe they'll smile on you and he won't turn out to be the last guy on your list."

He reached into his bottom desk drawer and drew out a bottle of twelve-year-old Macallan whiskey. After raising an inquiring eyebrow at Kenji, who politely declined, he poured a tot into his empty teacup.

"You in a hurry to get home?" Oki asked, recapping the bottle and stowing it.

"Not particularly," Kenji said, as lightning flashed outside, followed closely by a rumble of thunder. "Why?"

Oki pulled out the envelopes that held the accident reports inside. "Get yourself a fresh cup of tea and give me a few minutes with these." He surveyed the empty interview rooms. "Meet me in Number Three. The chairs in there at least try to be comfortable."

As Oki headed for the interview room with his whiskey, Kenji scooped up his teacup and made his way down the hall to the staff room. Standing with his finger on the button of the hot water pot, he waited for the trickle of water to turn a handful of cheap police-issue tea leaves into something drinkable. He'd managed to forget about the envelopes all day, but now that he knew Oki was opening them, looking at the contents, his stomach began to churn. He carried his tea back down the hall, his steps slowing as he neared the door. He stopped outside. Through the window, he could see Oki hunched over the table, studying a diagram.

Be a detective, he admonished himself, not a victim. Taking a deep breath, he walked in.

Oki sat in one of the armchairs, papers spread out on the coffee table before him. He'd pushed aside the plant that was struggling to disguise the interrogation room as a lounge. Rain rattled against the small windows near the ceiling.

Kenji perched on the chair opposite. He recognized the documents on the table, even though they were upside down: incident summaries, accident diagram sketches, forms stamped with the red seals of multiple officials.

"No investigator's notes?" Kenji asked. "Or anything from the medical examiner?"

"No," Oki said, looking up. "In fact, as far as I can tell, most of this stuff boils down to ass-covering paperwork, the train company and the local police assuring each other that they conducted a thorough investigation and found nobody at fault."

"*Was* somebody at fault?"

"Hard to say. They didn't include copies of the original investigation materials, just summaries of their findings."

"I guess I shouldn't be surprised. The reports were written for survivors, not investigators. Is there anything I can follow up on?"

Oki picked up the summary with the train line's logo at the top. His eyes flicked between it and the document he'd been reading. "The police and the train company agree that the incident happened on December fourth, at a foot crossing between Toritsu-daigaku and Jiyugaoka Stations. They agree that—"

"Wait." Kenji sat up. "A foot crossing?"

"Yeah. Closer to Toritsu-daigaku than Jiyugaoka." Oki looked up. "You didn't know that?"

Kenji shook his head. "I assumed it happened at the station."

"There's a diagram," Oki said, handing him another piece of paper printed with the train company logo.

Kenji studied it. Tracks bisected the sheet of paper at a slight angle, an arrow at the top pointing due north. Safety fences ran alongside, interrupted by an opening where a narrow street crossed the tracks. Four boxes flanking the gap marked the machinery that lowered arms to bar the crossing when a train approached. Neat lettering labeled the warning signs, emergency train stop switches and cross-traffic mirrors. On both sides, signal boxes housed the flashing red lights and clanging bells designed to alert even the oldest grandmas and youngest kindergarteners that a train was coming.

How had his mother accidentally been hit at a foot crossing? The diagram made that look even less likely than falling from the station platform. A circle inside the fence on the east side of the tracks was marked "victim location." He swallowed.

Oki said, "The police and train company also agree that it happened close to midnight, probably right before the last train."

"How do they know that? Were there witnesses?"

"No, but in the door-to-door, they talked to someone from the neighborhood who had crossed there at about five to midnight, and there was no accident victim lying by the side of the tracks then."

"Who was the witness?"

"First name Rui, last name Okihara." He swiveled the report around so Kenji could copy the characters into his notebook.

Oki continued, "The reports also agree that it was an accident, not suicide."

"Why?"

Oki read from the train company's summary. "'Personal effects found with the victim suggest no plan to end her own life.'"

"Personal effects? What does that mean? The stuff in her purse? How could they tell from that?"

Oki sat back in his chair. "Was she carrying an appointment schedule? A calendar? People often don't make appointments for things like haircuts or dental work if they plan to kill themselves."

Kenji thought a moment, shook his head.

"What about money? Suicides know they won't be needing more than whatever it takes to get to the place they plan to do it, so they're often found with hardly any cash."

The ¥300,000 that was in her purse. Could that be the reason? The investigators must have found it when they went through her personal effects. Nobody would carry a fortune in cash that might be scattered to the wind after they threw themselves in front of a train.

"There was quite a bit of money in her purse," he told Oki. "Could that be the reason they decided it wasn't suicide?"

"Could be." Oki looked up. "Why? Did someone in your family suspect . . . ?"

"No. Everyone believed it was an accident. Everyone *wanted* to believe it was an accident." Kenji's voice grew bitter. "Everyone wanted it to be something nobody was responsible for and nobody could have prevented."

His father especially. Was that the reason his heart was suddenly giving out now? Because that suitcase had resurfaced, and he could no longer pretend his wife's death was an accident? Because he was finally facing the fact that he'd been lying to himself and everyone else for ten years? Why hadn't *he* ever investigated her death?

"Are you okay?" Oki was looking at him strangely.

"Sorry," Kenji said. He shook his head to clear it. "Who were the lead investigators on the case?"

Oki consulted the report. "Sergeant Toshio Arakawa from Toritsu-daigaku Station, and Superintendent Fusanosuke Harada from the Toyoko Train Line."

Kenji made a note. "And do they say how they think it happened?"

Oki read from the summary. "'Victim is believed to have approached tracks from the north and entered the restricted zone, although warning bells and lights were all found to be in working order. Proximate time window suggests victim may have disregarded safety to make it to Toritsu-daigaku Station before the last train departed in the Shibuya direction. Injuries were found to be consistent with coming into contact with a moving vehicle.'"

Kenji sat up with a jolt. They thought his mother had jumped the safety gates and tried to beat an oncoming train across the tracks? That was crazy! He knew kids who'd done stuff like that, but not anyone's mother. Certainly not *his* mother. If her death had been an accident, it hadn't been *that* kind of accident.

He pulled the diagram closer, studied it again. It looked like trains crossed barely a meter from where pedestrians stood. He shuddered, remembering the express throwing his muffler into his face at Toritsu-daigaku Station. How sturdy were the safety arms that came down to bar the way? Was the entire crossing closed off, or were there gaps? Could she have fallen through one of them? Tripped while she was running? Been pushed? He tried to picture it.

"I don't suppose they included photos of where it happened?" he asked Oki.

"No."

His heart sank. He'd been trying to avoid going to see for himself, but now it looked like he had no choice.

WEDNESDAY, JANUARY 7

•

The fragrance of grilling meat wafted from a nearby *yakiniku* restaurant and Yumi's stomach growled. It was almost noon, but lunch would have to wait until after she'd found the offices of Human Rights Traffic Watch.

When today's translating job had been cancelled at the last minute, she'd seized the opportunity to use the information she'd mined from Jack Goldman yesterday to go after an even bigger prize—the woman who got away. If she could track down the organization that had helped the two foreign women escape, they might be able to tell her where the second woman was living now. She might even learn her name.

Yumi smiled, imagining the look on Kenji's face when she delivered that choice piece of information. She'd already reserved a private booth for them tomorrow night at a nice *izakaya*, to tell him everything she'd learned from Jack. It would be the perfect romantic place to hand him an unexpected new witness. For the first time since this all started, she allowed herself to hope that this difficult chapter would soon be over, that they could go back to thinking about the future. *Their* future.

But first, of course, she had to track down the group that had helped the women escape. She studied the front of a gravestone carver's building, searching for a street number, as a life-sized dachshund carved from black granite regarded her from the display window. The traffic watchers' headquarters was somewhere on this stretch of the street, but Tokyo buildings weren't numbered in order. It could be anywhere on this block.

Finally, she spotted a small metal plaque next to the tombstone maker's door, stamped Shin-Okubo 2-7-18. She was getting close, but the building she was looking for was 2-7-22. She moved on.

It was next to the building beyond. None of the mailboxes were assigned to Human Rights Traffic Watch, but 3F's had no card taped to the front. That must be it. An outfit offering enslaved women a way out probably wouldn't advertise its location, in case the traffickers came after them.

She climbed three flights of stairs to a locked door, painted dark blue. Rang the bell. A tinny voice asked her name, and she told the speaker box that if this was the office of Human Rights Traffic Watch, she was the person who'd called earlier, referred by Shoko Kawasaki at ITEMP.

The door buzzed, and she walked into a small room carpeted in brown, dominated by a wooden desk. A girl who looked barely out of her teens sat behind it, her eyes framed by the kind of oversized black glasses without any lenses that were favored by girls affecting the "cute nerd" look. Behind her, a closed wooden door was labeled "Office." The waiting room was filled with the smell of shrimp-flavored instant ramen, wafting from the receptionist's half-finished lunch. The edge of the comic book she'd been reading stuck out slightly from beneath a stack of paperwork.

"Excuse me," Yumi said. "I was wondering if I could speak with Director Matsubara."

"Sorry, but she's out," the girl said.

"Oh no. Is it after twelve? She said she'd talk to me if I was here before twelve!"

Actually, the director had shut her down over the phone, claiming that all information about rescued women was confidential. But among the organizations on the list she'd gotten from ITEMP, this was the only one that had been around ten years ago and had both "traffic" and "watch" in its name. She figured if she showed up in person, maybe the director would at least explain how they operated, and she could find out if it was possible they'd been involved with the foreign women at Korankei.

"You can wait for her if you'd like," the girl said, nodding toward an uncomfortable-looking visitor chair wedged into the corner. "Or you could call her later and make an appointment." She pulled a pamphlet from the stand on her desk.

Yumi glanced at the brochure and put a worried expression on her face. "I don't know. What should I do? The thing is, I have to get back to work. And I came all the way from Komagome. Do you think she'll be back soon?"

"Not before one," the girl said, apologetically. "Do you want to leave your name and number? I can ask her to call you when she gets back . . . ?"

"I really need to talk to someone in person. It's about a, a situation. I came here to find out what your organization does for the women who come to you. Can you help me?"

"Uh, that depends on you want to know," she said, stealing a glance at the cup of rapidly cooling noodles on her desk.

"Please go ahead and eat your lunch before it gets cold. I don't mind."

"No, no," the girl said quickly. "I'm not really supposed to eat at my desk," she admitted.

"I know. Me too." Yumi gave her a sympathetic smile. "But I bet you've got something important to do on your lunch break. We can talk while you're eating. Please."

"Well, if you're sure. Thanks." She picked up her chopsticks and slurped up a bite of noodles. "What do you want to know?"

"Can you tell me what kind of women you help? Are they foreigners, or Japanese?"

"Foreigners," the receptionist said, digging for another bite. "We rescue women who were brought here and told they'd get good jobs, but end up being forced to work in massage parlors. Or worse."

"How do they hear about you?"

"We put up flyers and stuff, in places women like that might see them. You know, like in Shinjuku and Ikebukuro and Shibuya. There's a number they can call."

"And you're the one who answers?" Yumi nodded at the phone on the desk.

"No, it goes to one of our staff. She speaks a bunch of languages. Most of the women who call can't explain their situation very well in Japanese."

"And what happens after they contact you?"

"We listen to their story, then figure out how to help them escape."

"Escape? You mean they're actually locked up? Like slaves?"

"It's not like they're kept in chains, exactly—they have to go to work, after all—but they might as well be, because they can't leave the country or change jobs without money or papers. The men who bring them to Japan take their passports and tell them that they have to pay for their housing and food and the cost of bringing them here before they can get back their IDs and start keeping any of the money they earn. Every day their debts get bigger and bigger, and pretty soon they're so desperate, they agree to do things they don't want to."

"Why don't they go to the police?"

"Usually by the time they realize that they're never going to be able to pay back what they owe, their ninety-day tourist visas have run out. If they go to the police, they might get their passports back, but they'll be deported. And they're really scared of that happening, because most of their families paid a lot for them to come here and work. If they go home without the money they were supposed to be earning, they'll get in big trouble."

"So how do you help them?"

"I'm not sure exactly how it works," she admitted. "You'll have to ask the director. But I know we help them get away from the traffickers, then we help them stay in Japan."

"You get them visas? Jobs?"

"I don't know the details—I just answer the phone—but yeah, we have these partners who help them with that kind of stuff. Help them get resettled, like that."

"Resettled? You mean they don't stay in Tokyo?"

She shook her head. "Never. That's one thing I do know—they're always moved at least a hundred kilometers away, to smaller towns. I guess that's so there's less chance the traffickers will find them."

"Places like Korankei?"

"Korankei? Where's that?"

Yumi showed her a map on her phone.

"I don't know. Maybe." The receptionist squinted at her through the fake glasses, puzzled. "Why Korankei?"

"I'm trying to track down two foreign women who disappeared there, ten years ago. They were on a bus tour to the Ise Shrine, and when the bus stopped at Korankei, they didn't get back on. My friend's mother was on the tour, and the driver told her they'd decided to come back to Tokyo later. Nobody thought much of it, but yesterday I was at a lecture about human trafficking, and I remembered. So I asked Shoko Kawasaki at ITEMP how I could find out if they'd been victims of human traffickers. She gave me Director Matsubara's name." Yumi glanced at the computer sitting on the reception desk and put a little desperation into her voice. "But I have to get back to work soon. Is there any chance you could check to see if they were working with Human Rights Traffic Watch? If they're safe?"

"Um," The receptionist looked doubtful. "Sorry, but I don't think I so. I'm not really supposed to go into the records, except to check things if the director asks."

"Oh. I see." Disappointment. "Of course, I don't want to get you in trouble. But you wouldn't have to give me any details, just tell me if this is the organization they were working with or not. Can't you just tell me if they're safe?"

"Well . . . . " She bit her lip. "Maybe if you tell me their names, I could check. But I really can't tell you anything else."

"One was Li Qian," Yumi said, reciting the name she'd gotten from Jack's article about the second Painted Doll victim. "I've tried and tried to remember the other one, but I can't. I do know that ten years ago, they were both at Korankei on November twenty-eighth. Is that enough for you to check?"

The receptionist thought for a moment, then moved a bulky old mouse around on the pad next to her keyboard and clicked several times. Scanned the results.

"Oh."

"What?" Yumi said. "Did you find them?"

"No. Cases from that long ago aren't on here. The files must not have been computerized back then."

"Where would they be?"

The receptionist hesitated before replying. "They might be in the director's office."

"Could you take a look? Please? Before I have to go back to work?"

The girl shifted uncomfortably in her chair.

"It's only twelve twenty-five," Yumi pressed. "You said she wouldn't be back before one. Please."

"Well . . . . " The young woman glanced at the closed door. "You just want to know if they're safe, right?"

"That's all," Yumi assured her.

"Okay." She opened the door behind the desk and flipped on the lights. Yumi heard the rumble of a file cabinet drawer opening. Shutting. Another one opening. Silence. Then, "I found it. I think."

Yumi heard the drawer roll shut. The girl returned, switching off the lights behind her and closing the door carefully.

"I found a file matching the date and place that you told me," she said. "Was the other woman's name Wu Yin?"

"Yes," Yumi said. Score! She had the missing woman's name. "I'm so relieved. Except, why is there only one file? What happened to Li Qian?"

"I don't know. The cases are organized by date, and that's the only one for the month of November that year. Maybe her friend got resettled at a different time . . . ?"

Or, Yumi thought, her resettlement had failed because she'd been abducted before she reached her destination. And then she became the second Painted Doll victim.

•

"*O-tsukare-sama*," Kenji said to Suzuki, as they packed up their laptops and called it a day. They'd been camped out in one of the interview rooms since early that morning. So far, they'd run 223 possible underwear thieves through the police database.

There wasn't anybody who'd been arrested for panty snatching among the men working regular routes in Komagome, but they'd discovered sixteen with sealed juvie records, five with assault charges, three previously arrested for petty theft, and one computer hacker who'd been run through the justice department wringer for malicious mischief.

"See you tomorrow, sir," Suzuki said, bowing before heading for the elevators.

Kenji's phone buzzed. He checked the caller ID. Unknown number.

"*Moshi-moshi*?" he said. "This is Nakamura."

"Nakamura-*san*? This is Harada. I believe you called me about an incident on the Toyoko Line . . . ?"

Harada was the train company supervisor who had signed his mother's accident report. Kenji had discovered that he'd retired three years ago, but it hadn't been hard to find him, because there was only one Harada in Tokyo with the unusual first name of Fusanosuke.

Kenji explained that he had a few questions about an accident at a foot crossing between Toritsu-daigaku Station and Jiyugaoka. That he was the son of the victim, and wanted to hear about it from someone who had been involved in the investigation. Would it be possible to meet face to face?

The man hesitated, then agreed.

Half an hour later, Kenji was waiting outside the coffee shop the retired supervisor had suggested, in the vast underground mall adjacent to Shinjuku Station. At precisely five minutes to six, a man with neatly barbered white hair appeared. His bearing suggested he'd worn a uniform for most of his life, and the muffler looped around his neck bore the mascot of the Toyoko Train Line.

"Supervisor Harada?"

"Yes," the ex-trainman said, stopping to bow. He straightened and studied Kenji's face. "You must be Detective Nakamura." He added, "I'm sorry for your loss."

Kenji murmured the polite response, then held the door. They settled themselves at a corner table, and by the time they finished commenting on the unusually cold winter and discovered they were both Yomiuri Giants fans, two black coffees were steaming before them and Kenji felt it wasn't too soon to ease into the subject they were there to discuss.

"Were you with the Toyoko Line for your entire career, Harada-*san*?"

"Yes." The ex-supervisor sipped his coffee and his face softened with nostalgia. "I'm a gold watch man—started as a conductor trainee, moved up to driving trains, ended up driving a desk."

"*O-tsukare-sama deshita*," Kenji said, bowing over the table to acknowledge the man's long years of service. "I'm sure you investigated many accidents in your long career, so you probably don't remember the one involving my mother, but . . . ."

"Actually, I do."

Kenji couldn't hide his surprise.

Harada put down his coffee cup. "Accidents are, in fact, quite rare. People who throw themselves in front of trains on purpose are sadly common, but during my entire career, I only saw three accidental deaths. It's easy to get past the safety barriers if you're trying, but not so easy if you're not."

"I guess that's why I have questions, Harada-*san*. From the diagram you included with the report, it looks, well, impossible."

Harada frowned at his coffee, but didn't disagree.

"Is that why you thought it might have been some sort of judgment error on my . . . on the victim's part?" Kenji asked. "Did you have evidence she was doing something she shouldn't have been doing?"

"No," Harada said, sharply. "And that's not what I thought happened. That was Sergeant Arakawa's theory. He—" Harada fell silent.

"He what?" Kenji leaned toward the ex-trainman. "He wanted to rule it an accident? Why? So he didn't have to investigate?"

Harada sighed. "He did investigate. Just maybe not enough. He was two weeks from retirement. I tried to talk him into keeping the case open, assigning someone to dig deeper, but he said it would cost time and money, and in the end, they wouldn't be able to prove anything. He said it would be kinder to your family to call it an accident and let everyone move on." Harada shook his head. "And I couldn't prove he was wrong, even though the drivers all swore there hadn't been any 'human body incidents' that night, and there was no evidence that any of the engines had come into contact with a human being."

"Could one of the drivers have been lying?"

"To save himself from an inquiry? No. Hitting someone, ah, makes a noise. Everyone in the first three cars knows something happened."

"How carefully were the cars examined?"

"By the time your . . . the victim was discovered the next morning, the engines had all been washed and put back into service. But I went out to the yard myself and looked them over. There was no undocumented damage to any of the trains that came through Toritsu-daigaku Station in the hour before midnight."

"So why did you sign off on it as an accident?"

"I didn't. After we eliminate suicide, driver error and equipment malfunction as possible causes, the train company's job is finished. It's up to the police to take it from there and make a ruling. I did my part, but all I could do was advise further investigation, not tell the police how to do their job."

"But . . . ?"

The trainman's eyes met Kenji's. "Are you really okay talking about this? I mean, the victim was your mother."

"It's difficult, yes. But I'm a police detective and I need to know. Tell me, please."

Harada nodded. He pulled a napkin from the dispenser on the table and brought out a pen. "After you called, I went back over my notes. You remember the diagram we attached to the report?"

He sketched in the tracks and the crossing, drew wiggly lines to stand for the fences alongside, and made a circle marked with an "x" next to the fence.

"This is where your mother was found. Inside the fence, east of the tracks, on the side of the crossing closer to Toritsu-daigaku."

He drew an arrow across the tracks from the victim's location, pointing toward Shibuya. Labeled it "train direction." Then he did the same on the victim's side, after writing the characters for "Jiyugaoka."

"A week after we delivered the report, I checked back with the police, to see what they had discovered. Sergeant Arakawa had closed the case as an accident, with a vague mention of 'contact with a moving vehicle' as the cause of death. I went back to the only witness who had been anywhere near that crossing between eleven-thirty and midnight, and asked if she'd been running for the last train that night.

"She said yes, but she wasn't trying to catch it, she was meeting her husband. She always waited for him outside the station, even when he came home late. But that night, she had fallen asleep in front of the TV. She didn't think she'd make it, but there had been a delay on the line and the train was late, so she still made it to the station in time to meet her husband, as usual.

"I went back and checked the records, and sure enough, at 11:43 that night, someone called in a report of debris on the tracks near Den-en-chōfu. The couple of minutes it took to move the cardboard box off the rails stacked up trains in both directions. Everything on the line was running seven minutes late.

"If your mother had been hit by the only train to traverse that crossing between when the witness was there and midnight, it wouldn't have been the last train headed toward Shibuya. It would have been the one that should have gone by seven minutes earlier. The one headed in the other direction."

He looked at Kenji. "It would have thrown her towards Jiyugaoka. She would have been found on the other side of the tracks, and the other side of the crossing." He made a circle across the tracks from the one he'd labeled "victim."

Kenji studied the diagram. "So, what are you telling me? The accident actually happened at a different time?"

"No. What I'm saying is, I don't think she was hit by a train."

Kenji stared. "She wasn't hit by a train? What hit her, then? A car? A truck?" *A brown van?*

"Don't know," Harada said. "Was there a post-mortem?"

"I don't know. All I've got are the reports that were written up for my father. Did you go back and tell Sergeant Arakawa what you found out?"

"I did. But he shut me down. Told me I was out of line. Said it was too late, that the case was closed. That your family was satisfied." Harada looked Kenji in the eye. "Forgive me for saying this, but I'm glad he was wrong."

•

Yumi poked her head in the door at the Mad Hatter.

"*Irasshaimase!*"

Tonight, Boshi the bartender was wearing a red plaid deerstalker hat with earflaps. Yumi had never seen this one before—it must be new, because there was no gap in his collection of haberdashery on the shelf behind the bar. Nobody had ever seen Boshi-*san* without a hat; rumor had it that he'd even chosen his high school because the uniform included an odd, peaked cap.

Tonight the Hatter was packed, but most of the usual Goths and Lolitas had abandoned it for parts unknown, because a group of giggling college students from some faraway prefecture had invaded the place, pretending to take pictures of each other, but actually aiming their cameras at the exotic costumers they never saw in their hometown. This kind of nuisance had become commonplace at the Hatter since a travel blogger had named it one of her Top Ten Underground Tokyo Must-Sees. If Coco hadn't already grabbed them a table, they'd be standing tonight.

The bartender expertly stirred the White Rabbit he'd started making for Yumi the moment she walked in, tapped the bar spoon with a flourish, and slid the glass across the bar.

"She's over there," he said as Yumi laid a ¥1000 note on the pay tray. "At the table under my new Alice."

Yumi followed his gaze. A reassuringly re-princessed Coco was sitting next to a wall where more than a hundred Alice in Wonderland figures of various sizes were displayed. Yumi squinted at the new offering. Alice's signature blue dress, white pinafore and golden tresses had been meticulously painted on a model of . . . a paunchy old man? Then she laughed as she recognized the face that scowled at her nearly every morning from the newsstand.

"That's not the prime minister, is it?"

"It is." Boshi grinned. "My friend Stinger isn't a big fan of his right-wing policies." The freshly painted politician fit right in with the Godzilla, Totoro and Gundam robot Alices that Boshi-*san*'s army of model-making friends had crafted for him over the years.

Yumi accepted her change, then threaded her way through the crowd toward Coco's table. Her friend was bent over her phone, scrolling intently.

"Hey," Yumi said, setting down her White Rabbit and plopping into the chair opposite.

Coco looked up, startled. "Oh. Hi. Did you get anything from Hoshi yet?"

Yumi pulled out her phone and checked. "Nope. But I told him I was busy this weekend, remember? How about you?"

"Yeah," Coco said. "Just now."

"And . . . ?"

Coco made a face. "I don't know why Hoshi thought *this* guy was my type."

She passed her phone to Yumi. On it was a photo of a slightly plump man with the kind of short, conservative haircut that instantly branded him a corporate warrior or the servant of some government ministry.

Yumi scrolled down to his particulars. Ren Noda. 32. Mitsubishi Bank. Blood type: O. Hobbies: Golf.

Hoshi's stylist had tried hard, but Ren Noda's nervous smile made his waxed hair look like it was standing up in alarm at the prospect of going on a date. She handed back the phone.

"Are you going to say yes?"

Coco looked up, uncertain. "Do you think I should?"

"Why not? It's not like you have to marry him after one date. The first one is just drinks, right? If it's too painful, you can chug your cocktail and bolt. Besides," Yumi added, "even if he's a jerk, he can't be any worse than Mr. Pregnant Wife. Anything would be better than seeing *him* again."

Coco's eyes teared up and she quickly looked away.

"Hey," Yumi said, peering into her friend's face. "What's the matter? Don't tell me—"

Sniff. "He came into the club last night. And he . . . he asked for Misty."

"What? I thought once you chose your favorite hostess, you couldn't switch?"

Sniff. "You're thinking of host clubs." Coco dug in her bag for a tissue. "The rules are different at hostess clubs. Women customers can't switch. Men can."

"What? Why?"

Coco dabbed at her eyes. "Because men and women are different. Men like to chase, women like to be caught. Men can play the field, women can't."

"Well that's stupid."

"No it's not. It's how things are. It's biology."

"Who told you that?" Yumi snorted. "Oh, let me guess—a *man*?"

She took Coco's phone from her, studied Ren Noda's picture again, handed it back. "I think you should say yes to

Noda-*san*. At least he looks like he wouldn't dare give you a biology lecture."

"True," Coco admitted. She stared at his picture for a moment longer, then sighed. "Okay. I'll do it."

She keyed in a reply, pressed Send, then took a gulp of her Lemon Jabberwock.

Yumi's phone chimed. She glanced at the display and frowned. Subject line: Meet Your Perfect LuvLuv Match!

Hoshi really wasn't used to taking no for an answer, was he? She opened it. Hearts and stars danced across the top, with a message inviting her to consider a date on Friday at seven, with the very eligible candidate she'd been matched with. Clicking on her so-called dream date's profile, she recognized the one handsome man she'd glimpsed among Hoshi's photos.

Taro Takahashi. Age: 37.

Thirty-seven? Kind of old not to be married yet, wasn't he? Where did he work? Yikes, Ministry of the Environment. Plum job. What was wrong with him?

"Who's it from?" Coco asked.

"Speak of the devil."

Coco snatched the phone from her. "What? That's the guy I wanted!" She scrolled down and read, "Blood type: B. Maybe that's why Hoshi put him with you. You're type B too, aren't you?"

"Yeah," said Yumi, without enthusiasm. That had been one of the unpleasant surprises she'd encountered after moving back to Japan. In America, few people knew their blood type or cared. But in Japan, blood type was believed to predict everything from what kind of employee you would be, to how compatible you'd be with your mate. Type B was the least desirable, belonging to a small percentage of creative, yet supposedly selfish and unreliable, individuals.

Coco read on. "Hobbies: Foreign travel." Her lips turned down in a pout. "Hey, I like foreign travel! At least I would if it was with him. We could go to Hawaii, sip cocktails on the beach at sunset . . . . "

"Yeah," Yumi said, taking back her phone. "With all the other government hacks on Golden Week package tours, taking the only three vacation days a year they can't refuse." She scrutinized his profile again. "Ministry of the Environment—I bet this wonk hasn't taken a real vacation in years. Maybe never."

"So turn him down. Maybe he'll choose me next." Her cheeks dimpled as she took a sip of her drink, then excused herself to run to the ladies' room.

Yumi moodily stirred her drink. She *would* turn Taro Takahashi down, because she couldn't get any of her LuvLuv Match obligations out of the way until she'd told Kenji about the blunder she'd made. She'd meant to say something by now, but he'd been so obsessed with his mother's pictures and finding that bus driver, there hadn't been an opportunity. Maybe she could tell him tomorrow night, after she gave him the second victim's name. He'd be so grateful for the time and effort she'd spent helping him, he wouldn't dare go all Japanese Man on her.

Men can play the field, women can't. Yumi scowled. What a load of hogwash. Outdated, sexist, hogwash. Sometimes, she really missed America.

"So, you're going to accept, aren't you?" Coco was back.

"Let me think about it," she replied. Meaning, she'd wait to turn down Taro Takahashi until Coco wasn't there to ask why.

THURSDAY, JANUARY 8

•

"Well, sir, at least we were able to help Detective Oki," Suzuki said, as Kenji wearily shut down his laptop. It had been a long day.

The underwear thief had not been among the deliverymen they'd interviewed, but one suspect had seemed a little too prepared with exact details when asked about his schedule on several of the days the thefts had occurred. His alibis for the times of the underwear snatchings checked out, but while asking around, they discovered that the perpetually broke deliveryman had recently bought a new flat screen TV and blown a couple hundred thousand yen at a *pachinko* parlor. They'd passed his name along to Oki, in case the source of his new-found wealth was stolen goods from the string of shop burglaries.

As Suzuki headed toward the elevator, Kenji's phone buzzed. Inspector Mori.

"Nakamura," Kenji answered.

"Mori here. Wanted to thank you for sending those pictures. Sorry I didn't get back to you sooner. I've been reassigned to the Painted Doll case."

"Congratulations, sir."

"Thank you, but I'm not sure that's in order yet. The good news is that I have access to the old files again. The bad news is that I can't share anything that's in them."

Goddamn Mori. Why was he not surprised?

"It's regrettable," the Inspector added, the closest he could come to apologizing to an inferior.

"I see." Kenji said, trying not to sound as disappointed as he felt.

"If it were up to me, I'd help you."

Like hell.

Kenji made himself say, "Well, then, good luck, sir. I hope you get a solve."

"Thank you." Mori hesitated. "I won't forget. If the time comes when I can release information that might help you find out what happened to your mother, I will."

Kenji thanked him with a gratitude he didn't feel.

Dammit, dammit, dammit. He knew Mori—the Inspector and his compadres had probably been on Keiko Sato's doorstep before dawn, grilling her. And the First Investigative Division specialists would already be analyzing the pictures. They'd zero in on the bus driver's arm, track him down, squeeze out the information he'd refused to give Kenji and Yumi. And hell would freeze over before they'd share.

Now what? He was on his own. Back to square one. Scowling, Kenji pulled up the photos again. How could he get around the Painted Doll investigation's locked door? He zoomed in on the shot showing the van's license plate. He'd held off asking Oki if he knew anyone in Motor Vehicle Registration, counting on Mori giving him access to the file. But now Oki was his only hope.

The door to Interview Room One opened, and Assistant Detective Kurosawa emerged, marching the *pachinko*-playing deliveryman before her in handcuffs. Detective Oki accompanied them into the elevator to head down to Booking.

Kenji was still staring moodily at his computer when the big detective returned.

"Hey, I owe you one," Oki said, plucking his jacket from the back of his chair. "Looks like that case is on its way to the prosecutor."

"Congratulations," Kenji said. "Glad to put away an evildoer, even if he's not our evildoer." He paused. "Actually, there is something you can do for me. Do you have any friends in Motor Vehicle Registration?" He explained about Mori's refusal to give him information about the brown van's license plate.

"Ha, when are you going to learn? Information only flows one way when you're dealing with headquarters. Let me get on the phone to my friend Mimi-*chan* at Motor Vehicles, see what I can shake loose."

Kenji thanked him. Once he got the name of the company that owned the van, he'd work on getting a list of employees who'd been there ten years ago.

Oki stepped out to make the call, but returned a few minutes later, shaking his head. His contact had just gone out on maternity leave and wasn't expected back at her desk for three months, if ever.

Kenji thanked him for trying, offered his condolences for losing a valuable source in such a useful department, and gave a halfhearted wave as Oki disappeared toward the elevator. He slumped back into his chair. Now what? All the legal avenues were blocked. All the *legal* avenues. But what about . . . .

Ghost.

Last year, Kenji had been working a case where he'd run into a similar dead end. Oki had found them a hacker calling himself Ghost, who'd been able to slip through the phone company's firewall as easily as strolling into a rice cracker shop. Could he do the same with Motor Vehicle Registration records? Or even . . . task force records?

It would be illegal. Career-endingly illegal, if anyone found out. But nobody needed to know. And information about the brown van's ownership didn't have to stand up in court—it was strictly for his own use. Once he knew the name of the company, he could use by-the-book methods to track down the employees who had access to the van. Nobody needed to know how he discovered where to start looking.

Kenji pulled out his phone and sent Ghost a message.

While he waited for the hacker to get back to him, he looked up the note he'd made about the witness Harada had mentioned. Would Rui Okihara remember if she'd seen any brown vans near the foot crossing the night his mother died? It had been ten years, but it was worth a try.

He flipped back through the accident report, but neither her address nor her phone number had been included. He could go to the Toritsu-daigaku police box and ask. Or he could ask Keiko Sato. If Toritsu-daigaku was anything like Komagome, everybody knew everybody else. And Mrs. Okihara would probably be happier to talk to him if he were introduced by a neighbor, rather than a police badge.

He took out his phone, but his finger hesitated over Keiko's number. She'd probably just spent an unpleasant day being grilled by Inspector Mori and his merry band. He'd be lucky if she even answered when she saw his name on her caller ID.

Still, he had to try. He dialed. Got her voicemail. Left a message.

•

Yumi scowled as the numbers over the elevator doors counted upward. The lift at the address where Kenji had asked her to meet him was slower than if it were being hoisted by a team of ailing grannies. The stairs would have been faster. She tried not to be irritated, but failed—too many unwelcome changes of plan had been foisted on her in the past two hours.

First, Kenji had moved the location of their dinner. Instead of an intimate evening in a private booth at the romantic *izakaya* she'd chosen, they were now eating at— *ugh*—an Akihabara maid café.

But that wasn't the worst part. He'd invited some computer hacker to join them. They wouldn't even be alone. Not that being alone would be the least bit romantic anyway, if what she'd heard about theme restaurants like Café Jaunty were true.

The elevator doors finally shuddered open, and she poked her head out. She'd never been to a maid café before, but this one pinged all the stereotypes. Waitresses in ruffled black and white uniforms flitted from table to table among a geeky clientele that looked like they'd be far more comfortable slaying zombie Nazis than speaking to the female half of the human race.

The pigtailed girl who was manning the register sparkled at Yumi and chirped, "Welcome, Honorable Princess! How may we serve you?"

Yumi wasn't surprised when none of the customers seated at the white Formica tables looked up. Apparently, women were invisible unless they wore lacy over-the-knee socks, furry cat ears, and maid uniforms that stood out like ballerina skirts. Not that there *were* any other women enjoying themselves at the Maid Café Jaunty.

"I'm meeting someone," Yumi explained. "Kenji Nakamura?"

The maid frowned as she failed to find his name on her reservation list.

"Or, uh, it might be under 'Ghost'?"

The maid's face brightened. "Oh, Ghost-*sama*! He has a standing reservation. But I'm afraid you're early—he's never here before seven thirty."

Yumi fumed. Had Kenji told her the wrong time?

The elevator doors opened.

"Sorry I'm late," Kenji said.

The maid turned her beamage on him. "How may we serve you, Master of the House?"

He returned her smile. "We're meeting Ghost, but he won't be here for half an hour. Is it okay if we sit at his table and order something while we wait?"

"Your wish is my command, Master of the House."

She curtseyed and plucked three menus from the rack behind the counter, flouncing ahead of them to a table in the corner. It was situated under what appeared to be a window with a view onto a sunny European hillside, but was actually a light box fitted with frilly curtains. The walls were papered in a faux stone pattern, like a medieval castle.

The lighting was anything but romantic, and the tables were so close together Yumi could pick out the scales on the flying dragon that the customer to their right was riding on screen. This definitely wasn't what she'd had in mind for tonight's date. She knew she ought to make an effort to hide her bad mood—after all, Kenji didn't have any idea he'd postponed more than a nice *izakaya* dinner, didn't have any idea how hard she'd been working to find out what happened to his mom— but making her mouth curve into a smile still wasn't working.

Sliding into one of the seats and accepting a menu, she asked Kenji, "Have you been here before?"

"Yeah," he replied, taking the chair opposite her. "This is where Ghost works. After hours, that is."

"What does he do? For a living, I mean." Yumi opened her menu.

"I suspect he has an IT job with the phone company," Kenji said, dropping a flat brown bag on the table. "But . . . well, when you meet him, you'll understand."

Yumi nodded toward the package. "What's that?"

"Payment." Kenji slid a cellophane-wrapped comic book from the bag. "First edition *Naruto, Volume One*. Ghost is a collector. That's why I was late. I had to stop by a special comic book store to buy it." He slid it back into its wrapper.

The customer to their left lost a game of rock, paper, scissors to his maid. As punishment, he apparently had to drink a tumbler of milk mixed with any ingredient the winner chose, because he was watching anxiously as his maid stirred something green into his glass.

"Don't worry," Kenji said. "You have to pay extra for that kind of abuse."

Yumi turned her attention to the menu. Pizza, curry, omelets filled with ketchup-sauced rice. She looked around at the other tables. It didn't seem like the young men glued to their laptops missed the salads and vegetables conspicuously absent from the offerings.

Kenji pushed the bell on the table and their maid arrived with a cat's-paw wave and a "*Nyan, nyan*, how may I serve you tonight?"

They ordered—omelet for Kenji, curry rice for Yumi—then Kenji told her about his meeting with Supervisor Harada.

"So, he doesn't think my mother was the victim of a train accident after all," he concluded. "He thinks she might have been hit by a car. Or a truck."

"Or maybe a brown van?"

"Or maybe a brown van. Which is why I'm hoping Ghost can help us tonight. If he can get us the name of the company that owned it, then I can figure out who worked there."

Their food arrived, and they waited while the maid drew a bewhiskered cat on Kenji's omelet with a ketchup bottle. She bobbed a curtsey and *nyan*ed her farewell.

Yumi spooned up a few bites of her curry rice. It wasn't bad. Actually, it kind of hit the spot. Her irritation receded a bit. Maybe she was just hungry. They ate in silence for a few minutes, pursuing their own thoughts, then Kenji heaved a great sigh.

Yumi looked up from her curry. "What's wrong?"

"You know what's really bothering me? I understand why my mother would refuse to tell Mori anything if my dad told her not to. But why didn't she go to the local police in Korankei, right after it happened?" He shook his head. "She didn't even tell her friends."

That *was* hard to believe. But Yumi didn't have the answer.

"The bus driver was there," she said. "You could try asking him."

"Ha." Mirthless laugh. Kenji poked at his omelet. "I wish there were a way to track down the woman who got away."

Yumi swallowed her bite of curry rice. Should she tell him? This wasn't the way she'd planned to do it, but—

"Actually," she said, "I found out her name."

"What?" Kenji stared. "How?"

Yumi told him about how she'd arranged to meet Jack Goldman, how they had gone out for coffee and he had given her the names of several groups that helped trafficked women escape their situations.

"One of them is called Human Rights Traffic Watch," she said. "Today I went to their offices to find out if they were the ones who were helping the two women at Korankei ten years ago, and guess what? They were. The survivor's name is Wu Yin."

"That's incredible! Are you sure?"

"Yes. According to their files, she was successfully 'resettled' ten years ago. The receptionist told me that the women they help are moved out of Tokyo, to places where the traffickers won't find them. To small towns, like Korankei. She didn't know the details, but when I asked about visas and working papers, she said they had 'partners' who helped the women stay in Japan. There's a chance that Wu Yin is still there, that they found someone to sponsor her visa."

Kenji put down his chopsticks, his eyes shining. "There can't be many Chinese women living in Korankei. Do you think we could find her if we went there and asked around?"

"*Konban wa.*"

They looked up at the figure that had suddenly appeared at their table to wish them a good evening.

Yumi tried not to stare. This had to be Ghost. His skin was shockingly pale, and the razored hair standing in spikes atop his head was pure white. She wondered what color his eyes were behind the violet contacts he wore. She'd never met an albino person before.

"Hey, long time no see," Kenji said, rising and greeting him with a grin.

Why hadn't he warned her? Then Yumi was immediately ashamed. She should be able to ignore the fact that Ghost looked different from most people.

"This is Yumi Hata," Kenji said. "We've known each other since we were kids, and she's helping me with the thing I want to ask you about. Yumi, this is Ghost."

"Pleased to meet you," Yumi said, making herself look him in the eye.

He was watching her, his mouth curved into a half-smile. She felt her cheeks grow hot.

"He didn't tell you, did he? Why I'm called Ghost?"

Yumi stammered, "Well, no."

"It's okay. I'm used to it. And," he said, pulling out his chair, "I don't blame you for being surprised, although there are a lot more of us in Japan than you think. I save the hot blue flame of loathing for those who show their surprise in, ah, more painful ways."

"Not that they'd get close enough to lay a finger on you." Kenji laughed. "Ghost-*san* is a second degree black belt," he told Yumi. "In judo."

Ghost ordered a cake set from the maid and pulled out his laptop. He looked at Kenji expectantly. "Did you bring it?"

Kenji pushed the brown paper bag across the table. Ghost peeked inside and a grin spread across his face.

"Been wanting this one for a long time," he said, sliding it out, but resisting taking it from the cellophane until he'd earned it. He set it aside. "So, who are we playing hide and seek with tonight? More online stalkers?"

"No," Kenji said. "I didn't want to be too specific in a message that someone might be able to dig up later. I'm hoping you can help me take a look at some police files."

Ghost's smile faded. "Police files? What kind of police files?"

"First Investigative Division. A cold case."

Oh." Ghost looked with longing at the Naruto bag and pushed it back across the table. "Sorry. I could have saved you a trip."

"You can't do it?" Kenji said, dismayed.

"It's not that I couldn't get past their watchdogs, but there's just too much downside. I mean, if a company catches me poking around, all that happens is their so-called security department threatens to call in the lawyers. They bark a lot, but in the end, if I didn't take anything they think is valuable—like credit card numbers, stuff like that—they back off. But the police—" He shook his head. "Life as we know it would be over if the All-Seeing Eye of the Tokyo Metropolitan Police started clocking my every move."

"Oh," Kenji said, disappointed. "Sorry. I didn't realize—"

"How come *you* can't get into the file? I mean, you're in the police, right?"

"Not my turf. This cold case I'm interested in got sucked into something bigger. Something password protected."

"And you don't have any friends in high places? Or enemies who owe you?"

"I do, but they're not paying up."

Ghost brooded for a moment, then said, "Why don't you tell me what's in those files you want so badly? Maybe there's another way to get the info besides poking the sleeping dragon."

Kenji explained about the Painted Doll case, then told Ghost about his mother and what had happened at Korankei. Yumi added what she'd found out that day from the human trafficking group.

By the time they finished, Ghost had forked up the last bite of his mille-crepe cake and asked for a coffee refill. He sat there, thinking, then pulled his laptop toward him. Fingers flying over the keys, he entered a password so complex Yumi wondered how he remembered it.

He shot an apologetic glance at Kenji. "I'm sorry I can't hack into motor vehicle registration for you. But," he said, turning to Yumi, "what was the name of that trafficking group again?"

"Human Rights Traffic Watch."

Ghost returned to his keyboard.

"You won't find anything online, though," Yumi said. "The records from ten years ago aren't on their computers. I had to talk their receptionist into sneaking into the director's office to look through the file cabinet."

"I'm not looking for the file," Ghost said. *Clickety, clickety.* "I'm searching their phone records. Once we get the numbers they called, I think we might be able to find out—" a predatory grin spread across his face, "—who their 'partners' are, the ones who help the victims stay in the country. And from there," *clickety, clickety,* "we might be able to discover who resettled your missing Chinese girl. Maybe even her last known address."

He stopped, and code spooled past on the screen. Then it stopped. The cursor blinked, waiting. He tapped a key, and the screen filled with telephone numbers.

"Got it."

He opened another window and fed the numbers into a subroutine. As his program spit out the names to which they were registered, he smiled with satisfaction.

"Looks like they were getting work visas for the women at . . . let's see: Lucky Wok? Banyan Thai? Those sound like restaurants. And this here—Golden Needles Fabricators. Sewing shop?" Then confusion replaced his triumph. "Wait, this can't be right. Happily Ever After? Princess Bride?" He frowned. "Those sound like . . . hostess clubs."

"Or," Yumi said, "marriage brokers."

Ghost and Kenji turned to stare.

"Marriage brokers?" Ghost echoed.

"Yeah. I could be wrong, but marriage brokers have names like that."

Yumi explained about the building she'd recently visited with Coco, the halls lined with small offices catering to every type of marriage hopeful, including foreigners seeking to tie the knot with Japanese men in exchange for being allowed to stay in the country and work. Then she frowned at the screen of names.

"What I don't get is why a human rights organization would be 'rescuing' women from sex work, then turning around and marrying them into a different kind of servitude."

Kenji's head snapped up. "You think of marriage as servitude?"

Yumi colored. "Well, not all marriage, obviously. But honestly, why should women have to marry men they never met, just so their families don't have to live in poverty?"

"Wait a minute, not all women who use a marriage broker are forced into it," Ghost objected. "I mean, I grew up in a small town, just like Korankei. I knew some farmers' sons who married foreigners, because none of the local girls wanted to get stuck in rural nowhere for the rest of their lives. The guys I knew must have met their wives through marriage brokers, because the local matchmaker sure didn't know anyone from China or Thailand. And the women in my town definitely weren't trafficking victims, they were willing participants. Last I heard, most of the couples are still happily married, with kids." He turned to Yumi. "If you live in Tokyo, it's hard to imagine why someone would leave her home forever and sign up to work the rice fields in rural Aomori for the rest of her life, but believe me, that's a walk in the park compared to rural Hunan, with no doctors or indoor plumbing."

"And it does look like the women were offered other options," Kenji added. "They could choose piecework or restaurant jobs over getting married, if they wanted to." He returned his attention to Ghost. "But it's getting late. Any chance of finding out where our second victim is now?"

Ghost looked at Yumi. "The person you talked to at the anti-trafficking office said her 'resettlement' was successful, right? Which means if they were working with a matchmaker, there must be a marriage record between a Japanese man and a Chinese woman filed at the nearest ward office."

He cracked his knuckles, then bent over his keyboard, fingers blurring as his avatar prowled around the back doors of small-town government offices.

"Lucky for us," he said, a smile playing across his lips, "officials in the provinces are much less sophisticated than the ones in Tokyo." He dove in again, typing. The scrolling stopped. He read the results and grinned. "Found it. A ten-year-old marriage registration at the Korankei Ward Office, dated November thirtieth."

Kenji and Yumi peered at the screen. Wu Yin had married Nobu Hayashi two days after her friend was abducted at Korankei.

"So now her name is Wu Hayashi," Kenji said. "Or would it be Yin Hayashi? Is Yin her first name, or her last?"

Yumi replied, "She's Chinese, so Yin would be her first name, I think. If she's still married. But I heard that a lot of foreigners who marry for residence permits disappear soon afterward with their husbands' savings."

"Then let's hope Yin was a nice girl like the ones from Ghost's hometown, and that she still lives in Korankei," Kenji said. He turned to Ghost. "Is there an address attached to that marriage record?"

"There is, but it's ten years old." Ghost's fingers blurred again. He stopped to read. "Nope, you're in luck. Still good. The mobile phone number on the paperwork is still billed to 4-21 Korankei."

Kenji grinned. He pushed the comic back across the table and said, "All yours."

•

On the way back to the station, Kenji volunteered to rent a car, so they could to drive to Korankei on Saturday. He figured they could get there and back in a day, and if he stopped to pick up the car on his way home from the judo workshop he'd signed up for on Friday night, they could leave really early.

Belatedly, he remembered to ask Yumi, "You're not working, are you?"

"No."

Kenji glanced at her face as they beeped their way into the train station and headed down to the platform. She'd been awfully quiet since they left the maid café.

"If only we could figure out who the guy with the scratches on his face is," Kenji said, scanning the platform for the least-crowded spot to wait for the next train.

Yumi sighed as he steered her into a line. "Actually, I discovered a way to do that too. You know that reporter I met, Jack Goldman? He didn't just write the newspaper articles about the Painted Doll killer, he covered the *yakuza* for over twenty years. He knows a lot of people, and he says he remembers what they looked like ten years ago. He thinks the guy with the scratches on his face might have been one of the gangster wannabes who drive those right wing vans. If you send him the photos from your mom's camera, he might be able to help us."

Kenji stared. Was she crazy?

"*Help us*? You're kidding, right? A reporter?" He couldn't believe she'd suggested it. "He's not interested in helping us— he just wants to grab eyeballs. The minute we give him anything, my mother's death will be all over the internet!"

"No, it won't," Yumi retorted. "He can't publish anything until some high heejun at police headquarters gives him the okay. Jack told me that after the second murder, they put together a secret task force and gagged the media. But it's still under wraps, because the investigation has been a total failure. In ten years, the same guy has killed five women, and they still haven't caught him."

"What? There are five victims?" Kenji stared at her, stunned. He lowered his voice. "That's why Mori isn't giving me the time of day. There's a task force."

The train came, and they pushed aboard the already crowded car, maneuvering themselves into a space by the door.

Five victims. Kenji's head spun. And Mori was on the task force. Damn. It would be a cold day in hell before Mori shared anything with him now. They were almost to Komagome when he realized he'd been so wrapped up in his own thoughts, he'd almost forgotten Yumi was there. He tried to catch her eye, get her to smile, but she stared at the ground, refusing to look up.

Uh oh, something was wrong. He hoped she wasn't pouting because he'd refused to let her new best friend Jack plaster his mom all over the Internet. That foreign shark certainly had been quick to drag her all the way to Ginza just to drink coffee. How old was he, anyway? Kenji did the math and relaxed a bit. If the journo really had been writing about the *yak* for twenty years, that would put him on the far side of forty. Still.

When the doors opened at Komagome, Yumi was still in a mood, so they rode the escalator up to the ticket gate in silence. At the end of the corridor by the shuttered bakery where they'd agreed to part, Kenji's steps slowed, stopped. Yumi nearly bumped into him, looked up with a little frown on her face.

"What's the matter, Yu-*chan*?" he asked. "Aren't you happy we're making such good progress?"

"Yeah," she said, with a little edge to her voice. "*We've* learned so much in the past two days."

"And we'll find out even more on Saturday when we go to Korankei," Kenji said confidently. "It'll be worth the trip. I just know it."

Yumi didn't reply.

He felt a spark of annoyance. "What's with you tonight? Is it something I said?"

"More like something you *didn't* say." She shot him a hurt look. "Good night." She turned and walked away.

Buh? Kenji stared after her, bewildered. What had he done to deserve that? He shook his head. He'd never understand women. One minute they were all cheerful and helpful, and the next . . . .

He sighed, pocketed his train pass, and set off toward home.

•

Yumi fumed, stopping to buy a bottle of hot tea at the vending machine around the corner from the station. Why should she waste a whole Saturday, driving for hours and hours, to *maybe* talk to a witness? A witness *she* had found. A witness Kenji and Ghost wouldn't have been able to track down if it weren't for her and Jack Goldman. She savagely twisted off the cap off her tea bottle. What the hell was the matter with Kenji, anyway?

She knew what Coco would say: "Duh, he's a Japanese man." Yumi downed a slug of tea. Had she ever heard her father say "thank you" to her mother? No. Had Ichiro ever said "thank you" to her? No. They could both use a serious session with Hoshi.

But Kenji was the worst of all. Not only had he failed to appreciate all the legwork she'd done for him, he still hadn't mentioned anything about doing something fun together this weekend, something that in no way resembled a police investigation. All he'd talked about was that stupid drive to

Korankei. She stopped in her tracks. Surely he didn't think a nine-hour road trip to chase down a witness counted as a romantic getaway? The very thought made her furious. Kenji didn't just need a session with Hoshi, he needed a complete makeover.

She stalked down the street. What she needed was a good girltalk session with Coco. The #5 Hostess at the Queen of Hearts would know exactly what to do about a Japanese Man Problem.

Yumi stopped to dig out her phone. Coco would be working tonight, but maybe they could get together tomorrow night—she usually reserved Fridays for her real social life. Yumi flicked her phone on to send a message, but was stopped by the notification that popped up on her screen. It was a reminder that she hadn't yet replied to Hoshi's LuvLuv Match invitation to meet Taro Takahashi on Friday, at 7:00. She groaned, remembering Coco was supposed to meet her LuvLuv Match at the very same time.

Gloom. With Coco out on a date, she'd be stuck at home with her problems. And her parents. The idea of sitting in front of the TV with them—watching soap operas she'd never seen before, but could all too easily guess how they ended—was too depressing for words.

Yumi navigated to her LuvLuv invite. Her finger hovered over the "No Thanks" button, but she hesitated. If she got her first matchup out of the way, she and Coco could meet up later to compare horror stories.

The "Yes, Please" button pulsed pink. No, she decided, she couldn't. She hadn't told Kenji yet. If he found out, he'd be . . . what? Mad? Hurt? *Welcome to the club, buddy.* And how was he going to find out, anyway? He'd said he was going to some judo workshop after work, way out in northwest Tokyo. If she and Mr. Suspiciously Old To Still Be Unmarried met somewhere far from Bunkyo-ku, there was zero chance they'd cross paths with Kenji.

She tapped the pink "Yes" button before she could change her mind. A box appeared for sending a personal message, confirming the place and time. Yumi paused, thinking. Hoshi had recommended they meet at a fancy restaurant in Shinjuku, but that would require dressing up and an expensive trip to the hairdresser. It wasn't worth taking time off work for a man she never intended to see again. She bit her lip, then keyed in a message suggesting that instead, they meet at 7:00 for drinks and a bite to eat in Harajuku, at the Mad Hatter.

Then she sent a message to Coco, begging her with whipped cream and a cherry on top to join her there afterward.

•

"*Tadaima?*" Kenji called out the traditional greeting as he slid the front door shut behind him.

"*O-kaeri,*" came his dad's voice from the kitchen, welcoming him home.

Kenji closed his eyes and took a deep breath. It was now or never.

Every time he'd tried to track down the identity of the brown van's driver, he'd run into a brick wall. After Yumi had walked away from him, he'd detoured to the Komagome Shrine before heading home, figuring he could use a little guidance from the gods.

And he got it. While tossing his coin and ringing the bell, it occurred to him that the *kami-sama* might be stonewalling him on that license plate for a reason. Something besides grief had come packed in his mother's little blue suitcase, and his father had spent a decade avoiding it. Maybe the gods were giving him a sign that he should ask his father who owned that van. Maybe his dad needed to get it off his chest before it gave him a heart attack.

Kenji exchanged his shoes for slippers and came through the door into the kitchen as his dad muttered, "Idiots!" and rattled his newspaper.

A paper copy of the Mainichi Shimbun was still delivered to their doorstep every morning. But even though it didn't get read until after Internet news made everything in it obsolete, his father stubbornly refused to give up his after-work ritual of washing down the latest political scandal with rice crackers and beer.

The absence of cooking smells told Kenji his dad hadn't eaten yet, even though it was late. He glanced at the level of beer in the large bottle of Ichiban Shibori sitting on the table, surprised to find it down by only one small glass.

Kenji was still a little hungry, despite the rice omelet he'd wolfed down at the maid café. He crossed to the fridge to see what there was for dinner, and was surprised by a plastic shopping bag from Seibu, filled with take-out cartons. He took it out, peered inside. What could have possessed his father to buy food at a fancy Ikebukuro department store?

"That's Ayako's doing," his dad muttered. Setting aside his newspaper, he pulled the snack bowl toward him. Frowned. Poked around in it with his finger. Gave up. Kenji came closer to see what was in it. Unfamiliar brown nuggets had replaced his father's usual salty rice crackers.

"These damn things are only healthy because they taste so bad nobody eats them," his father groused, taking another sip of beer as consolation, returning to the paper.

Kenji unwrapped the cartons in the bag. Plain skewers of chicken, unadorned with *yakitori* sauce or tasty black char marks. Was the thin sauce in the sealed packet supposed to go with them? He set it aside, trying to keep an open mind. The next carton contained a multicolored salad packed with more vegetables than they usually ate in a week. The third held rice. Brown rice.

Kenji piled the chicken skewers onto a plate, wondering whether to put the sauce on before or after reheating. He decided to stick them in the microwave as is, and fetched a bottle of *yakitori* sauce from the fridge, just in case. While the chicken warmed, he dumped the salad into a saucepan, because he couldn't remember where they kept bowls big enough for a tossed salad. *Bing.* Took out the chicken, replaced it with the rice. Punched "Reheat." Seven skewers for his dad's plate, three for him, salad bowls, chopsticks. *Bing.* Rice was done. His dad folded his paper and poured Kenji's beer, then held his own glass while Kenji topped it up.

"*Kampai.*"

They took their first sip together, then eyed their dinner. Kenji dished out a serving of salad for his dad, then helped himself, while his father sniffed suspiciously at the healthy chicken sauce.

"So, how was your day?" Kenji ventured.

"Fine." He shot Kenji a defiant look. "It was fine. Somehow I managed to sit behind the desk in the police box all day and not collapse once."

He studied his salad bowl and picked up a slice of Japanese pumpkin with his chopsticks, examining it thoroughly it before taking a tentative bite. "You catch your panty raider yet?"

Kenji updated him on their pursuit of the underwear thief, watching his dad push aside the unfamiliar vegetables in his salad bowl and eat only the ones he recognized.

"The only progress we made today wasn't on our own case," Kenji said, finishing his last unsatisfying bite of chicken. "While we were looking for Mr. Panty Snatcher, we caught the guy Detective Oki's been after."

His father nodded. "Always good to have someone owing you one."

Kenji topped up his father's beer. "Actually, I already tried to cash in that chip, but Oki-*san* couldn't help me. I asked him to get someone to run a license plate for me, but his friend in vehicle registration is out on maternity leave."

"Why didn't you ask me? I know someone who might be able to help you."

"Actually," Kenji said, "that's exactly what I'm going to do. Do you remember the name of the company that brown van's plate traced back to?"

His father looked up. "What brown van?"

"The one in Mom's picture."

"What picture?"

"The one you told Inspector Mori you didn't have."

"I don't know what you're—"

"Yes, you do." Kenji said. "I found it on mom's camera chip."

A chicken skewer stopped halfway to his father's mouth. "What camera chip?"

"The one with pictures on it from her Ise Shrine trip. She took it to the camera store to get prints made, and nobody ever picked it up. They still had it." Kenji leaned in. "Who did the van belong to?"

"I don't know." His father bit off a piece of chicken. Chewed. "I never found out."

"Dad. Cut it out. I know your buddy at Shinjuku Station traced it. I talked to Mori."

His father lowered his skewer. "You talked to Inspector Mori? About what?"

"About the crime Mom witnessed. The crime you wouldn't let her tell him about. The crime that was committed using the same van that the Painted Doll victims were dumped from. Now tell me—which company did the plate trace back to?"

Silence.

"Which one?"

"Ace," his father croaked. "Ace Office Cleaning."

"It wasn't the one in the building that collapsed in the earthquake, was it?" Kenji said. "The one where they found mom's suitcase?"

His father didn't deny it.

"You knew," Kenji accused, putting down his chopsticks. "When Toyama-*san* appeared with mom's bag, you knew exactly which unsolved case Mori was talking about, didn't you? That's why you didn't want me to go with you. I called Mori after you refused to tell me anything. He gave me an earful. Why didn't you let mom tell him what she saw?"

His father didn't answer.

"Why?" Kenji persisted.

His father picked up his beer. Glowered at it. Drank it down. Then he fixed his son with a cold stare and answered him in a voice to match.

"Who do you think owns Ace Office Cleaning?"

"You tell me."

"I'll give you a hint: they run everything from guns to money laundries, and they don't like people who snitch to inspectors in the First Investigative Division. I didn't want the *yakuza* coming after your mother. Or you. Or your brother." He clamped his lips into a thin line, struggling for control. "But Mori—" He pounded the table. "Fucking Mori! Ten years later, and he's still badgering me about some picture she didn't have."

"But she did have pictures," Kenji said. "They were on that chip I found. Including one of a big man forcing a woman into that van, then coming after her friend."

"What? There were pictures?" His father's face went slack with shock. "She didn't tell me. Why didn't she tell me?"

"I don't know. To be honest, she might not have known what she had. It looked to me like she was trying to take a picture of some leaves and accidentally caught the abduction in the background. The one of the guy's face is close up, but off center and blurry, like the shutter tripped as he was trying to grab her camera."

"The sonofabitch who snatched those women saw her taking pictures?"

Kenji nodded. "I think that's how her camera got broken. She didn't tell you?"

"No. I didn't even know it got broken until . . . . "

"Until what?"

Silence.

"Until you saw that suitcase," Kenji guessed. "Until Sho told you her camera was in it, along with the Painted Doll victim's clothes?"

His father didn't say anything. Then he looked up at Kenji, confused. "How did Mori know? If *I* didn't know there were pictures, how did Mori know?"

"He didn't," Kenji said. "He was guessing. He couldn't believe Mom would remember a ten-digit license plate number if she didn't have a picture of it. He didn't know we used to play 'Eyewitness' with her when we were kids, and she always won. Mori was bluffing."

And then it hit him.

"Goddammit." Kenji felt like he'd been punched. "Mori was *bluffing*."

Inspector Exam Study Guide, Chapter Three: *You don't have to have incriminating evidence as long as the suspect believes you have incriminating evidence.*

"What's wrong?" his father asked.

"Mori lied. He lied to the piece of scum who killed Mom." Kenji grew more agitated as the logic unspooled. "He got a list of Ace Cleaning employees and narrowed it down to the most likely suspects. Then he called them in, one by one, and told each of them that someone had taken a picture of him and the van at Korankei. That he had photographic proof and an eyewitness who would testify. That the conviction would be a slam dunk. Told them they'd get a lighter sentence if they confessed. He was hoping to get a quick solve if the perp bought his line."

"It didn't work," his father pointed out. "Nobody confessed."

"But the sonofabitch who actually did it believed him, and went running to his boss." Kenji stared at his father, stricken. "Then mom had her . . . accident."

His father's face went white as a sheet.

"No," he cried, throwing down his chopsticks. Breathing hard, he scrambled to his feet, turning to flee. "No!"

Kenji grabbed his arm. "Dad. *Dad.* Stop."

"No!" His father wrenched his arm from Kenji's grasp, backed away, his face ripped with agony. "How could he do that? How could he . . . . "

"Dad, listen to me," Kenji pleaded. He hadn't seen his father this upset since his mother died. "What Mori did was standard procedure. It's a technique they teach all detectives at the Academy—"

"That doesn't make it right!"

Kenji tried to put an arm around his dad's shoulders, but his father flung it off and charged out of the kitchen, careening to his room, slamming the door. Kenji went after him. Pounded on his door. Tried the handle. Locked.

"Dad? Dad, are you all right?"

He put his ear up to the door and listened. Muffled sounds came from within. Was he having a heart attack? Kenji stood there for a minute, but now he couldn't hear anything.

"Dad?" Kenji rapped again. "Are you all right in there?"

Silence. Then something that sounded like, "Go away."

Kenji let go of the breath he didn't realize he'd been holding. He waited a moment more, then gave up and dragged himself back to the kitchen. Picked up his nearly full beer glass. Stared at it. Went to the sink to pour it out.

He made himself a cup of tea and saw that his father had kicked his cushion halfway across the floor in his panic to escape. He crossed the room and bent to retrieve it.

That doesn't make it right.

Mori. *Fucking* Mori. Kenji hurled the cushion against the wall, and stood there, shaking.

Mori thought he was so smart, bluffing like that. But there really were pictures of the abduction on his mother's camera. His mother really *had* been an eyewitness. The Inspector didn't know that, but the angry man in her last photo did.

Mori had played it by the book, but he had still signed Sachiko Nakamura's death warrant the moment that lie left his lips.

•

Kenji's father stood there, swaying, throat closed, vision blurred.

Breathe, dammit, breathe.

But it wasn't working, not this time. The agony inside him swelled, and he stumbled across the room, falling onto his futon and burying his face in his pillow, trying to stifle the shameful sounds that were escaping against his will.

Mori had lied. He choked back a sob. *Mori had lied, then Sachi had died.*

Coughing and gasping now, he pounded the futon as the full weight of his guilt crashed down on him. The sobs broke free, and he was helpless against the tears that were now soaking into his pillow.

Forgive me, Sachi. I tried. But it wasn't enough. It wasn't enough. I sold my soul, but it wasn't enough . . . .

A yawning hole opened up inside him and swallowed everything he'd been telling himself for ten years. Face buried in his pillow, he wrestled with his despair, raging against the infernal truth, but finally he gave up and lay there, gasping, spent. And in the darkness, as his body stilled and time passed, he realized that even though everything he believed had been snatched from him, he'd been left with one cold, hard truth.

He knew who had killed her.

But that made everything worse. Much worse.

Forgive me, Sachi. Because he wouldn't tell. *Forgive me, Sachi.* Couldn't tell. Because if he took the killer down, the killer would take him down too.

FRIDAY, JANUARY 9

•

An exhausting Friday spent fruitlessly chasing panty thief suspects had turned into an even more exhausting evening of getting slammed onto the judo mat. And it wasn't over yet. Kenji bundled his damp workout clothes into a duffel bag and hustled out of the locker room at the Bunkyo Ward Sports Center. He wanted to catch Detective Kurosawa before she left, and he was pretty sure Aya wouldn't bother with the girly stuff that took most women an hour. The daughter of one of the biggest gang bosses in Kabuki-chō had grown up in a house full of boys, and she would beat him out the door if he didn't hurry.

Bypassing the slow elevator, he trotted down the stairs, wincing a little as post-workout muscles began to stiffen. Stationing himself beside the exit so he wouldn't miss her, he took out his phone and navigated to his mother's photo of the angry guy's face. He'd shown it to Detective Oki, who had grown up in Kabuki-chō and gone to school with players from every gang in town, but Oki hadn't recognized the man in the ten-year-old picture.

"Ask Aya," he'd advised. "She's younger than me, knows the hustlers who appeared after I joined the good guys."

The stairwell door opened and the assistant detective emerged, a workout bag nearly as big as she was slung over her shoulder. No makeup, wet hair pulled back into a ponytail, the high cheekbones she shared with her handsome younger brother still pink from her workout.

"Kurosawa-*san*."

She turned, belatedly sketching a bow as she remembered that off the mats, Kenji was her superior.

"Good workout tonight. Sir. I think you're improving."

"I don't know about that," Kenji said, wincing. "I still spend more time on the mat than on my feet when I spar with you."

"Well, yeah," she acknowledged. "But you really dished it out to the other students. Two of those guys outrank you on the mat, but tonight you handled them like they were yellow belts. If you practiced a bit more, you could test for your second degree, you know. Sir."

"Thanks, maybe I will," he said. But not anytime soon. Right now, Kenji couldn't afford to spend his free time at the gym.

"Can I ask you something before you go?" He showed her the close-up of the man in the Korankei parking lot. "Do you recognize this guy? This is from ten years ago, but—"

Her face froze.

"Why are you asking me? Sir."

"He used to work at Ace Cleaning Service, which my father says is a gang front. And I thought maybe—"

Aya turned and stalked out of the Sports Center. Astonished, Kenji ran after her.

Outside, she turned to him and said, in a tight voice, "And you thought because I was a Kurosawa, I'd recognize him?"

"Do you?"

"Why do you want to know?"

"Because I found that picture on my mother's camera."

Confusion. "Your mother's camera? Why did your mother have a photo of that thug on her camera?"

"It's . . . a long story," Kenji said. "Do you know him?"

"It's . . . a long story."

They stared at each other as cops fresh from the locker room began emerging from the Sports Center.

Aya muttered, "Not here."

"Oh. Right. Sorry." Kenji kicked himself for momentarily forgetting she'd been transferred from previous postings three times in four years because her colleagues discovered that the reason she knew so much about the underworld was that she was related to half of it.

Where could they go that would be more private, but not *too* private? The fact that Assistant Detective Kurosawa was female didn't matter when they were working together, but after hours he didn't want anyone putting two and two together to make five.

"Ramen?" he suggested, choosing the least romantic kind of restaurant he could think of. "Curry rice?"

Ten minutes later, they were seated in a corner booth at a Jonathan's American Style Family Restaurant. Neither particularly liked the food, but it was brightly lit and filled with senior citizens stretching their pensions. They'd ended up there after spotting fellow judo workshop attendees already chowing down at the other three places they'd tried.

"So, the guy in the picture," Kenji said. "Who is he? Does he work for your family?"

"No. He's Yamamoto-*gumi*. His name is Ryo Maeda, but everyone calls him Shark."

"Shark?" Kenji laughed. "Why, did he bite someone?"

"Yeah."

Kenji waited. Aya didn't elaborate.

"You know where I can find him?"

"He works for the Yamamoto-*oyabun*'s number two son."

"Koji Yamamoto? In the porn biz?"

"No, he runs their human trafficking trade. But he started out in janitorial."

"Janitorial, as in Ace Cleaning Service?"

"No, as in, when Koji made a mess, Shark cleaned it up. Ace Cleaning just happens to be where he's on payroll."

"Ten years ago," Kenji ventured, "if a couple of foreign women escaped the Yamamoto-*gumi*'s sex trafficking outfit, would Koji have sent Shark to bring them back?"

"Sent him where?"

"To Korankei. Near the Ise Shrine."

"No. Too far away. Is that where that picture was taken?"

"Yes." Kenji explained about his mother's trip and the incident in the parking lot with the foreign women.

Their food arrived, and they shoveled in the first few bites to take the edge off their hunger, then Aya said, "But that all happened ten years ago, right? Why are you asking about him now?"

"I just found out about it."

"Your mom waited ten years, then out of the blue she mentioned she'd witnessed an abduction?"

"No." He hesitated, then added, "My mom passed away ten years ago."

"Oh." Aya colored. "Sorry, sir. I'm . . . I'm sorry for your loss."

"It happened right after that trip to the shrine. Right after she witnessed the abduction. At the time, we all thought it was an accident, but two weeks ago, they found her missing suitcase in a building filled with human trafficking victims. Now I'm not so sure."

"You think Shark . . . ?"

"I don't know. But Inspector Mori found out my mother had seen the van he was driving, and its tag matched one used in a murder they called the Painted Doll killing. The plate traced back to Ace Cleaning Service. Mori called my mother in to question her, but my dad told her not to say anything. He was worried that—" Kenji stopped, remembering whom he was talking to.

"It's okay." Aya looked away. "I know how dangerous life can be for inconvenient witnesses."

"Yeah, but it's not all my dad's fault. I blame Mori too."

"Mori? Why?"

"I think when he questioned the Ace Cleaning employees, he lied to them. He told the suspects he had pictures and an eyewitness, tried to trick them into confessing. The problem was, it was true. My mother did have pictures. She was an eyewitness. And this guy Shark knew it."

"You think he killed her?" Aya considered the possibility, then shook her head, unconvinced. "The thing is, that's not really his line of work. I mean, not that he'd have a problem whacking someone, but it's unlikely he'd have done it unless Koji was in real danger."

"What do you mean?"

"Well, back then, Shark was Koji's minder." She tossed a pickle in her mouth and crunched. "Which means that his only job was to take care of Koji. Personally. Day and night. His father died protecting Koji's uncle, and his brother went to jail for Koji's cousin in Osaka. So, first of all, if Shark killed your mother, it's because he thought she was a serious threat to his boss. And second," she dug a bite of barbequed eel and rice from her bowl, "if Shark was in Korankei ten years ago, that means Koji was there too."

Koji Yamamoto was in Korankei? Kenji flashed back to the photos. He was sure there had been two men in the brown van. Was Koji the driver?

"But what were they doing all the way down in Korankei?" he wondered aloud. "Do you think they drove for five hours just to hunt down two escaped sex slaves? It's awfully far from their territory, isn't it?"

"You're right," Aya agreed. "There must be more to it. They wouldn't have bothered chasing those small fry nearly to Nagoya if there hadn't been some kind of major fuckup. One that involved Koji personally. One he had to fix himself, because—" She fell silent.

"Because what?"

"Because ten years ago, Koji Yamamoto couldn't afford another fuckup," she said. "Not after what I did to him."

Kenji stared at Aya as she scooped the last bite of eel and rice from her bowl. She sighed and put down her chopsticks.

"My father wasn't happy when I joined the police," she explained, picking up her soda. "But the real reason he kicked me out of the family was that I threw Koji Yamamoto's shoes in his face."

"His shoes?"

"Yeah. You've got to understand—my father is old school. Third generation head of the Kurosawa-*gumi*. My older brother Hiro will be the fourth, if there's anything left to lead." She paused. "And if there isn't, it'll be my fault."

"Why?"

She sighed. "When I was in high school, my family was getting squeezed pretty hard by foreign gangs moving into Kabuki-chō, all with pipelines of drugs and smuggled weapons to finance themselves. We weren't big enough or rich enough to compete with them on our own. My brothers wanted to move into drugs and guns, but my father was against it. Then Yamamoto-*oyabun*—the head of the other major outfit—contacted him. The Yamamoto-*gumi* was about twice the size of the Kurosawa-*gumi*, but he saw the writing on the wall too. The only way they could survive was to get into dirtier and more dangerous businesses, or join up with us.

"The problem was, there's enough bad blood between our families that there was only one face-saving way to make an alliance—an arranged marriage between me and Yamamoto's second son, Koji. I was seventeen at the time, he was thirty-one."

Aya stirred her soda. "At first I thought he was okay. He's not bad looking, and everywhere we went, people treated him like a prince. He's the second son, but his older brother Yoichi is a chump—no edge, likes his saké too much, has a bit of a gambling problem. Their father gave each of them control of some of his businesses when they turned twenty, but even back then, bookies were giving odds that when Number One Son stepped up to take over when the *oyabun* died, he would follow his dad faster than he'd like. These days, Koji runs eighty percent of the business, including most of the ones that matter: stock fixing, real estate, insurance fraud, human trafficking, porn. The only ones his brother still controls are gambling and loan sharking."

She shook her head. "It took me a while to figure out what a pig Koji was, but by the time someone sent me a DVD with an anonymous note asking if I knew that my fiancé's hobby was making movies, I was beginning to guess why he wasn't married. The business he was running behind his father's back went way beyond pornography." She shuddered. "I only watched five minutes before I had to run to the bathroom and throw up."

"So you broke it off?"

"Yeah. In front of both families, at a cherry blossom viewing party. I took off the fancy high heels he'd bought me as a *hanami* present and pitched them at him in the middle of a sixteenth century garden. They were French. Expensive. The kind with red soles."

"Why didn't you just tell your father? Call it quits quietly?"

Her smile faded. "I tried, but he didn't want to know. I was only seventeen, and I couldn't make myself describe the sadistic violence I'd seen on that DVD. He thought I was just being a delicate flower, shocked by garden-variety porn." Aya's voice took on a bitter edge. "He said I needed to grow up, to learn that a good wife shouldn't ask her husband how he put rice in her bowl, just thank him for doing it."

"So he kicked you out?"

"Not for that. But seeing the filth Koji was producing really opened my eyes. I know it's hard to believe, but before that, I never really thought much about what my father's 'company' did. He went to work in the morning, came home late, had a nice office in a tall building and people gave him lots of respect. The only way he was different from other dads was that he was embarrassingly old-fashioned—making formal offerings to the ancestors every morning, striking sparks over our backs with a flint for good luck when we went off to the first day of school. My brothers called him 'sir' and we ate dinner together every night, along with a sort of extended family of his lieutenants. I never realized that the 'older brothers' who sneaked me sweets from my favorite candy shop and played catch with us after school spent their days shaking down store owners for protection money and going after people with baseball bats if they couldn't pay back their loans.

"Breaking the engagement was such a public slap in the face for the Yamamoto family that my father had to send me to his brother in Nagoya while he dealt with the fallout. His solution was to demand that I return and apologize to Koji on my knees; mine was to apply to the police academy. My father said he'd disown me if I went, and he kept his word. I haven't seen my family since."

"But I don't get why Koji would be especially scared of screwing up after that—he's the one who got dumped."

"Well, Yamamoto Senior was furious when the alliance he'd humbled himself to arrange fell through, and twice as mad when he found out that the reason I refused to marry Koji was because he was making movies so disgusting his father couldn't even bear to watch them. He told Koji that if he couldn't manage to land himself a suitable wife—meaning a decent girl, not a sex worker—he couldn't promise to back him when it came time to take over. That he'd better get busy, because there were rumors."

"What kind of rumors?"

"About why Koji didn't have a girlfriend, even though he was thirty-one." She shook her head. "In that world, guys with kinky tastes are for making money off of, not swearing allegiance to."

"What kind of kinky tastes?"

"I didn't stick around long enough to find out. But that video I saw? It wasn't just sex, it was violence. Extreme violence. The kind of violence that would make any normal person sick. The anonymous note that came with it said Koji didn't just produce it, he directed it."

"Sounds like you've got plenty of reason to hate him," Kenji said.

"So do you," she replied. "If he arranged your mom's 'accident.'"

"If he did, I'll bury him."

"If he did, I'll help you."

•

"And then, oh my god, he crunched his way through every last piece of ice in his scotch glass!" Coco complained.

Yumi laughed, enjoying the gory details hinted at by the string of texts she'd gotten from Coco throughout the evening.

oh god. he's waiting for me with a big bouquet of red carnations. nooooo!!!

tried to forget flowers in cab. unsuccessful

told me I had beautiful hair. tempted to take off wig and scare the pants off him

Coco had gone on her date made up like the photos in her LuvLuv Match profile, and had come straight to the Hatter to meet Yumi afterwards. In her knee-length suit and black hair, she looked as out of place as the provincial gawkers. Yumi hadn't recognized her at first, when Coco appeared next to her table.

Coco sipped her drink moodily, then said, "What about your date? Please tell me Mr. Dreamboat's not your type, but you loyally put in a plug for me."

"Actually—" Yumi took a sip of her White Rabbit. "I think you'd have a lot in common."

"Really? Like what?" Coco leaned in.

"Well, first of all, his underwear probably cost more than my whole outfit, shoes included."

"You saw his *underwear*?"

"No, but I'm guessing it was the cheapest thing he was wearing," Yumi said. "And he was disappointed Boshi-*san* didn't have any Dom Perignon Pink."

"My favorite!"

"And his fantasy dream vacation is a beach weekend in Hawaii."

"That's *my* dream vacation!"

"And you both like men."

"We both—" Coco stared at her. "He's *gay*?"

"As they come."

Coco groaned. "Then why's he wasting money with Hoshi, pretending to look for a wife?"

"He's not pretending."

"I don't get it."

"He's the son of the Minister of the Environment. The only son. Only child, actually."

"And his parents don't know?"

"He told them when he was in college, but they just sat there without saying a word, then his mom asked if he wanted fried pork cutlets or eel for dinner. After that, the offers for arranged marriage meetings began arriving."

"Can't he just say 'no'?"

"He doesn't want to let down his family. Says it's his duty to make them happy, give them grandchildren."

"Then why doesn't he just pick one of the girls they're trying to set him up with and be done with it? Why spend money with Hoshi?"

Yumi stirred her White Rabbit and sighed. "Because he's a nice guy. He didn't want to marry someone without telling her she'd be marrying a friend, not a lover. And even though the women his parents tried to set him up with weren't all prize specimens, they came from rich and powerful families and they all had better options. He chose LuvLuv Match because he figured women who signed up with a brand new matchmaker would be more desperate. And he picked me because Hoshi told him that I'd just broken off an *o-miai* with the heir to the Mitsuyama Department Stores. He figured that meant I'd pass the parent test and be more likely to say yes."

"Why would you be more likely to say yes than, say, me?"

"Because I'd already made compromises. He figured nobody would marry into a long line of notorious womanizers without agreeing that 'wife' and 'lover' might be two different people."

Coco sipped her drink moodily.

"So what are you going to do?" Yumi asked. "Will you ask Hoshi to dish you up another one?"

"Well, actually . . . . "

"You're giving up already?"

"No." Coco signaled to Boshi-*san* for another Lemon Jabberwock. "I agreed to go out with Ren again." She glanced at Yumi. "Don't look at me like that! I felt sorry for him, okay? He's so awkward, but he's not hopeless. I thought he'd get all huffy when I told him to order another drink instead of eating his ice, but he just turned red and asked for more. Begged me to help him, to go out with him again and tell him everything he does wrong." Her drink arrived. She took a sip and reached for her phone. "I was still going to say no, but when I got home, there was a note waiting, asking to meet him again on Friday night. It came with flowers, from a fancy florist. So I changed my mind."

"Flowers made you change your mind?"

Coco passed Yumi her phone with a piece of sent mail on the screen.

From: cocomoco@docomo.co.jp

To: ren_noda@mitsubank.com
OK, I'll meet you in Roppongi at 19:00 on Friday, as long as you promise never to do this again:
Below, she'd sent two phone snaps. The top one was of a single pink rose stuck in a glass, labeled YES. Below was a picture of what Yumi recognized as Coco's bedroom, stacked to the ceiling with more pink roses than Yumi had ever seen in one place before.

Below, Coco had typed NO.

Yumi laughed. "Looks like you've got your work cut out for you." She held out the phone for her friend to take it back, but Coco was distracted, scanning the room over her shoulder.

"Who are you looking for?" Yumi turned to look too, puzzled.

"No one," Coco said quickly, taking a sip of her drink. "Well, actually," she admitted, "I forgot to tell you, but your buddy Kenji texted me earlier. Said he tried to call you, but you weren't picking up. I told him you were meeting me here later."

"He's coming here? Why?" Yumi scowled, remembering how mad at him she was.

"Dunno." Coco peered at her, suspiciously. "Is there something you're not telling me, missy?"

"No!" she answered quickly, then muttered something about needing the ladies' room.

Locking herself into a stall, she checked her phone. Sure enough, two missed calls from Kenji, no voicemails. Was it possible he was calling to apologize? Ha. That'd be the day. It was probably something about that accursed trip to Korankei tomorrow. He probably wanted to change the godawful 6:00 a.m. departure time to even *earlier*.

She stuffed the phone back in her purse, feeling cranky. Now she couldn't even beg Coco for advice about how to train up an ungrateful Japanese man. Coco would know exactly who she was talking about. It would have been the perfect opportunity to come clean and confess all, if she hadn't noticed

Coco surreptitiously glancing toward the door every time someone new arrived. Until she figured out why Coco was so eager to see Kenji, she'd have to figure out how to deal with his shortcomings herself.

•

Kenji took a miserly sip of the beer he'd been nursing for over an hour, then resumed staring out the window at the door of the Mad Hatter. He was in the bar across the street, and had been ever since he'd walked into the Hatter, scanned the room to see if Yumi was there yet, and discovered her sitting with her back to the door, across the table from a *man*. And not just a man— a very handsome man in an expensive suit, who was sharing an intimate-looking laugh with the woman Kenji had been thinking of as the love of his life.

Kenji had been so shocked, he'd beat a hasty retreat to the less popular Bar Texas, and snagged a window table so he could corral his stampeding thoughts and wait for her to emerge.

The Texas was the kind of place that attracted people who drank alone, staring down into their beer, contemplating whatever wasteland their life had become. The melancholy twanging that Kenji vaguely recognized as "American country & western music" wasn't helping his mood, and he couldn't help but feel that the empty eyes of the bleached animal skull over the bar were regarding him with pity.

Since he'd been there, he'd watched as the man who had been with Yumi left the Mad Hatter and her friend Coco arrived. He'd cycled through shock (Yumi was dating other men behind his back!), denial (surely there was some other explanation), anger (Yumi was cheating on him!), hurt (she didn't care about him, never had) and, finally, fear (what if he'd lost her forever?)

What he couldn't figure out was *why*. Twenty-four hours ago, everything had been fine, then— What had happened between the maid café and Komagome Station that made her walk away from him last night? He'd refused to let that reporter drag his mother's name through the mud, but that wouldn't be enough to make her dump him, would it?

How could they be working so well together—like a well-oiled team, he'd thought—then suddenly, *boom*? Hadn't their search for what happened to his mom been bringing them closer? He'd taken her enthusiasm for finding the bus driver and the name of the second victim as a sign of how much she cared.

He regarded the last inch of beer in his glass. It had gone flat. Re-checked the time. It was late. Yumi would have to come out soon.

And then she did. As she stopped in the narrow street to wait while Coco pulled on her gloves, Kenji shot from his seat and pushed through the front door.

"Yumi!" he called.

She turned.

Coco took one look at him, then fixed Yumi with a meaningful glare and said, "Call me." Fluffing her muffler, she disappeared in the direction of the train station.

"What are you doing here?" Yumi asked him, taking a step closer.

He crossed the street. "You first."

A clutch of Gothic Lolitas emerged from the Hatter and Kenji pulled Yumi around the corner into a quiet alleyway.

She was looking cuter than ever in that flippy skirt and those little red shoes, but that just made him madder. She had picked them out for *another man*.

Now that he was face to face with the source of his suffering, the self-pity he'd been nursing at the Bar Texas was curdling into outrage. He tore into her. "I ran all the way across town after judo practice to see if you wanted to go somewhere nice for a nightcap, but when I walked into the Mad Hatter, I caught you on a *date*."

"A date?" She gave a nervous laugh. "You mean with Coco?"

"No, with a *man*."

Alarm erased her smile. "How long have you been here?"

"Since nine." Kenji's hands curled into fists. "Who was he?"

"Nobody. It wasn't what you think."

"What was it, then? It sure looked like you were having a good time to me."

"I was," she retorted. She crossed her arms, hugging herself against the cold.

Good. That's what she got for wearing such a short skirt. Kenji glowered at her.

"I'm sorry I didn't tell you," she said, her face stony, sounding not nearly repentant enough. "But it wasn't a date. It was more like, uh, a meeting. I was doing it for Coco. She's my best friend and she's in a bad patch right now. Last week she dragged me with her to find out about this company Hoshi is starting—you remember Hoshi, right? From Club Nova?"

Hoshi the bar host was starting a business? What sort of man would pay that professional liar to do anything?

"And the thing is," Yumi explained, the words tumbling out, "I accidentally agreed to meet with three of his clients. I meant to tell you, but you've been so—"

"Clients?" Kenji exploded. "What sort of clients?"

"Well, it's sort of a matchmaking service, but—"

"*Matchmaking*?"

"No! I mean yes, but— It's not just matchmaking. First, Hoshi coaches them on how to treat women, then he—"

Kenji couldn't believe what he was hearing. "You're telling me that cash-hoovering gigolo is making money teaching men how to treat women? What does *he* know about that?"

"A lot more than you!" Yumi's eyes blazed. "The guy I had dinner with tonight actually asked me about what's happening in *my* life, actually said 'thank you' for taking the time to meet with him." She glared at Kenji. "Which is more than I can say for *some* people. Who never say thank you for *anything*."

Kenji stared at her. Is that what last night was about? She expected him to thank her? For what? They were in a relationship, weren't they? Sure, she'd been helping him find out what had happened to his mother, but didn't it go without saying that they'd do things for each other without being thanked all the time?

"I don't understand," he said.

"Well, it's time you did," she said, hotly. "Of course I want to help you find out what happened to your mother. I'm glad there's something I can do. But for the past week you've been treating me like . . . like I was your *kōhai*, or something. Like that's all I am to you, just another assistant detective."

What was she talking about? She knew how he felt about her! "Yu-*chan*, how can you say that?"

"Because it's true! When was the last time we talked about anything besides how to track down witnesses?" She vibrated with indignation. "Last night after the maid café, I halfway expected you to say '*o-tsukare-sama-deshita*' instead of 'goodnight'. Or maybe *that's* even expecting too much. You probably don't even say 'thank you for your hard work' to your real assistant detectives."

"That's not true!" Kenji objected. "I—"

Then he stopped short. Had he said 'thank you' to Aya after she helped him tonight? Now that he thought about it . . . no. Had he thanked Oki for staying late and going through the accident reports with him? Well, actually, no. But they didn't expect to be thanked! They knew he'd do the same for them. They were colleagues.

Then he looked at Yumi, shivering in her short skirt and little red shoes, her face full of hurt. He felt a stirring of guilt. Yumi wasn't his colleague. It wasn't her job to investigate suspicious deaths. But she'd done it anyway. In fact—now that he thought about it—she'd spent pretty much all her free time since New Year's helping him find out what had happened to his mother. She'd tracked down the bus driver. And the name of the second victim. And—all right, he had to admit it— even the information she'd gotten from that reporter was a goldmine.

The anger drained out of him. He *hadn't* thanked her. Not once. He'd been grateful, of course he had, but he hadn't said it. Remorse hit hard.

"Yu-*chan*, I'm sorry," he said. "You're right. I'm sorry I didn't tell you how much I appreciate your help." He stepped toward her, wanting to take her in his arms instead of saying all the difficult words, but something in her face told him he couldn't get out of it that easily.

"I know it's way too late," he said, "but I do want to say thank you. For . . . for finding the bus driver. And the second victim. And even . . . " it was hard to say it, but he knew he had to. ". . . for getting all that stuff from the reporter. Thank you for understanding. For caring about what happened to my mom, as though," he swallowed the lump in his throat, "as though she were your mom too."

Yumi's face softened, and he stepped up to take her hands in his. She hadn't said she'd forgive him yet, but she didn't pull away either.

"I'm sorry I didn't say all this before," he said, bending down to look into her eyes. "From now on, I'll try to remember, I really will. But—"

"But what?" Wary again.

"I'm a little worried that— I mean, I know how I get when I'm on a case and—" He blurted, "Will you be mad at me if I don't say 'thank you' all the time? If I don't say it *every* time?"

"No," she conceded, with the beginnings of a smile. "I won't be mad if you don't say it every time." Then she looked into his eyes. "But I need you to say it *sometimes*."

He pulled her into his arms in a flood of relief, and she didn't back away. After a moment, her arms stole around him too.

•

It was at times like this that Takeo missed smoking the most.

One of the kitchen staff had stopped showing up for work two nights ago, and the second-best filleting knife had disappeared with him. He sighed, not wanting to be the one to tell his father-in-law. Maybe it could wait until tomorrow, when they weren't both so tired.

Shouldering open the back door of the restaurant, he dragged the heavy bag of burnable trash to the can, heaved it in. He paused for a moment to savor the cold air, letting it wash away a little of the weariness.

A wedge of light suddenly stretched out over the alleyway from the next building, and Takeo stepped into the shadows. Two of the neighboring restaurant's workers emerged, joking. Darkness returned as the door closed behind them, and a lighter flared in the darkness. It was soon joined by the burning embers of their after-work smokes. The scent of tobacco filled his nostrils and he closed his eyes, wanting a Seven Stars so badly he could taste it.

At the end of a long, hard day, he could have done without the craving that reminded him of the grave where he'd smoked his last one. Every time he denied himself, he thought of the day everything changed. He only allowed himself to taste tobacco once a year now, but it brought him no pleasure. It was small but necessary atonement, for costing his mother her life.

SATURDAY, JANUARY 10

•

"Korankei, seven kilometers," Kenji announced, pointing to the large sign over the road that only someone too blind to drive could miss.

"I know, I saw it," Yumi replied, already making the turn.

She'd been behind the wheel since they switched at the rest stop near Nagoya, and she was beginning to regret the two coffees she'd drunk along the way. They hadn't passed a rest stop for the past hour.

The highway wound alongside a river lined with trees, and they could hear the snowmelt tumbling over boulders in the stream, see the whitewater through the bare branches. Mist veiled the valley ahead, even at midday. How much farther? She checked the scrolling navi map on their rent-a-car's dashboard. Good, they were close.

"Next right," Kenji said.

"I *know*." And not a moment too soon. She sped up. On the right, she spotted the bus lot. Zipping in, she parked haphazardly in the first extra-long space, flung open the door, and dashed to the ladies'.

A few minutes later, feeling better, she emerged to find Kenji standing outside, next to a leafless cherry tree. His breath formed little clouds as he held up his phone, comparing the photo from his mom's camera with the view across the parking lot.

"We were right," he said, with satisfaction. "I'm sure this is where my mom stood when she took those pictures." He pointed to the far corner of the lot. "That's where the brown van came from."

Kenji switched to his GPS and keyed in the address Ghost had provided for the missing Chinese woman. The map swung around and pinpointed a building on the outskirts of town.

"Walk?" he asked. "Or drive?"

Yumi's stomach growled. "What about lunch?"

"Oh, yeah. Sorry." Kenji looked sheepish. "When I get excited about a case, sometimes I forget to eat."

Across the street, they found a homely café that promised the kind of old-fashioned comfort food still common in the countryside. Ten minutes later, Yumi's red-bean-and-butter sandwich was half gone, and Kenji was ordering another bowl of noodles.

Revived, they drank their tea, then pointed the car toward the address Ghost had given them. It turned out to be a farm equipment repair shed, with an old-fashioned steep-roofed farmhouse beyond. Sounds of metal-on-metal banging came through the wooden walls as they skirted the shed on their way to the house.

The farmhouse's original roof had probably been thatched, but the reeds had been replaced with tile so long ago that moss and tufts of grass had grown into miniature gardens between them. The breeze changed, bringing the scent of old-fashioned charcoal smoke.

They knocked. Waited. Tried again. A dog's face materialized behind the pebbled glass. It barked, once. A moment later, the door slid open, and a woman appeared in the gap.

"*Konnichi wa?*" she said, turning the greeting into a question.

A slight lilt was all that remained of her accent. Wu Yin was still beautiful, ten years after she'd posed with a shy smile in front of the Ise Shrine. Lines were beginning to crinkle the corners of her eyes and her face was thinner, but her lips were still lovely and full, her skin clear.

"Are you Mrs. Hayashi?" Kenji asked.

A cautious, "Yes?"

Kenji introduced himself and Yumi, explaining that his mother had met her ten years ago on a trip to the Ise Shrine. He was wondering if she could answer a few questions about an incident in the parking lot.

Her eyes widened. "No, I'm sorry. I don't know what you're talking about." She began to shut the door.

"Wait!" Kenji said, shoving his foot into the gap before it closed. He pulled out his police ID. "I'd hoped we could have a friendly chat, but if you prefer, we can go to the police station and—"

"I didn't do it," she cried.

"Didn't do what?"

"Take something that wasn't mine."

"You mean the suitcase?"

"It wasn't me. I swear. I didn't, I'd never—"

Kenji held up a hand and said, "Perhaps we could talk about it inside?" He glanced back at the repair shed. "You might prefer that your husband didn't . . . ?"

Her eyes widened, and she hastily slid the door open, waving them in. Yumi and Kenji left their winter boots behind and stepped into the woven straw slippers awaiting visitors on the *tatami* mats. A square fire pit in the middle of a spacious room beyond beckoned them closer, glowing with the charcoal fire they'd smelled earlier. An age-darkened fish-shaped counterweight hung from the rafters far above, a battered teakettle hooked below it. Yin Hayashi knelt anxiously on one of the floor cushions, and gestured for them to use two others. She didn't offer tea.

"Tell us what happened the day you came to Korankei," Kenji said as they seated themselves.

The woman's eyes flicked nervously to Yumi, then back to Kenji. "What . . . what do you want to know?"

"Everything."

"I can't. I can't." She wrung her hands. "If my husband finds out . . . . "

"There's no reason he needs to know, unless you refuse to help us. Then I'll have no choice but to make this more formal. But if you tell us everything, it ends here. Why were you and your friend on that bus tour?"

"She wasn't my friend." Yin's face clouded. "Li Qian and I just had the same matchmaker and were going to the same place, that's all. Both of us were far from home, trapped in terrible situations. We came to this country to make a better life for ourselves, but when we got here, we found out that everything we'd been told was a lie."

"So you ran away?"

She nodded. "We both found flyers about the Traffic Watchers. They helped us. Introduced us to honorable men, who wanted good wives. Gave us bus tickets to the Ise Shrine."

"And they told you to leave the bus tour when it stopped at Korankei?"

"Yes. Someone from the matchmaker was supposed to meet us in the parking lot, so we let everyone get off, then we asked the driver for our luggage."

"And how did you end up with a suitcase that didn't belong to you?"

"It wasn't me! It was Li Qian! The driver went back in the bus to get a form we had to sign, and she switched her bag with one that looked like it. I tried to stop her, but she said shut up, she needed the money in it worse than the lady who owned it. It was then I realized Li Qian was not sincere. She didn't want to get married; she was only using the Traffic Watchers to get away and get money. I told her she should take this opportunity to change her life and start fresh, but she just laughed and said I was a fool. The bus driver didn't understand, because we were speaking Mandarin, but he was looking at us suspiciously, so I just signed the form and walked away. I knew what she was doing was wrong, but I was afraid if I said anything, he'd go to the police and they'd arrest us and throw us out of the country."

A tear slipped down her cheek, but she brushed it off.

"So you walked away," Kenji prompted. "What happened then?"

She took a breath. "A van drove up to meet us. We thought it was the lady from the matchmaker, but when a big man got out, I was confused. Li Qian started to get in, then saw something wasn't right and tried to back out, but the man shoved her in. All I could think of was the suitcase. I thought he saw her take it and was there to arrest us. I dropped my bag and ran. He chased me all the way to the bathroom.

"A lady from the tour was standing outside, taking pictures. I ran past her and locked myself in a stall. A few minutes later, she came in and said that the man was gone.

"When I came out, the bus driver was there too. He was arguing with the camera lady about something, but my Japanese wasn't so good back then. All I know is that she wanted to tell the police what happened and he didn't. I was crying and begging her not to go to the authorities, when the woman from the matchmaker came. She talked to them for a while, then we left without calling the police." Tears filled her eyes. "But I never stopped being afraid they would come for me. That someday I'd open the door and . . . and . . . . " She looked at Kenji helplessly and tears streamed down her cheeks.

Yumi opened her bag and handed Yin her handkerchief. "Don't worry. We're not going to turn you in. Do you know what happened to Li Qian?"

"No."

"Weren't you worried about her?"

"Yes," she whispered, and hung her head. "But if my husband heard that I was mixed up with a thief, or if he found out the kind of things I had to do before I met him—"

"Did you hear from her at all, after that day?"

Yin dabbed at her nose with the handkerchief. "I talked to her once. The next day. I locked myself in the bathroom and called her, left a message asking if she was okay, asking if she wanted me to tell the Traffic Watchers what happened. She called back and said not to tell them. That she'd decided not to get married after all. It turned out the men in the van weren't police—they were the bosses of the bad men we worked for in Tokyo. I thought she'd be scared, but she told me that getting caught and taken back was the luckiest thing that ever happened to her. The one driving the van was an important man's son. He had a movie business. He said he was going to make her a star."

•

"The driver of that van had to be Koji Yamamoto!" Kenji couldn't hide his excitement as he climbed back into the car.

"How do you know?" Yumi started the engine.

Kenji told her what Aya had said about Koji's porn business.

Yumi wrinkled her nose and pulled onto the street. "Do you really think he was planning to turn Li Qian into an adult video star?"

Kenji pondered the possibility. The abduction had happened on November 28th. The second Painted Doll victim had died five days later.

"He would have had to work awfully fast to put her in a movie," Kenji said. "She died less than a week later."

Yumi nodded.

"You know," she said, "according to Jack Goldman's article, she was wearing professional makeup when they found her—maybe that was because she'd just finished a video shoot. Wouldn't that suggest her murderer was involved in producing it?"

"Yes," Kenji agreed.

But how could he find someone who had helped Koji Yamamoto produce his sick trash? If the videos violated obscenity standards—for sex or violence or both—he wouldn't be able to just go online and comb the net porn, looking for Li Qian's face, hoping to get lucky. Illegal stuff was sold on sites you needed an invitation to access.

"Jack told me there were five Painted Doll victims," said Yumi. "I wonder why he thought they were connected. All of them must have crossed paths with the killer somehow—maybe if you looked at the other cases, you'd find the common thread." She hesitated. "Are you sure you don't want me to ask him?"

Kenji watched the bare trees flashing by outside. Jack Goldman might be able to give them new information, but was it worth the risk? What if the reporter started digging again, and Koji found out they were looking at him for the Painted Doll murders? The *oyabun*'s second son hadn't escaped prison all these years by being stupid—he'd constructed an elaborate web of informants around himself, and the moment he felt the slightest tremor at the far edge, he'd send an underling to deal with it and sever any threads connecting the problem to himself. In the process of distancing himself from the Painted Doll murders, he might also destroy evidence linking him to Kenji's mother's "accident."

Kenji sighed. "I'm sorry, Yu-chan. I just can't take the risk."

They eased to a stop at the junction with the road that would take them back to Tokyo. The arrow pointing in the opposite direction read "Ise Shrine."

"We're awfully close," Yumi said. "What do you think?"

Kenji hesitated. A detour to the Ise Shrine would mean they'd get back to Tokyo long after midnight. On the other hand, for years he'd felt he owed the Shrine's *kami-sama* a prayer of thanks, because building a model of the main building was what had first thrown him and Yumi together.

"Yes," he said. "Let's go."

•

The late-afternoon sun slanted through the branches overhead as Yumi and Kenji inched up the steps to the Grand Shrine at Ise, waiting to pay their respects. All around them, lofty green sentinels brooded in fragrant silence. This grove of ancient cedars had already been towering over the shrine buildings when samurai trod the wide granite stairs. Ahead, a massive pi-shaped *torii* gate crafted of peeled logs marked the spiritual gateway to a portal set into the high fence surrounding the sacred ground. A wide, slatted, offering box crouched below the roofed gate, and purple curtains emblazoned with the imperial chrysanthemum crest hung behind, shielding the holy of holies from commoners' eyes.

Kenji advanced another step, wondering how he was going to find a porn video featuring a Chinese girl with a gap between her front teeth. If it even existed. He needed someone with special knowledge of the underground distribution sites. Maybe Oki knew someone in Vice who—

Yumi handed him a hundred-yen coin, and Kenji looked up to see that only two couples now stood between them and the offering box. His cheeks burned, ashamed he'd been thinking about sifting through porn sites while approaching the holiest spot in Japan. They climbed another step, and Kenji tried to compose his thoughts.

The couple in front of them turned aside, and Kenji stepped up to the box next to Yumi. Together, they tossed their coins, heard them clatter between the slats. Bowing twice, they clapped their hands.

Thank you for good health. Please let my dad be okay. Thank you for Yumi.

How many times had he stood next to his mother like this, on the steps of the Komagome Shrine?

Show me what happened to her. Tell me what to do.

A breeze riffled his hair and Kenji looked up as the wind lifted the curtain that hung behind the offering box, giving them a glimpse into the holy places beyond. A collective sigh rose from the crowd behind and he felt a jolt of the power that centuries of intense prayer had given this spot. Stunned for a moment, he stood motionless, then remembered to step aside to let the next petitioners approach.

Had Yumi felt it too? She looked up at him and took his hand. Without a word, they made their way back toward the entrance.

Peasants and merchants and warriors and princes had all brought their hopes and fears and desires to this place. How many had gone away with what they sought?

Feeling lucky, he knew that today the gods had spoken to him. The curtain had lifted, and he'd understood. The *kami-sama* could open doors, but it was up to him to walk through them. There was one standing wide open in front of him, but he'd been refusing to take advantage of it. It was time to take a leap of faith.

He turned to Yumi. "Your friend. The journalist. Do you really think we can trust him?"

SUNDAY, JANUARY 11

•

Yumi looked up from the vocabulary she was studying for her next translating job, as Jack Goldman's shadow fell across her table. All around, Bo Peep Lolitas and Sailor Moon lookalikes were enjoying their afternoon tea.

"Hi," she said, pulling out her earplugs. "Thanks for coming."

He slid into the seat opposite and looked around curiously. The Tea Four Two was a favorite meeting spot for cosplayers, serving up cake sets and cream puffs, with a slice of fantasy. Pink was the predominant color, and each booth was swagged with lacy curtains, allowing the customers to enjoy just the right mix of privacy and exhibitionism.

"Is this where you always work?" he asked.

Yumi laughed. "No. But every once in a while it cheers me up to be called Your Highness."

"I'll remember that."

She rang the little brass bell on their table and their waitress arrived. Jack ordered coffee, black, then pulled a thick manila envelope from his briefcase.

"This is it," he said, handing it to her. "But I'm curious—why did you want hard copies?"

"I need to share them with my detective friend, but his computer belongs to the station where he works. If I send him electronic files, he's afraid the task force might get their hands on them."

"Ah. He's almost paranoid enough to be a reporter."

She picked up the envelope.

"Okay if I look?"

"Sure."

She opened the flap, then hesitated. "Is there anything in here I shouldn't take out in public?"

"If you mean autopsy photos, no. My friends at the crime lab aren't that friendly. And the shots I took at the crime scenes all look like stills from TV dramas. Japanese dramas," he added, "not American."

Yumi smiled. On Japanese crime shows, victims died fully made up, the violence that killed them communicated by a few artistic bruises or an attractively pouty split lip.

She drew five paperclipped stacks of paper from the envelope.

"They're in order—first victim to last," he said.

The Korankei victim's was halfway through the pile. Yumi looked up.

"I thought the girl abducted at Korankei was the second victim?"

"So did I, at the time I wrote that article. But she's actually the third. I discovered there was another death that matched the killer's pattern six months before the 'first' Painted Doll killing. That girl was Thai, illegal, worked as an office cleaner, but moonlighted making adult videos. She was found dumped in a gutter in Adachi wearing full makeup, her hair styled. The police didn't connect her to the second victim because she was dressed like a classic Office Lady. And she'd been strangled, not stabbed."

"What about the others? Did they die the same way?"

"Not all of them. Three were strangled, two were stabbed."

"By Shark?" Kenji had given her permission to tell Jack what they knew, so she'd brought him up to speed when she called to ask for his files.

Jack frowned. "I don't doubt Shark is capable of killing, but he'd only do it as a means to an end. He's a brute, but he was smart enough to start out as Koji's minder and end up managing the Yamamoto-*gumi* sex trafficking trade. He didn't get there by killing off the girls who bring home the bacon." He finished his coffee. "On the other hand, Koji Yamamoto's got a reputation for liking it rough, and there have been rumors about him for years. He's a more likely suspect, but if I could prove that, I'd have half a dozen shiny awards on my shelf."

He stood, fishing in his pocket for change.

"No, this is on me," Yumi said. "Remember? I owe you."

The reporter laid a five-hundred-yen coin on the table, and smiled. "I prefer to keep it that way. I'll be in touch."

MONDAY, JANUARY 12

•

It was the longest Monday morning Kenji could remember, as the clock ticked slowly toward noon. The envelope Yumi had dropped off radiated temptation from his middle desk drawer. Finally, the squad room began to empty. Kenji retrieved the journalist's files and toted his laptop to Interview Room Three. He twirled the blinds shut.

Laying out the pictures of all five victims on the coffee table, he stood back and surveyed them. Were they really connected?

Opening his laptop, he began to take notes as he read through the material Jack Goldman had collected. All five had been found on back streets, but in different residential neighborhoods all over Tokyo: Adachi, Ueno, Shimbashi, Kita-Senju, Uguisudani. They'd all worked in the lower echelons of the sex trade: adult videos, sex services "health clubs," costume fetish bars. They were all Asian, and they'd all been professionally styled and made up.

Looking at their photos side by side, he noticed a few other similarities. The clothes they wore could almost pass as ordinary street wear and uniforms, but the roles they represented were common in fetish fantasies: Office Lady, flight attendant, nurse, schoolgirl, tour guide. They'd all been found without shoes. And all but the first one had the same haircut.

The profilers would say that meant the Painted Doll killer was a psychopath, compelled to kill a certain "type" again and again. But had the victims all died in the same way? Kenji flipped through Jack's notes. No. Strangled, strangled, stabbed, strangled, stabbed. That didn't fit the typical serial killer model—usually psychopaths didn't stray that far from their sick personal scripts.

He looked up the victims' former employers and plotted their addresses on a map with his GPS. All within half a kilometer of each other, in Kabuki-chō. Yamamoto-*gumi* territory? He moved to the window and parted the blinds to see if Oki had returned. Yes, he was standing by his desk, showing Aya a photo of one of his judo students. Kenji pulled out his phone and called.

The big detective came through the door, and Aya closed it behind them. Kenji showed them his map.

"Sorry, can't say for sure," Oki said, studying the five dots as Aya drifted toward the photo array on the table. "The territory lines have probably shifted a dozen times since I grew up."

"That's her!" Aya gasped, snatching up the first victim's photo.

Kenji and Oki turned.

"On that DVD I told you about. The one that made me sick. A guy was chasing this woman through a forest."

Kenji joined her. "Are you sure?"

"I recognize that striped sweater and I remember her stumbling in that blue skirt, because it was so tight, she couldn't run very well. But where are her shoes? She was wearing high heels." She glanced at Kenji. "The kind that have red soles."

No wonder she'd thrown them in Koji's face.

"When she stopped to hike up her skirt and kick off her shoes so she could run faster, they fell on their sides. The soles were the only red things in the forest, until—"

She stopped, swallowed.

"Do you remember the name of the DVD?"

Aya paced the interview room, trying to recall. "Something about hunting," she said with a shudder. "I think it was something about hunting."

"And it was shot in a forest, you said? Where?"

"I don't know. When I first started watching, I thought it was a horror movie about those creepy suicide woods near Mt. Fuji, but then the guy caught her and ripped off her clothes and—" She stopped.

"And what?" Kenji prompted.

She flushed and dropped her gaze. "He raped her and—"

"And killed her?" Oki supplied, his face grim.

"I ran to the bathroom to throw up after the violence started. I was only seventeen, and it looked so real."

"Maybe it was," Oki said.

"You mean they actually killed her on camera?" Kenji said, shocked. That would explain why Koji couldn't allow anyone to connect him or Shark or his van to one of the victims. "Do you know where I could get a copy?"

Aya looked at him with horror. "Sir?"

Oki tapped his chin with his pen. "I have a friend on the Vice Squad at Shinjuku Station. He shoots pictures of flowers in his spare time, says it helps him forget the filth he has to watch for his job. He's a walking encyclopedia of what's out there, though—if that film was made in Japan, he'll know about it. Maybe he'll even have a copy."

•

"Where did you get these?"

Oki's friend Detective Takei looked up from the photos Kenji had spread out on the table in the Shinjuku Station interrogation room. A slight man with sad eyes, he and Detective Oki had grown up together in Kabuki-chō and been partners as rookies. They must have made an odd pair, the bulldog and the chihuahua.

Takei had shut the blinds and closed the door when Kenji appeared with Jack Goldman's Painted Doll files, making sure nobody with ties to the elite murder squad could walk by and see what they were looking at. According to Oki, the Vice detective had quite a collection of commendations he'd received for "assisting" the First Investigative Division after they swanned in to commandeer one of his cases, and he had no desire to add to it.

"Do you recognize any of them?" Kenji asked.

"Yeah, except for that first one, they all look like Mana Pink Star."

"Who?"

"Porn actress," he said. "Are these Mana wannabes, or what?"

"They're murder victims."

Takei frowned, picking up the first photo. "Same guy did them all?"

"I think so."

"There's a serial killer on the loose and nobody knows about it?" Takei said skeptically. "Don't tell me—the almighty profilers think it's some creep who gets his kicks from whacking Mana-*chan* again and again?"

"That's one theory," Kenji said. "Tell me—if someone was making knock-offs of this actress's videos, where would I look?"

"Depends."

"On what?"

"Whether you're looking for the garden-variety ones or the famous ones."

"Famous ones?"

"They're what we call 'Special Interest Items.' Distributed over the internet, on sites you need an introduction to find. I could give you a couple of URLs, but you'd have a pack of Headquarters boys on your doorstep the second you click the 'I'm a legal adult' button."

"Why?"

"Mana churned out plenty of everyday *ero*, but she got famous by dying. Her specialty is sex and violence, way beyond anything you'll find in the S&M section at your local video store. I had to watch one of hers, about three years ago. It looked like the real deal. To this day, I'd swear it was a genuine snuff film, not faked. I saw the knife go in, saw Mana's blood spray in a classic arterial arc, saw the light go out of her eyes." The corners of his mouth turned down in disgust. "Took a few days off after that, went to Hokkaido to shoot about a thousand pictures of late-blooming cherry trees."

"She died on camera?"

"No, that's the problem. She didn't. Mana Pink Star died five, maybe six times, on screen. All totally believable. If they gave Oscars for death scenes, she'd have a shelf of 'em." He shook his head. "Something about those movies stinks, but we've never been able to get our hooks into the guy who made them."

"Koji Yamamoto?"

"Yep. Ten years ago, when he made those films with Mana, he was just getting started. Made a couple for practice, then discovered Mana and made her a star. We came close to nailing him one time when a guy we had in lockup for distributing that garbage told us Koji not only financed the video, he produced it. He said the violence wasn't faked, that a girl really died at the end."

"And?"

Takei gave a short laugh. "Our informant was ashes in an urn before he could sign a statement."

"Koji got to him, even in jail?"

"Like a knife going into a block of tofu."

Kenji picked up Jack's photo of the woman from Korankei. "Koji told this girl he was going to make her a star. You recognize her from any of his videos?"

Takei took the picture, studied it, then a strange look passed over his face. He pulled his laptop over, typed in a password, did a search, scanned the screen. Clicked a link, then swiveled the laptop so Kenji could see.

"Look familiar?"

The figure in the video frame he'd pulled up was wearing a nurse's uniform just like the one the woman from Korankei had been found in, but her cheekbones were wider, her lips slightly fuller. And she didn't have a gap between her front teeth.

"That's not her," Kenji said, disappointed. "It looks like her, but it's not."

"I know. This is Mana Pink Star. In her second video, the one where she's stabbed twenty-three times." He looked at Kenji. "Tell me, how did your victim die?"

Kenji flipped through Jack's notes. Stopped. Read. Read it again.

"She was stabbed," he replied slowly. "Twenty-three times."

"Body doubles," Takei said, his voice rising with excitement. "They're all body doubles."

He leaned forward with a feral grin. "You know what I think? I think you and I are going to put Koji Yamamoto away for murder." He stood. "Let's go to the Vice Division library and check out that video. I hope you slept well last night, because this one will give you nightmares for weeks."

•

"There," Kenji cried.

Takei paused the video. The screen froze on a close-up of the actress's face. She looked more surprised than anything, in the moment when she realized she'd been stabbed. Her narrow eyes were widening, her lips parting to scream. And the gap between her teeth was something that hadn't been there a split second before, when she'd been begging for mercy and doing things that had been hard to watch.

The Vice detective captured a screen shot, a look of profound satisfaction on his face.

"I'd say it's a match," he said, holding up the crime scene photo of the girl from Korankei. "Do you want to request her autopsy records, or should I?"

"You might have better luck than me, but I have a feeling they won't give them to either of us."

"Why not?"

"There's a task force."

"What task force?"

Kenji told him what Yumi had learned from Jack.

Takei sat back in his chair. "Mori, huh? You think he's in charge?"

"Acts like it."

"Fucking career wonk. Thinks his fancy piece of paper from Tokyo University means the rest of us poor grunts live only to serve."

Kenji's own fancy piece of paper from Tokyo University hadn't gotten him any better treatment from Mori, but he didn't think it would help to mention that.

"You got any friends at the crime lab?" the Vice detective asked.

"Just Tommy Loud."

"The foreigner who married the SG's daughter?" Takei snorted. "If there's one guy who's lower on the totem pole than us, it's him." He shook his head. "That means we're shit out of luck, because my best source there retired last month."

"What about witnesses?" Kenji suggested. "There was an 'actor' whose face we never saw. And what about Mana Pink Star?"

"I'm afraid she won't be telling us anything. She's dead."

"Koji did her too?"

"Nah, she got hit by a truck."

"A brown van?"

"No idea. It happened in France. She went on holiday with a girlfriend and looked the wrong way before stepping off the curb. They drive on the other side of the road there."

"What about the actor? Or the cameraman? Any chance we can find them?"

Takei shook his head. "If they're still alive, the only reason is because they never talk about Koji Yamamoto."

"I guess we'd better give Mori what we've got, then. Let him try to put the guy away."

"No." Takei pounded the table. "I've been after Yamamoto since he first skated on a distribution charge. I want him to look me in the eye in court, and know that it wasn't some fancy-pants elite murder squaddie who took him down." He heaved himself up from his chair. "Keep thinking. I'm going to take a piss."

The door closed behind him and Kenji checked the message that had vibrated into his pocket earlier. It was from Yumi.

jack called, says shark was arrested this afternoon because his name is on the lease for the collapsed warehouse in shinjuku where a girl died. he's at shinjuku station now but jack says hurry because koji yamamoto will get him out before the 48 hours are up

Shark was downstairs in a holding cell right now? Kenji checked the time. 6:47. He groaned. The message had arrived nearly an hour ago. He should have checked his phone earlier. Had Koji already sprung him?

Detective Takei returned.

"We might have an alternative to taking this to Mori, if we're not too late," Kenji said, handing him his phone.

Takei's eyes darted over the message. "How will talking to Shark get us Koji? Even if he was there when they made those snuff flicks, he'll never roll over on his boss."

"What if he thinks he's the one who'll get the big drop instead?"

"How are you going to convince him of that?"

"I'll tell him I can prove he abducted the girl with the gap between her teeth, in the van that was used by the Painted Doll killer, five days before she died."

"How?"

"I'll show him the pictures."

"What pictures?"

"The ones my mother took."

Kenji filled the Vice detective in on how his investigation into his mom's death had sent him in search of the Painted Doll killer.

When he finished, Takei sat, staring at the photos of the abduction, then he nodded. "I think we can put this sonofabitch away." He looked at Kenji. "But you're the one with the evidence, so you take the lead. How do you want to play it?"

"Well, first we have to find out if Shark's still here. And who arrested him—Shinjuku locals or Mori's team?"

Takei stood and pulled out his phone.

"Good news," he said a few minutes later, ending the call. "He's still here. Mori's the one who picked him up, but we're in luck—the gatekeeper tonight down at the jail was my *kōhai*, and I'm sure he'll do his old mentor a favor. If we want to have a little chat with Shark-*san* off the record, I'm sure I can arrange it."

"Okay." Kenji stood. "Let's think this through."

He paced over to the whiteboard and began to write. "Here's what we can prove: Ten years ago, on November twenty-eighth, Shark abducted an illegal foreign woman at Korankei, using the van that was subsequently used by the Painted Doll killer. Five days after her abduction, she was killed on screen in the snuff video you just showed me, and her body was dumped in a way that matched the Painted Doll killer's pattern."

He paused. "And here's what we believe, but can't prove." He drew a line and started another column. "That Koji Yamamoto was driving the van that day at Korankei. That he's the one who made her the movie offer, dolled her up to look like his prize porn actress, and killed her—or had her killed—on camera. That he's the one who ordered someone—probably Shark—to get rid of the body afterwards."

Takei shook his head. "It's too circumstantial for the prosecutor. And if it's too circumstantial for the prosecutor, it'll be too circumstantial to get Shark to turn on his boss."

"The abduction isn't circumstantial. We can hook Shark on that, with my mom's photos. Photos he thinks he buried ten years ago, when he made sure my mother had an 'accident,' so she couldn't testify about what she saw."

"But even if he's convicted of abduction, what'll he get? One year? Two? That's not nearly serious enough to get a guy like Shark to take the stand against Koji Yamamoto." Takei thought for a moment. "Unless we can convince him that's not all we've got. We don't actually have to have the evidence as long as—"

"I know." Kenji frowned. "As long as he *believes* we have it."

"We'd need to find a weak point. Or make one up. Some detail so small he might have missed it at the time. Something that would really scare him if he thought we could prove it."

"If only we could get into those files." Kenji muttered, frustrated. He returned his attention to the five victim photos on the table.

Takei picked up the first one and studied it thoughtfully. "Maybe we can. Didn't this girl die before the first official Painted Doll victim? If your press piranha is right, Mori doesn't know it's connected."

"Which means," Kenji said, catching his drift, "the file wouldn't be behind the task force firewall."

Takei returned to his computer, accessed the police database, and ran a search. He clicked on a result, and breathed the word, "Yes!" He looked at Kenji. "No one has opened this file since it was shelved. Now we just have to find the video she starred in. You have any idea what it was called?"

"Yeah. It's got 'Hunting' in the title."

•

After three hours of mining the Vice Division files, Kenji was ushered by a turnkey into one of the visiting rooms in the bowels of Shinjuku Station.

The cold fluorescent lights did nothing to dispel the miasma of despair and longing that lingered in the room where prisoners could see through the glass to an open door, but not walk through it. Two molded blue plastic chairs sat in front of the speakhole in the partition, but only one of them would be used tonight. They'd decided it would be best if Detective Takei waited down the hall with the guard, listening in from a small room lined with video feeds. Kenji had welcomed the older detective's suggestion that he ask the questions, even though his less-than-flattering reasoning was that Shark would be less on guard if he thought he was being questioned by an inexperienced rookie.

Kenji pulled out one of the chairs and sat, a copy of the first victim's file on his lap. He closed his eyes and took a deep breath to steady himself. He felt like a kid, waiting to make a report in front of the class. A report that wasn't quite true. A report containing something sketchy that he hoped the teacher wouldn't catch. He moved the folder to the chair next to him. Opened it to make sure the pictures they'd printed out were in the right order. Wished he had a glass of water.

The door in the room beyond the glass opened, and a man dressed in a gray prison jumpsuit filled the doorway, followed by the guard who'd fetched him.

The passing years hadn't been kind to Koji's right hand man. Shark looked bigger now than when the picture at Korankei had been taken, and not all of the new bulk was muscle. Bags under his eyes were bruised dark with fatigue, and time had puckered a scar on his chin that he'd acquired since Korankei. Without his knit cap, the jailhouse stubble shadowing his scalp gave away the fact that he'd been trying to disguise his receding hairline by shaving his head. His file said he was thirty-eight.

Relieved of his chains, Shark stalked up to the glass and squinted at Kenji. "Who are you, asshole? Kinda young to be one of Mori's, aren't you?"

Kenji stood. "Detective Kenji Nakamura."

"Detective? I don't talk to anyone lower than Inspector," Shark grumbled, but he dropped into the waiting chair. "Let's get this over with so I can go back to bed."

Kenji sat and picked up the file. "All I want you to do is listen to a story. And look at some pictures."

"You're shitting me. It's the fucking middle of the night!"

Kenji pulled out the crime scene photo of the woman Jack Goldman believed was the first Painted Doll victim.

"Remember her?"

Shark glanced at her face. He leaned closer.

"No," he said, slouching back in his chair with studied disrespect. "Should I?"

"She starred in a little film called 'Girl Hunting' and she's the first woman Koji Yamamoto killed on camera," Kenji told him. "Before he got the idea of using foreign illegals as body doubles."

Shark snorted. "Okay, I get it now. Mori's just trying to fuck with me, waking me up in the middle of the night and sending in a newbie to hit me with every unsolved he's got. Tell him it ain't gonna work. Call him now. Wake *him* up." He stood. "I'm going back to bed."

"I guess I shouldn't be surprised you didn't remember her right away," Kenji said quickly. "She didn't live long enough to become a star, just long enough for your boss to discover how much money he could make from snuff films. She was the first Painted Doll victim, though, wasn't she?"

Shark returned to the window, eyes narrowed. "What did you say your name was?"

"What happened that night, Mr. Maeda? Was it an accident? Did Koji get a little carried away? Cross the line from acting to the real thing?"

Shark turned away and strolled to the far end, as if it afforded a better view.

"Afterward, he panicked, didn't he?" Kenji said. "Told you to get rid of the body. You dumped it all the way across town in Adachi. You even remembered to take off her shoes, to save them for the next movie. Because they were expensive, right? The French kind, with red soles? Bit of an artist, old Koji. Used them in all his movies, didn't he? He really shouldn't have given a pair to his fiancé, though. I hope they weren't the same ones."

Shark froze. Then he countered, "Anyone can buy shoes."

"Yeah, but he should have been more careful with things that are a little more personal. Like that ring. You never see his face in the video, but he forgot to take his ring off before he strangled her."

Shark turned. "What ring?"

"The ring he used to wear, ten years ago. You don't remember it? I'm sure you'd recognize it if I showed you the video. You never noticed it, did you?"

Shark stared at him, then threw back his head and laughed.

"You dumb fuck. If you're going to lie to me, do your homework, asshole. If the guy in the video was wearing a ring, you've got the wrong brother. Koji never wears rings. No rings, no chains, no watches. He hates shit like that. Says all it does is show people you've got money to burn and make them want a piece of it."

He stalked back and leaned close to the glass, putting his mouth right up to the speakhole. "Interrogation 101? You flunk, rookie." He straightened and turned to the guard. "We're done here."

"Wait!" Kenji said, as the guard stepped up to re-chain the prisoner. Kenji pulled out a printout of the photo Keiko had taken at the Ise Shrine. He pressed it against the glass. "What about these girls?"

Shark didn't even bother to look. "Don't know 'em."

"That's funny, because two weeks later, the one on the right ended up like this." Kenji held up the crime scene photo he'd gotten from Jack Goldman. "After you dumped her from a brown van with license plate Shinjuku-zero-seven-ma-four-four-oh-nine."

Shark flicked a glance at the picture Kenji was holding up to the glass. "Like I told your boss, I never saw that girl or drove a car with that plate number."

"Really? Because you're in a picture with it, chasing her friend through a parking lot at Korankei."

Shark turned, a pained expression on his face. "Oh, fuck me. Didn't Mori tell you he already tried that one? It's bullshit."

Kenji held up the photo from his mom's camera. Shark squinted at it, then he shuffled closer. Kenji pressed it against the glass.

"Where did you get that piece of photoshoppery?"

"It's not a fake. A witness took it."

"What witness?"

"The woman who was standing outside the bathroom at Korankei when you abducted the third Painted Doll victim. You don't remember the nice lady with the camera? She saw everything. And she'll testify. There's no statute of limitations for abduction leading to murder, you know. Whoever killed this girl is going to go down for all the others. So unless you tell us who the second guy in the van was, and convince us you were just an accessory, you'll take the weight for all of them when we put her on the stand."

Shark stared, then he gave a bark of laughter.

"Good luck with that, asshole. Ghosts don't make the best witnesses."

Kenji stood there, stunned, as Shark shuffled away and the guard followed him out the door. The only way Shark could know whom Kenji was talking about was if he'd been the one who killed her.

He leaned his forehead against the glass and pounded it with his fist.

Fuck. Fuck. Fuck.

He'd gotten nothing. Nothing but confirmation of what he suspected, but couldn't prove.

The door to the visiting room opened behind him.

"Well, it was worth a try," Takei said. Reading the disappointment in Kenji's slumped form, he added, "Don't be so hard on yourself, Detective. It couldn't be helped—the jewelry thing wasn't in Koji's file. It's just bad luck we tried the ring trick on the one gangster in Kabuki-chō who knows his boss never wore one."

Kenji dropped into the chair, still reeling.

"Go home and get some shut-eye," Takei advised. "You'll feel better in the morning."

"I won't." Kenji raised his eyes to the empty room beyond. "Because we both know this was our only shot. Tomorrow I'll have to call Mori and turn over what we've got."

TUESDAY, JANUARY 13

•

After a morning of interviewing more potential panty thieves, Kenji released Suzuki for lunch and wearily pulled out his phone. He no longer had any excuse to avoid calling Inspector Mori. Detective Takei had finally agreed to hand over what they had to the task force and hope Mori had better luck.

Kenji frowned at the display. Missed call, 11:12 a.m. Mori's number. He returned the call, was shunted to voicemail.

"Mori-*san*, this is Kenji Nakamura. I'm returning your call, but I also have some information that might be useful to you on the case you're working. Please call me back at your convenience."

He'd barely hung up when the phone began vibrating in his hand. Mori.

"This is Nakamura."

"What the hell did you think you were doing, interrogating my witness at one in the morning?"

"I—"

"What did you tell him?"

"Nothing, sir. I only asked him about some things having to do with my mother's death. And a few questions about a cold case that's not part of your investigation. But it's good you called me back, because I've uncovered some information that might help you get him for the Painted Doll killings. There's actually—"

"You're too late."

"What? What do you mean 'too late'?"

"Too late to make a case against Shark *or* his boss. Because I just spent the past hour listening to 'Stumpy' Utagawa confess to all the Painted Doll murders."

"Who is 'Stumpy' Utagawa?"

"Yamamoto-*gumi* lifer."

This was wrong. All wrong.

"Don't believe him," Kenji said. "He's lying. Koji Yamamoto is the one who—"

"Funny you should mention Koji Yamamoto," Mori spat. "He personally picked up Mr. Utagawa from his room at Tokyo General Hospital this morning and chauffeured him to the station."

"But that's crazy! Shark dumped those bodies, and Koji is responsible for their deaths. I'm sure of it."

"So am I." Mori's voice was ice cold. "But unless 'Stumpy' blows his lines and confesses to something that doesn't match the evidence, I'll be forced to take him before the prosecutor. Oxygen tank, wheelchair and all."

Kenji sat, dumbfounded. "I don't get it. He's admitting to multiple murders he didn't commit? Doesn't he know he could get the death penalty?"

"You ever play baseball, Nakamura? Ever heard of a sacrifice?"

"No way," Kenji said. "He's willing to die for Koji Yamamoto?"

"He's dying anyway. Cancer. Probably won't make it to trial, if there is one. And his family will be taken care of for life."

"No."

"Yes. Thanks to you, the real killer will go free."

"Inspector Mori, I swear, I didn't tell him anything that would compromise your investigation."

"Well, you certainly said something. Because last night when I went to bed, I had an accessory to quadruple homicides cooling his heels on a trafficking charge while we put together a strategy for getting him to roll over on his boss. This morning I awoke to find him packing his bags and debating whether to go to Yoshinoya or Mosburger for dinner."

"You're letting him go? You can't let him go. What about the trafficking?"

"That's going away too. Mr. Utagawa has apparently been very busy, despite the fact that he trails an oxygen tank like a pet dog everywhere he goes. So far he's confessed to four murders and being the kingpin of the trafficking branch of Koji's business. Those Chinese girls in that collapsed warehouse building? According to Utagawa-*san*, they were his. Shark didn't even know what was going on, he just signed the lease and paid the bills." Mori paused, then in a voice that could freeze the Shinobazu Pond he added, "As soon as I'm done with this fiasco, I'm going to bury you."

Kenji felt like he was going to black out. How could this have gone so wrong? All he'd done was talk to Shark about Korankei, and ask a few questions about the first victim, who—

"Wait!" Kenji cried. "Sir. There's another victim. One he probably didn't confess to, because nobody realized she was a Painted Doll victim. He killed her before your first case. On camera. Just like the others."

"'On camera'? What are you talking about?"

"You know the Painted Doll victims were all body doubles used in snuff videos, right? Videos that Koji and Shark—"

"Stop! Don't say any more." Mori lowered his voice and hissed, "Cellphones aren't secure. Get your ass over to Shinjuku Station right now."

•

"And you're sure that's all of them, Utagawa-*san*?" Mori asked. "The four victims whose pictures I showed you earlier, plus the Chinese girl who died in the earthquake?"

Through the one-way mirror, Kenji watched the wizened man in the wheelchair nod.

"Could you answer out loud, for the record, Mr. Utagawa?"

"Yes," the man wheezed, emphysema vying with the stomach cancer for which would kill him first. "I did all five of them."

"What about this woman?" Mori showed him the printout Kenji had held up to the glass last night for Shark. "Do you recognize her?"

Confusion suffused the old man's face. "Is this one of the ones you showed me before?"

"Look carefully. Take your time," Mori said, handing him the photo.

The old gangster pushed his reading glasses up on his nose and peered at the first victim's face. Frowned. "Can I speak with Mr. Yamamoto before I answer?"

"I thought Mr. Yamamoto had nothing to do with these crimes. Are you saying you think he might know something about this one?"

"No," the man answered quickly. "Of course not. It's just that—"

"Surely you remember if you killed her or not, Utagawa-*san*. That's not the sort of thing most people would forget."

"You're right," he said, his chin quivering. He handed the photo back. "Yes. I did it."

"Did what?"

"I killed her too."

"How?"

Utagawa's eyes darted around the room, as if looking for an answer.

"How?" he stalled. "I . . . oh!" He clutched at his chest. "I . . . the pain . . . I think I need a doctor."

Mori threw down his pen and stalked out of the room.

Kenji watched as Utagawa hunched over in feigned agony, then jumped as the door to the observation room flew open. Mori entered.

"Looks like you were right, Nakamura. He doesn't know anything about it. But that's not going to be enough to put away Koji Yamamoto unless we find more evidence tying him to that first murder, then link it up to the Painted Doll cases."

"What about the shoes, sir? With the red soles."

"I'm getting a warrant, but Koji would be an idiot if he still had them, and he's no idiot. What else do you have?"

He had nothing. Kenji sighed, shaking his head. If he'd had more, he wouldn't have had to try the trick with the ring.

"I'm sorry, but that's all, sir."

Mori gave him a cold stare. "Then you're dismissed."

"Yes, sir." Kenji bowed. He picked up his laptop and turned to go.

"Nakamura."

"Yes, sir?"

"If you ever interfere in one of my cases again, you'll be manning a police box in rural Hokkaido."

"Yes, sir. I understand, sir."

Mori moved to the one-way mirror and watched as two officers wheeled his prisoner out the door to the infirmary.

WEDNESDAY, JANUARY 14

•

It was only Wednesday, but it already felt like Friday. Kenji stared into his morning tea as it sat cooling on his desk, trying not to think about how much damage he'd done to his career in the past twenty-four hours. He'd never get into the First Investigative Division now. And the way things were going, he'd be lucky to be kept on at Komagome Station, because he couldn't even catch a panty thief. Yesterday, he and Suzuki had struck out with suspects 201 through 215.

"Sir? Excuse me for interrupting."

Kenji looked up. "Yes, Suzuki?"

"I had an idea last night, sir. My family bought a new TV this week, and while I was calling the oversize garbage haulers to take the old one away, I realized they weren't on our list."

Kenji sat up. Suzuki was right. They'd forgotten about the *sodai gomi* men. Trucks that picked up oversize garbage regularly crawled through every Tokyo neighborhood, broadcasting their pitch to relieve homeowners of old bikes, appliances and electronics—anything too unwieldy or troublesome for Tokyo Sanitation to haul away. Everyone tuned them out, unless they had some oversized trash that needed getting rid of.

"Good work, Suzuki. Call around and find out which ones operate in Komagome, and whether they have scheduled routes."

"I already did, sir. And we're in luck—he'll be making his rounds this afternoon, starting at two."

Kenji checked the time. "Okay. But we've got a few hours before then. I'll meet you at the elevator in ten minutes to go after the rest of the deliverymen on our list."

"Yes, sir."

Suzuki strode back to his desk with a spring in his step.

"What's with him this morning?" asked Aya, arriving to leave a file for Detective Oki. "He looks like he just won the lottery."

"No, just some *sodai gomi*."

"Oversize junk?" she said. "Ah, is this about your panty thief?"

"Let's hope." Kenji said.

Aya lingered.

"What can I do for you, Assistant Detective?"

"I was just wondering what happened when you met with Detective Oki's friend on the Vice Squad. Sir."

"We found your *Girl Hunting* video. It was every bit as revolting as you said. Turns out, the victims were body doubles for a porn actress known as Mana Pink Star, who's famous for films in which she seems to die at the end. Only she wasn't the one who died—the real victims were those poor foreign illegals, made up to look like her."

Aya didn't attempt to hide her disgust. "That sounds like something Koji would do. Do you think it'll be enough to get Shark to turn on him?"

"Unfortunately, no. We knew we didn't have quite enough to convince him, so Takei suggested a bluff he'd used before. The 'actor' in the video wasn't wearing a ring, but whoever strangled the woman in the final scene was. I told Shark we knew it was Koji's, and that's when we lost him. He just laughed, said Koji hated jewelry."

Aya groaned. "Why didn't you ask me, sir? I could have told you that Koji's brother is the one who does the bling."

"Wait a minute. Shark said the same thing. 'If he's wearing a ring, you've got the wrong brother.' Do you think it could have been Koji's older brother who killed the girl in that movie?"

"Was the ring gold? With a sort of dragon design?"

"Yes."

"That's his, all right," Aya said. "He won it from a Chinese gang boss in a dice game, then pissed the guy off by refusing to give him a chance to win it back. He made matters worse by wearing it around, telling the story to anyone who'd listen. The *tong* leader was so mad, he— Well, let's just say it was bad for business."

"How long ago was this?"

"I must have been in high school. So . . . eleven, twelve years ago?"

"Thanks, Kurosawa. I'll see what Mori's merry men can do with that."

Kenji dialed the Inspector.

"What now, Nakamura?"

"I might have a lead on that ring."

"What ring?"

"The one Takei-*san* and I spotted in the first snuff video's death scene. The one I lied about when I told Shark it tied the girl's murder to Koji Yamamoto. The actor in the first part of the movie wasn't wearing any jewelry, but the guy who strangled her was. Something Shark said to me last night was just confirmed by another source—Koji never wore a ring with a dragon design, but his brother did."

"Yoichi?"

"Yes. Apparently he took it off a Chinese gang boss. Wore it around to piss the guy off."

"Do you have a picture?"

"No, but Detective Takei at Shinjuku Station can make a screen shot if you want one."

"Get it to me ASAP."

•

"And at the next corner, he's going to turn right," Suzuki predicted, consulting the color-coded incident map as he and Kenji followed a slow-moving pick-up truck with a rusty washing machine in the back and a row of stuffed Rilakkuma bears strapped to the bumper. They'd been following the oversize garbage man on foot for over forty-five minutes. Kenji's feet hurt, but at least it wasn't raining today.

"Old bicycles . . . broken microwaves . . . television sets . . . appliances. . . ." sang a voice from the loudspeaker mounted on the truck. The recording had been made by a honey-voiced woman, but the driver was a man.

Sure enough, the truck rounded the next corner, perfectly tracing the route the panty thief had carved through Komagome. When they reached the corner, they found he'd pulled over in front of a small apartment building and was ringing the doorbell at one of the units.

"What do you want to do, sir?" Suzuki asked.

"Let's see what he comes out with."

They retreated across the street to watch. A few minutes later, the junkman reappeared, wheeling a rusty bicycle with two flat tires. He hoisted it into the back of the truck, then grabbed a clipboard from the front seat and returned to the unit. Five minutes later he reappeared, tossed the clipboard into the cab, and set off again.

"We don't have probable cause to search him for any underwear he might have picked up along with that rusty bike," Kenji said. "But let's do a little 'traffic stop' and find out his name, shall we?"

They approached the truck, and Suzuki asked for the man's driver's license, copying the particulars into his notebook. He passed the license to Kenji, who glanced at it before returning it to the man in the truck.

"Were you aware that your right brake light appears to be out, Mr. Aoki?" Kenji asked him through the open window.

"No, officer. It must have just happened."

"Good thing we noticed it, then. Is this your regular route?"

"Yes. Once a week."

"Same day every week?"

"No, it varies. Why?"

Kenji smiled. "Actually, I might need to have some garbage hauled."

The man handed him a flyer. "Ten percent off your first pickup, if you call first."

Kenji nodded. "See you get that light checked, okay?"

As the truck pulled away, Suzuki showed Kenji the map, on which he'd checked off eight of the eleven victims' addresses as they passed. "Looks like a pretty close match to me, sir," he said.

"What about these other three?" Kenji asked, pointing to the ones off the route.

"Could be special pick-ups," Suzuki suggested. "Like the one I arranged for my family's old TV."

"Okay, call the company and find out if they collected oversize garbage near those addresses on the days of the panty thefts. Meanwhile, I'll run a background check on Mr. Aoki."

•

"Sorry," Kenji apologized again, as he and Yumi turned onto the narrow street in Toritsu-daigaku where Keiko Sato lived. "I know this isn't exactly the romantic evening we'd planned. You aren't mad at me, are you?"

Yumi smiled and shook her head.

Kenji's dad was working at the police box again tonight, so he'd invited Yumi to his house to make *sukiyaki* together. But Keiko Sato had returned his call from several days ago, just as they were unpacking the fixings. She apologized for being slow to respond to his request for an introduction to the witness that the trainman Harada had mentioned—she explained she'd been in Nagoya, visiting her new grandson.

Keiko hadn't recognized the witness's name, but she suggested that Kenji talk to her husband. Shin had worked at the neighborhood police box for nearly twenty years before being given the command at Jiyugaoka, and he knew everybody. She was sure he'd be happy to arrange a meeting, if they could come tonight. It was the only night this week he was free.

So here they were, stomachs growling, ducking through the old-fashioned gate in front of the Satos' building.

Kenji rang the bell. The door was opened by a slightly older version of the husband he recognized from Keiko's family photos.

Shin Sato introduced himself and invited them in, remarking that he hadn't seen Kenji since he was a boy, but he wasn't surprised at how tall he'd grown—his mother had been tall. Yes, he'd be retiring in a few years, just like Kenji's father, but he'd heard Kenji was on the elite career track. He was proud to say his own son had done the same.

When the pleasantries had been concluded, Kenji said, "Your wife may have mentioned that I tracked down the Toyoko Line supervisor who investigated my mother's death. Harada-*san* told me he thought my mom was hit by a car or truck, not a train."

Sato's eyebrows shot up.

"There were no witnesses to the accident itself," Kenji continued. "But one of your neighbors crossed the tracks shortly before it happened. I was hoping to talk to her, ask her if she remembers any vehicles parked near that crossing when she went to the station that night."

Sato nodded. "What's her name?"

Kenji pulled out his notes to check the *kanji*. "Looks like . . . Rui Okihara?"

"Okihara?"

Kenji passed him the notebook.

"Ah!" The older policeman smiled when he saw the characters. "Not Okihara. Ogiwara. Everybody knows her, and

everybody mispronounces her name. But they only do it once—
she gives you hell if you don't say it right."

"Do you think you could you introduce us?"

"I'd be glad to. Let me give her a call. She doesn't go out
much anymore, but I know she'd appreciate it if we gave her
some warning. Excuse me a moment."

He disappeared down the hall to phone, and returned a
few minutes later. Ogiwara-*san* would be happy to see them,
although she apologized in advance for the quality of her tea.
Sato ushered them back out to the street, and steered them
down the narrow lane, away from the tracks.

As they turned onto a cross street, Kenji took the
opportunity to ask about a loose end that was still bothering
him. "Sato-*san*, do you happen to know why my mother was in
this part of town on the night she died? Toritsu-daigaku is kind
of far from Komagome, so it doesn't seem as though she'd just
be passing through on the way home from doing one of her
usual errands."

"I believe she came to see Keiko," he replied. "They'd just
been on a trip together."

"But Keiko-*san* told me she wasn't home when my mom
arrived. That she'd been out visiting her mother, and was
surprised to find the two of you talking in the entry when she
returned. The thing is, my mom used to lecture me and my
brother about calling before we went to see anyone, because
otherwise we might catch them at an awkward time. We used
to laugh about it, since our baseball buddies would never drop
what they were doing to serve us tea. I can't believe my mother
would come all the way out here to see Keiko-*san* without
calling first, to make sure she was home. She must have been in
the neighborhood for some other reason, but I can't figure out
what it was. Did she say anything to you?"

Sato thought for a moment, then he shook his head.
"Sorry. I wish I could help you."

The gate squeaked as they turned in at an old-fashioned wooden house wedged between two apartment buildings. Instead of an entry garden, hundreds of different-sized *maneki neko* cat figures were crowded onto the small patch of dirt in front of Mrs. Ogiwara's house, welcoming them with raised paws. Sato led the way up a narrow path.

The tiny woman who answered his knock was so hunched, she had to twist her head to the side to look up at Kenji.

"Well, you're a handsome young man. Come in, come in." She stood aside, so they could enter. "It's too cold in the *genkan* for introductions," she called over her shoulder, scuttling down the hall like a little crab. "Put on some slippers and come in, while I fetch us some tea."

They reluctantly gave up their winter boots and donned hard straw slippers sized for people who had grown up before the war. Their heels hung off the backs, but it was better than walking on the chilly *tatami* mats in their socks. The fact that Mrs. Ogiwara had answered the door bundled in layers of sweaters and a fleecy scarf told them she probably wouldn't be offended if they kept their jackets on. They caught up with her in the kitchen, but she shooed them into the main room, where a heated *kotatsu* table sat, draped with a faded indigo quilt. They lowered themselves onto the floor cushions and gratefully stuck their legs into the island of warmth beneath the low table.

"Now," Mrs. Ogiwara said, appearing with a tray of lacquer saucers and thick Mino-ware teacups. "What were your names again? Sato-*san* told me over the phone, but I forgot."

They scrambled to their feet to bow and introduce themselves.

She twisted her torso to peer at Kenji, then Yumi, and waved them back under the *kotatsu*, saying, "Sit, sit, stay warm. My name is Ogiwara. That's Ogi, not Oki, and Wara, not Hara. Sorry, I can't bow too well anymore. Pretend I did."

She hobbled back to the kitchen for the teapot and a bowl of seaweed-wrapped rice crackers.

"Help yourself, help yourself," she said, pouring tea first for her guests, then herself. She settled the teapot onto a ring made from woven rice straw, then fetched a pair of enormous black-framed spectacles that looked like they'd been made for a man. Settling them on her nose, she twisted to the side and studied her visitors with interest.

Shin Sato explained, "We wanted to ask you about that accident at the train crossing."

"Accident? There was an accident?"

"Ten years ago," Kenji answered. "I know it's ancient history, but the one I'm interested in happened ten years ago, in December."

"Oh, that one. How could I forget? My back's gone, not my brain. Not sure what I can tell you, though. Didn't see it myself." She took a sip of tea and reached for a cracker.

"Can you just tell us what you remember about that night?" asked Kenji.

"Well, what I remember is that I fell asleep. In thirty-seven years, I'd never been late to the station to meet my husband, but the night before our thirty-eighth wedding anniversary, I fell asleep. Woke up five minutes before the train was supposed to be pulling in. So I grabbed my coat and ran out the door. But I shouldn't have wasted my breath—there was a delay on the line. Got there in plenty of time to tidy my hair and put on some lipstick before my husband came through the gate. He never guessed I almost missed him that night, and I never told him." She leaned toward Yumi conspiratorially and said, "You've got to learn to keep a few secrets when you're married thirty-seven years."

"And when you walked back," Kenji said, "you didn't see my mother?"

"Your mother?" Mrs. Ogiwara turned to Sato. "You ought to have told me the lady who had the accident was his mother."

Sato bobbed his head. "Sorry, ma'am."

"I'm sorry for your loss," she said to Kenji. "How old were you?"

"Sixteen."

"Hard to lose your mother like that. Hard."

Kenji took a sip of tea. "So, you didn't see her on the way to the train station. But what about when you returned?"

Mrs. Ogiwara shook her head. "Didn't see her then either, because we went home a different way. My husband liked to have a few skewers of *yakitori* at the standing bar near the *pachinko* parlor, so on the way home, we always crossed the tracks at the underpass down by the station, instead of the one up here."

"Did the police ask if you saw any strange vehicles parked in the neighborhood that night? Cars? Trucks? Vans? Ones that weren't usually here?"

"No."

"'No' you didn't see any, or 'no' they didn't ask?"

"They didn't ask." Her brow furrowed in concentration for a moment, then she shook her head. "I can't remember if I saw anyone on that night or not. But I do make a habit of keeping a lookout, because sometimes people park illegally outside the Lawson, that convenience store on the corner opposite the Satos' house. The 'no parking' notice is a little faded and hard to see; people don't realize that if they park there, nobody can turn. It was really a nuisance before I started reporting them."

"Reporting them? At the police box?"

"Yes. I'd march straight to the *koban* next to the station and tell them, then the officer would get on his bike and ride over to make them move. After paying the fine once, they didn't do it again. Now we don't have much of a problem, except with first-timers."

"But you didn't see a van that night? A brown one?"

She shook her head, unsure. "I can't remember. I saw vans parked there plenty of times, but I can't say if that night was one of them. You could ask at the police box, though. If I reported something that night, they'd have a record of it."

•

"Let me see if I can find that for you, sir," said the officer on duty at the Toritsu-daigaku police box. "I'm afraid the date you're asking about was too long ago to be in our computers, so I'll have to dig up the old logs in back. It might take a few minutes."

"Thank you," Kenji said, putting away his badge. "Take your time."

A few minutes later, the officer returned with a thick tome and set it on the desk with a *thunk*.

"December fourth, right?" He heaved the log over to start at the back. *Flip, flip, flip.* Then he stopped, his finger tracing a line down a column on the right hand page. Frowned. Looked at Kenji. "Are you sure it was the fourth, sir?"

"It might have been reported after midnight," Yumi suggested. "Which would have made it the fifth."

The officer turned the page and said, "Ah. Is this it?"

He swiveled the log so Yumi and Kenji could see the first entry.

Incident #1702, Sunday, December 5, 12:11 a.m.—Illegally parked van, blocking fire lane. Dark brown, license plate 目 黒 0 7 は 3 0 2 9. *Investigating officer: Ryo Iwata. Incident reported by: Rui Ogiwara.*

Damn. The description of the van matched the one his mother had seen at Korankei, but the license plate didn't. Kenji double-checked the date and time, hoping there was some mistake. There wasn't. But next to Rui Ogiwara's name there was a notation written in red ink, circled. 12/6 01738

Hoping the first numbers referred to a date, Kenji paged ahead to Monday the sixth, and ran his finger down the column until he reached

Incident #01738 Stolen license plate.

Two days after his mother's accident, a neighborhood man had reported that someone had stolen the license plate from his car, which he had left parked in his carport while he was on a business trip. They'd replaced his plate with one he didn't recognize. The stolen plate was 目黒０７は３０２９. The one that attached in its place was 新宿０７ま４４０９.

It matched the number on the brown van in the photo taken at Korankei.

THURSDAY, JANUARY 15

•

The sun had not yet cleared the horizon as the night crew in the squad room wrapped up their shifts. Kenji set his tea on his desk, and called Inspector Mori, hoping a voicemail would get his attention faster than a message buried in his email. It rang. He waited for the recorded greeting to kick in.

"This is Mori."

Kenji blinked. At six-thirty in the morning?

"Uh, this is Kenji Nakamura, sir. Sorry for calling so early. I didn't think you'd pick up. Can I, uh, ask you something about the van used to dump the second Painted Doll victim?"

Mori grunted.

"After you learned it was owned by Ace Cleaning, did the crime techs go over it?"

"No. It had disappeared by the time we discovered who owned it."

"Disappeared? How?"

"Stolen, supposedly. Why?"

"Because last night I talked to a witness who saw Shark's van in Toritsu-daigaku on the night my mother was killed, but it had Meguro plates. The van's Shinjuku plates were later found on a car parked a few blocks away. They'd been switched."

"What was the number on the stolen plates?"

"Meguro-zero-seven-ha-three-oh-two-nine. I know it's a long shot, but if that tag went through a toll plaza or Shark got a ticket while he was driving it . . . . "

"Don't get your hopes up." Click.

Kenji stared at his phone, not sure if he'd just been blown off.

"Sir? I think we've got him!"

Kenji looked up, startled. Suzuki was here already? The assistant detective hovered next to Kenji's desk, vibrating with excitement. He handed Kenji a copy of last night's incident report.

"Look here," he said, pointing to an entry halfway down the page. "Number oh-oh-oh-two-six-five. Another underwear theft. When this woman came home from work yesterday, she went out to her balcony to take in the laundry, and noticed that her panties were missing. Look at the address."

The same building where the *sodai gomi* truck had picked up the bicycle yesterday.

"Good work, Suzuki!"

"Thank you, sir. Should we bring him in for voluntary questioning?"

Kenji pondered the possible courses of action.

"No," he said with a grin. "Let's catch him in the act."

•

Yumi smiled at the officer manning the Toritsu-daigaku police box and said, "Excuse me?"

"How can I help you?" he replied, sitting a little straighter and adjusting his hat.

"I was here last night with Detective Kenji Nakamura, who was asking about an incident in the crime log from ten years ago. I'm sorry to bother you, but I was wondering if you'd let me take another look at it?"

"What was the date?"

"December fourth."

"Just a moment, please."

He disappeared into the back and returned with the log they'd seen last night. He opened the front cover.

"It might go faster if you start at the back," Yumi suggested.

"Oh. Right." He reddened and flipped the book over. Paged through it until he found the date. "Which incident are you looking for?"

"If you could just show me the page, I can find it."

He turned the book around.

Last night, while the officer had been searching for Rui Ogiwara's report of the illegally parked van, an earlier entry had caught her eye.

Incident #1697, Saturday, December 4, 1:16 p.m.— Vandalism and underage drinking. Suspect: Takeo Nakamura. Investigating officer: Shin Sato.

She closed the log and thanked the officer. An underage suspect with the same name as Kenji's older brother had been arrested on the day his mother had inexplicably gone to Toritsu-daigaku.

Yumi retraced her steps to the station and got on a train headed toward Jiyugaoka. The police box that Shin Sato commanded shouldn't be hard to find.

•

The day was nearly over by the time Kenji finished making arrangements to catch the panty thief. He'd called Yumi to ask if she'd help, and she'd agreed to make an appointment with the oversize garbage collector to pick up an old floor lamp and a bundle of broken umbrellas at ten the next morning. She'd also volunteered to hang two pair of underwear on the drying rack by the back door, so they could catch the thief in the act if he tried to steal them.

His phone rang. Yumi, calling back to confirm.

"Hi, Yu-*chan*. Did you have any trouble setting everything up?"

"No, he's coming at ten, just like you asked. Are we still on for dinner tomorrow night?"

"Yes. If everything goes to plan, I'll have to take the underwear thief in to book him and collect evidence from wherever he's keeping the stolen goods, but I should be done before dinnertime." He paused, trying to think of a meeting place. Remembering the *sukiyaki* ingredients they hadn't used last night, he said, "Tomorrow is my dad's regular poker night, and he won't be back until late. Why don't you come to my house and we'll make dinner together?"

"Sounds good. And guess what? I've got something to tell you."

"Really?"

"I went back out to Toritsu-daigaku today."

"Toritsu-daigaku? Why?"

The landline on his desk began to ring.

"Excuse me, Yu-*chan*, I'm sorry, but I've got another call and I have to take it, because it's the office line. Can I call you back?"

"That's okay, this can wait. I'll tell you over dinner tomorrow."

They ended the call and Kenji answered his landline. It was Inspector Mori.

"We found Shark's van," he said without preamble. "The license plate matched the one you gave me. He ditched it at a farm that belongs to his cousin, out in hell-and-gone Niigata. Some young cop who doesn't want to spend the rest of his career in rural nowhereland actually read the bulletin I sent out, and he pulled the cousin over when he spotted the plate. The van is on its way to Tokyo now, and I've got techs standing by to go over it with cotton swabs and tweezers."

"After all this time, do you think they'll find anything to tie it to the Painted Doll killings?" Kenji asked, his heart hammering.

"It's a long shot. Frankly, it's more likely we'll find something that will tie it to your mother's. Which is why I'm calling. I need a sample of her DNA."

Damn, how was he going to get that? His mother had been gone for ten years.

"I'll see what I can find, sir."

Mori muffled his phone and talked to someone, then came back to say, "They're telling me the van should be in Tokyo by midnight, so get the sample to me before then."

"I'll do my best. Thank you, sir."

"Don't thank me, Nakamura—I'm not doing it as a favor to you. If I can't get Shark for the Painted Doll murders, I damn well want to put him away for something."

"Yes, sir. I understand. I'll try to find something the techs can use for a DNA match. I'll get back to you."

What might still have some of his mother's DNA on it after ten years? Kenji called Tommy Loud, who picked up on the first ring.

"Thanks for taking my call, Rowdy-*san*," Kenji said, returning to his desk. "Got a quick question for you. What kind of things do people routinely leave their DNA on, besides hairbrushes, toothbrushes and drinking glasses?"

"Man or woman?"

"Woman."

"Is she a smoker?"

"No."

"Too bad. Can you trick her into drinking from a can of coffee? Or a bottle of tea?"

"Sorry," Kenji said. "She died ten years ago."

"That makes it harder. DNA degrades over time and—" Loud stopped. "Wait, is this about your mother?"

"Yes," Kenji admitted. "Inspector Mori found the vehicle that might have hit her, but if they find any evidence on it, we'll need a sample for a match. I was hoping you could help me figure out what to look for."

"Right," Loud said. He considered the possibilities. "It needs to be something that could only have been used by her, something that might still have intact cells or body fluids stuck to it. What about Kleenex? Any used tissues in the pockets of her clothes?"

"My aunt gave all her clothes away, I think."

"What about her purse?"

"I checked the pockets and didn't find anything like that, but I'll look again."

"Make-up," Loud said. "Do you still have any of her makeup?"

Kenji thought about what he'd taken from his mother's purse that night. Wallet. House keys. Reading glasses. Lipstick.

"What about lipstick?" Kenji asked.

"Possible."

"Nail file?"

"No."

"Okay. I'll give Mori the lipstick and hope for the best."

"And if you can't find any samples that belonged to her, the DNA of direct descendants—that means you—can be used to correlate hers with reasonable accuracy."

"'Reasonable'?"

"Fifty percent."

"Okay. I'll bring in the lipstick, and have them take a swab from my mouth, just in case. Can I do it tonight after work? Will anyone be there?"

"Yeah, a couple of my guys are working some rush thing Inspector Kobayashi got overtime approval for. When you get to the lab, call Shimoda and he'll come down to meet you in the lobby." He recited a cellphone number.

"Thanks, Rowdy-*san*." Kenji jotted it down. "I really appreciate it."

"Anytime," the crime tech said. Then he added, "I hope you catch the bastard."

•

Kenji handed the cotton-tipped swab to Tommy Loud's colleague Shimoda, and watched him seal it in a plastic evidence bag. It joined the one holding the carryall from the morgue, with the inventory sheet inside. He'd decided it would be better to give the lab the whole thing, so there would be no doubt about the chain of evidence.

Kenji stood. "Thanks. I appreciate you taking the time to help me."

"No, thank *you*," said Shimoda. "Rowdy-*san* is looking forward to watching Inspector Mori faint when he actually gets his test results 'yesterday.'"

Kenji's phone buzzed as he bowed his good byes. Out on the sidewalk, he checked to see who had called. Assistant Detective Aya Kurosawa. He returned her call. When she answered, her voice was nearly drowned out by the sound of traffic.

"Could you speak up, Kurosawa? I can't hear you."

"Sorry, sir. Just a minute, let me get behind this—" The background noise lessened somewhat. "Is that better?"

"Where are you?"

"Outside Koji Yamamoto's office building in West Shinjuku, sir. And so is Shark."

"What do you mean?"

"He's standing at the curb, with two big suitcases— Shit. *Shit*," she cursed. "That's Koji's car. It just pulled up to the curb. They're putting the bags in the trunk. *Fuck*. It looks like he's running."

What the hell? Mori had cut Shark loose this morning for lack of evidence. He was off the hook, home free.

"You sure he's not just taking a vacation?"

"Shark doesn't take vacations."

So why would he leave town? Unless his cousin had called him to tell him that Mori found the van and was hauling it back to Tokyo for testing. Maybe Shark feared they'd find something in it to tie him to Kenji's mom's 'accident.'

"Sir, he's getting in the back. The driver is closing the door. What do you want me to do?"

"Get in a cab. Follow them. As soon as you see where they're headed, call me."

"Yes, sir. I'll call you back."

No time to arrange for a squad car. He had to get to a train station, so he could set an intercept course as soon as he knew where they were headed. Ikebukuro Station would give him the most options. He took off at a trot.

His phone buzzed. Aya.

"Narita, sir. It looks like they're headed to Narita."

The international airport.

"Okay, stay with him while I figure out how to stop him."

"Uh, sir?"

"Yes?"

"I don't think I have enough cash to get me all the way to the airport."

Kenji groaned. Narita was a notoriously expensive ninety-minute taxi ride from metro Tokyo.

"Okay, stay on his tail and just sit tight while I figure this out."

"Hold on, sir." She covered the mouthpiece and exchanged a few sentences with the driver, then got back on the line. "My driver says that the Skyliner train out of Ueno will probably beat both cars there, because there's construction between here and Nippori."

"Right. I'm on my way. I'll get myself to Ueno Station and get back to you as soon as I have a plan."

"Yes, sir."

Kenji dodged into Ikebukuro Station and pelted down the steps, leaving commuters spinning in his wake. Slowed by the Friday night crowds pouring off eight separate train lines, he doggedly swam upstream toward the nearest Yamanote Line ticket gate. Taking the stairs two at a time to the platform, he jumped aboard a train just as the doors closed.

It was 7:18 now. According to the train route finder on his phone, it was possible to be at Terminals Two and Three by 8:36 or Terminal One by 8:41. Kenji groaned. He'd never been to Narita Airport, never flown anywhere outside of Japan. He hadn't realized there was more than one terminal.

He hunched over his phone and flouted train etiquette to call Aya. Cupping his hand over the mouthpiece and speaking in a low voice, he said, "I should be at the airport in an hour and twenty, but we don't know which terminal, so I need you to stay with him until you see where he's getting off. I'm going to call Mori and tell him what's going on, ask him to send back-up."

"Yes, sir." She hesitated, then said, "Uh, the driver tells me the fare will be about twenty thousand yen, sir."

"Tell him not to worry, I'll make sure he's paid. But now I've gotta run—I'm almost at Ueno."

The doors opened. Beeping himself through the exit with his train pass, he snaked his way through the crowd, cursing baby strollers, lovers, and lost tourists who stopped or changed direction for no apparent reason. Down the corridor and up the stairs, he finally hit a stretch of clear sailing that allowed him to sprint, slaloming between travelers sedately rolling their luggage. Five minutes later, he leapt aboard the train, and the doors sighed closed behind him. *Safe.* He leaned against the bulkhead, breathing hard. The train eased away and began to gather speed as a mellifluous voice welcomed him aboard the Skyliner.

He called Inspector Mori. *Damn.* Not picking up. Kenji left a message, telling him that Shark was en route to the airport, requesting instructions and backup.

He rang Aya.

"Where are you now?" he asked.

"Nishi-Nippori, I think."

"You've still got Shark in sight?"

"Yes."

"What's your estimated arrival time?"

"The driver says nine o'clock."

"Okay. Stay with him."

Kenji checked for a callback from Mori. Nothing. He made his way to his seat and stared out the window. If he didn't hear soon, there would be no time for backup to reach the airport. He and Aya would be on their own. But even if they figured out a way to make Shark miss his plane, they couldn't keep him from getting on the next one. They needed a legitimate reason to keep him in the country, and for that, they needed Mori.

Kenji returned to the no-man's-land between the cars and tried the Inspector again. This time he left a message about the DNA samples he'd dropped off at the lab, and urged him to call with something, anything, they could use to arrest Shark before he went through Security.

•

Kenji stepped off the train at Terminal Two, gambling that Shark would be using one of the many airlines that served smaller countries in Asia. It would be easy for him to disappear among the thousands of Japanese tourists who thronged the streets each day in countries like Thailand and Cambodia, places where the Yamamoto-*gumi* might have human trafficking partners or arrangements with gunrunners.

He called Aya as he stepped onto the escalator.

"I'm here," he said. "Terminal Two. If it looks like he's planning to fly out of Terminal One, call me right away. I'm going to find an ATM, then locate the terminal shuttle, in case I have to move in a hurry. Where are you now?"

"About fifteen minutes away." She hesitated, then asked, "Is Inspector Mori sending back-up?"

"I haven't been able to reach him yet." Kenji showed his badge at the ID check at the top of the escalator and was waved though. "If he doesn't get back to me in time, we're on our own. We can't let Shark get past Security, or he's as good as gone."

"I understand, sir. What's the plan?"

"I'm working on it." He ended the call and looked around for an ATM. Saw the information desk instead and ran over to ask where he could get cash and catch the terminal shuttle.

He was stuffing ¥30,000 into his wallet and waiting to cross to the shuttle stop when his phone buzzed.

Mori. Finally.

"What the hell is going on, Nakamura?"

"One of my colleagues spotted Shark getting into Koji Yamamoto's car with two big suitcases around seven-fifteen tonight, sir. She's on his tail, and as of five minutes ago, he was about fifteen minutes from Narita. It looks like he's fleeing the country, sir. Is there anything we can do to stop him?"

"Goddamnit. *Goddamnit.*" Mori fumed. "Is your colleague alone?"

"Yes, but I'm at Narita, Terminal Two, waiting to meet her and intercept Shark. If you give me the go-ahead, sir."

"Okay," Mori said. "The flatbed with the van on it will be here in less than two hours. I called Loud and he'll be there when it arrives, but even if we find something, it'll take time to run DNA tests on the sample and get a warrant for Shark's arrest."

"Are you telling me to let him go?"

"No. Stall him. Be creative. Knock him out, if you have to, but don't let him get on that plane. I'm on my way with backup, but it'll take at least an hour, even with flashers and sirens."

"Yes sir. I'll do my best."

A shuttle bus stopped at the curb and the doors opened. The line began to move.

While he'd been on the phone with Mori, he'd missed a call. Aya.

"We just pulled up to the curb at Terminal One," she said.

"On my way."

The bus door was closing, but Kenji hammered on it, fumbling his badge up to the glass. The door opened and he jumped on.

"Thanks," he said to the driver, grabbing a handhold near the door. "How long will it take to get to Terminal One?"

"Ten minutes, sir."

Kenji prayed for long lines and inefficient clerks at whatever airline Shark was flying. His phone buzzed again. Aya.

"I'm at the Terminal One curb with the driver, waiting for you to get here and pay him, but I can see through the glass that Shark is standing in the check-in line at Thai Airways."

"Is the line long?"

"Long enough, I hope."

"I'm on the bus. Be there in three minutes."

When the shuttle doors opened, he hit the ground running. Kenji shoved two ten-thousand-yen notes into the hand of the taxi driver, then he and Aya dashed into the terminal, dodging travelers and porters.

Up ahead, they could see that Shark was next in line.

"What about Inspector Mori?" Aya asked, as they badged their way past the customer service rep and trotted to a position between the check-in desk and Security.

"He's on his way. But we've got to keep Shark on this side of Security until he shows up."

They watched an attendant help Shark navigate the check-in kiosk. His suitcases were hoisted onto the scale, one by one. They looked heavy.

"How are we going to stall him, sir?"

"Mori said to knock him out if we had to, but as tempting as that is, I'm afraid that'll just get airport security on our backs. We've got to figure out a way to convince them to detain him. What do you think is inside that carry-on?"

"Money," she said grimly. "And lots of it. But I doubt that will help us—it'll all be perfectly legal."

"What about his passport? Could it be a fake?"

"Doubtful. All the really guilty guys keep legit papers, in case they have to disappear."

"Shit," Kenji said, as Shark took his boarding pass and began wheeling his carry-on bag in their direction. "Looks like we're going to have to do this the hard way."

•

Kenji and Aya set an intercept course with Shark. As he detoured around a Chinese tour group sitting on their bags, Kenji stepped in front of him, badge out.

"I'm going to have to ask you to come with me, Maeda-san."

"Huh?" Then he recognized Kenji and frowned. "What are you doing here, rookie? Get out of my way."

He tried to sidestep them, but Kenji blocked his way.

"We've got some unfinished business, Mr. Maeda. You're not going anywhere until you tell me what happened that night in Toritsu-daigaku," Kenji said, trying to keep his voice steady.

"What are you talking about?"

"I'm talking about the night you killed my mother."

"Your mother?" Shark stared at him, then threw back his head and laughed. "The lady with the camera was your *mother*? Okay, now I get it—the midnight visit, the half-baked case. You think I made your mommy have an accident?" He narrowed his eyes. "Then get a warrant. And get out of my way, asshole, I've got a plane to catch."

He tried to shoulder past, but Kenji held his ground, grabbed his arm. Shark tried to break free and suddenly all the anger Kenji had been holding at bay found its target. He hooked his leg through Shark's and swept him off his feet with one of the judo moves he'd practiced last week with Aya. Shark went down hard on his back with a grunt, the wind knocked out of him, and Kenji was on top of him, pulling his fist back to give his mother's killer the punishment he deserved.

"Stop, sir! Stop!" Aya cried. She grabbed his wrist, pulled him away.

Shark scrambled to his feet, furious.

"You sonofabitch!" he gasped. "That's assault!"

"Then report it," Kenji replied, voice shaking. A team of security officers was converging on them. "Go ahead. File a complaint."

Shark shoved him. "Go to hell. I'm not missing my plane."

"What seems to be the problem here?" said the point man, planting himself in front of Shark while his partner drew Kenji aside.

"Nothing, officer," Shark said. "I apologize for the disturbance. I, uh, tripped and we had a little misunderstanding, that's all. Now if you'll excuse me, I have a plane to catch." He grabbed his wheelie and turned to limp away.

Snick.

Shark moved, but his carry-on didn't. He spun around. Aya held up her left arm, now handcuffed to his bag's extended handle.

"Fuck me!" Shark's face reddened with rage as he recognized Aya. "Why, you little Kurosawa bitch! What the fucking fuck are you—"

More security arrived. "Sir? Ma'am? What's going on here?"

Shark pointed a shaking finger at the handcuff. "Take this thing off. Take it off right now and we can all walk away without starting a war."

Aya looked him in the eye and smiled, then flung the key as hard as she could, sending it skittering over the polished floor. It disappeared between the feet of the crowd waiting to check in.

"Why, you . . . !"

He shoved her hard with both hands. Kenji watched with astonishment as the third degree black belt who was nearly impossible to throw staggered backward and toppled as dramatically as a stuntman, dragging the handcuffed carry-on with her.

The security officer grabbed Shark in an arm lock from behind, as reinforcements arrived at a trot. A newcomer bent over Aya.

"Are you all right, ma'am?"

She grimaced in apparent pain, as she reached into her jacket pocket with her free hand and produced her badge.

"After you call the medics, would you please detain this man for assaulting a police officer?"

•

"Well played," Kenji said to Aya, as they sat in the security office, waiting for the First Investigative Division team. "How's your, uh . . . ?"

"My butt?" She winced and shifted on the hard chair. "I don't think I'll be practicing rolls for a few days. And I need you to promise not to tell Oki-*sensei* that I ignored my training while being assaulted by a suspect."

"Done."

She grinned. "But we kept him from getting on that plane, didn't we?"

Kenji nodded. "Now we just have to wait and see if Mori can make it stick."

He looked across the office toward the interview room where Shark had been sequestered while the security chief was on the phone, confirming Kenji's story with Inspector Mori. Through the glass, he could see Shark hunched over his own phone, his body language tense. Who was he calling? His lawyer?

Kenji turned to Aya and lowered his voice. "So, Kurosawa? Before Mori gets here and starts asking questions, there's something I need to know."

"Yes, sir?"

"How did you just happen to be in West Shinjuku, right outside Koji's building, when Shark's ride came for him? I'm having a hard time believing it was a coincidence."

She hung her head. "It wasn't. Sir."

"Did someone in your, uh, family tell you he was going to run?"

"No, sir. I wasn't lying when I told you I haven't talked to any of them for three years." She sighed. "But I still know people. One of them is Shark's ex-wife—we went to grade school together. She called me after work today, told me that when she went to pick up their daughter at school, he'd been there. He wanted to say goodbye."

"I don't understand. Why did she call you?"

"Because she wanted to know if it was true. She knows I . . . . " Aya fell silent.

"You what?"

"I follow him, sir. Him and Koji. In my spare time." Her fists clenched. "Someday they're going to do the wrong thing, at the wrong time, and I'm going to be there."

The door to the security office opened and Mori sailed through it, followed by his entourage of assistant inspectors. He exchanged introductions with the airport security chief, and was led to the room where Shark was being held. Stopping outside, he sent his men in first and pulled the chief aside to ask if there was somewhere he could talk to Detective Nakamura in private before interviewing the detainee.

The security chief showed Kenji and Mori into his office and the Inspector took the seat behind the desk. The door closed softly behind them.

"Okay, what happened?" he said. "Don't leave anything out."

Kenji filled him in, then asked if the van had arrived.

"Yes. But it's going to take time to search it. I need your help." He drew a small evidence bag from his pocket and held it up. Inside was a dirty button. "This is from the nurse's uniform the third Painted Doll victim was wearing."

Kenji was surprised. "You found it in the van?"

"No. We found it at the scene, but Mr. Maeda doesn't know that. I'm going to let him think we found it in the van. One of my men is going to call me halfway through our interview, so I can make him think we're pulling evidence off the vehicle left and right. I'm going to insist he come back to headquarters for questioning. You're going to be his driver, with one of my men riding shotgun."

"Yes, sir."

"Your job between here and headquarters is to get him to admit something we can use to hold him until we pull some hard evidence from the van."

"On the first Painted Doll murder, or my mother's 'accident'?"

"Either. Get me anything at all that'll give us a legitimate reason to detain."

"Yes, sir. I'll do my best, sir." Kenji hesitated, then said, "He might not talk to me with someone else in the car, though, sir. He's good at not incriminating himself in front of witnesses."

"Which is why," Mori said, "if you arrive at headquarters and he hasn't slipped up, I'm going to assign you to be the note-taker in the interrogation room. At some point in the interview I'm going to leave you alone with him, and you're going to convince him to tell you what happened with your mother, without any witnesses present."

Kenji shook his head, doubtful. "He's a pro, sir. He knows those rooms are wired, and there are observers behind the mirror."

"So turn it all off. Make a big show of flipping off the switches to the mikes and video, so he knows we won't be able to hear anything he says. He'll think he's safe, because you're the only witness."

"But won't that defeat the purpose, sir?"

Mori flipped open the latches on his briefcase and pulled out a little black box. "Not if you're wearing a wire."

•

Over the top of the interview room laptop, Kenji watched Shark ponder the latest in the long line of questions Inspector Mori had posed. He hadn't said a word since being put into the patrol car at the airport. Not to Kenji, not to Mori, not to anyone.

A frustrated Mori threw down his pen. "Do you understand the seriousness of the charges we're about to bring against you? Right now, my team at the lab is going over that van with black lights and tweezers, and you can bet that if there is even a speck of evidence tying you to one of these crimes, we'll find it. The longer you wait to answer my questions, the closer we get to being able to convict you on the evidence, regardless of whether you confess or not." He shook his head. "I doubt you murdered that girl alone, but if you don't tell us who helped you, you'll take the weight for it, all by yourself."

Shark sighed and let his head fall back. He stared at the ceiling for a long moment, then looked Mori in the eye and said, "Okay. See if I got this straight. You think I was there when someone was videoing this porn actress lady getting killed."

"We know you were there."

"But what if I got called in afterwards? By the idiot who did it? Who was in a panic, because it was an accident."

"If you disposed of the body," Mori said, "that makes you an accessory. Tell us who did it and we'll recommend a lighter sentence. Instead of growing old behind bars, you'll be out in a few years, while you're still a young man."

Shark gave a short laugh. "I'd be out in a few days, on my way to the crematorium. The people I work for don't believe in light sentences for snitches." He leaned forward. "If I give you the real killer, I need you to bury everything you've got on me and put me on a plane to parts unknown, the minute I finish testifying."

"I can't do that," Mori said.

"Then I guess I can't help you put away the son of the biggest boss in Kabuki-chō."

Mori's eye's narrowed. "You're telling me if we ignore any connections you have to other open cases, you'll take the stand so we can convict your boss."

"If you do that, I'll help you put away the real killer."

Kenji stiffened. Shark would never offer to deal unless he knew they were going to find evidence in the van that would convict him.

"All right," said Mori. "But I have to check it with the higher-ups."

"Sir?" Kenji shot to his feet. "What are you doing, sir? You can't agree to that!"

Mori turned a cold eye on him. "Yes, I can. This is about results, Detective, not personal vendettas. Shut up and sit down. Remember your place." He turned back to Shark. "If I make all our open cases against you go away, you'll give us Koji Yamamoto?"

"No," said Shark. "I'll you give you his big brother, Yoichi."

•

"I'm going to call the Superintendent General," Mori announced, gathering his files.

He turned to Kenji. "Nakamura, monitor Mr. Maeda while I'm gone."

Then he addressed the assistant inspector who'd been standing behind Shark during the interview. "Honda, hook Mr. Maeda up again, then you're with me. I need you to go to the lab, tell them to hold off booking any evidence they're taking from that van."

The assistant inspector stepped forward to replace Shark's shackles, then followed Mori out the door.

As it clicked shut, Kenji rose and crossed the room. He stood, swaying, over the prisoner.

"Too bad for you, chump," Shark smirked. "Nobody cares about your mom."

"Tell me," Kenji said, through clenched teeth. "Before he comes back. I need to know what happened. Even if you never spend a day in jail for what you did, I need to know."

Shark laughed. "You're joking, right? You think I don't know they're watching and recording?" He looked up at the video camera mounted in the corner, smiled and waved.

Kenji spun around and strode to the switches next to the door. He flipped them all to OFF, killing the recording devices and microphones. Then he swept up the chair Mori had been using and set it down facing Shark. He sat.

"They can't hear us now."

Shark frowned and said, "How do I know you're not wearing a wire?"

Kenji whipped off his tie and began to unbutton his shirt. Pulled it apart to show Shark the black box taped to his chest. Without a word, he ripped it off and flipped the switch. The little red power light died.

"Now I'm not," he said, casting it to the floor between them. "But we only have a few minutes before they figure that out. And once Mori returns, you're going to disappear into First Investigative Division custody. You'll be out of the country." He took a shaky breath. "I'm going to get a reprimand for this. A demotion. They might even fire me. So before Mori comes back and all hell breaks loose, tell me what happened."

Shark gazed at the little black box on the floor and his lips twitched into a smile. He lifted his foot and stomped the transmitter, grinding it to pieces beneath his boot heel. Then he sat back in his chair and narrowed his eyes. "Okay. I'll play."

Kenji stared at him, not quite believing the ploy had worked. He took a deep breath. "All right. You saw my mother taking pictures of you abducting those two women in the parking lot at Korankei. How did you find out who she was? Did the bus driver tell you?"

"Nope." Shark snorted. "But if that Chink girl hadn't swiped her bag with the nice neat luggage tag on it, that's who I'd have asked."

"How did you know my mother would be in Toritsu-daigaku that night?"

Shark raised an eyebrow. "I think you'd better ask your brother about that."

"My brother?" What was Shark trying to pull? Takeo had gone to judo practice early that day, he'd said. He hadn't seen her at all.

The asshole was lying. Playing him.

"Cut the crap, Maeda. My brother wasn't even around that day," Kenji said, grabbing a fistful of Shark's shirt and yanking him out of his chair. Through clenched teeth, he growled, "He wasn't the one who laid in wait, who ran over her in cold blood, who tried to make it look like an accident."

"She didn't give me a choice!"

"Like hell." Kenji shoved Shark back in his chair. "How did you know where she was going that night?"

Shark winced, shifted in his seat. "She took a cab. I followed her. But I'm not shitting you—all I was after was her camera. And the pictures on it. If she'd told me the chip wasn't in the fucking thing when she handed it over—" He scowled. "Did she think I wouldn't notice? I opened it up and saw right away that she was lying about not giving that shit to Mori—"

"What are you talking about? She didn't give the chip to Mori! It was at the camera shop. She dropped it off to get prints made. Ten years later, it was still at the camera shop. I found it last week. She must have told you that."

"She sure as hell didn't," Shark snapped. "She didn't say a fucking word about the pics not being inside."

"Well, she didn't give them to Mori. She didn't give Mori anything. My father wouldn't let her. He was afraid of what you'd do to her."

"That's what he told you?" Shark gave a derisive laugh. "Well, that makes him a lying sack of shit, doesn't it? Because if there was one thing your old man knew, it was that no one would touch a hair on his pretty little wife's head as long as he kept his end of the bargain."

Bargain? Kenji felt the color drain from his face.

"I guess he didn't tell you that part, did he?" Shark sneered. "But I was there. I was right there when that dirty cop cut a deal with the bossman."

Kenji reeled. No. It wasn't possible.

"Don't let him tell you anything different," Shark continued, his voice dripping with scorn, "because I was also front row, center, when that lying sonofabitch broke his word. Must have set a new world record for speed snitching—less than an hour after swearing on his mother's grave, your pa was shoving your ma into a police cruiser that took her straight to the downtown cop shop."

"That doesn't mean she told Mori anything when she got there. She couldn't refuse to go in when my dad's higher-ups summoned her, but my dad swears she didn't say a word."

"She did." Shark shook his head. "If she didn't give him the pics, why did the good Inspector call me in the very next day and tell me he had photos and an eyewitness?"

"He was guessing," Kenji countered. "It's standard procedure. He was bluffing."

"Right," Shark scoffed. "Nice try. But the truth is a whole lot simpler: Your old man's been lying to you, and so has that asshole Mori. You're more of an idiot than I thought, if you believe them."

Kenji shot to his feet. "I'd be an idiot to believe *you*!"

"You think so? Then tell me this: If your dad wasn't in it up to his neck, why didn't he ever come after us? Why didn't he investigate your mom's 'accident'?" The prisoner cocked his head, waiting for an answer. "You want me to spell it out for you? Your pa knew that if he took us down, we'd take him down with us."

No. Shark was lying. He had to be lying.

"And I'll tell you one more thing," Shark added, "in case you don't quite get it. When my boss makes a deal, he keeps his word. If your old man had done the same, your old lady would still be alive."

No. It couldn't be true. Shark was fucking with him. He was—

The door burst open, admitting Mori and company.

The Inspector stopped before the shackled man and said, "The Superintendent General has agreed not to pursue any of the open cases against you if you agree to testify against Yoichi Yamamoto." His eyes flicked to the shattered black box on the floor, but all he added was, "Nakamura, take notes."

•

It was after two in the morning by the time Mori finished his questioning. Kenji shut down the computer and stood, mute and numb, as the Inspector thanked everyone for their hard work, and Shark was led away to parts unknown as a protected witness.

Kenji was not invited to be on the team that was now withdrawing to a conference room to strategize how and when they would arrest Koji's brother, Yoichi Yamamoto. He tensed as the last assistant inspector filed out of the room, leaving him alone with Mori.

It would come now. The reprimand for taking off the wire and letting Shark crush it. But Mori merely scooped up the mess of wires, grabbed his files and muttered a hurried "*o-tsukare-sama-deshita*" as he slipped through the closing door to join his team.

Kenji stood there, puzzled. Didn't Mori care? Of course, he might just be waiting to mete out punishment until he wasn't busy arresting a major gangster. It would be a mistake to feel lucky just yet.

Not that feeling lucky was at all likely, after what he'd heard tonight. Had his father really made a deal with the *yakuza*? Kenji had never felt so confused, so betrayed.

Trudging past the deserted reception area, he spotted a small figure slumped in one of the chairs. Detouring, he bent over the assistant detective.

"Kurosawa-*san*?"

She awoke with a start.

"Yes? Sir? What happened, sir?"

"Time to go home."

She pushed herself out of the chair. "Did they get him? Shark? And what about Koji?"

"He didn't give them Koji," Kenji said. "He gave them Yoichi."

"Yoichi?" Aya stopped in her tracks.

"You were right," Kenji said wearily. "About the ring."

"It was Yoichi in that video?"

"Yes, according to Shark." They began to walk toward the elevator. "He says he got a call from Koji late one night, saying that Yoichi was in trouble and begging for their help. When they got to the shoot, they discovered that Yoichi had been doing more than producing and distributing the videos—he'd been, uh, participating. The night they were shooting *Girl Hunting*, he got a little carried away. The woman he was supposed to pretend to choke died. He panicked and called his little brother. Koji hustled Yoichi away and passed the cleanup off to Shark, who hauled the body across town and dumped it in Adachi."

"I can't believe it," Aya said, frowning. "Why would Shark agree to testify against a Yamamoto? When the *oyabun* finds out, he's a dead man."

"Not if Mori gets him out of the country first."

Ping. As they stepped into the elevator, Kenji told her about the deal Mori had okayed with the Superintendent General, how he'd promised not to prosecute Shark in any open cases, and allow him to leave the country if he gave them Yoichi.

"*All* the open cases?" she cried. "But what if they find out he killed your mother?"

"He did kill my mother. He admitted it tonight."

"He did?"

"When Mori left me alone in the interview room with him, I switched off all the recording equipment and microphones, then I ripped off the wire. He confirmed that he followed my mother the day she died, and killed her."

"That's terrible, sir." She hesitated. "But it'll just be your word against his."

"No, it won't."

Kenji reached into his pocket and pulled out his phone. Held it up, so she could see the jagged white lines of a voice recording on the screen.

Aya's face lit up. "Well done, sir! Has Inspector Mori heard it? Maybe he'll reconsider the deal."

"He doesn't have to," Kenji said, as the doors opened. "Mori agreed not to pursue any open cases against Shark, but my mother's death isn't an open case. It's still classified as an accident."

FRIDAY, JANUARY 16

•

Kenji wearily pressed the button on the electric hot pot, and a stream of boiling water shot into the teapot that had sat on the Nakamura family breakfast table for as long as he could remember. The window was still dark, dawn still more than an hour away.

His head ached, his eyes felt gritty and sore. He'd slept like a dead man for a few hours, but the moment his alarm jolted him awake, Shark's words had returned to taunt him. He'd dragged himself out of bed, determined to ambush his father before he left for work, make him admit the truth.

Who was lying? Shark? Or his dad? He couldn't stand the thought of spending even one more day wondering if the familiar face he saw across the kitchen table every day was just a mask, hiding a man he no longer knew.

The hot pot grumbled as the teapot filled and Kenji heard the toilet flush behind the bathroom door down the hall. He scooped up his phone and moved the steeping tea to the kitchen table, then retrieved his cup from the drying rack. He hesitated, then set it down in front of his father's usual spot, instead of his own. His dad's cushion faced the door, and Kenji didn't want to give him a chance to spot him waiting there and escape.

His father had been avoiding him since the night he'd barricaded himself in his room to wrestle with what Kenji had told him about Mori's bluff. Sergeant Nakamura had been up and out of the house long before his day shift started, and filled his evenings with don't-wait-up-for-me "poker nights," and "night shifts" that had probably been spent on Toyama-*san*'s couch, not behind the desk at the Tabata police box. But Kenji had let him get away with it, telling himself that eventually his dad would stop being so hard on himself and they'd be able to come to an understanding that both of them could live with.

But Shark's accusations had changed everything. Kenji checked his phone, made sure it was cued to the recording he'd made last night. He poured himself a cup of tea and lowered himself to the floor cushion, then leapt to his feet to turn off the lights. No sense alerting his father that a reckoning was waiting for him in the kitchen. Settling down to wait in the dark, Kenji took a sip of tea. The bitter taste of the supermarket's economy brand matched his mood.

The fan in the bathroom shut off. A door slid open, and Kenji heard his father stump down the hall. The kitchen light flicked on. A surprised Sergeant Nakamura stood in the doorway, already in his blue uniform. He frowned. "What are you doing up?"

Kenji didn't answer.

His dad crossed the kitchen to pluck his cup from the drying rack and looked around for the teapot.

"Already made," Kenji said. "Have a seat."

Then his father saw the grim look on Kenji's face and noticed that he wasn't sitting in his usual spot.

"Actually," he said, replacing his cup, "I've got some paperwork to do, so I'll think I'll just grab a cup when I get to—"

"No."

His father opened his mouth to protest, but Kenji cut him off.

"Sit down, Dad. Last night, Inspector Mori and I spent a little time in an interrogation room with your friend Ryo Maeda, better known as Shark."

Alarm slapped across his father's face.

Kenji reached over to his phone and pressed Play.

As Shark's voice filled the room, Kenji's father closed his eyes, as if in pain. The recording ended. In the distance, a drum at the shrine began beating.

"Why didn't you ever try to find out what really happened to Mom?"

"I never had any reason to." His father's chin jutted. "I trusted the investigators. They said it was an accident."

"But it wasn't an accident, was it?"

His father exploded. "Fucking Mori! It's all his fault. If he hadn't—"

"No!" Kenji shot to his feet. "It's your fault. If you hadn't— If you hadn't sold out to that gangster—"

"You believe him?" his father sputtered. "You believe that lying—"

"Yes. I believe him. Koji Yamamoto thought you broke your word, so he killed Mom."

His father spun around, bracing himself against the sink, breathing hard.

"Dad," Kenji insisted. "I need to know. Now. No more lies."

"I didn't lie," he said, through clenched teeth.

"Did you, or did you not, cut a deal with the Yamamoto crime family?"

As if the words were being ripped from him with red-hot pincers, his father admitted, "We had . . . an agreement."

"What kind of 'agreement'?"

The shrine drumming stopped, and the only sound in the kitchen was his father's labored breathing. He stared down into the sink. The silence stretched.

"We're not leaving this room until you tell me," Kenji warned.

Slowly, his father turned to face him. In a cracked voice, he said, "When your mother came home after that damned trip, she told me what happened. Wasn't sure she'd done the right thing, letting the woman who showed up to collect the foreigner talk her out of reporting it. I wasn't sure either, but I told her I'd look into it. I'd take care of it."

"But you didn't."

"I couldn't!" his father cried. "Not without knowing more. I didn't know what we were dealing with. *Who* we were dealing with. Your mother . . . . " His voice caught. "Your mother gave me the van's plate number, and the next day, I had my buddy at Shinjuku Station run it. He told me it was registered to Ace Cleaning. And that Ace was a Yamamoto-*gumi* front. Then he got a little too curious. Wanted to know why a *koban* officer from Tabata was running a *yak* plate." His father looked away. "Told him the car ran a red light. He said it was lucky I didn't write them ticket, because the Yamamoto-*gumi* had all kinds of juice, and it didn't pay to get in their crosshairs. Especially for a 'minor infraction.'"

"So, what did you do?" Kenji's voice dripped with sarcasm. "Redefine an abduction as a 'minor infraction'?"

"No. I didn't know what to do. Your mom told me a crime had been committed, but I didn't understand why the victim who got away begged her not to report it. Was afraid to let your mother get involved until I knew who the lowlife with the scratched face was."

"You mean, how much protection he had."

His father didn't reply.

"How did you find out?" Kenji crossed his arms over his chest.

"First thing I did was talk Toyama-*san* into trading shifts with me. I staked out Ace Cleaning, waited for a guy with scratches on his face to show up for work. But he didn't. Waited all morning. Nothing. By quitting time, I figured Ace was a bum lead, that the goon didn't work there after all. Was waiting for the train when Mori called. He got pinged when Shinjuku Station ran the plate, wanted to know why I was looking for the owner of that van."

"But you didn't tell him."

"No, I *did* tell him." His father scowled. "Biggest mistake of my life. Was so surprised a muckity-muck from headquarters was calling me, I answered his questions. Told him my wife thought she saw someone shoving a woman into a van with that plate. I thought that'd be the end of it. That something she saw way out near the Ise Shrine couldn't have anything to do with his Tokyo case." His face pinched with regret. "But when I got home, guess who was waiting for me outside our house?"

"Mori?"

"No, Shark. In a white Ace Cleaning van, parked in front of the Ikedas'. Couldn't believe I was seeing the scratched face I'd been looking for all day. I crossed the street to ask him who he was and what the hell he was doing there, but soon as he saw me, he threw the van into gear and gunned it. Nearly ran me over."

"Did you get the license number?"

"Didn't try."

"Why?"

"Saw his arm."

"His arm?"

"Full sleeve tattoos."

"So . . . you guessed he was Yamamoto-*gumi*? You suspected the *yakuza* were involved in the abduction Mom witnessed? Why didn't you take her in to tell the Organized Crime squad what she knew?"

"I didn't have a chance!"

"Didn't have a chance? Or didn't want it?" Kenji couldn't keep the accusation from his voice. "Did you go to Koji Yamamoto instead? Did he pay you to withhold evidence?"

"No!" His father's face purpled with rage. "I don't have to listen to this!"

In two strides, he was across the kitchen, but Kenji beat him to the door. They stood, nose to nose, his father's face livid.

"Get out of my way."

Kenji didn't move.

"I said, get out of my way."

"All right," Kenji replied, his voice shaking. "I will. But if you walk out that door without answering my questions, I'll be gone when you get home." He paused. "And I won't be coming back."

Kenji slowly stepped aside. His dad took two steps, then stopped. He stood there, trembling with suppressed fury, then Kenji watched the fight drain out of him. Shoulders slumped, head bowed, he stood there, swaying.

Kenji returned to the table and poured his father a cup of tea. "Dad?"

His father dragged himself back into the kitchen and sank onto the cushion across from his son. Kenji pushed the teacup across the table and his dad wrapped his hands around it, even though the tea had grown tepid and offered scant comfort.

"Dad," Kenji said. "Tell me the truth. And don't stop until I've heard it all."

The clock ticked. Kenji's father sat there, staring unseeing into his tea. Finally, he heaved a great sigh.

"It didn't take the Yamamoto-*gumi* long to track me down. The day after Maeda nearly ran me over, the *oyabun*'s son was waiting for me when I got off work at the *koban*."

"Koji?"

His dad nodded. "Sitting in a car with blacked-out windows, half a block from the police box." He didn't try to hide his disgust. "Had his driver stop me, 'invite' me to join him. Let me know it would be a mistake to refuse. I stalled, told him I didn't want to be seen getting into a gangstered-up car in my uniform, but he just pulled around the corner and opened the back door. Koji was blabbing on his cellphone when I got in. Didn't even say hello before handing it to me. Just said, 'Talk to my friend Shark.'"

He fell silent.

"And . . . ?" Kenji prompted.

"The bastard told me you were having a crappy day at baseball practice, couldn't hit the side of a barn. That yesterday you'd pitched much better. But maybe that was because your mom brought you some rice balls after school, before she went to the shopping street to buy that nice mackerel for dinner." His father's face pinched with suppressed emotion. "I handed the phone back to Koji, asked him what he wanted. He said he didn't want anything, as long as I kept my mouth shut. All I had to do was keep my wife from saying a word to anyone who asked about her trip. If we did that, we'd never hear from him or Shark again."

"And you . . . agreed?"

"I had no choice!" his father sputtered. Then his eyes filled with defeat. He looked away. "The asshole made me drink three cups of saké on it. Then he drank three cups, to seal the deal. Like he was the fucking *shōgun* or something."

"And then Inspector Mori asked Mom to come down to headquarters?"

"*Asked*? You think he gave us a choice? A cruiser was waiting outside the house when I got home. Barely had time to warn your mother. Told her not to say a word to Mori, no matter what he threatened her with, no matter how long they kept her there."

"And she went along with it?"

"No. Until I told her what Shark said about your pitching. Then she went white as a sheet."

"So Koji didn't pay you?"

"Pay me?" His father's voice shook. "You think I'd take money from that . . . that . . . . " He scrambled to his feet, breathing hard.

"I don't know," Kenji cried, now on his feet too. "I don't know anything anymore." His throat closed, and his eyes filled. "I don't know *you* anymore."

Kenji's father stood before him, fists clenched, and the words tumbled out. "He didn't pay me. He didn't have to pay me. All he had to do was show me he could hurt you. And your brother, and your mother. That's why I never asked questions about the accident." His face crumpled. "I wanted it to be an accident. I needed it to be an accident. I couldn't bear to think I made a deal with the devil for *nothing*." He shook his head helplessly as tears spilled down his cheeks. "But I did. And I did it for free. I betrayed my goddamn police oath for *free*."

He turned and lurched toward the door, but Kenji stepped in and wrapped his arms around him. Sobs wracked his father's rigid body, as the pent-up remorse spilled out. As his father wept in his arms, Kenji was saddened to feel bones that were so much closer to the surface than they looked in his blue uniform, to feel how much smaller his dad had become with the passing years.

At last the sobs subsided into great shuddering sighs.

"Dad?" Kenji said presently. "Are you okay?"

Slumped against his son's shoulder, his father moved his head helplessly, turned his face away. Didn't answer.

Kenji stared out the window, at the sky that had lightened to blue while they fought. Did he really blame his dad for what he'd done? For the decisions he'd made? What would he have done, in his father's place? The truth was, he didn't know. Might never know.

But at last his dad had told him the truth. At last he'd finally given up the secret that had been tying him in knots. Kenji shook his head at the cruel twists of fate that had upended all their lives. He held his father tighter, and said, "Dad?" Took a deep breath. "Thank you for telling me. Thank you for . . . for telling me the truth."

His father didn't say anything. Then Kenji felt a clap on his back. And another. And another. Kenji reciprocated. They stood there in the middle of the kitchen for a long while, awkwardly pounding each other on the back. Telling each other in the only way they knew how, that they were still a family.

•

Several hours later, Kenji was standing on Yumi's front step, stamping his feet against the cold. He pushed the Hatas' ailing doorbell. *Bing-blunk.* After the emotional cataclysm with his father, it was something of a relief to have a nice, solid panty thief sting scheduled for this morning.

The Hatas' door opened and Yumi stood there, holding a small shopping bag.

"Thanks for helping us catch this guy," Kenji said. "Are your parents home?"

"No," she replied, stepping out and closing the door behind her. "But they were quite happy to hear someone was coming to pick up the junk we've been meaning to get rid of for ages, even if the guy *is* a thief." She peered at him, frowning. "Are you okay?"

"Yeah," he said, dropping his gaze. "I'm fine. I'll tell you later."

She nodded and suggested they follow her down a graveled path that meandered crookedly around the house toward the back garden.

"I put the stuff I arranged for pick-up next to the fence," she explained. "And I asked our next-door neighbors if I could hang our laundry rack by their back door, right on the other side. He can't miss it."

They rounded the corner, and Kenji stopped to survey the small enclosed area behind the Hatas' old house.

The only green in the winter-bound garden was the moss tracing the cracks between the paving stones. A handful of pink blossoms had popped open on the Hatas' plum tree, but the branches were still mostly gray and bare.

Kenji glanced up at the neighboring houses. In old parts of town like Komagome—where nearly every square inch had been built on over the years—the windows overlooking the Hatas' back yard were all made of pebbled glass or had curtains blocking the too-close-for-comfort view of their neighbors' lives. Just as he'd expected, it was an excellent set-up for a thief. Or a sting.

He spotted the bundle of broken umbrellas tied with a red rag that Yumi had propped against the fence, under a broken floor lamp trailing a frayed cord. Then he raised his eyes to the large square rack hanging from the eaves next door. It was fitted with clothespins holding drying laundry. Excellent. The scant space between the buildings made anything on it an easy arm's reach from the Hatas' yard.

Yumi reached into her shopping bag and brought out two pair of panties.

"Will these do?" she asked, holding them up for inspection.

Suzuki blushed, but Kenji nodded his approval as he examined the white lace bikini and a thong printed with a bunny face. "Perfect. Depending on what kind of mood he's in today, one of these should be just his style."

Yumi reached up to remove one of her father's undershirts and clipped the panties in their place while Kenji and Suzuki surveyed the ambush possibilities.

"Inside the trash enclosure seems like the best choice, don't you think, sir?" Suzuki suggested, nodding toward the fenced-in garbage area.

"Agreed."

They had just finished identifying which gaps in the fence would yield the best video angle, when they heard a truck rattle to a stop out front.

"Good luck," Yumi whispered, then slipped inside to answer the doorbell.

They hid behind the fence, positioned themselves and waited. A breeze stirred the undershirts hanging from the laundry rack. The sound of voices drew nearer as Yumi brought the garbage man around the side of the house.

Suzuki aimed the video camera they'd checked out of the police station's equipment room. *Recording.* Through his own gap in the fence, Kenji watched Yumi lead Aoki into view.

"These are the things we need taken away," she said. The man nodded. "You can go inside, miss, while I put these in the truck. I'll ring the bell again for payment."

Yumi thanked him and went back inside. Aoki paused to study the laundry over the fence, then picked up the lamp and disappeared the way he'd come. A few minutes later, he was back. He hoisted the umbrellas onto his shoulder, then flicked a furtive glance around the small enclosure. Quick as a snake striking, he snatched the lacy white panties from the drying rack and stuffed them into his pocket, then disappeared around the side of the house.

Kenji and Suzuki exchanged grins of triumph, then switched off the camera and followed, catching up with him just as he tossed the bundle of umbrellas into the back of his truck.

Badge out, Kenji stepped up to him. "Mr. Aoki? I'm going to have to ask you to come with us. You're under arrest."

The garbage man turned.

"Under arrest? For what?" Confusion suffused his face as he recognized Kenji and Suzuki. "For a broken taillight?"

"No," Kenji said. "For theft. I don't think this customer's underwear was on your work order, and I'm betting you have quite a collection at home. Perhaps you'd like to show us?"

•

"You're awfully quiet tonight," Yumi observed, moving green onions and shredded cabbage from a brown pottery plate to the bubbling *sukiyaki* pot on Kenji's kitchen table.

Kenji's dad had left a message reminding him that tonight was his poker night and he'd be out late. Even if it hadn't been, Kenji suspected his father would have made some excuse to give himself more time to figure out how to face him again with a minimum of embarrassment, after what had happened this morning. And, to be honest, Kenji was relieved to postpone that awkward moment himself.

He was also acutely aware that he needed to show Yumi he was doing his best to make good on his promise to appreciate her help more. They couldn't have trapped the panty thief without her, and he didn't dare let her feel she was being taken for granted again.

But the past twenty-four hours had taken their toll. Kenji stifled a yawn, muddling the raw egg yolk in his dipping bowl with his chopsticks.

"Sorry, I guess last night is catching up with me," he said.

"Here. Help yourself." Yumi pushed the plate of thin-sliced beef closer to him. "This morning you mentioned you didn't get much sleep, but you didn't tell me why."

"Oh. Yeah. Sorry." He shook his head to clear it. "We arrested Shark. I didn't get home until after three."

Yumi eyes widened as Kenji told her how he and Aya had intercepted Shark at the airport, and that Mori had offered the gangster a deal to testify against Yoichi Yamamoto.

Yumi congratulated him, then frowned. "But what about your mom? Does that mean you can't go after him for the hit and run?"

"No. He can still be prosecuted for that. But—"

"But what?"

"I just . . . I have to work out how to do it."

She ladled out two bowls of *sukiyaki*. "You still don't have enough to arrest him?"

He didn't answer. Couldn't. Before Yumi arrived, he'd listened to the recording he'd made of last night's session with Shark, and decided he couldn't bring himself to use it. Nailing Shark wouldn't bring his mother back, and his dad was all he had left. As much as he yearned for justice, he needed his family more. He wasn't going to give up trying to jail Shark, but he'd have to find another way.

Accepting the bowl Yumi handed him, he breathed in the aroma of beef and vegetables simmered in the savory broth made from his mother's recipe. Folding his hands, he gave thanks with a quick "*Itadakimasu*," then dipped a steaming shred of meat in his egg yolk and brought it to his mouth. So good. He ate a few more bites and took a sip of beer. Helped himself to more. Looked up to find Yumi cooling a piece of cabbage, watching him through the steam rising from the pot.

"What?" he asked.

"I was wondering if you wanted to hear what I found out yesterday."

He'd forgotten about it entirely. Seeing his blank look, she added, "You know, the thing I mentioned on the phone."

"Oh. Yeah. Of course. Sorry I didn't ask about it sooner." He fished another steaming shred of meat from the pot and gave her his attention. "What's the story?"

"I know what your mother was doing in Toritsu-daigaku the night of her accident."

He stared.

"She didn't go out there to look at Ise Shrine pictures at all. She was rescuing your brother, Takeo."

SATURDAY, JANUARY 17

•

Kenji stood outside the glowing windows of the sushi bar where his brother worked. The street was lined with trendy boutiques and pricey eateries catering to the upwardly mobile young families that were colonizing the outer suburbs as they navigated the stroller-pushing phase of life. Couples promenaded arm-in-arm, occasionally pausing to admire an elegant lamp or precious baby dress, spotlit behind one of the many plate glass windows.

It was just past closing time, and Takeo's restaurant had emptied, except for two men lingering at the pale wooden counter. A man in a tall toque and white coat stood attentively behind.

Kenji's older brother had become stockier and grown a neat goatee since he'd seen him last. The chef who was now raising a teacup with his customers in a final toast of the night looked more like their father every day. Kenji had never seen Takeo in his professional role before, and was surprised by a swell of pride. His brother looked almost . . . distinguished.

Takeo bowed as the men pushed back their chairs, then he came around the end of the bar to fetch their mufflers and coats from a tall wooden cabinet. He accompanied his customers to the door and bowed deeply as they left, holding the position and waiting for the door to close behind them. When it didn't, he looked up to see why.

"Hey," Kenji said.

Takeo's eyes widened. "Little brother?"

"Uh, yeah. Long time no see."

"What are you doing here?" Alarm. "Is it Dad? Is he all right?"

"Oh! Don't worry, he's fine," Kenji assured him, with a twinge of guilt. He'd left a message after their dad's scare at the shrine, promising a progress report after his tests. A report he'd never delivered.

"The docs did a workup, and they finally decided his collapse was caused by dehydration," Kenji explained, as Takeo waved him into the restaurant. "But they've scheduled an ultrasound for Tuesday, because they suspect he might have heart problems too."

Takeo nodded. He pushed the door closed and locked it behind them before flipping the Open sign to Closed. He turned to face Kenji.

"Good. I'm glad to hear he's okay. But if this isn't about Dad, what brings you here so late?" He retreated behind the bar to begin tidying up. "I mean, it's nice to see you and all, but . . . ?"

"There's something I need to ask you."

"About . . . ?"

"Some things that happened around the time of Mom's . . . 'accident.'"

Takeo's hands stilled for a moment, then he resumed piling knives onto a tray for washing.

"Kind of ancient history, isn't it?" he said. "I mean, why now? It's after eleven. I won't actually be off work for another hour and you'll miss the last train. I still have to clean the kitchen and sharpen the knives and—"

"Grab yourself some dinner from the back and get your brother a beer," a gruff voice commanded. A graying chef in an even taller hat than Takeo's stood in the doorway to the kitchen. "Go ahead. I'll clean up tonight."

Takeo mustered a smile. "Thank you, sir, but—"

"You don't see your family often enough," admonished his father-in-law. "Go."

Kenji's brother thanked him and excused himself to do as he was told.

A few minutes later, Takeo appeared with a plate of curry rice and a beer. Without his coat and chef's hat, he looked more like the brother Kenji remembered. He crossed the room to a table in the corner. Setting down the curry rice for himself, he handed Kenji the beer.

"You're not having one?" Kenji asked, as they sat.

"No," Takeo said, busying himself with his chopsticks. "I haven't had a drink since the day Mom died."

His words hung in the air between them.

"What happened, Takeo?" Kenji blurted. "Why did you get arrested?"

His brother's head snapped up.

"Where did you hear that?" Throwing an anxious glance at the door to the kitchen, he lowered his voice. "I didn't get arrested. Well, I did, but a friend of Mom's got the case dismissed. Sent me home and talked to the guy whose window I broke. We paid for the damage, he didn't press charges, and that was that."

"But why did they arrest you for breaking a window?" Kenji persisted. "Wasn't it an accident?"

"No." His brother hesitated, then said, "I was drunk. And angry. Not in that order."

"About?"

Takeo studied his face. "Don't you remember what it was like? Around the time Mom passed away, Dad and I weren't even speaking to each other."

Kenji stared. He'd had no idea. He'd always thought the fighting started after his mom died, when Takeo decided to become a sushi chef instead of a policeman. Wrapped up in his own high school ups and downs, Kenji only saw his father and brother together at the dinner table. They didn't say much to each other, but he hadn't thought anything of it. He'd assumed Takeo was simply turning into a man of few words. Like his dad.

"What were you fighting about?" Kenji asked. "You guys always seemed so—"

"Alike?" His brother shook his head. "Just because I look like him, doesn't mean I *am* like him."

Kenji had never really considered that possibility. He couldn't remember a time when people hadn't smiled at his brother, saying, "like father like son" and "are you going to grow up to be a policeman too, just like your daddy?" As a child, Kenji had been a little envious. No one ever said that to *him*.

"Why were you fighting?"

"Because it was December of my senior year, and I had no idea what to do with my life."

"But hadn't you already been accepted to the police academy?"

"Yeah. But I didn't want to go."

"Then why did you apply?"

Takeo sighed, poked at his curry. "Because I wasn't like you—good at sports, good at taking tests. It's not like anyone forced me, but all my life, everyone just assumed that's what I would do." He looked up. "But I've never felt more trapped than the day I got my acceptance. I went to Dad and told him I wasn't sure. That maybe I didn't want to go into police work after all."

Even imagining that conversation made Kenji's hair stand on end. "I guess he wasn't too happy to hear that, huh?"

"He was furious. What was I, a coward? I needed to be toughened up, he said. The police academy would make a man out of me. He demanded to know what I was planning to do with my life if I didn't go to the academy. I couldn't give him a good answer, so that night after I went to bed, he stamped my seal at the bottom of the acceptance form and took it to the mailbox without telling me. When I found out, I was beyond furious, but he wouldn't listen. Said he did it for my own good, that I'd thank him someday.

"But from that day on, I spent every waking moment trying to figure out how to get out of it. I stopped talking to Dad. Stopped talking to everybody." Takeo shook his head. "After a while, I guess he thought I'd given up, because he started trying to give me advice, telling me stories about how tough it was to be a cadet, back in the day. One night, he was going on and on about how hard the training was, how many guys washed out, and he started nagging me to take up running, to work on getting myself in better shape.

"I didn't say no to his face, but I didn't start working out either. Next thing I knew, he'd arranged for me to train every Saturday with this retired cop he knew in Toritsu-daigaku." Takeo shook his head. "The guy was older than the gods, but he was a real slave driver. If I was even three minutes late, he'd call Dad to ask where I was, then make me drop and do push-ups until my arms gave out. If I didn't understand how to do a throw, he wouldn't explain what I was doing wrong, he'd just send his biggest black belt at me again and again until I accidentally got it right. If I got too tired to finish a set with the weights, he'd give me more reps. Sometimes I'd throw up afterwards, but I couldn't quit, because even though I hated Dad more than I'd ever hated anyone in my life, I . . . I didn't want him to be ashamed of me either."

"So what happened the day Mom had her 'accident'?"

Takeo sat there silent for a long time. Then he gave a deep sigh. "I'd been out late the night before, but I dragged myself as usual to Saturday morning training. I was moving slow that day, a little sloppy because I was hung over, and I screwed up my shoulder, practicing falls. The trainer didn't believe me, accused me of faking, but I really was hurting. I grabbed my bag and walked out.

"I sat in the park for a while, then found a Family Mart. I went in looking for some aspirin, but walked out with a pack of

Seven Stars and a six-pack of beer. Sometime between beer number five and beer number six, I had this brilliant idea: if I had a police record, it would disqualify me from going to the academy. So I walked down the alley and found a crate of empty saké bottles sitting outside a bar. I hauled it back to the Family Mart and chucked it through the big plate glass window. Then I just stood there, while the guy behind the counter freaked out and called the cops." Takeo shook his head. "I couldn't stop laughing, thinking how sorry Dad would be for making me do all that strength training."

"And the cop who arrested you was Dad's friend from the Academy? Shin Sato?"

"No, it was some other guy. But Sato-*san* arrived at the *koban* just as they were logging the incident, and recognized me. He outranked the officers who brought me in, and he told them he'd take over. He brought me some coffee to sober me up, then sat me down to talk before he called Mom and Dad. I thought I was totally screwed when I found out he went to the police academy with Dad, but when I told him why I'd trashed the window, he actually listened. Told me he understood, but there were better ways of getting out of it. That having a police record would shut me out of a lot more than the academy. He sent me home, and told me not to say anything to Mom or Dad until he'd talked to the Family Mart manager."

"And what happened?"

"I got back to Komagome around four, but I didn't go home. I was afraid someone would ask where I'd been, and I didn't want to explain before Sato-*san* called. I hung around in the smoking area next to the station for about an hour, and was on my last cig when my phone rang. I was pulling it out to answer it when I saw Mom leaving the bank across the street. I tried to duck behind those big planters surrounding the smoking area, but she spotted me."

"You saw her that day? Why didn't you say something when we discovered she was missing?"

"Because she told me not to!" Takeo cried. "Sato-*san* had called her and explained what happened, told her that if we paid for the damage right away, the manager wouldn't press charges. But it was going to cost thousands to replace that big plate glass window, so she'd gone to the bank before it closed and taken money from their savings. She hadn't told Dad yet, because she knew he was going to freak out." Takeo sighed. "She couldn't understand why I'd done such a thing. What was I thinking, shaming him in front of his colleague? Acting more like the son of a gangster than the son of a police officer?

"I told her I was tired of being the son of a police officer, tired of him telling me what to do. That I'd find some way to pay them back, but I wasn't going to apologize. She just shook her head, that way she always did. Said I'd better cool off before coming home, that she'd take the money to Toritsu-daigaku, but then we'd have to sit down and talk about how to tell Dad. Then she walked away, and that's the last . . . that's the last—"

Takeo hung his head. In a choked voice, he blurted, "I know it's my fault. If I hadn't thrown those saké bottles through that window, she wouldn't have been in Toritsu-daigaku that night, wouldn't have been running for the train. She wouldn't have . . . . "

"Takeo," Kenji said, reaching across the table. "Listen. Mom's death had nothing to do with you. I'm serious. It wasn't an accident."

Takeo looked up. "What do you mean, 'it wasn't an accident?' She was hit by a *train*."

"No, she wasn't." Kenji pulled out his phone. "Have you ever seen this man before?"

He showed his brother Shark's picture. Takeo frowned at the display, then grabbed the phone and his eyes widened.

"How did you . . . where did you . . . who is this?"

"The man who killed Mom."

"The man who . . . ? What?"

"His name is 'Shark' Maeda and he was following her. He laid in wait for her near a foot crossing in Toritsu-daigaku, then he hit her with his van." Kenji took a deep breath. "Where did you see him?"

Takeo frowned at Shark's picture. "He was standing outside the Komagome train station." Takeo looked up, stricken. "It was the money, wasn't it? Did he kill her for the money?"

"No," Kenji said. "Sato-*san* told me it cost twenty thousand yen to pay for the window, but I found the rest of it in her purse."

"You found her purse?"

"Yes. The morgue gave it back with her things in it, but Dad was too shell-shocked to even open the bag. Aunt Ayako decided to stash it away until he could handle it, and I guess she forgot about it, because I discovered it a few days ago in a storage well under the pantry floor." Kenji leaned in. "Tell me what happened."

Takeo handed back Kenji's phone. "When Mom caught me outside the station, she showed me the money. She wanted me to see how much it was, make me sorry I'd done it. But while she was talking, I saw that guy behind her, leaning against a van, smoking. He had scratches on his face like he'd been in a fight. He made me nervous, so I told her to put the money away, not to wave it around.

"She said she was meeting Sato-*san* after he got off work, and they planned to take the cash to the Family Mart manager together. She didn't know for sure how long it would take, because she wanted to go to the Satos' afterwards and thank them, so she might not get home until late. That she expected me to wait up for her, because we had to figure out how to tell Dad." Takeo's face pinched. "I stayed up all night, called her again and again. But she never picked up. She never came home."

"It's not your fault."

In a bleak voice he said, "It is."

"No, Takeo, it really isn't." Kenji shook his head. His father hadn't blamed himself enough for his mother's death; his brother had blamed himself too much. "Listen to me. If Shark hadn't caught up with Mom that night, he'd have got to her another day, somewhere else. She was a witness to a crime he committed. While she was on that trip to the Ise Shrine, she saw him do something that would land him and his boss in jail for life."

Takeo raised his head, cautiously. "How do you know?"

Kenji drank off the last of his beer. "Hang on a minute, and I'll tell you the whole story."

Kenji stood and carried his empty glass to the kitchen door. When he returned, he was carrying two beers, He raised an eyebrow at Takeo. This time, his brother took one.

There was only an inch left in the bottom of Takeo's glass by the time Kenji finished telling him everything that he'd found out since the blue suitcase had been returned to them on New Year's Eve. Except, of course, for the parts their father would have to confess to his eldest son himself someday—Kenji didn't feel that was his to tell.

They sat in silence for a long moment.

"Will this guy Shark go to jail now?" Takeo asked.

"I'd like to put him there." Kenji reached into his pocket and set his phone on the table between them. "But I could use your help."

He pushed Record.

Tuesday, January 27

•

Plum trees that had nearly finished blooming whizzed by, as the police cruiser sped toward Narita airport with Aya at the wheel. Kenji had missed them at their peak because he'd been busy for the past ten days, putting together the case against Shark.

The file sat on his lap in a plain manila envelope. Inside were copies of the statements made by all the witnesses who had supplied pieces of the puzzle. After Takeo gave him the final missing link, he'd realized he had enough to arrest Shark without using the recording that would tar his father with a corruption charge.

His mother's photos put Shark and a brown van at the site of Li Qian's abduction, five days before she became the Painted Doll killer's third victim. Yin Hayashi identified Shark as the man who chased her through the parking lot at Korankei and forced Li Qian into a brown van. A Motor Vehicle Registration search had tied the license plate to a van owned by Ace Cleaning Service in Shinjuku. Payroll records named Shark as an employee of that company. Kenji's brother had signed a statement placing him and his van in a position to follow his mother's cab to Toritsu-daigaku that night, and police box records confirmed the van's presence near the accident scene on the night Kenji's mother was killed. The logs also documented the license plate switch, and the crime lab team had managed to tie six blood samples taken from bolts and crevices in the van's front bumper to DNA samples Kenji had supplied. With a little persuading, Shark's cousin had signed a statement that Shark had delivered the van to him the day after Sachiko Nakamura's death.

All that was left was to intercept the unsuspecting gangster before he got to the airport.

Inspector Mori had let Kenji know that if he arrived at a particular *yakiniku* restaurant with a warrant between 7:00 and 8:00 that night, Mori wouldn't stand in his way. The Inspector had successfully managed to keep Shark's whereabouts secret for the past two weeks, while the wheels of justice turned slowly against Yoichi Yamamoto.

Yoichi had protested his innocence for two days, telling anyone who would listen that he'd been set up, that he hadn't even been there when that girl was killed on film, that someone had stolen his ring and used it to frame him.

Then he'd been visited by his younger brother Koji. An hour later, a defeated Yoichi asked for Mori and told him if he was charged with manslaughter instead of murder, he had a story to tell. Yoichi was now in a holding cell at Shinjuku, awaiting transport to a maximum-security prison.

And Shark had a price on his head. It was common knowledge that the Yamamoto *oyabun* would reward anyone who brought him proof that Shark had been made to pay for his betrayal. But Mori had played it smart, moving his witness around between love hotels and other unofficial residences instead of putting him in protective custody with inmates and guards who might be tempted to cash in on the *oyabun*'s generous offer. And instead of advertising Shark's whereabouts with the usual cadre of uniformed officers, Mori had rotated an around-the-clock roster of single, plainclothes bodyguards. Which meant that only Mori, the guard, and Shark would be stopping for one last Japanese meal before the snitch got on a plane to a country with no extradition treaty.

The car's GPS voice announced, "Next exit on your left."

Aya changed lanes.

"If you were leaving Japan forever, sir," she mused, "would you choose *yakiniku* as your last meal?"

Kenji considered the question. He was a big fan of the thin-sliced meats you grilled yourself at your table before dunking them in garlicky soy sauce, but it wasn't really Japanese, was it? Restaurants all over Asia served some version of the Korean delicacy.

"Nah," he said. He decided the hardest thing for him to leave behind would be skewered chicken with barbeque sauce. "I'd probably go to a *yakitori-ya* and order everything on the menu. I've heard that in foreign countries, you can't get hearts or cartilage or skin, just plain meat. What about you?"

"*Motsu nabe*," she said, without hesitation.

"Pork intestine hotpot? Isn't that kind of a guy thing?"

"I grew up with guys," she said defensively. "In the winter, we used to sit at a table so long we needed three burners. My mother filled three big black pots with this secret broth it took her days to make. Me and my parents and my brothers and all my dad's lieutenants would start with what looked like a mountain of green onions and cabbage and *tōgarashi* peppers, but by the end of the night, it would all be gone."

"Your destination is ahead, on the left," interrupted the voice of the GPS. Sure enough, there was the sign for the restaurant. Aya pulled into the parking lot and cruised the rows, looking for Inspector Mori's police-issue Toyota.

There it was. Not hard to spot the budget sedan sitting between a top-of-the-line Lexus and a Mercedes. Mori's driver/bodyguard sat behind the wheel, keeping a vigilant eye on every car that came and went. The guard raised a pair of binoculars to peer at their car as they passed. He lowered them and waved. Mori and Shark must already be inside.

There were no parking spaces open in the front lot, so Aya took the car around to the rear. But as they cruised past the restaurant's back door, she slammed on the brakes.

"Sir," she said, suddenly tense. "Look. There. That black Lexus with tinted windows. That's Koji's car."

"What?"

Their eyes met, and Aya wrenched the wheel, throwing the car into the first available space. They yanked open their doors, sprinting for the restaurant.

Kenji burst through the back door, Aya close behind. Startled kitchen staff in white coats and toques froze as Kenji pulled his badge from his pocket.

"I'm Detective Kenji Nakamura and this is an emergency."

He pushed his way through the workers, then stopped by the door to the dining room. Peering out the service porthole, he scanned the tables for Koji Yamamoto, then realized Aya would be better at spotting him. He'd only met the gangster's son face-to-face once, and had been surprised to find him so unimposing and—frankly—forgettable-looking. He might not even recognize Koji unless he was close enough to see the thin white scar running through one of his eyebrows.

"Kurosawa," he said, stepping aside. "Do you see him?"

Aya took his place at the window, stood on her tiptoes and scanned the room. "No, sir. But isn't that Inspector Mori? Why is he alone?"

Kenji peered over her shoulder and saw Mori eating at a table near the wall. Where was Shark? And where was Koji Yamamoto?

"Cover me," he said to Aya, then pushed through the door and made his way across the dining room. He slid into the other seat at Mori's table.

"Right on time," said the Inspector, flipping a slice of meat that was sizzling on his grill.

"Where's Shark, sir?" Kenji asked, his voice tense.

Mori nodded at one of the doors in the back wall. "Private room. Figured that was the most secure way to do this. No one can go in or out except through that door."

"What about Koji Yamamoto?"

"Managed to avoid seeing him all week," the Inspector said with satisfaction.

"Well, I'm afraid we're about to, sir. His car and driver are in the back lot."

"What?" Mori stared. "You must be mistaken. No one followed us. I made sure of it myself."

"Maybe he wasn't following. Maybe he got here before you did. Someone could have told him you'd be here."

"That's impossible. Nobody but—" The Inspector stopped himself, catching Kenji's urgency. "We can ask questions later. Let's get this thing done before Koji turns this restaurant into a bad gangster movie." He rose, unsnapping his weapon. "I'll cover you."

Kenji waved him back down. "Don't you think it would be better if you stay here, sir, and keep a lookout for Koji while I go in with my warrant? That way, you can stop him if he tries to intervene before I get Shark out. My partner's waiting in the kitchen. She can cover me."

Mori eased back into his seat and Kenji stood, nodding to Aya through the kitchen door porthole. She joined him outside Shark's private room. The door was fitted with a small window at eye height for the wait staff. Kenji peeked in.

Their quarry was sitting in lonely splendor on the far side of the room, at the end of a table that could probably seat twenty. He'd tied a large white bib around his neck. Nearly empty plates of sliced meats surrounded him, and smoke rose from a piece that was browning nicely on his table grill. As Kenji watched, Shark put the last few pieces on to cook, and emptied the dregs of a beer bottle into his glass.

"Okay," Kenji whispered. "He's alive and he's alone. I've asked Inspector Mori to stay where he is and keep a lookout for Koji. You're my backup, but I want you to cover me from here, in case Mori needs your help more than I do."

"Yes, sir," she said. "I understand, sir."

"Okay. Let's get him out before Koji has a chance to get what he came for."

Kenji drew the warrant from his breast pocket as Aya took up a ready stance against the wall next to the door.

"Going in."

He pushed through the door.

Shark looked up. A piece of grilled meat wrapped in a *miso*-smeared lettuce leaf stopped halfway to his mouth.

"What the . . . ?" He squinted at Kenji. "What are you doing here, asshole?"

Kenji strode the length of the table, eyes locked with Shark as he pulled out the warrant.

"Ryo Maeda, you're under arrest for the murder of Sachiko Nakamura."

"Huh?" He shook his head, scowling. "You really don't give up, do you? Read my lips: I can't be prosecuted for any open cases."

"Then you shouldn't have tried so hard to make my mother's death look like an accident."

"What the fuck are you talking about?"

The meat began to burn. Shark hastily plucked it from the grill.

"The crime lab found all kinds of evidence in that van they hauled back from Niigata. The van you used to kill my mother."

"So?"

"So, her death was still classified as an accident until the prosecutor signed this warrant yesterday. This is a brand new case, a case that's outside your deal with Mori."

"You are fucking joking. Gimme that."

He snatched the warrant from Kenji's hand, but as he read, fear crept into his eyes.

"You're not going anywhere," Kenji said.

"I can't go to jail. They'll kill me." Shark dropped the warrant and scrambled to his feet. "I'm getting on that plane."

"No, you're not," Kenji said, pulling out his handcuffs.

"I'm not going to jail!" Shark was sweating. He looked toward the door. "You promised you'd help me leave the country if I testified!"

"I didn't promise you anything," Kenji said.

"But I did."

Kenji spun around. A man in a chef's coat and hat stood in the far corner next to the door, pointing a gun. Chef? Gun? What was a chef doing with a gun? The kerchief around his neck had been pulled up to cover his face.

The man gestured with his weapon. "Hands where I can see them."

Kenji raised them, slowly, as the man advanced. He was slight, like Koji Yamamoto, but he couldn't be Koji—before Kenji arrived, the chef had been alone in the room with Shark, and he was armed. If the chef was Koji, Shark would be dead already.

The man stopped a few feet from him, raised the weapon.

Kenji said, "Don't shoot, okay? Don't shoot." Recalling his academy training, he spread his arms wide and began waving his hands helplessly to confuse the gunman's peripheral vision, trying to put him off guard.

"Get the bag," the man said to Shark. "The car's out back, by the door."

Kenji's left arm swung up to grab the gun barrel, twisting his head and body out of the line of fire and bringing his right hand up to chop at the inside of the gunman's wrist. The man's grip on the gun broke before he could pull the trigger and Kenji took the weapon from him as Shark stumbled for the exit, clutching a bulging plastic bag.

Aya came through the door like a rocket and threw the big gangster to the floor like a sack of rice.

Kenji pointed the gun at the chef and shouted, "Freeze!" but the man in white ignored his warning, dashing for the open door.

Kenji raced after him as he made for the kitchen. The chef pushed through the swinging door, barreled past the dishwasher's sink, and grabbed the handle of a frypan on the counter, sweeping a stack of dirty dishes into Kenji's path.

Kenji stumbled and fell as the man disappeared out the back door. He scrambled to his feet and followed, but by the time he barreled into the parking lot, the back door of Koji Yamamoto's car was slamming shut, the car pulling away.

Fishtailing around the side of the building, the driver gunned for the exit.

Kenji pulled up, breathing hard, staring after them. He reached for his phone to call it in, have a patrol car stop them, then he remembered Aya. Shark was their priority. She might need help.

He ran back inside, but by the time he came through the door to the private room, Shark was face down on the floor and Aya was tightening a set of detention ties around his wrists. Inspector Mori stood over the gangster, gun drawn. Mori's driver burst through the door, breathing hard.

"I just saw Koji Yamamoto's car speeding out of the parking lot, sir," he gasped, bowing to Mori. "If we hurry, we can—"

Kenji crossed the room and picked up the chef's toque that had fallen from the gunman's head as he escaped. He turned to Mori. "How did he know you'd be here, sir?"

Mori shook his head. "Not from me. Or my men. The only ones who knew are the people in this room."

"Do you want me to call in the license plate?" the driver asked. "I can have a patrol car stop them."

"Do it," Mori said. He turned to Kenji. "Are you sure it was Koji?"

"No. He had his kerchief pulled up. I didn't get a good look at his face."

Kenji examined the weapon he'd taken off the chef. Chinese nine-millimeter. Serial number filed off. Probably untraceable. He pulled out the magazine. Empty.

Kenji wasn't all that surprised, although he hadn't been willing to take the chance when it was pointed at his head. The penalties for firing a gun in Japan—even if you didn't hit anything—were so severe that smart gangsters carried them unloaded.

"We might be able to pull his prints off this," Kenji said.

'Yeah," Mori said. "But if that was Koji Yamamoto, they won't officially be on file. He's never been arrested. When he denies that gun is his, it'll just be your word against his." He jerked his head toward the hogtied Shark. "Unless our friend wants to get himself a double death sentence for putting away the Yamamoto-*oyabun*'s other son."

Kenji crossed the room and picked up the bulging plastic bag Shark had dropped when Aya took him down. It was heavy. Filled with . . . take-out cartons? He pulled one out and opened it. Inside was a thick roll of ¥10,000 notes. He peered into the bag. There were five more boxes, just like the first.

Kenji sat back on his heels. The chef's uniform. The car parked out back. A fortune in cash. It all pointed to something that had been carefully planned. Kenji crossed the room and crouched down next to Shark.

"That was your boss, wasn't it?" Kenji said. "And it was you who told him you were going to be here. When I saw his car out back, I assumed he came here to kill you, but now I think he was making a delivery."

Kenji thrust the roll of bills in Shark's face. "Why didn't he send someone else to do this little errand, Mr. Maeda? Why did he risk coming here himself?" Kenji's voice hardened. "What service did you perform for Koji Yamamoto that he's willing to take this much personal risk to pay off the man who put his brother in jail?"

WEDNESDAY, JANUARY 28

•

It was only ten in the morning, but it had already been a good day. Less than twenty-four hours after Kenji and Aya had intercepted Shark at the *yakiniku* restaurant, the prosecutor had agreed to go to trial in the matter of Kenji's mother's murder.

Kenji smiled as he and Aya walked down the hall. First he'd tell Yumi. And then his father. Then his brother. He glanced at the assistant detective, who had barely said a word all morning. They stepped into the elevator and began to descend.

"What's wrong?" he asked.

"He played us, sir." Her face was stony as she watched the numbers over the door count down.

"What do you mean? The prosecutor's taking the case to court. Shark will go to jail."

"But Koji is free. He won. He's about to become more powerful than anyone but his father." Her fists clenched at her side.

Yesterday, a patrol unit had pulled over Koji's car ten minutes after they left the *yakiniku* restaurant and found the Yamamoto-*oyabun*'s second son in the backseat, dressed in a suit and talking on his phone. No chef's uniform was found in the car.

"I wish we'd been able to pin something on him too," Kenji said. "But at least—"

"Do you know what he said to me at that cherry blossom party?" Aya interrupted. "After I threw his shoes in his face? He leaned over and whispered, 'Thanks, sweetheart. I knew you'd do the right thing.'"

The doors slid open and they stepped out.

"I didn't figure out what he meant until now. He's the one who sent me that DVD. He was the anonymous 'well-wisher' who wanted me to know my fiancé was making sick porn. Koji didn't want to marry me—a seventeen-year-old his father had picked out for him—but he couldn't afford to cross the *oyabun*. So he sent me that piece of filth, knowing I'd break the engagement. He knew his father would want to know why I'd backed out, and demand to see the video. The *oyabun* would recognize Yoichi's ring—the ring Koji swiped from his brother and used in the death scene—and his father would think Yoichi was going off the rails. He'd welcome the suggestion to let his second son take over the porn business."

"Wait," Kenji said, stopping in his tracks. "You're telling me Koji framed his own brother? Yoichi didn't kill that girl?"

"He probably wasn't even there."

Kenji stared. "How do you know?"

"I saw that gold dragon ring in Koji's room."

"Why didn't you say something?"

Aya gave him a withering look and stalked toward the exit.

Kenji sighed. He couldn't really blame her for not wanting to go public about how she happened to be in Koji Yamamoto's bedroom. He caught up with her as the automatic doors opened, and they emerged into the crisp spring air.

"So you think Koji arranged it all, in order to take over the Yamamoto-*gumi* porn business?"

"Yeah. Just like he's going to take over everything else, now that Shark helped him put his brother in jail."

"But we can't prove it, can we?"

"No," said Aya. "We can't."

"Well, at least we made some holes in his web. The next time he makes a mistake, I'll take him down."

"And I'll be there to help you."

•

Yumi paused in the doorway of the Mad Hatter and closed her eyes, going over what she planned to say, one more time. She had to tell Coco about Kenji tonight. This afternoon she'd run into Haru Toyama with her husband Sho and their new baby at the Family Mart, and somehow Haru already knew about her and Kenji. The only thing that would hurt Coco more than hearing that Yumi had a new boyfriend was hearing it from someone else.

The bartender began mixing Yumi's White Rabbit as soon as he spotted her, but when she dropped a thousand-yen note on the pay tray, he handed it back. "Not tonight. Your friend Coco says she's buying."

Coco was buying? Why? Yumi picked up her drink and turned, searching the tables for her friend's familiar bleached curls.

"Over there," said Boshi, pointing to a table under the shelf displaying his Iron Man dressed as Alice.

Oh. Coco was wearing another LuvLuv Match costume— a black wig and a blue suit with a skirt that was a mere two inches above her knees instead of eight. That's why Yumi hadn't recognized her at first. Tonight she was also wearing a pair of tortoiseshell-rimmed glasses as she smiled and keyed something into her phone.

Yumi set her drink on the table and pulled up a chair.

Coco looked up, saw who it was, and regarded her with a frown. "When were you planning to tell me, missy?"

"About what?" Yumi asked, suddenly nervous.

"Quitting LuvLuv Match."

Oh. *Whew.* She didn't know about Kenji yet. But how did Coco know that she'd called Hoshi this afternoon, begging him to let her out of the other two dates in her contract?

"I, uh—"

"You think my business partner wouldn't tell me something like that immediately?"

Yumi stared. "Your what?"

"My new business partner. Hoshi."

Yumi sat there, speechless.

Coco grinned. "Remember I told you how Ren Noda begged me to go out with him again and point out everything he was doing wrong? Well, I told him that he had absolutely zero chance with me and he'd be wasting his time, but he still wanted to do it, just for the practice. And after a couple more dates—with me stopping him every time he did or said something lame—he actually became quite presentable. When we met for dinner on Thursday, he said that would be our last 'date' because he'd asked Hoshi to set him up with another candidate, this time for real. Before he said goodbye, though, he wanted me to have something. He handed me an envelope, with a hundred thousand yen inside."

"A hundred thousand? Wow. Nice work, if you can get it."

"I know, right? He told me that signing up with Hoshi was the best thing he'd ever done, and that if Hoshi was smart, he'd make me his partner, because I was such a good coach." Coco sipped her Lemon Jabberwock. "So I got to thinking—Hoshi's got the backing and contacts, but Ren was proof that I could deliver the coaching. I talked to Hoshi, and he agreed."

"So, just like that, he gave you half the company?"

"Well, he didn't exactly give it to me," Coco admitted. "But I'd been thinking of investing my savings in a hostess bar anyway, and this seemed like more fun and a better bet."

"But . . . what about finding a boyfriend for yourself?"

"Who do you think gets first pick of the new clients?"

Yumi shook her head, smiling, and raised her glass, clinking it with Coco's in a toast. They drank, then Coco said, "But back to my original question: Why are you quitting?"

"Well," said Yumi, taking a deep breath. "You know how you warned me about Kenji Nakamura? Well . . . . "

"Ha! I knew it!"

"Shh!" Yumi glanced around nervously. She lowered her voice. "What do you mean, you 'knew it'?"

"I knew you two were doing more than solving crimes, Little Miss Pants On Fire. When did it start?" Coco narrowed her eyes. "It was while you were still with Ichiro, wasn't it?"

Yumi hung her head.

"Ha! It was!" Coco crowed, triumphant. "I was right all along."

"What do you mean, you were 'right all along'? When did you guess?"

"Oh, about the time you started getting nervous every time I mentioned him." Then Coco frowned, hurt. "Why didn't you tell me?"

Now it was Yumi's turn to roll her eyes. "Maybe because I was still engaged to Ichiro?"

Coco gave her a best-friends-would-tell-anyway glare.

"And," Yumi admitted, "I was afraid *you* were interested in him."

"Me?" Coco gave a snort of laughter. "You're kidding, right? How many years have you been trying to set me up with 'respectable' men?"

"Um, as long as I've known you?"

"And how many times has that worked out?"

Yumi cracked a smile. "Zero?"

Coco gave her an arch smile and said, "Which doesn't mean hope doesn't spring eternal." She lit a cigarette and took a puff, then raised her glass. "To happily ever after, for both of us."

Yumi grinned and raised her own. She could drink to that.

Saturday, January 31

•

Kenji squinted into the setting sun. It was playing hide and seek through the late-blooming plum branches arching over the Nakamura family grave. The skinny sapling they'd planted on the first anniversary of his mother's death had really grown. Each spring, the slender tree bloomed a little more exuberantly.

"*O-tsukare-sama deshita.*"

Kenji turned, to find Yumi smiling up at him. "Funny, that's what my dad said too, after I told him about catching Shark."

"He must have been happy," Yumi said.

Happy wasn't really the word Kenji would choose to describe what his father was feeling right now.

"It might take a while," he said. In the past two weeks, they had returned to their normal gruff exchanges about mundane things, with one exception. Kenji and his father had begun to unpack the storage well beneath the pantry together.

His father couldn't bear to see more than a few reminders of his wife at any one time, before retreating to his room, overcome with feelings he still felt uncomfortable displaying. But over the past few nights, they had made it through the mail bag and started on the photo albums. The objects Aunt Ayako had hidden away *did* spark the memories she feared would undo her brother, but now he was able to talk about them, even laugh a little. And Kenji was learning things about his mother he'd never known before.

"What about your brother?" Yumi asked. "Has he talked to your dad yet?"

"Not really."

"He still hasn't told him about the arrest?"

"No. I told my dad about my mother going out to Toritsu-daigaku to pay for the broken window, because I had to set his mind at ease about the money she withdrew from their account. But I didn't explain why Takeo did it. That's part of a much bigger thing they'll have to work out between them."

"So you didn't tell your brother about your dad either? About his making a deal with Koji Yamamoto?"

"No. But I'm not putting pressure on either of them to tell each other anything until they're ready. Ten years of being estranged is going to take time to fix. On both sides."

"Will tonight really be the first time they've seen each other in ten years?"

"Pretty much."

"Well, I'm looking forward to trying the seasonal menu at your brother's restaurant. And to meeting your family."

"They're looking forward to meeting you too."

They stood silently for a few moments as one crow chased another overhead, cawing. Then Yumi looked up and nodded at the flowers on the late-blooming plum tree, bursting like pink popcorn.

"You know that means it's going to snow again," she said.

Kenji smiled. "It always does."

He took the bundles of white chrysanthemums she'd brought, and stepped up to pluck the old flowers from the gravestone vases. He stopped, seeing they were fresh. And they were pink, the kind that came from the shop by the station. His father must have visited today. Kenji hoped that was a good sign. He stripped the cellophane from Yumi's bunches and made room for them next to his father's.

Drawing a plastic trash bag from his pocket, he brushed in the ashes from the incense altar. There was another cigarette butt, but Kenji didn't need Tommy Loud to tell him who'd left it there. Takeo had admitted making yearly pilgrimages to apologize to their mother for his part in her death. Kenji suspected the ancestors were going to have a lot more company than usual while everyone made their peace with the past.

Drawing two sticks of incense from his pocket, he handed one to Yumi. He flicked the lighter and they held the ends in the flame until they glowed red. Wisps of fragrant smoke began to stream toward heaven. Yumi laid hers next to his on the stone altar and joined him as he knelt before it and closed his eyes.

Kenji still didn't feel anything. But at least now he knew why: Sachiko Nakamura wasn't here. She'd never been here. He'd realized that, when he took a bunch of flowers to leave at the crossing where she died. She hadn't been there either.

But every time he ate o-hagi, she reminded him not to eat too many or he'd get a stomachache. She was right behind him when he detoured to the Rikugi-en garden on his way home from work, because even though the changing leaves looked exactly the same to him as they did every year, there was a chance they *might* be even more beautiful than last year. And every day, she reminded him that if he didn't like the weather, just wait. That eventually, all things came to those who waited.

He smiled, and took Yumi's hand.

GLOSSARY OF
JAPANESE WORDS AND PHRASES

Japanese Phrases:

"*It-te ras-shai*"—Farewell called to someone as they leave the house. Literal meaning: "After going, please return"

"*It-te ki-masu*"—Said by someone leaving the house. Literal meaning: "I'll go and come back"

"*Konban wa*"—"Good evening" greeting

"*Konnichi wa*"—"Good day" greeting

"*Ta-dai-ma*"—Announcement made by someone as they arrive home. Meaning: "I'm home"

"*Moshi-moshi*"—What people say when they answer their phones.

"*O-kae-ri na-sai*"—Acknowledgement that someone has just come home. Meaning: "Welcome home" Sometimes shortened to "O-kaeri"

"*I-ta-da-ki-masu*"—"I humbly receive this food." Typically said before beginning a meal, like grace.

"*Ir-as-shai-ma-se!*"—"Welcome to my shop/restaurant." Greeting when someone arrives at a shop, used only in commercial situations.

"*O-tsu-ka-re sama-deshita.*"—"Thank you for working hard today." Typical end-of-work departing words, said to co-workers. Also used at the end of a big project/job. Colleagues often shorten it to the more casual, "O-tsu-kare-sama." Literal meaning: "You really became tired by working so honorably." May also be used to show respect or gratitude to someone for finishing a big job or concluding a long career.

Japanese words:

dai-ginjo—The highest quality of saké, made from rice that has been polished down by 65%

eki-in—Train station attendant

genkan—Vestibule inside the front door of a house where outerwear is shed and shoes are exchanged for slippers before stepping into the living areas

hanami—Cherry blossom season

izakaya—A restaurant/bar serving a wide variety of appetizer-sized dishes, often designed with private booths and rooms instead of one large dining room

kami-sama—Shinto gods, worshipped at Japanese shrines

kanji—The multi-stroked characters used to represent Japanese written words.

kinpira—A sautéed and simmered dish made with slivered carrots and other root vegetables

kōhai—Apprentice/subordinate

kotatsu—A low table covered by a quilt that drapes all the way to the floor, with a heater mounted underneath to warm the legs of people sitting around it

maneki neko—Small statues of white cats with one raised paw, often found inviting good fortune into shops and restaurants

miso—A savory flavoring paste made from soybeans

nyan—The Japanese equivalent of "meow"

o-hagi—Traditional Japanese sweet. An apricot-sized ball of soft, sticky, pounded rice, covered in sweet red bean paste.

okashi—Traditional Japanese sweets made from white bean paste, usually shaped into motifs that fit the season.

oshiri—Bottom, behind, butt

oyabun—The top boss in a Japanese organized crime organization

ozōni—A clear soup served at New Year's, filled with auspicious ingredients and gooey, softened rice cakes

pachinko—A game of chance played by pouring buckets of steel balls into a pinball-like machine

sempai/kōhai—Master/Apprentice. This relationship exists in professional as well as in skilled labor careers in Japan. The *sempai* (mentor/superior) trains and looks out for the career of the *kōhai* (apprentice/subordinate), and in return, the *kōhai* gives the *sempai* support, loyalty and allegiance.

shamisen—A traditional Japanese string instrument that is played with a plectrum

shōgun—Japanese ruler during the samurai era

shōji—Old-fashioned Japanese sliding windows/doors, framed with wood and covered with paper instead of glass

sodai gomi—Oversize garbage

sukiyaki—Japanese hotpot made from beef and vegetables, simmered in a savory broth at the table

takoyaki—Balls of fried batter studded with pieces of octopus and vegetables, topped with a sauce and eaten as a festival snack

tatami—The woven grass mats that cover the floors in old-fashioned Japanese houses.

tōgarashi—A variety of hot pepper often used in Japanese cuisine

yakiniku—Plates of sliced raw meat grilled at the table and dipped in a garlic-soy sauce *yakitori*—Skewered chicken and vegetables, grilled in a sweet and savory sauce

yakuza—Japanese organized crime gangs

yen—Japanese unit of money. Roughly: 1 yen = 1 cent.

Honorifics used with names:

-chan—added to the name of a childhood friend or a young woman (instead of *-san*), to show a close relationship.

-gumi—Added to a name to mean "organization" (often used for organized crime families)

-kun—added to the name of a young man or young professional colleague (instead of *-san*), to show a close relationship.

-sama—the most formal level of honorific, often added to the names of revered customers

-san—added to someone's name like Mr., Mrs., Ms. or Miss.

-sempai—added to the name of someone who is either 1) a mentor (in the case of work or sports teams) or 2) senior to you in class level at the same school or on the same work/sports team

-sensei—used to indicate teacher, doctor, martial arts or other skilled master teacher

ABOUT THE AUTHOR

Jonelle Patrick is the author of four *Only In Tokyo* mysteries. She has spent many years living in Japan, and is a graduate of Stanford University as well as the Sendagaya Japanese Institute in Tokyo.

She's also a member of the International Thriller Writers, the Mystery Writers of America, Sisters In Crime, and the Japanese women's club, Nadeshiko-kai.

Jonelle divides her time between Tokyo and San Francisco.

Follow Jonelle at:

Her website (jonellepatrick.com),

Her Only In Japan blog (jonellepatrick.me),

The Tokyo Guide I Wish I'd Had (jonellepatrick.com)

Facebook (JonellePatrickAuthor).

Twitter: @jonellepatrick

Books by Jonelle Patrick

NIGHTSHADE

FALLEN ANGEL

IDOLMAKER

PAINTED DOLL

ACKNOWLEDGMENTS

To my saintly readers—Paula Span, Mary Mackey, Darlis Wood, Lisa Hirsch, Craig Tanisawa, and John Kalinka—eternal thanks for taking time from your busy lives to make the pithy remarks, thoughtful critique, and spot-on comments that made this book better in every way.

I'd also like to dish out a helping of gratitude to my editor, Stacy Donovan, for suggesting cuts where there was too much, additions where there was too little, and doing it all without making me want to give up writing for a career in street sweeping.

To April Eberhardt, my fine agent, thank you always and always for pulling out all the stops to find good homes for my books.

And finally, eternal gratitude to my longsuffering family. Thank you for never rolling your eyes and always cheering me on.

Are you just discovering this series?

Take a peek inside the first
Only In Tokyo mystery:

NIGHTSHADE

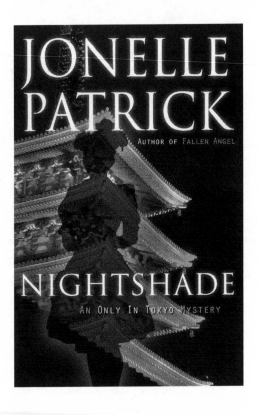

NIGHTSHADE

FRIDAY, APRIL 5

•

9:00 P.M.

The girl walked toward him across the moon-silvered parking lot, the long ribbons on her tiny black top hat fluttering behind. As she passed through the shadow of the looming Komagome Shrine, all he could see was the glow of white lace on the stiff petticoat peeking out from under her flouncy black frock.

She just wanted someone to hold her hand, so she didn't have to be alone anymore.

He smiled. Holding girls' hands for the very last time was his specialty.

SATURDAY, APRIL 6

•

8:00 A.M.

"Yumi, it's time to get up! You'll be late!"

Pulling her pillow over her head, Yumi Hata groaned. She was never going to drink again. Never. At least not at the Mad Hatter with Rika's Goth-Lolita friends. The ones she'd been with last night looked like little girls in their Bo-Peep frocks, but they could put away cocktails like sumo wrestlers. Yumi wasn't a Lolita herself, but her best friend had been dragging her along for so many years she'd become an honorary member of their Circle. If Rika hadn't left so early for her mysterious date last night, they'd have gone home together as usual at a reasonable hour and Yumi wouldn't have this pounding—

"Yumi, please," her mother persisted, now standing over the bed. "You know that Ito-*san* is coming in early just for you. Don't be late."

Crap. Now she remembered. Her haircutter was booked solid, but he'd offered to come in at the ungodly hour of 9:00 A.M. as a favor. Tonight she had Date Number Five with Ichiro Mitsuyama. Actually, Date Number Four if she didn't count their *o-miai*, the formal matchmaking introduction lunch with both sets of parents making stiff conversation at the other end of the table. After tonight it would no longer be too soon for Ichiro to raise the subject of marriage. She burrowed deeper.

"In twenty minutes you need to be on the train to Harajuku," her mother insisted mercilessly.

Wincing, Yumi threw off the covers and struggled to her

feet, making her way to what used to be the room's bedding cupboard. Hugging herself against the cold, she pushed aside hangers until she found her green pants. A light touch was required; the clothes bar had been improvised when they'd retrofitted the eight-mat parlor as Yumi's bedroom, and sometimes the entire thing collapsed. The Hata family had moved in with big plans, but over time, as the money needed to modernize failed to materialize, temporary fixes had settled into permanence.

As she picked out a sweater, her mother couldn't resist adding, "If you hadn't stayed out so late with Rika and her Freeter friends . . ."

Yumi grabbed some underwear and quickly shuffled to the bathroom to avoid the familiar lecture. It wasn't unusual for grown children to live at home until they married, but after being pushed and prodded through school, a growing number of Japanese graduates just stepped off the treadmill. If they didn't land a job in their chosen fields, they refused to get married or launch any kind of career. Freeters lived at home, worked part-time day jobs, and cruised the clubs at night.

At least I've got a real job, thought Yumi, shutting the bathroom door. Sort of. Translating professorial ramblings on "The Splendor of Longing in *The Tale of Genji*," wasn't exactly something to brag about to her former English Lit professors at Boston College, but at least she wasn't working at a tea ceremony sweetshop like her friend Coco. She sighed, regretting for the thousandth time that she hadn't been able to land a job in America with a permanent resident visa attached.

Glancing in the mirror, she hoped her haircutter had made a big donation at his local shrine this year. Today it would take some divine intervention to transform her into anything remotely resembling a potential Mrs. Mitsuyama.

Pulling her shoulder-length hair into a spiky ponytail, she splashed water on her face. Better. Did the way her eyes crinkled when she smiled made up for her sickly pallor? Better not answer that before chugging a bottle of Ukon no Chikara hangover cure on the way to the subway station. Nose nearly touching the glass, she inspected the dark circles under her eyes and prodded the slightly painful spot next to her nose, hoping it wouldn't turn into something red and hideous by tonight. Fortunately, Ito-*san*—makeup wizard as well as haircutter— used industrial-strength foundation that had proven effective before at fixing the ravages of the Mad Hatter.

In the kitchen she found her mother settling a pickled plum into the middle of a bowl of breakfast rice. She handed it to Yumi and poured her a cup of green tea. Yumi noticed a large empty sake bottle sitting by the back door next to the nonburnable trash. Uh-oh, it hadn't been there yesterday when she'd come home from her interpreting job.

"Did Dad come home early yesterday?" she asked, picking the plum off her rice and squinching up her face at its salty sourness.

"Yes," her mother sighed. "Remember that professorship that's going to be vacant next year? His interview was yesterday at three."

"How did it go?" Yumi asked, dreading the answer.

"He says it went well." The worry line between her mother's brows deepened. "But he's already predicting they'll give it to the retiring professor's protégé."

"The skinny guy with the terrible teeth?" Yumi frowned. "Isn't he a lot younger than Dad?"

"Yes, but apparently he won a prize recently. And his area of specialization is popular right now. He's already written three books."

They contemplated that fact in silence. After twelve years, Yumi's father's magnum opus still wasn't quite done. His angry outbursts on the "publish or perish" dictum he blamed for his series of temporary professorships were never mentioned within the family. Every time he'd been passed over for a permanent position during their years in America, he'd spend the first week nursing his disappointment with liberal doses of sake, then he'd dig in for several weeks of feverish writing and research on *After the Black Ships: Japanese-American Trade as an Instrument of Change.* Eventually he would run out of energy and put the project aside until inspiration returned—usually when another coveted chair was awarded to a rival.

Then his mother died, leaving them this house in Tokyo. Yumi was transplanted from the third grade class at Boston Elementary to Komagome *Shōgakko,* and Dr. Hata took a lecturing position in the history department at Toda University. They'd all hoped that moving back to Japan would bring a change in his fortunes, that perhaps at Toda he'd be judged by the quality of his scholarship, not by his failure to publish. But as the years slipped by and he continued to be passed over for promotion, the plans for renovating the drafty old house grew outdated and Yumi learned to make herself scarce when she saw her mother's lips set in a thin line and empty sake bottles by the back door.

Yumi rinsed out her bowl, detoured to her room to toss her phone into her purse, then scuffed on some shoes by the front door, calling a hasty "*Itte kimasu*" as she escaped the dim, cramped house.

A handful of cherry blossom petals fluttered by in the fresh spring wind, and Yumi began to feel better. At the Family Mart on the way to the station, she ducked in to buy a can of hangover elixir and downed it right outside the store, tossing the empty can into the recycle bin.

Crossing the bridge near the subway station, she discovered that a few of the trees lining the tracks had turned into princesses overnight. It still thrilled her each spring when, among the regiments of bare, brown trees, a few suddenly revealed themselves as blossom-crowned royalty. Even the hoary old cherry tree at the Komagome Shrine was beginning to flower, changing from a crusty old man to a dowager queen. A gust of wind swayed the heavy, rice-straw rope on the *torii* gate as she crossed the intersection to the subway station.

Waving her train pass over the turnstile sensor, she didn't even slow as it beeped her through. A train was still paused at the platform, but the doors closed with a sigh just as she came within range. The train pulled away.

Four minutes until the next one would arrive. Time to call Rika. Pulling out her mobile, Yumi flipped it open and was surprised by a picture of the scary, rooster-haired band Moi dix Mois on the display.

She groaned. This wasn't her phone.

She and Rika had gone to the Docomo store together to buy new phones a few weeks ago. As usual, they'd decided on the same model, and, after a brief argument, the same color. There'd never been any danger of a mix-up before, because Rika always transferred her collection of phone ornaments. The thick tassel of little figures on their strings was a living record of Rika's enthusiasms and travels since first grade, but she hadn't switched her collection to this phone yet. Rika must have scooped up the wrong one when she left the Mad Hatter.

Yumi would have to remember not to answer any calls today, unless the display showed they came from her own number.

Scrolling through Rika's address book, she found her own name and hit Send. The call went immediately to voicemail. She asked herself to leave a message. That was strange—Rika always picked up, even when she was sound asleep. Was she . . . *with* someone?

Rika had been awfully closemouthed about where she was going last night and whom she was meeting. The only thing she'd admitted was that she'd seen a new editor that afternoon, some guy interested in a freelance piece she was pitching.

That was why she'd been dressed so strangely. Well, strangely for Rika, anyway. Ever since middle school, Yumi had rarely seen her in anything but thigh-high, lace-edged stockings, frilly pink dresses, and eccentric little French-maid mobcaps. Rika was the queen of the Sweet Lolitas, girls who demonstrated their commitment to each other by dressing in variations on Little Bo Peep. Outsiders often made the mistake of thinking the Lolitas were trying to appeal to men with weird fetishes, but that was before they saw the scorn Rika and her friends heaped on salarymen who looked at them the wrong way. All the Lolitas—Sweet, Goth, Elegant, Punk—put on confidence and style when they tied the ribbons of their frothy hats beneath their chins, no matter how shy or awkward they'd been before. One end of the spectrum was defined by petticoats, Mary Janes, and bonnets, the other by artfully tattered dresses, black-buckled boots, and top hats.

That's why all Rika's parasol-toting friends at the Mad Hatter had turned to stare when she'd appeared last night in a navy blue suit and high heels. Clearly the new editor she'd been meeting didn't work at *GothXLoli* magazine, where Rika was a staff writer. And whoever she'd had a date with last night hadn't been a member of her Circle, either.

Yumi heard the train approaching as the phone's low-battery icon glowed red. She texted, dying to hear about last night CALL ME, and pushed Send.

•

Tokyo Metropolitan Police Detective Kenji Nakamura leaned his tall frame against the side of the squad car and watched as Assistant Detective Suzuki arranged roadblocks across the entrance to the Komagome Shrine's parking lot. A slight breeze lifted the wings of his thick, nearly-black hair, reminding him he ought to get it cut on the way to judo practice tomorrow. Once a would-be girlfriend had embarrassed him by saying it drew attention to his dreamy eyes, but Kenji found it annoying to have his hair in his face all the time.

He squinted as the sun began to break through the trees. It was a good thing Shinto priests started work early—one of them had noticed the lone Lexus shortly after 7:30 A.M. and had called the police as soon as he saw what was inside.

Kenji had been a detective for nearly a year, but these were the first suspicious deaths he'd been called to investigate. Crime in Tokyo tended toward burglary and assault; murder was rare, usually the work of drunken family members who dutifully turned themselves in afterward and confessed.

Not that these deaths would require much investigation—it looked like a garden-variety suicide pact, the kind that had become all too common. Now that the Internet made it so convenient, the despairing could plan their final deadly get-togethers as easily as cherry blossom viewing picnics. A flurry of spent petals whirled past him like a small blizzard, the classic Japanese reminder that life is fleeting.

Kenji sighed and pulled on his police-issue white cotton gloves.

He bent to peer through the window at the three bodies inside. A middle-aged man and woman in front, a young woman in back.

The twenty-something girl was obviously a Goth-Lolita, one of the doll-like eccentrics who dressed exclusively in black and white, right down to the Buddhist rosary she'd chosen to clasp while saying her final prayers. She wore thigh-high, black stockings and platform Mary Janes under lace-edged, white petticoats and a short, ruffled, black dress. A tiny top hat, jauntily canted over one ear, tied under her chin with ribbons that trailed to her waist. In her fingerless, black velvet gloves and studded-leather choker with dangling crucifixes, she must have made an arresting mixture of innocence and decay. Her heavy makeup gave her an artificial appearance, yet there was something familiar about her.

Kenji frowned. What was a twenty-something Goth-Lolita doing in a car with a couple old enough to be her parents?

He opened the front door on the passenger side and unlatched the glove box. Inside, registration papers listed the owner's name: Mr. Tatsuo Hamada, with a Shirogane address.

"Excuse me, sir?"

Suzuki stood at attention on the other side of the car, having secured the shrine entrance with multiple barriers against incursion by worshippers, tourists, and passing imperial armies. Kenji wasn't quite used to having a *kōhai* to mentor yet. Being called "sir"—as all *kōhais* properly called their *sempais*—still made him look around to see whom Suzuki was addressing.

His new assistant's attention to the finer points of the regulations was impeccable, if a little hard to take first thing in the morning. Suzuki had graduated from university two years behind Kenji and was on the same National Public Servant Career Group fast track, but he was so new to the Komagome detective detail that his suit hadn't even been to the cleaners yet. And his haircut would have to grow out for months to even slightly threaten the dress code.

"What shall I tell the priests, sir? There's apparently a wedding scheduled later and they're becoming anxious."

Kenji glanced at the knot of men muttering to each other under the cherry trees. Shinto shrines and Buddhist temples divided the business of life and death neatly down the middle: Everything to do with life and the living fell to the Shinto priests, while the Buddhists took care of death and the afterlife. It was such bad luck to have a death at a Shinto shrine that the priests would have to do some serious parking-lot purifying before the wedding party arrived.

"I'll talk to them in a minute. I doubt this is anything but suicide, but we should cover ourselves. Could you give the crime tech unit a call? And arrange transport for the bodies?"

"Which hospital, sir?"

Kenji thought for a moment. Komagome Hospital was closest, but if it turned out there was anything suspicious about the deaths, the bodies would be transferred to the Tokyo University School of Legal Medicine.

"Let's decide after the tech team finishes. Call them first."

"Yes, sir. Right away, sir."

Suzuki walked away, pulling out his phone. Kenji called after him, "Suzuki-*san*? Could you fetch some tea? If the priests don't have any, try the Family Mart across the street." Being a *sempai* did have its advantages.

He returned his attention to the bodies.

The man in the driver's seat had died holding hands with the woman next to him. Two unlabeled prescription bottles sat near the gearshift, and a half-empty bottle of good sake lay on its side by the driver's foot. Matching cups sat on the dashboard, the one on the passenger side stained with pale pink lipstick.

They were conservatively—but expensively—dressed. The woman's hair was glossy black, but would have been peppered with gray if she hadn't colored it. Lines on her face were beginning to show through her careful makeup. She was close enough to the man in age that Kenji suspected she was his wife, not his mistress.

A thick, business-size envelope sat propped behind the steering wheel. Given the empty pill bottles and the old-fashioned charcoal burner he'd spied squatting on the floor in the back seat, Kenji bet he'd find a suicide note inside. He'd read it after photos were taken.

He pulled open the back door. The girl still puzzled him. How did she fit in? The small handbag on her lap most likely contained her ID, but he didn't want to disturb anything until the tech team was finished examining the scene.

Unfolding himself from the Lexus, Kenji turned in a circle, surveying the surroundings.

What a beautiful place to die. Kenji had grown up in the neighborhood, but had seldom stopped to appreciate the serenity of the shrine while cutting through it on his way home from school. The *sugi* trees lining the parking lot cast long shadows over the asphalt. Their subtle cedar fragrance perfumed the breeze, a scent evoking the very soul of Japan. A red lacquer *torii* gate stood solemnly over the entrance to the shrine path, which passed beneath it into a frothy pink tunnel of blooming cherry trees. Beyond, the shrine stretched its red and gold wings above the awakening gardens. It would have been a fine day for a wedding.

"The crime technicians are here, sir," said Suzuki, appearing at his elbow with a steaming cup of hot green tea. He leaned in to whisper, "Just to warn you, we got the *foreigner*."

Kenji accepted the tea and information with thanks and watched as his assistant jogged over to move the roadblock. He'd never met Crime Technician Tommy Loud, but that name had frequently been the subject of Australian stereotype jokes in both English and Japanese, as had his employment in the notoriously clubby National Police Administration. According to the gossip, Loud's appointment had nothing to do with his degree in Legal Sciences from Jikei University. Everybody knew he'd been hired because of his wife.

The daughter of the Superintendent General of the Metropolitan Police had inexplicably and defiantly eloped with this gangly red-haired foreigner who shared her passion for the novels of Yasunari Kawabata. Only the news of an imminent grandchild and a job offer in Sydney had finally convinced the Superintendent General to abandon his hopes for a speedy divorce and pull strings instead.

A van rolled to a stop just inside the entrance and the Australian jumped out, toting a digital camera. He jogged toward them, stopping a few feet away to bow at the proper angle for greeting a Detective-grade officer. "Good morning, I'm Tommy Loud, from the crime lab. Sorry it took me so long to get here," he said in impeccable Japanese.

Kenji's mouth dropped open. It was like hearing a dog speak. He stammered his own name in reply.

"Ah, Nakamura-*san*, a pleasure to meet you. Nice day for some suspicious deaths, *ne*?"

"Not so suspicious, Rowdy-*san*," Kenji replied, recovering

from his shock but mispronouncing Loud's name in the typical Japanese fashion. "Group suicide. Looks pretty open and shut."

Suicide wasn't a crime, but they had to go through the motions, just in case. Unless compelling evidence emerged to the contrary, the file would be inscribed "*jisatsu*," the case closed, and the bodies released for cremation within a day or two.

Loud nodded, already fiddling with his camera. "Shall we start with the car?"

Kenji nodded. "I'll be over there, talking to the priests if you need me. If we need a wider perimeter, I'll let you know."

Loud directed his three blue-jumpsuited assistants to fetch evidence bags and begin searching a grid around the Lexus while he photographed the victims.

Grabbing his cooling tea and still marveling at hearing fluent Japanese from such an unlikely source, Kenji approached the priests. Bowing respectfully, he said, "Good morning, *kannushi-san*. I'm Detective Kenji Nakamura. Who discovered the bodies?"

A thin, nervous man in white robes and the traditional, black, oven-mitt-like headdress stepped forward. "I was the one who called 110. When I came out shortly after sunrise to make sure there was nothing inappropriate in the parking lot before the wedding today, I found . . . this." His eyes flicked unwillingly to the silver car, then back to Kenji.

"What do you mean by 'inappropriate,' *kannushi-san*?"

The priest exchanged glances with an elderly priest, robed in green, with a long, thin beard.

"The parking lot is surrounded by trees," he explained. "It's one of the few places in Tokyo that can't be seen from neighboring buildings. Sometimes young people come here for . . . privacy."

"Ah. Couples that can't afford a love hotel?"

"Sometimes. And sometimes it's kids, raiding the Suntory vending machine behind the *pachinko* parlor and bringing their cans of *chū-hai* here to get drunk."

"Foreign kids," interrupted the older priest.

"Well, not always," said the young one. "But when I saw the mess by the path, I was pretty sure it was just young people sleeping it off in their parents' car before driving home. I was hoping they spoke some Japanese because my English isn't so good. I went over to roust them, but when I looked in the window . . ." He shuddered.

"Where is this 'mess by the path' you mentioned?"

The priest stood aside and pointed to a splat of vomit in the bushes next to a sign pointing the way to the shrine. Kenji stepped over to look, then bent down to peer into the thicket of azaleas surrounding the cherry trees.

"When can we start cleaning up?" asked the old priest. "I don't know if your colleague mentioned it, but . . ."

"Yes, I know, the wedding." Kenji looked back at the car. Loud was bent awkwardly into the back seat, his camera flash bouncing around inside like caged lightning. "Let me get our crime scene specialists over here to collect any evidence that might relate to our investigation, then we'll let you do whatever you need to do."

Kenji began to walk back toward the Lexus, then turned and asked, "What will you tell the wedding party?"

"Nothing they'll be happy to hear." The young priest sighed.

Kenji returned to the car as Loud was putting away his camera. "Okay if I look in her purse now?" he asked.

"Go ahead," said the tech. "But put everything back when you're done. Let me know when you're finished so I can bag it up properly."

"While you're waiting, there's a white mobile phone in the bushes over by the path to the shrine. Collect that and anything else that looks like it was dropped since the last rain, including a sample of the vomit by the phone."

"Will do." Loud grabbed two of his assistants and steered

them toward the *torii* gate.

Kenji leaned into the car and gently pulled the handbag from the girl's hands. He unsnapped it and peered inside. Cheap gel pen, a piece of paper smeared with something that was the same color as the vomit by the path, and a thin, spiral-bound notebook. No phone, no ID. A ¥5,000 note was tucked into a side pocket. As he replaced the bag on the girl's lap, he noticed the corner of a rumpled, white envelope poking from her skirt pocket. Kenji teased it out and read the front. Clearly it wasn't intended for the "Mother and Father" in the front seat, who wouldn't be around to read it. Maybe there was a name on the note inside. Careful not to tear the envelope, Kenji lifted the flap and drew out a sheet of folded stationery.

It was blank.

•

To continue reading NIGHTSHADE...

Download the ebook from:

amazon.com

barnesandnoble.com

itunes.apple.com

kobobooks.com

Or order the paperback from:

amazon.com

Books by Jonelle Patrick

NIGHTSHADE

FALLEN ANGEL

IDOLMAKER

PAINTED DOLL

Made in the USA
San Bernardino, CA
10 May 2019